THE SOCIETY

THE SOCIETY BOOK ONE

JONATHAN SOL

The Society

Cover Illustration by Jane Chen

ISBN 978-1-7340814-1-1 (eBook)

ISBN 978-1-7340814-2-8 (mass market)

ISBN 978-1-7340814-0-4 (trade paperback)

ISBN 978-1-7340814-3-5 (hardcover)

For my parents
who have always encouraged me to follow my dreams.

CONTENTS

LIST OF CHARACTERS

Victor Stanley – captain, *New Gaia*
Ishani Jha – social media star, *New Gaia*

Nethean(s)

Endless Green Sky – doctor, Earth Embassy
Fresh Snowfall on the Lake – cultural historian
Last Rain in Autumn – Society envoy, Earth Embassy
As the Gentle Wind – Society ambassador to Earth

Xindari

Ahmon – captain, *Fulcrum's Light*
Sarjah – dimensional technician, *Fulcrum's Light*
Tuhzo – lead security, *Fulcrum's Light*

A'Quan

t'Zyah – lead metatech, *Fulcrum's Light*
n'Dala – Society envoy to Earth
sa'Xeen – doctor, Earth Embassy
tuu'Karo – aide to n'Dala

Ta Wei

K'lalaki – Protectorate investigator/ditec, Earth Embassy
M'zazape – communication technician, *Fulcrum's Light*

Axlon(s)

Kleedak Pah – security officer, *Fulcrum's Light*

Zin Ku Lai

Ja Xe 75 05 – lead officer, *Fulcrum's Light*

Oodandi

Ujexus of Seven – sensor technician, *Fulcrum's Light*
Yeizar of Eleven – dimensional technician, *Fulcrum's Light*

Zythya(ns)
Ky'Gima ma Redstripe – navigation technician, *Fulcrum's Light*

Yotara(ns)
Saa Sinju – bioneer, *Fulcrum's Light*

Koroukh(s)
Jahnas Bb – lead bioneer, *Fulcrum's Light*
Zeinon Gg – tactical technician, *Fulcrum's Light*

Fent'r(i)
Haxi Leikeema – lead doctor, *Fulcrum's Light*

D r. Nina Rodriguez stood under the hot Egyptian sun, staring in bewilderment at the angry mob of protesters who filled the sidewalk and street in front of the train station. The smell of car exhaust was strong, but the sounds of the congested traffic were drowned out by the hundreds of shouting people being held back by police barricades. She read a lot of signs saying things like REAL HUMANS ONLY, NO ALIENS, ET GO HOME, and EARTH TRAITORS.

Nina's new coworkers crowded out of the shuttle bus behind her, their faces showing the same travel-weary confusion over what was happening. United Nations officials had warned them on the shuttle that the embassy's itinerary had been leaked to the press and that there was a growing crowd of protesters gathering at the train station. But everyone had been too tired to take the warning seriously; at least, Nina had been after thirty hours of traveling. She dozed on and off during the shuttle ride from the airport to the station on the outskirts of western Cairo. Then the yelling crowds had woken her to her new reality. Earth's first embassy to an interstellar civilization, and this was their send-off.

"Please, everyone, keep moving," a UN official said over the noise of the protesters while trying to herd Nina and the others into the train station. Staffers were starting to stand around in groups, talking to colleagues or just trying to process the angry crowd. Nina recognized a few faces from neural science conferences and social media, but so far, she hadn't seen anyone she actually knew, which wasn't surprising. The embassy was made up of over three hundred people from all over the world.

"Our bags—" Nina said, trying to get the man's attention.

"Everyone's luggage will be put on the train," he said over the noise, not sure who had spoken. "Please, let's all move inside."

Nina's olive skin was already starting to perspire in the heat, and she put her long black hair in a ponytail as she shuffled forward with the others and looked around. A lot of the protesters were native Egyptians, but not nearly all. There were more bareheaded women than those wearing hijabs, and while some men wore jellabiyas, most wore Western-style clothes. She saw many European and Asian faces in the crowd and felt the only obvious difference between the protesters and her international group of delegates and staffers was the yelling and signs. Nina had done some marches herself when she was young, new to college, and drunk on teenage freedom. For most of them she couldn't even remember why now. Somebody's violated rights, or injustice, things she believed in, but still, as she got older, it was hard not to grow desensitized to the ugly nature of the world. Yet she had never been on the other side of the line, the side being protested against. And Nina honestly wondered for a moment if she was a sellout, if her desire to do what she thought was right overshadowed her ability to see what was right.

"Can you believe this?" a woman next to her asked with what Nina thought might be an Australian accent. Nina guessed she was mid-twenties, a few years younger than herself. She was an inch or two taller than Nina's five-and-a-half-foot frame and of a similar complexion. The young woman had just pushed her sunglasses up, as she looked from person to person in the crowd. "God, it's starting to feel like the Long Year all over again."

"Let's hope it doesn't get that bad," Nina said, thinking of the bomb-shelter drills she had practiced with her little nieces back in Albuquerque. "Public outrage does seem to be getting worse lately, but people have been protesting since the Society first arrived."

A man walking behind them joined in. "But organized, multinational protest groups like this? Popping up in every country? No, these aren't just local fringe fanatics. Globally, many people are still scared of what's coming."

"Yeah, well, of course," the young woman said, readjusting her sunglasses and wiping disheveled black hair out of her brown eyes. "I'm scared too. Hell, we're going to live on an alien planet. My point is, I don't think it's been this bad since the Crash."

"That might be why," Nina replied, thinking of arguments with her ex-boyfriend and her mother about the Society's influence on the modern world. America was still trying to balance itself after the divisiveness of the Trump and Biden presidencies. The new president had only been in office a couple of years when first contact happened. And a lot of people just didn't want to trust the Society, although personally, to Nina, that was a knee-jerk reaction based on fear, not facts. "I think between our embassy finally leaving

Earth and the maiden launch of *New Gaia* coming up, it's all getting shoved in everyone's face again."

"You may be right," the young woman said, fanning her face with her hand because of the heat. They both wore casual clothes, jeans and T-shirts with no logos, but Nina was beginning to wish she had worn shorts and a tank top because of the heat. They moved forward slowly with the group toward the station entrance. The man was now talking loudly with a couple behind him. The continued yelling of the crowds made it hard to hear anyone not next to you. "They're pro-contact, at least."

Nina looked to where the woman pointed and noticed for the first time that some of the crowd on this end had pro-Society signs. The police weren't doing a good job of keeping people separated. She saw a man with a sign saying ALL HUMANS ARE HUMAN get in a shoving match with another guy in a T-shirt saying REAL HUMANS ONLY.

"Hard to believe it's already been six years since the bioship crashed," Nina said. "To me, the media is just hyping it up more and playing on the fear of the unknown. What's gonna happen now that we get to see behind the curtain? As if Earthers haven't already been out there for a couple of years." After the Society starship crashed on Earth, the most significant shock hadn't even been that there were aliens but that the aliens were saying they were human. C-human: cousin species to *Homo sapiens* just as Neanderthals and Denisovans had been—and they claimed an ancient hominin race had seeded this entire region of space. As they evolved, all the spacefaring C-human races eventually joined together to form the Society, a vast, unified, interstellar civilization. And now Earth was being allowed to petition for membership.

"It did go quick after the first year," the woman said.

"Since I got accepted, that's definitely all anyone wants to talk about. *Are you going to live with C-humans? Will you get to meet them? Have you ever met them?* And on and on and on."

"Yeah, me too," Nina said. "Sorry, I'm Nina, from the States," she said, extending her hand to the other woman.

The young woman smiled brightly, shaking hands, but before she could respond, they were both distracted as a limo pulled up at the curb and a light-purple male stepped out, followed closely by a short, bald woman with sky-blue skin. They were quickly flanked by aides and guards. Nina bumped into the man in front of her, who had stopped at the sight. She knew the woman was an envoy from the Society but had only seen her a few times. The man, however, had been on TV more than most celebrities over the last few years. He was the Society's ambassador to Earth with the memorable name, As the Gentle Wind, and he was from the planet Nethea, almost two thousand light-years away. That equaled so many miles Nina couldn't recall the actual number used, but she always remembered a news sound bite that described one light-year as almost six trillion miles. Trillion. One light-year: a six followed by twelve zeros. And their planet was two thousand light-years distant. It just wasn't something she could visualize.

The ambassador had light purple skin, curly, short black hair, eyes with overly large golden irises, and an easy smile. His height and facial features were mostly Earth human-looking, although where ears should be, there were bone-like protuberances extending from the jawline, up each side of the head, and blending into his hair. The blue woman's race was called A'Quan. On average they were shorter than Earthers, about five feet, and aesthetically beautiful with exaggerated cheekbones that swept back into a slightly oblong, hairless cranium. They both wore Earth-style professional clothes, which, to Nina, always made them stand out more.

Even though C-humans had been the major topic of the media since their arrival, it was still rare to see one of the hominins in person. Of course, every member of the embassy delegation had met and been interviewed by numerous C-humans over the course of the selection process and training. And as a doctor, Nina, and others in the medical contingent, had met more C-humans than most. But it was always in an official, controlled environment. Now just seeing C-humans get out of a car, like anybody else, and to know she was about to ride a train with them, made everything seem a little more real to Nina in a way that even the screaming crowds hadn't managed.

"Ahh...Manaia, from New Zealand," the young woman said releasing Nina's hand. They both laughed having been so distracted they didn't even realize they were still shaking hands.

The ambassador and envoy walked as if the protesters weren't even present, but there was no question they heard them. Nina could almost see the news of the C-humans arrival ripple through the crowd. The yelling of the protesters got even louder, and some people shouted the most vile, hateful things. Ambassador As the Gentle Wind seemed unfazed, smiling at Nina's group, shaking some hands, and even greeting one person by name, as his entourage was quickly ushered inside. Nina and Manaia looked at each other, their expressions acknowledging that this was their new normal, more than any words could.

INSIDE THE TRAIN station was no less hectic, but there it was the general confusion of travel and not angry idealists. None of the protesters were allowed inside the building, but the station was still full with arriving embassy personnel, UN security, station staff, a flood of reporters, and retail-store clerks. Even though some areas of the station and shops were still under construction, a number of stores were open for business. People had been arriving all morning from various destinations, and Nina knew she was in one of the last groups to arrive. She started to mention something to Manaia and realized they had gotten separated in all the groups of people.

Nina overheard more than one person upset about what they felt was unnecessary traveling. While the Nethean ambassador worked mostly out of the United Nations in New York, it was Sahara City that would serve as a starport for people going into space and for C-humans visiting Earth. But no one, not even Earth's new ambassador, was allowed to fly off planet directly yet. Nina hadn't been involved in the decision, but she knew higher-ups in the medical fields had studied the Society's contact protocols and agreed with them that psychologically, it was important to not rush the experience of people leaving their planet for the first time. The journey would give everyone time to appreciate the scale of the trip before them. And since Sahara City was built in the middle of the desert, everyone had to fly into Egypt, ride shuttles to the station twenty miles from downtown Cairo, and from there take the train across the desert to the city. Not until tomorrow would they board a ship and leave Earth.

Leave Earth.

She took a deep breath to collect herself at that thought. For the past year she had been so busy going to various governmental training sessions that she had spent more time on the road than back home in New Mexico, something her family reminded her of relentlessly at her going-away party. But all were proud of her, even more so than when she had become a neurologist. Only a few like her ex, Tony, and her mom were really against her going. But she refused to let the depressing trail of those thoughts over-shadow that she was in Egypt.

Nina thought the building was beautiful, modern archi-tecture with a bit of old-world style. Looking around, she felt a stab of disappointment that she had made it all the way to Egypt yet wouldn't get to see the pyramids, especially since the station was only about eleven miles away from Giza Plateau. She had unthinkingly promised some of her cousins pictures before she left, not realizing she wouldn't get the chance. The train station was located in 6th of October City, a suburb of Cairo and one of the largest industrial zones in Egypt even before the Society decided to build its station there. It was a modern town with numerous universities, amusement parks, and apartments which was growing into a major area. And now with the station to Sahara City—the only Society-made place on Earth—it was also bringing in the ultrarich cosmopolitan crowd and major international investment.

Nina adjusted the bag on her shoulder and moved along with others toward the far end of the station. The rear of the building was a large glass wall that gave a clear view of the back of the train parked outside. At first glance, it looked like a typical high-tech train, its sleek, metallic shape stretching off into the distance. Then Nina noticed it was about twice as wide as a normal train and it floated a couple of feet above the ground—there were no rail tracks at all. The platform the train was parked at was wide, with a moving sidewalk section taking up one half, and Nina could see delegates and staff all along its length, boarding the train. The medical contingent had a car somewhere in the middle, and she was looking forward to sitting down and relaxing.

Tomorrow, before the embassy boarded the spaceship to Jupiter, its first stop, there would be an official leaving ceremony open to the media. But to Nina it seemed as if every newsgroup in the world had managed to get access to the train station now. Most were blocked off from questioning delegates, but some of the big-name news companies were moving about, trying to interview or photograph anyone high up the embassy food chain. Nina saw the Society ambassador off to the side, talking to a mass of reporters with TV cameras, while a few other C-humans she hadn't noticed outside were also surrounded by people and talking. As she continued walking, she could see the Society's envoy had also been stopped by the media before she reached the platform entrance and was smiling and answering questions. The lights and the cameras flashed as they spoke. Nina grinned to herself as she passed behind the short, bald, blue-skinned woman, wondering if she would be seen on the news. She was still smiling when the first explosion went off.

PAIN. Confusion. Were those legs running past her? Nina blinked and shook her head to clear it, but that only made the ringing in her ears louder than the screams. She realized she was on her knees and was starting to get up when another explosion went off on the other side of the station. Nina was bumped and jostled by screaming people as she finally stood and tried to get her bearings. She coughed, only then realizing that she had also been yelling. The air was full of smoke and debris. She coughed again, tripped—over someone, maybe—and stumbled a few feet.

One of the TV cameras was on the ground, its light cutting a luminous shaft through the dust, the beam strobing as people passed through it in their panicked rush. Nina looked around trying to cut through the fuzz in her brain and make sense of what was happening. There had been, a bomb. Two bombs. Was her cousin okay? No, she was alone. She had only been thinking about family. She was in the station. Nina oriented herself when she saw the train and moved in that direction, stumbling again when she bumped into someone in a blue mask, no, blue skin? It was the A'Quan envoy helping a woman who had fallen to the ground. And just past the envoy, two UN guards were wrestling fiercely, which made Nina blink in confusion. She only realized they were fighting a second before the gunshot. As one guard fell, the other with the gun turned toward her. Nina froze—her hands rising automatically—the echoing bark of the shot having cut through the chaos and madness to focus her entire being on that gun. But he pointed the weapon at the envoy, who was a step or two closer.

"Fake human!" the guard screamed in spittle-filled, zealot-like rage, and shot the blue woman in the chest and neck.

Time seemed achingly slow as the envoy fell back into Nina's arms. She instinctively clamped her hand to the C-human's neck as they stumbled backward. Two more guards tackled the shooter, and his third shot went wide into the dusty, fear-soaked air. The would-be assassin wailed as he struggled against the guards pummeling him, and one more shot went off before the gun was knocked away.

"Help us!" Nina screamed as she tried to drag-carry the

envoy's limp body away from the fight. This was crazy—Nina looked around in a panic and for one irrational moment was mad at her mom, who had never liked the Society and would be the first to say *I told you so.* Then Nina's foot slipped, and she almost fell herself, but someone steadied her from behind, and more UN guards were suddenly around them.

"She'll bleed out if I move my hand," Nina yelled at one of the guards as he started to push her out of the way.

The guard relented, covered the envoy's chest wound, and swept Nina along with their group as they carried the envoy toward the last train car. There was still a lot of screaming and yelling, people jostling against them almost every step. Nina's heart was pounding, the muted fear only now seeping into her consciousness that she could have been shot, bleeding her life away like the envoy. And amidst all the chaos, now that she had noticed it, Nina couldn't stop staring at the blood on her hands as she pressed into the envoy's neck. The blue liquid stained her skin and clothes. Blue! Maybe... No. She shook her head, trying to focus on what was at hand. A living being might be dying in her arms, and she was wondering how to classify her! Before she realized it, they were on the train, in one of the passenger lounge cars.

"Lay her here," someone said, and the guards obeyed.

Nina knelt, keeping pressure on the woman's neck, as they lowered the moaning, barely conscious envoy to a couch. The shot had to have ruptured her carotid artery. And her chest was bleeding badly. Nina didn't see any way the woman could survive, but Nina had to try. She started to ask for a first aid kit but stopped short when she saw another alien was there. He was Nethean, which reminded

Nina she hadn't seen what had happened to the ambassador during the attack.

"Hold on, Envoy n'Dala; we have you," he said to the envoy whose blue eyes fluoresced briefly before they closed in pain. Nina realized he was a doctor as he pulled a long cylindrical tube from a baseball-sized sphere that hovered next to him and touched it to n'Dala's neck. The envoy lost consciousness immediately.

"I have it now," the doctor said to Nina, letting the cylinder go. It floated back into the sphere. Nina was familiar with the medical spheres but had never seen one used in the field. It was biological, like most of the Society's technology. There was a faint bioluminescence to its off-white shell, which seemed to ripple like a pond's surface, and if what she had heard was true, part of it was always in another dimension. The doctor held his hand up, and a small dark ball popped from the sphere; gently moving Nina's hands aside, he put it in the hole in n'Dala's neck, then another one in the wound in her chest. The envoy's sky-blue skin was bruised and puckered.

"What is... Oh," Nina started to say when the ball seemed to shimmer and glisten as it began to liquefy and flow over the wound. Nina looked from the wounds to the sphere and to the doctor, trying to understand everything she was seeing. She hadn't felt this out of her depth since she was a first-year resident.

"No major arteries hit; now, where is the— Ah, there," the doctor said with a distant look on his face as he stared at the wounds. At least it looked that way to Nina, although she knew many C-humans' body language could be completely different. But it seemed like he could "see" what was going on inside the envoy's chest and was actually controlling something. She expected to see holographic ideograms or digital displays floating above the envoy's body, but there was nothing.

"Extract those," he said.

Nina was about to ask what when the material over the wounds puckered and the bullets came out, as if squeezed from a tube of toothpaste, and floated up into the still-hovering sphere.

"Good, that should do it," the doctor said absently to himself.

The sphere emitted two beams of light that shone on the envoy's wounds, then expanded to cover her entire shoulder and left torso for a moment before winking out. Then the sphere hovered back up to a place just above the doctor's left shoulder and even seemed to shrink in size a little. He turned to Nina with a big smile.

"Well, that was some orientation, huh, Dr. Rodriguez?"

Nina stared at him for a moment, mouth open, trying to find the words to voice the million questions swirling in her head. "Jesus," was all she managed to get out.

The doctor looked quizzical for a moment; amazing, the similarities in body language. "Oh, I'm sorry. We don't have a nickname on file. Is that what you prefer to be called? I'm Endless Green Sky, one of the doctors that will be working with your embassy."

"What? Oh, God, no, I'm...I mean..." Nina took a breath and started over. "It's just an English expression, sorry. Call me Nina."

She extended her hand, then pulled back in shock seeing it was still covered in blue blood. "Oh, God."

"Don't worry. We'll get you cleaned up. Kevin, can you show Dr. Rodriguez the bathroom, please?" The last was directed at one of the many people Nina hadn't realized had crowded into the cabin.

She stood, looking down at the unconscious blue woman. "Will she be okay?"

"She'll be fine." The doctor smiled. "A'Quan blood clots a lot faster than mine or yours, but their sensitivity to pain is a little greater also. Don't worry. You thought quickly, and it's appreciated."

"But...her neck wound," Nina said. "How did she not bleed out?"

"Neck?" the Nethean asked then continued with understanding. "Oh, I see. A'Quan don't have a major artery in that area of their neck."

"Really?" was all she managed to say, knowing her simple responses made her look foolish. But to hell with pretense, now that the immediate crisis was over, events were starting to catch up to her. She was still finding it hard to believe that the "operation" for two major bullet wounds had taken less time than them getting on the train.

"Dr. Endless Green Sky," a woman's voice said, and Nina turned to see Xian Xu, the deputy chief of Earth's embassy, second only to the ambassador. She nodded to Nina, but her focus was on the sleeping envoy, and she and the Nethean doctor started talking in quiet tones.

"Dr. Rodriguez, this way, please." An aide gently steered Nina out of the cabin and toward the front of the car. She looked back once; the range of emotions playing across the deputy chief's face reminded Nina of the broader implications of what was going on and that this attack could affect their mission—if not the entire Earth.

NINA STOOD in the bathroom for a long, long time, trying to compose herself. She didn't think she was in shock but knew the reality hadn't sunk in yet that the blue liquid she was washing off her hands was blood. The aide was gone when she came out, replaced by a couple of UN security agents in suits. She relayed what she had seen and answered their questions as best she could, purposefully not letting herself think about the fact that she could've died.

"Was anyone killed?" she asked when they had finished. With all the screaming and panic, she didn't know. "I didn't see what happened to the Society ambassador."

"I'm not sure yet, ma'am, sorry," one of the agents answered before they left. "And you can't move between cars while the train is moving, so you can't go to the medical contingent's car, but you can find a seat anywhere here."

Moving? Nina looked over to see scenery sliding by the window; she hadn't even realized they had started moving. The landscape went by so fast that even the horizon didn't feel like a constant. She hadn't paid attention at the time, but the aide had brought her to the bathroom in the next car before they started moving. It wasn't even half-full, and the train's large size made it seem even emptier. Rows of big, comfortable seats lined each side, the flow only broken by occasional cabins like the one they had put the envoy in. But Nina didn't want to be in a room now; she needed to see people, if not interact, so she went to find a seat. As she walked, she couldn't stop staring out the windows; how had she not known they were moving?

The approaching and receding dunes seemed to undu-late like waves as the train eased its way across the desert. To Nina—growing up in the Southwest—desert meant some-thing different: shrubs, brush, hard cracked earth, rocks, even cactus. In her mind, a desert was a living, breathing thing—harsh, unforgiving, and dangerous, yes, but full of life. She knew much of the Sahara was like that also. But this part of the Sahara was...nothing, a vast emptiness. Like

God had taken a tan tablecloth and thrown it over the ocean, freezing the waves in place. And the Society had built their city, Sahara City, right in the middle of it. In an area of the Sahara Desert known as the Great Sand Sea, an erg approximately seventy-two thousand square kilometers that stretched from western Egypt to eastern Libya.

Everyone was talking animatedly about what had happened, but they had all been on the train when the attack happened, so it was all speculation. As she made her way down the wide aisle, looking for a seat, Nina finally realized what had been bothering her subconsciously. The train didn't move. Oh, it moved forward, of course. No, it was that it didn't rock or sway in the slightest. If not for the passing scenery outside, she wouldn't have any idea she wasn't walking down a hallway in a building. No sound other than that made by the passengers filled the car. No rushing wind outside, no rolling over tracks, no creak of the cars, nothing. It was a smooth, quiet ride.

And utterly alien.

She found an empty seat and sat down heavily. The conversations of the few people near her were about the attack, as well as grumblings that cell reception wasn't working, something she hadn't realized but was surprisingly relieved by. She needed a moment to just breathe. The flight from Albuquerque Airport, the layover in LaGuardia, the flight to Cairo, the shuttle ride to the train station, the terrorist attack, and the operation on an alien...it was a lot to accept. And here she was almost at the end of her trip, but really it was just the beginning of her journey.

2

D imensional Technician Marcus Greer watched the exterior image from his station as the Society Protectorate starship *Fulcrum's Light* emerged into standard space just outside of the Travanis star system. The biological ship was an elongated ellipsoid over two hundred meters long from bow to stern, and sixty meters wide. The windowless hullskin was grayish with bioluminescent streaks of white and blue, giving the ship the appearance of some exotic sea life. Along its back upper and lower half were four morphogenic tentacle-like extensions that were coiled tightly when not in use but could extend over fifty meters and move independently, allowing the ship to latch on to things like stations or asteroids.

"Transition complete. We're twenty light-hours from Travanis primary, on the inner edge of this system's Oort cloud," Ujexus of Seven, the bridge sensor tech, said out loud. It was standard procedure even though everyone was connected through the shiplink, and access to ship's location and status was not only available with a thought but something bridge crew was always aware of on an unconscious level. To Marcus, it was like the background hum of an air conditioner.

Marcus had only been on board a week, yet as strange as his new reality was, he felt at home. Just a year earlier, he'd been a recent college grad from Atlanta doing visual effects compositing and programming for the booming film industry in Georgia. And now there he was, exploring the star system of an alien race thousands of light-years from Earth.

Are you scanning? the voice asked, as clear in his head as one of his own thoughts, yet unquestionably from an outside source. To his credit, Marcus didn't startle—visibly —but his involuntary surprise, and guilt, of having been caught daydreaming was unmistakable in the private link he shared with his trainer Sarjah through their biowebs. She was Xindari, a reptilian C-human race, about the same size as people from Earth, with scales that were a deep, rich purple. Xindari faces had more prominent brows, cheek bones, and chins than Earthers, and their eyes were always green, but the shade could vary from person to person. The Mohawk-style wavy black hair on the top and back of her head tapered down her back to a point at the center of her shoulder blades, as with all Xindari women.

"Scanning now," Marcus said.

They sat at their stations in the dimensional technician cavity located right off the bridge. There was a closable membrane between the two cavities in case of an emergency, but since they were near the center of the ship, direct damage was unlikely. The circular space had four ditec stations adjoining the wall, spaced evenly around the room. They were facing inward so crew could see everyone else, but Marcus and Sarjah were the only ones currently on duty. The organic chair that grew from the wall formed to his body, providing the maximum amount of comfort and usability. And while most of their job was done mentally with a bioweb, petal-like protrusions grew from the floor in front of Marcus to provide a workstation console for manual controls. The connecting bridge cavity was also circular but large enough for the six-officer crew. Facing toward the center, five workstations circled the walls: lead officer, navigation, sensors, communication, and tactical, while the captain's station sat in the center of the cavity. There was also enough room for other specialist stations to be grown if needed. The bioluminescent ceilings gave off clear, steady light, and the chromatophores of the wallskin could adjust color to serve as a viewscreen showing any image needed, including an exterior view, although most crew used biowebs to *see* in their mind's eye. The entire ship held a crew of seventy-five, most from C-human races that hadn't even been seen on Earth yet.

"Preliminary scan shows no dimensional discrepancies," Marcus reported after a few moments.

"Negative on artificial transmissions," M'zazape, the comms tech, said. And even though she didn't look at him, Marcus felt a wave of encouragement from the tall, orange-skinned Ta Wei, and he realized, as per procedure, she had been waiting for him to give his report before she did. He pulsed a smile at her in thanks.

"Ujexus," Lead Officer Ja Xe 75 05 said. "Natural-phenomenon threat assessment?"

"Stellar activity normal, commander," the sensor tech said. "And no current extinction-level asteroids intersecting the inhabited planet's orbit. Still scanning terrestrial bodies."

"Be sure Dr. Ueda has access to the nonrestricted data," Captain Ahmon said to the Oodandi sensor tech.

"Aye, sir," Ujexus responded.

Marcus could feel a number of the crew observing their mission status through the shiplink, but Marcus was currently the only Earther in the bridge area. The bridge crew were all different C-human races except the captain, who was also Xindari like Sarjah. Instead of hair on the top of their head and going down their back like females, males were bald but had a thick mane all the way around their shoulders, like a fur collar that tapered down to points on each side of their torso. Marcus couldn't decide if it made the purple C-human look like a lion or a pimp.

In fact, all Society government and Protectorate uniforms accommodated each race's physiology. So, although they had the same color scheme, light gray and black with white highlights—and the Protectorate symbol, which was a stylized double helix—the uniforms could still be very different between C-human races. Marcus's own ship suit had Earther-standard long sleeves, pants, and boots. Oodandi tops had no sleeves because of their shoulder quills, and their pants had a hole for their tail; Ta Wei like M'zazape wore a sheer cassock to regulate the humidity for their amphibian origins; and Zythyans, like the navigator-pilot, only wore boots and a wrap around their waists because they found covering their feathers distasteful. The captain's uniform was the same as Sarjah's, a knee-length sarong-type bottom over pants and boots, that was belted at the waist and rose to just below the chest, with separate sleeves. The first time he had seen the bare chest, Marcus did a double take, but since Xindari were reptiles and laid eggs, the women didn't have breasts, so their chests were as flat and nippleless as the men's.

"Reviewing near metaspace now," Marcus said to Sarjah.

She hadn't reminded him, but through their private link he had felt she was about to.

"Maintain standard protocols," she said aloud. "This is no different than training."

"Copy that."

Sensor pores in the ship's thick, windowless surface absorbed EM spectra, which the crew could process into visual and other data, giving full three-hundred-and-sixty-degree perception, while more powerful sensors reinterpreted extradimensional data in a way biological minds could comprehend. Even with his awareness focused on what was going on outside the ship, because of his bioweb, Marcus also had a peripheral understanding of what was happening in the bridge and ditec cavity around him. His bioweb implant allowed him to mentally interact with and use the Society's biological technology, from simple things like controlling his quarter's doors and lights, to nonverbal communication with other people, to more complex nonphysical things like dimensional technology.

With a thought, his bioweb connected to the ship sensors; data appeared in his mind's eye and was directly encoded into his short-term memory, allowing Marcus to suddenly "know" things as if he had just studied them.

Travanis was a standard yellow dwarf star orbited by seven planets: four terrestrial and three gas giants. Past the farthest planet lay the system's Kuiper Belt, which held a few dwarf planets but was mostly a mass of planetesimals made of ice, rock, and dust grains that were concentrated into a belt centered on the plane of the ecliptic. Past the Kuiper Belt was the star system's Oort cloud, a spherical shell of trillions of icy bodies gravitationally bound to the star and surrounding the entire system. Yet space was so vast that the average separation of these icy rocks was about ten million kilometers. It was there on the inner edge of the system's Oort cloud that *Fulcrum's Light* now flew.

The star system's only inhabited planet, Travanis 4, was a UHC, uncontacted human culture, just as Earth had been six years before. It wasn't lost on Marcus that what they were doing now was the exact same thing other Protectorate starships had done around Earth's solar system for thousands of years. And that the Society bioship that had crashed on Earth was an example of what happened when UHCs were not protected correctly.

Four major hominin civilizations had risen and fallen over the course of the ancient past, each in their way spreading humanity in this region of the galaxy. The Society was the fifth mega-civilization and was made up of all the currently advanced C-human cultures that had developed technology and eventually started to explore beyond their star systems to find not only other "humans" but a shared genetic history. But due to the vast timescales involved, there were always many other planets with native C-human races at various levels of evolution and development: Stone Age, preindustrial, hunter-gatherers, medieval, et cetera, and like Earth before the Crash, these civilizations had no idea their planet, their very DNA, was part of a larger galactic community.

In addition to defending the Society and enforcing its few laws, part of the Protectorate's job was to ensure that those uncontacted human cultures were able to grow and evolve at their own pace without outside influence. Influence like an entire planet thinking the object plowing through the atmosphere was an asteroid about to end all life on Earth, only to find out aliens were real and things might even be worse. The Society had been in damage control ever since then, trying to guide Earth through a cultural paradigm shift that had almost led to World War III many times. New Human Culture (NHC) status, the ditec program, Earther envoys, and the new embassy were all the Society's ways to try to help Earth not tear itself apart as it figured out how to navigate this new era.

While Marcus had never felt like the military was the best analogy for the Protectorate—the Society in general seemed almost too laid-back for that type of comparison— they took the protection of UHCs very seriously. He didn't know if it had always been like that or if they were overcompensating for what had happened on Earth, but the main feeling that permeated the shiplink was one of protectiveness for their unknown cousins in this system.

"The closest buoy is forty-seven light-minutes system-spinward," Ujexus said from sensors.

Marcus immediately detected the Society metaspace buoy and confirmed the coordinates on the shiplink. There would be a number of them spread around the star system in a sphere, not gathering data on the inhabitants but monitoring local space and any incoming traffic. While *Fulcrum's Light* could access all the buoys from one position, it was standard procedure to circumnavigate the system. Through the shiplink Marcus observed the avian C-human navigator Ky'Gima ma Redstripe. The Zythya's seven-foot tall, blue, and yellow feathered, lean form was lying back in her station seat and using the data to plot a course around the system. *Fulcrum's Light* would never actually go in-system unless there was a serious emergency, and with the ship's sensors, everything was easy to identify even from this far out.

"Nav, let's check the perimeter," Captain Ahmon ordered once all stations were reported.

The bioship accelerated away from its emergence point,

following the star system's rotation, its D-field molding the fabric of metaspace and allowing the ship to move through dimensions. Nav Tech Ky'Gima mentally accessed the flight controls with her bioweb as she steered the ship on a path that stretched out before them in a mental image overlaid on the shiplink. The three spatial dimensions of standard space seemed to compress and contort around them, and the images of stars appeared to squeeze together and spiral as the ship traversed metaspace. Marcus felt no acceleration at all because it was offset by the ship's internal grav field, and the 1.13 g's, which was the averaged gravity of all the homeworlds of C-humans on board, was close enough to Earth that he didn't consciously notice being heavier.

Marcus had only applied for the dimensional technician program on a whim, and the selection process had taken over a year. So, by the time it did happen, he was shocked, and excited, of course. Unlike the people who were training to be a part of Earth Embassy, the ditec program required sophisticated Society technology like biowebs, and members could only be trained off Earth. He had studied for six months on one Society world, but this was his first practical training on a bioship. As a dimensional technician, he was learning to manipulate metaspace, but part of that training had been learning to navigate basic Society tech like the Nexus.

While the shiplink allowed for a subconscious knowledge of what was going on around the rest of the living starship, any of which could be brought to a conscious level with a thought, on a deeper level than that was an instinctual awareness of the Nexus. The Nexus was a completely separate dimension with the entirety of the Society's knowledge encoded into its substrate. It served as a communication and data hub that could be accessed instantaneously throughout the whole Society by its citizens using their biowebs. But it was far more than just a futuristic analogy of the internet. It was the central mental gathering place for a civilization that spanned a small fraction of the galaxy. It was as immersive as the user wanted it to be. So, someone could use it just to look up information, or they could download data into their memory, or they could create a complete mindscape, indistinguishable from reality, to interact with others. Whatever your interest, there was always some sub-community to talk about it, learn about it, argue about it, play it, or simply get emotional support about it in the Nexus. And that was the most difficult part for Marcus to get used to, even after months of learning—that the Nexus also conveyed emotional content. One could actually feel the emotions of other people as clearly as you felt your own. It was akin to being in an internet chat group where you were also aware of what others were feeling and doing as they surfed the web. And if he let himself get distracted, he could get caught up in what was happening thousands of light-years away instead of focusing on what was in front of him.

So, with effort, Marcus consciously forced himself away from the countless distractions across the galaxy and focused on where he was now. He accessed the sensors with a thought and attuned to the gravity map. Instantly, he was aware of every object within a million kilometers that was larger than a baseball. And when he focused, he could detect larger objects tens of millions of kilometers away.

"Is your goal to be a sensor tech, *Mr.* Greer?" Sarjah asked with a little emphasis on *mister*.

"What?" Marcus asked, his awareness drifting from outside back to his body as he glanced at her.

"Because if that's the case, we can get Sensor Tech

Ujexus of Seven to teach you and I can get back to important work."

"You know that's not why I'm here," Marcus said. His only issue so far was Sarjah, his C-human instructor; she was professionally cool—if not outright rude at times. He didn't think she actively hated him, but Sarjah made it clear that she had little patience for New Human Cultures, or baby cultures, as she called them.

"Then I suggest, *Ditec* Greer"—she emphasized his title this time—"that you move deeper than the surface and do what you were trained to do."

"Okay." He had started to give a curt reply, but he knew it was just her teaching style, and he was trying not to judge all Xindari by her. Sarjah didn't respond, but he felt the emotional analog of a raised eyebrow from her. No doubt what he had been feeling leaked into their private link. He needed to get better at avoiding that.

Marcus had only been looking at the basic sensor data, which he admitted was Ujexus's job at sensors. And he could feel the green-skinned Oodandi C-human closely examining all aspects of the star system, his yellow-orange head and shoulder quills twitching involuntarily as he focused on one object or another. As a dimensional technician, Marcus had to do more than just observe the physical characteristics of the system. He had to also monitor metaspace itself. Not just the one temporal and three spatial dimensions of standard space but all dimensions —metaspace.

It wasn't guaranteed that Earthers would even be able to adapt to that particular Society technology. The ditec trainees had spent six months on planet Ya'sung, doing what they had all considered the most basic of things, but only later did they realize it was integral to making sure they didn't go crazy. They rarely got to interact with each other, but as far as Marcus knew, everyone had passed and been placed with a personal trainer. With all the new programs happening because of Earth's NHC status, the dimensional technician program had seemed to slip under the radar in the media. Marcus believed that was intentional because it dealt with more advanced tech than usual, but he wasn't sure. Only one hundred people from Earth had been chosen. And unlike the other programs, like envoys, embassy personnel, and cultural exchanges, the various nations had no say in the selection process for ditecs. Limiting it to one hundred had left many countries out, but as usual with the Society, they had chosen from a completely representative sample of Earthers, regardless of nations, politics, religion, or anything else. So, although he wasn't the only Black person, Marcus was the only American in the program.

Marcus was also the only ditec from Earth on board the *Fulcrum's Light*. All the other Earther crew members were part of other NHC programs—and that unconscious stray thought brought a flood of new information into his awareness through his bioweb. He knew the location of the other four people from Earth on board and what they were doing. And that knowledge shocked him out of what he was supposed to be focusing on, because they were all using the Nexus to watch an attack happening on Earth!

Marcus gasped involuntarily as he tried to make sense of what was happening. The Nexus couldn't be thought of in physical size since it was a separate dimension. And with hundreds of billions of C-humans using it at any given moment, there was a lot to draw someone's attention. But things could still go viral—to use an Earth concept—and since new human cultures entering the Society only happened every few generations, there was always a lot of attention on them. So, when the attack started, news of it spread quickly and people across the Society perceived what was happening through the biowebs of the C-humans who were there on Earth—and the emotional impact of that overwhelmed Marcus for a second.

Biowebs had natural filters to keep outside emotions from overpowering the user, but they did nothing against the person's own memories. So, the pain, horror, and confusion flowing from a C-human in the train station on Earth, who was looking at the Society ambassador lying in a pool of blood, reminded Marcus of how suddenly life could change. How permanently. He had been in junior high school when he found out. It was a normal day, hanging out with friends and having lunch. He was scrolling through his feed when a local car accident caught his eye. A major intersection had been blocked off, and his heart dropped out when he saw the car upside down in the street. His parents' car. He couldn't even remember how or why he got to the office, and that's when he saw his grandmother with the principal, and he knew his life would never be the same. So, even though the attack back on Earth was a different type of tragedy, Marcus relived in an instant the full overwhelming sense of loss, horror, and sadness from unexpected death because of his bioweb's ability to give him total perfect recall.

Briefly, Marcus felt concern from Envoy Rahel, the Earth woman on board who was his mentor in the Society, but the hectic flood of feelings from so many people was drowning her out. He couldn't tell what was memory and what was now. That woman's leg was missing. His mom and dad were gone. That screaming man had shrapnel in his eyes. The fear. The panic. There were so many emotions, he felt he couldn't breathe. Then almost immediately, the outpouring of empathy across the Nexus was as intense as the shock. And that comforting flood of solidarity and compassion from others reminded him of his parents' funeral, of his grandparents' love and pride for him, of... Then Sarjah's presence was there, all-encompassing yet surprisingly gentle, filtering the emotional chaos in the Nexus and guiding his awareness back to *him*.

She stood before him, but only in his mind's eye. A dim part of him knew he was still sitting on the bridge with her sitting next to him, but her presence, her being, was in the forefront of his perception. He could see/feel her, the casually perfect posture all Xindari had, this royal-purple woman with focused green eyes, standing calmly in a maelstrom of emotion. She raised her open, flattened hand and laid the edge of her palm on the center of his forehead.

This is the point.

Marcus didn't know if she spoke words or if he just felt her meaning. Her green eyes held his and didn't look away.

Exist here.

The coolness of her scales against his flesh seemed loud and hot. Even more than the explosion, it pulled his focus.

Let everything else fall into balance.

He could feel her repeat the mantra, but maybe not in words. Over and over until his racing emotions and disoriented thoughts started to calm. This was the point. The now. There was still so much happening, but he was beginning to be able to perceive it as separate from himself. The shooter was caught on Earth; a feeling of relief (righteousness? justice?) spreading across the Nexus showed that.

Exist here.

He concentrated on what she said and was able to slowly

let the mental noise of the Nexus go and focus on his surroundings and where he was again.

Let everything else fall into balance.

He had a peripheral awareness that everyone on the bridge appeared to be motionless. His body was also still, not even breathing, but his mind's sight could take it all in. And Marcus realized his perception had sped up to super-fast processing, something the shiplink made possible but was usually only done when needed. It had all happened in a few seconds. Only Sarjah's mental state ramped up to keep pace with him.

Marcus took a deep breath and, as he exhaled, reintegrated with normal time and relaxed into his chair, letting the physicality of where he was now ground him. Others on the bridge were moving again. He could feel waves of concern coming from Ujexus and Ky'Gima, the two C-humans he had come to know best. Ky'Gima's feathers ruffled in a pattern his bioweb told him was compassion, and Ujexus's tail swayed back and forth anxiously but they never lost focus on their own jobs.

"And that," Sarjah said calmly from her seat next to him, "is why emotional sharing should be damped down while on duty, until you truly learn to be one with it."

Marcus was aware of Dr. Leikeema, in the medical bay, checking his vitals over the shiplink. Which led him to realize one of the strong waves of concern he had felt was from Envoy Rahel, somewhere else on the ship. And he knew she was having a mental discussion with the doctor and the captain about whether he needed to stop.

"They're talking about me," Marcus said more to himself as he composed his mind.

"About whether you need to be relieved from duty, yes," Sarjah said.

Marcus thought about that as he wiped his eyes, real-izing he had been crying. The attack had definitely affected him, and he could still perceive what was going on on Earth. But the emotional support everyone across the Nexus gave each other was also affecting him in a good way. He felt a cathartic release on some level and wanted to see the mission through. "I want to finish this," he said.

"Commendable. If you're able to do it." Sarjah's voice wasn't loud enough to carry over the bridge, and even though her words were direct, he felt an underlayer of empathy from her about what was happening on Earth. He also received more pulses of understanding and support, through the shiplink, from some of the bridge crew.

"I can do it," he said, already forming arguments in his head to counter her imagined objections.

"As I told them," she said simply.

"But I..." He stopped when he actually understood she agreed.

Marcus was under no illusions about saving Earth, or something like that. His small contribution was part of a larger whole. All the Earther ditecs had gone through a lot of training, and he could feel the residual effects some of them he personally knew were experiencing after the attack. Yet none of the other Earthers on board the ship had been affected as strongly, possibly because their biowebs were not as advanced as ditecs. This was one of the reasons for the ditec training: seeing if Earthers could handle full Nexus access without being overwhelmed by it. He honestly didn't know if Earth was ready for that; all he could do was his best in the moment.

The captain agreed to let Marcus stay on duty, over the objections of Rahel. Marcus knew she had a lot more expe-rience with the Society, but he thought she was overreacting some. He hadn't really been in any physical or mental danger. It was just confusing and emotionally draining.

Marcus's perception cautiously flowed back into the Nexus, bypassing what was trending—the attack at the train station—and he accessed the Nexus Index, searching specifically for what he needed. Information on the star system filled his mind: orbits, composition, history, such an excess of data that he began to have trouble distinguishing facts. He shook his head, blinking, but opening his eyes only made it worse. His physical senses were seeing the petal-like console in front of him. The bioorganic composite was light grayish in color, but it was overlaid with the information from the sensors that was in his mind's eye, and then there was the biographical data being dumped directly into his working memory. Not to mention the underlying current of strong emotion from the other Earthers as they still perceived what was happening back home. Four different types of stimuli were vying for his conscious attention. It was too much.

Stop fighting it. Sarjah's statement was another beacon that cut through the confusion and gave him something to focus on. *You feel like the information is in conflict, but it's not; you are.*

She reached over and tapped his temple with a purple-scaled finger. *Get out of there.*

"Where should I be?" he asked out loud, a little exasperated and trying to not worry about what was happening back home. He had done well training planetside, but on a ship, the process was a little more chaotic and distracting.

In your mind, she answered over the link.

He looked at her. *I should be in my mind but not in my head? Ooookay.*

You have to find the balance in what you're doing and also in what it's doing to you, Sarjah said. *Remember it's just like listening to music. You can hear a song and enjoy it, but that doesn't stop you from remembering something else at the same time, nor does it keep you from looking at something else simultaneously. Integrate the data and focus on what you need at the moment; the rest is background.*

Marcus exhaled and closed his eyes again. Whatever was happening on Earth right now, he couldn't do anything about, so he had to let that go. And he didn't need to know the mass and diameter of the second planet, or the atmospheric composition of the largest gas giant. All that was there, like a sidebar on a page when he surfed the web, but not something he needed to read. He let the maps of the star system focus his attention, and then he overlapped details from their historical records with current metaspace scans to get a full picture of the system and anything out of place. As *Fulcrum's Light* continued to circumnavigate the system, Marcus spent the next twenty minutes studying metaspace. There was an area of near metaspace that felt...wrong to him, but nothing specific he could name. It only lasted for a moment and was gone so quickly, it was probably his imagination or the residual effects of the emotional barrage he had suffered. The attack was still the talk of the Nexus, and even though he wasn't paying attention it was a constant background presence, like the sounds of the city outside your window.

He could feel Sarjah next to him, not physically, although that was also true, but in metaspace. She was piggybacking on his access and experiencing the sensory input he called up. Their connection was more than just checking his "keystrokes" because of the conveyed emotional content, and now there was an undercurrent of annoyance beginning to come from her.

Balance preserve me. She was very loud in his mind. *You need to trust your instincts. The annoyance is from you not paying attention.*

"I am," he said out loud, annoyed himself.

"Really?" she asked, green eyes locking on to him. *And you've accounted for all observed dimensional discrepancies?*

As soon as she said it, he picked up on two things. One, that her annoyance really wasn't aimed at him but something they both perceived, and two, that the fluctuation in metaspace that he had noticed but discounted as natural wasn't. That's why it had felt wrong. Marcus ran a discriminator program, bringing different aspects of the system to the forefront of his consciousness. He still almost missed it. There was an intermittent dimensional signature near the fourth planet that, without close scrutiny, would be taken for background fluctuations in shallow metaspace. He analyzed the pattern and found that it couldn't be from a naturally occurring phenomenon.

He brought more powerful sensors online and determined it wasn't from the fourth planet but one of its two small moons. Something on that rock was emitting dimensional energy. And since the natives of Travanis 4 were a Bronze Age–equivalent civilization, they couldn't possibly be responsible.

"Da hell is that?" he muttered.

Trouble, Sarjah answered after a moment. "Captain," she continued out loud. "Ditec Greer has discovered a possible incursion in the system."

Then Sarjah was no longer piggybacking his data—she reorganized it and opened it to the shiplink for all to see. Marcus was mildly surprised that Sarjah hadn't taken credit for the discovery, then realized she would probably sense that, and he cast a guilty glance at her out of the corner of his eye before he could stop himself. Sarjah ignored him as the bridge became a flurry of activity, everyone working as a group preparing to face the unknown.

Ujexus started an intense sensor scan of Travanis 4 and its moons. Nav Tech Ky'Gima began plotting a course to the planet. Captain Ahmon reviewed the data with Sarjah, while Marcus could sense Commander Ja Xe 75 05 consulting with the lead bioneer over the shiplink.

Attention, crew. The captain's call over the shiplink took priority over all other communiqués as he spoke. *We have just found evidence of outside interference in the system. I don't need to remind you of the importance of protecting UHCs, especially considering what's now happening to our cousins on Earth. Alert Status; we're going in-system.*

Even with the emotional controls on his bioweb, Marcus could feel the anticipation, worry, and even excitement from the crew as it percolated through the shiplink. As much as the situation back home affected him and the other Earthers, he could feel a unity and resolve among the crew. Had it been like this for those first ships responding to Earth years before? It was hard to even imagine how different his life would be if a Protectorate ship *had* stopped the Crash. That made him think of his grandparents again and guiltily realize it had been a couple of weeks since he had last called them. He knew they felt they had never been able to say goodbye to his mom, and if something also happened to him unexpectedly it would crush them. He promised himself as soon as he got some time, he was going to call home.

3

Nina watched out the window as the train slowed and she got her first live look at Sahara City. There was no gradual transition of suburbs into metropolis; the sand dunes simply ended and the city began. The station they pulled into seemed to be adjacent to a park, large trees lining one side of the trackless train path, and Nina could see green lawns and a small lake through breaks in the foliage as the train glided to a stop. The walls of the station itself were transparent, but she didn't believe they were glass. And even though the majority of the neighboring buildings were skyscrapers, there was no feeling of being closed in, because most of the structures had multiple floors with clear walls allowing her to see buildings behind buildings. The light from the desert sun shone through window after window, refracting in a multitude of ways that caused colored patterns to shift and move across the city as the sun journeyed across the sky.

The train doors opened, and for a moment, everyone just sat there, no mad rush to grab luggage and get off but a group hesitation before the unknown. Most of the people in this car had been on board when the attack happened, so they hadn't seen much, and there had been no real information forthcoming during the trip. Then UN staff appeared, helping people to disembark and directing everyone to wait on the platform for their guides.

As soon as she stepped off the train, Nina's phone started alerting her to messages and kept on alerting her. There were at least fifty texts, missed calls, emails, and post alerts. She immediately thought something must've happened to her parents until she started noticing the same thing was happening to everyone disembarking as they gathered on the platform. Then a few of the people looking at their phones started glancing at her. Nina opened a message at random and saw shaky video of the assassination attempt and her holding the envoy as they were rushed onto the train.

Apparently, it had gone viral.

Nina stood there shocked, staring at the screen. Everyone chosen for the mission already had a degree of notoriety; just being selected as part of the staff to join Earth Embassy was attention-drawing enough. Once names of delegates and staffers had been leaked, privacy pretty much ended. Candidates and their families were practically under siege by reporters, curiosity seekers, and conspiracy theorists. She had gotten marriage proposals and death threats. Most countries had ended up providing police protection for their selectees. All of which were things that had made her parents more and more nervous about her leaving. But to Nina it had been a generic type of popularity, one of hundreds—where she got recognized in the local grocery store but rarely in another state. Today she had gotten on the train a relatively unknown person with a famous job, but now her face and name were everywhere. Crap. She knew her family must be going crazy.

"You're famous now, eh," said a familiar voice with a New Zealand accent.

Nina looked to see Manaia walking up to her, big smile on her tan face and phone in hand.

"When the explosion happened and we got separated, I actually thought you had been hurt too," she said. "Then I didn't see you on the train, and I got scared. Then when we couldn't get reception, I was really like, 'Oh, shit.' Sorry, I'm babbling; are you okay?"

"Yeah," Nina said, looking from her phone to the crowd of people talking on the platform, many looking at her. "I... I was stuck in the last car."

Having no cell reception had annoyed Nina, but not that much. She hadn't considered how the rest of the delegation might be reacting without clear knowledge of what happened. Now with the sudden flood of social media returning, it was like the group could collectively breathe again. Everybody was talking at once, those closest to her asking questions. Manaia stayed next to her, talking to anyone in earshot. It was almost as hectic as the attack itself. Then the giant image of a man's head and shoulders appeared in the air over the crowded platform, and his amplified voice seemed to come from everywhere.

"Everyone, please give me your attention." He wore a business suit, was a few shades darker than Nina, and had a slight Caribbean accent. She realized who he was just as he said it.

"I'm Ambassador Zachariah Isaacs," he went on. "I know this trip has started in a horrific way none of us expected, and everyone has questions. I can tell you that there were no actual fatalities, although a number of people, including

Ambassador As the Gentle Wind, were critically injured. They were taken directly from the scene to medical facilities in orbit. Also, Envoy n'Dala, who was brought on board the train, is stable and expected to recover, thanks to the Society doctor and our very own..." His image glanced aside for a second as if someone were speaking to him. Looking around, Nina could see the ambassador standing not far off, listening to an aide, but she didn't see any cameras on him so had no idea how the image was being projected. "Dr. Rodriguez," he finished, and she was taken aback as some eyes turned toward her.

"For now," the ambassador's image continued, "go ahead and check into the hotel and call your families to let them know you're all right. I'm not ordering you not to talk to anyone—God knows the story has a life of its own now—but please, let's keep speculation to a minimum. This has the potential to be a very volatile situation, and as shocking as it is, this is part of the job we've all trained for. I know you'll do your best. The orientation and reception are in a few hours, and we will be able to give you more info then. Thank you."

There were a few shouted questions, but the ambassador's quick speech had gone a long way to calming everyone. All the embassy staff had gone through extensive tests and training to prepare them for the unexpected, and most people held themselves together surprisingly well. Ambassador Isaacs's image dissolved in the air and was replaced by a Nethean. The purple man started directing people which way to go. A number of C-humans on the platform also began helping the groups. Nina let herself be carried along with the crowd as she nodded, shrugged, and answered people's questions. This, of course, caused even more people to pay attention to her.

"Dr. Rodriguez?" a voice behind her called.

Nina turned around to see Dr. Endless Green Sky walking up to her.

"He's cute," Manaia said quietly. And it was so out of place, yet everyday-normal, that Nina felt herself relax a little for the first time since all the craziness had begun.

"Dr....Endless Green Sky," Nina said. "How's the envoy doing?"

"She's fine," he answered. "In fact, she wanted to thank the person who helped save her life personally. But the oxygen content on A'Qu, the envoy's homeworld, is higher than on Earth, so I had her taken to her room for now as she recovers."

"Wouldn't it be better if she was in a hospital?" Nina asked.

"No, we'll adjust the environmental controls in her suite," Endless Green Sky responded matter-of-factly.

"Wait." Manaia held her hands up. "Oh, I'm Manaia, by the way. You're saying the hotel rooms can create different atmospheric environments?"

"Certainly. Atmosphere, gravity, radiation." He smiled. "And nice to meet you, Manaia. We might've all come from the same base DNA, but the Society is a big place made up of a diverse group of hominins that evolved under numerous conditions. The hotel wouldn't be much use if it couldn't cater to everyone."

"I guess," Nina mused while thinking what it would be like to turn the gravity off in her room and float around.

"Of course, it's only done for necessary use," Endless Green Sky said, smiling at the two. "Wouldn't want someone to get hurt playing around."

"Of course." Nina blushed, half-wondering how obvious she had been.

"Anyway, I just wanted to give you a...heads-up? Is this the right term? A heads-up that the envoy wanted to thank you personally when she's feeling better."

"Yeah, anytime," Nina said. She was curious how the Society would react to what happened. She didn't want the actions of a few people ruining something she thought was so important for Earth. "You saw the news, right? I guess I shouldn't be surprised something like that went viral."

"Oh, that's nothing. Last month, a famous singer from Cree'lon had an embarrassing moment, and thirty billion C-humans saw it in the first hour. Anyway, I hope to see you tonight at the reception. Nina. Manaia." Endless Green Sky waved and walked over to another group of people.

Nina looked at him then at Manaia, not sure if he had been telling a joke or not. "I really hope he didn't just say there's reality TV in space."

AT FIRST, Nina took the large area they moved into to be the concourse of the train station but soon realized it was the lobby of their hotel. It was circular, with a large information desk in the center. Spiraling out from the desk were areas with elegant lounge seating, fountains, bars, and gardens. Along the walls, plants and trees perfectly blended into the architectural design like columns and stretched upward three stories, the topmost leaves becoming transparent and joining to form a clear dome over the entire lobby. Nina could see walkways encircling the second and third levels. And through the various transparent areas of the walls and ceiling she could see the four spires of the hotel rise into the distance, each located at one of the cardinal points of the lobby.

"If their rooms look half this good, I'm never leaving," Manaia breathed, looking around in awe.

"As long as their beds are comfy," Nina said. "I'm exhausted."

"Maybe that doctor Endless Purple Hottie will show you the room controls."

Nina laughed as they moved through the lobby, pointing out interesting things and chatting like everyone else. Nina saw a couple of doctors she recognized, then looked at Manaia in sudden realization. "You know, I don't even know what you do, Manaia. I'm a neurologist and neuroscientist."

"Oh, God, that's right," Manaia laughed. "So much going on, we never had a proper intro, huh. I'm Manaia Harris, from New Zealand like I said. I'm an anthropologist working in the public diplomacy office."

"So, you'll be close to all the political action?"

"Ha, don't know about that. My focus was on how indigenous cultures, like my own Maori, have adapted to and influenced modern life across the Pacific region," she said. "For now, we're mainly focused on the Society's New Human Culture Division, specifically their contact protocols, and eventually, I guess, we'll be dealing with Earth's nongovernmental groups."

After years of debate and politicking, the nations of Earth had finally agreed to allow a newly restructured United Nations to take point in all dealings with the Society. They oversaw Earth Embassy's delegation process and were also in charge of hiring humans from Earth to work in Sahara City. And every Earth human going into space now was subject to UN approval.

There were many Earthers of various races in hotel outfits, but to Nina the majority appeared to be from North

African countries, no doubt because this part of the Sahara was in Libya and Egypt. There were also dozens of C-humans in the lobby, mostly purple-skinned Netheans, working with the hotel staff. There were not as many C-humans as Earthers, but far more than Nina had ever seen at once in person.

"Any members of the theology contingent, please come with me," a middle-aged hotel staffer was saying to passersby.

Many of the lounge seating areas had a few hotel personnel, C-humans mostly, with glowing words hovering above them for the many different embassy groups like science, arts, or culture. There was no official check-in procedure, and everything seemed to have that organized casualness that she had come to expect from the Society. Thankfully, there was none of the chaos of the train station in Cairo.

Nina's hand rose to her chest involuntarily as she steadied her breathing. For a second, Nina felt the weight of the envoy as she fell back into her arms. The screams, the panic, that gun barrel—

"Are you okay, hon?"

Nina blinked to find Manaia holding her arm with a concerned expression on her face.

"Yeah... It's just, yeah," Nina started. "It's been a long day."

"Manaia, over here," someone called, drawing both women's attention. A man standing with a couple of others, next to a sign for the public diplomacy and affairs office, was waving to her from a little ways away.

Manaia smiled and waved but looked back to Nina. "I can walk to your room with you..."

"No." Nina shook her head, consciously ignoring how

the lobby was filling with more people. People she doubted had even seen the attack. "No, I'll be fine."

Nina eyed the sign for the medical contingent on the other side of the lobby. She pointed it out to Manaia and reassured the young woman, promising to meet later for the orientation. Manaia agreed, still looking a little worried, but moved off to meet her own group.

As Nina began to move her way through the throngs of people, she started to get noticed again. She wasn't an anxious person, but she was starting to feel a little penned-in, and she smiled, nodded, and/or excused herself as she moved past the questioners perhaps a little faster than would be polite. Thankfully, with all the C-humans around, most Earthers didn't notice her.

"You must be getting tired of that," a female voice said next to her.

Nina turned to see a Nethean woman standing at her side. "I'm sorry?"

"All the curiosity seekers." She smiled, casting a glance at some of the crowd. "If you want, I can show you your room; that way, you don't have to wait around with your group and get overwhelmed by more questions."

"That's..." Nina was about to automatically say *That's okay* but realized she really didn't want to be the center of attention right now. "Thank you; that'd be nice."

The woman smiled and with a hand gesture led Nina toward one of the walls. A few more people noticed and spoke to her, but as the lobby filled, she gradually became just another Earther talking to a C-human. As they neared the wall, Nina realized it was lined with elevators. Others were starting to use them, either alone, with a hotel clerk, or in small groups. The elevator doors didn't slide open so much as the wall appeared to dilate open.

"Did you also work for a hotel out in the Society?" Nina asked as they went inside.

"Me? Oh, goodness, no, but I have enough access to look up room assignments." The woman laughed and extended her hand. "I'm Fresh Snowfall on the Lake, a cultural historian. I do my best to make sure the Society doesn't make too many silly mistakes when talking to Earthers."

"Dr. Nina Rodriguez," Nina said, shaking her hand and not being able to keep the smile from her face. Of the few C-human races she had met so far, Netheans had the most interesting naming structure. "Will you be stationed on Earth?"

"Yes," the woman said, holding Nina's hand in both of hers and whispered almost conspiratorially. "I admit I'm excited. A new human culture joining the Society rarely happens in one's lifetime."

"I promise I'm just as excited." Nina smiled. At first glance, Fresh Snowfall on the Lake looked like someone in light-purple body paint until you really looked at her face. There were differences in facial structure around the nose, her yellow irises were larger than an Earther's, and, of course, she had the bonelike outcropping, instead of ears, that went from the jawline up to disappear into her curly black hair that swept back and fell down to her shoulders.

The elevator started to rise, and Nina's breath caught as she realized the walls were also transparent and gave a clear view of the city. Buildings rose into the blue desert sky, skyscrapers that were more cylindrical than rectangular. Elevated parks and rivers came into view, and in the distance, through a break in the buildings, she could see the starport at the edge of the city. Light reflected off the massive ship that would be taking them to Galileo City, on Jupiter's moon Io, tomorrow.

"I watched it on the news as the city was being built," Nina whispered. "But to see it in person...it's beautiful. Does your planet look like this?"

"Nethea? No, not at all," Fresh Snowfall on the Lake said, moving to stand next to Nina, who was pressed against the glass, looking out. "Our architecture is as different from this as it is from yours. Actually, these are mostly original designs made with Earther aesthetics in mind. But there are plenty of worlds remarkably similar to this."

"You know, I've been so focused on getting *out there* and starting work that I kinda ignored this," Nina said, still taking in the sights. "It just happened so quickly." With the exception of the cures for diseases like cancer, Sahara City was the example of Society technology that people on Earth were most impressed with, even more so than the building of *New Gaia* in low orbit. The city had gone from empty desert to full metropolis in barely three months' time. The global media was allowed free access during "construction," and the world had watched in amazement as the city grew out of the desert. Not raised up from but grew, like a garden over time. Scientists speculated on the fabrication technology but, by simply watching it, had no real way of explaining it. Parks, fountains, waterfalls from mega skyscrapers; all in all, it was a marvel to behold. The city was the size of San Francisco, not so big that it could not be walked but large enough for millions of inhabitants easily.

The entire city was the Society's embassy to Earth and the only place C-humans could live on the planet. It was open to every nation, but for now only diplomatic personnel were allowed to move in, and a UN police force was created. A global lottery was held to allow two million Earthers a chance to live in the city, but those "regular" residents would not arrive for another month.

"Once it opens, people will love it," Fresh Snowfall on the Lake said.

"I hope so," Nina said, remembering the disputes that had almost stalled the entire diplomatic mission. The Society had negotiated deals with Egypt and Libya to build the city in the Sahara. In exchange for agricultural improvements, the Society was given one thousand square kilometers of the Great Sand Sea, which sat on both countries' borders, and that had sparked outrage from other nations, especially the superpowers. America lobbied hard for it to be built in the Southwest desert and China for it in the Gobi Desert, but the Society had made it clear it would be in the Sahara. There were talks of sanctions by some countries, but it was an empty threat since the Society could provide anything Egypt and Libya needed, and they agreed to share the agricultural improvements with all other nations that wanted them.

Nina tore her gaze away when the elevator stopped on the thirtieth floor and the doors opened on a wide, high-ceilinged hallway with rooms on one side and windows on the other. Fresh Snowfall on the Lake stepped partly out, holding the elevator door for Nina.

"Your room is halfway down the hall on the right," she said. "Your luggage should already be there."

"Thank you," Nina said. "I hope we get to talk more at the reception."

"*You can bet on it*, I think, is the appropriate response," Fresh Snowfall on the Lake said. She looked at Nina for a moment before she continued more seriously. "Forgive me for asking but...are you okay? A lot happened today."

That gun.

The feeling didn't hit Nina like it had in the lobby, but it was there, and she honestly wasn't sure how she had been affected. The fact that she was standing there, talking to a purple humanoid born on another planet was easier to accept than the craziness of the train-station attack—even knowing that she could have died. She knew a neuropsychologist colleague that swore the whole world was living with mild PTSD since the C-humans' arrival.

The superpowers had almost gone to war multiple times over how to deal with the existence of aliens. Multiple times, World War III had been a real possibility. And Nina had lived that year after arrival like everyone else, in a perpetual state of shock and fear.

"A part of me still can't believe we didn't blow ourselves up," she finally said. "That attack was part of a larger issue we're all trying to cope with."

"I can't pretend to know how it was for you Earthers, living through that, but I can promise you we were also worried. And I probably shouldn't say this, but..." Fresh Snowfall on the Lake glanced around even though the hallway was empty. "We wouldn't have interfered with your wars, of course, but we wouldn't have let you go extinct, either."

Nina looked at the C-human—her face so human yet so not at the same time—a cousin species. To her, what Fresh Snowfall on the Lake had said didn't feel menacing or like an invader's comment but more like an enlightened civilization looking out for family. Not everyone agreed with her, of course—what had happened at the train station spoke to that—but she believed it.

"I'm glad," Nina said to her, sighing. "I think people will figure it out eventually."

. . .

NINA SAT on the edge of the bed in her hotel room, trying to make sense of everything that had happened so far. All embassy staffers had been notified of the time for the orientation later, but for now, everyone had a chance to rest. She wanted to stretch out on the bed and sleep but knew she had to call her family first. The room was very high-class Earth-looking, with a huge bed, separate sitting room, and a window that took up an entire wall. Outside, the new city stretched into the distance, and beyond that, the empty desert. Even though it wasn't open yet, the city didn't seem deserted. Nina could see workers everywhere. Human engineers and landscape artists from all over the world were working with their C-human counterparts to put the final touches on things.

The official opening of the city would coincide with the launch of *New Gaia*, Earth's so-called emergence vessel that was being built (grown) in low Earth orbit. Nina glanced up. She could clearly see the small shape that was the *New Gaia* in the sky, but from there, she didn't know if it was rising or setting against the horizon. Earth's first interstellar spaceship was about six miles wide. Its starfish shape shimmered and glowed with its own aurora, greenish swirls spiraling around the vessel. It was common knowledge that the aurora was from the interaction of Society grav tech and Earth's magnetic field, but that didn't take away from the beauty of the sight, especially at night. To her, it was a sign of the future. And yet to radical groups, it was just another symbol of alien intervention.

Nina sighed and looked at the phone on the desk, and then she pulled out her cell and video-called her parents.

Her mother's tear-streaked face filled the screen. "Oh, Dios mío, Nina! Are you okay? Your papa and I have been calling—"

"Mama—"

"—and calling, but you didn't pick up. Why didn't you pick up? Are you on your way back? We can—"

"Mama—"

"—pick you up at the airport. Luis, its Nina! Come quick. My God, it's all over the news. Where are you—"

"Ma, I'm not coming back!" It came out a little louder than Nina intended, but sometimes, that was the only way to get a word in with her mother.

"Excuse me?" Her mother frowned at her. There was no passive-aggressive guilt trip in Nina's house when she was growing up. Her mom let you know exactly what she thought. "Somebody tries to kill you, and you don't call, don't text, and now you tell me you're not coming home?"

"No one tried to kill me, Mother."

"Don't you *Mother* me! You better—"

"Hey, honey." Her dad's face squeezed into the camera view. "How are you?"

"Hey, Papa. I'm fine."

"She's bulletproof, apparently," her mother said.

"Honey, you really should've called us. We had no idea what was going on."

"I know, Papa. I'm sorry." She genuinely did feel bad about that. "There was no reception on the train, and I really had no idea that the media was running the story like that."

"Well, I'm not surprised, with aliens attacking," her mother said.

"Ma." Nina was tired. "I love you, and I'm sorry I didn't call sooner. But I'm not having this argument again."

"But they're not human."

"Well, actually, they are. Genetic cousins, at least. And

there are still people today who act like other races on Earth are less than human."

"So, now I'm racist?!"

"I didn't say that."

"But that's what you act like."

"Let's be honest, Ma. You're judging them more for how they look than by what they're doing."

"And if what they're doing is putting my child in danger and taking over—"

"Terrorists put me in danger, Ma. Not C-humans. Terrorists from Earth. A bunch of crazy people who hate anything different, the way you—"

"So, now I support terrorists!" Her mom threw her hands up, looking at her dad.

"Oh my God." Nina sighed.

"Nina," her dad said, forestalling her mother before she could get started again. "We're proud of you. You know that, right?"

"I know, Papa, but—"

"No. No buts." He raised his hand. "We're proud of you and everything you've accomplished. And at some point, every parent has to say this, and you will one day, when you have kids, no matter how old and independent they get, the way you worry is on a whole different level. Our only daughter is about to fly off into space and live on another planet for years. That's not something a parent has ever, ever had to prepare for before. Literally, as you young people say."

"I get it," she said. "I don't really know how to wrap my head around this either. But I believe it's something that has to be done. And I know that I want to be a part of the team doing it."

"Honey," her mom said. "Not a day goes by that I don't

think if the Society had come a few years earlier, your abuelos would still be alive. Or at the very least know who they were in the last bit of their life." Nina's grandmother getting Alzheimer's and her grandfather suffering from dementia had been the driving force behind her becoming a neurologist.

"So, I get it," her mom continued after a deep breath. "It's not that we don't want you to follow your dream. We just want you to face it eyes open. Maybe I do come down on these C-humans kinda hard. Partly, I feel, because you are too accepting of them. You distinctly put them on a pedestal, and that's what scares us."

Nina nodded. She was honest enough with herself to know there was some truth to what her mom said. She didn't believe the Society was above reproach, and she felt knowing that would allow her to face anything objectively.

"I hear you, Ma. I really do," she said. "And I promise you I won't go into anything with blinders on."

"That's all we ask, Mija," her dad said. "And we'll be here for you whatever comes."

Nina sighed. She knew they were just scared for her. And before the Society had come, she figured she would have been happy working at a hospital in Albuquerque. But their arrival had changed...well, everything, of course. The impact on the medical field was the most obvious to her. And now she had a chance to be at the forefront of how that medical tech would be involved in human, Earth-based medicine. Making sure it worked for everyone. Not just a select few but everyone.

"And you better call home," her mom said. "I don't care how many light-years away you are."

Nina smiled. "Yes, Mami."

They talked for a while longer, her reassuring them she

was safe and fine more than once. Nina had started college a couple of years early, and she felt her parents had naturally become a little overprotective to compensate for her growing up so fast. As the conversation died down, her parents looked at each other; she knew what was coming next. Her father said tentatively, "Tony's been worried also. Are you going to call him?"

She didn't want to, but she would; she owed him that much. She had loved him. Probably still loved him. He was a good man, but they had never seen eye to eye on the C-humans' arrival. He genuinely feared they would be the end of freedom as Earth knew it—just as she believed the opposite. And that had eaten away at their relationship for years before she finally broke it off. Unfortunately, that had also been around the time when she was notified she had been selected for the embassy's medical division. So, naturally, he blamed the Society for their breakup, and he hated them even more than her mom did. And then he made it worse by proposing to her even though he knew she would say no.

"I'll call," she answered her dad. "I will. Look, I'll talk to you all tomorrow before we take off. There are some other functions going on tonight, so I gotta get some sleep."

"You be careful, Nina," her mom said, a wave of unspoken things crossing her face until she settled on one. "We love you, Mija."

"I know, Ma. And I will be careful," she said. "Love you guys. Bye."

Nina disconnected and sighed, flopping back on the bed to browse her phone. She just had to see the video again, not being able to believe she was in something that had gone viral. The second the video started and she heard the first screams, she turned it off and had to take a moment to calm herself. She didn't need to keep seeing something she had lived through.

Everybody would probably live, given the Society's medical technology. She had been very relieved to hear that everyone injured was being treated by Society tech. She had seen, firsthand, people die when doctors put their pride above their patients' health. And Nina realized that seeing the envoy's surgery was a big part of the reason she wasn't more bothered by what happened. She had been absolutely certain n'Dala was going to die, so then to see her healed before her eyes made everything before that seem a little unreal to Nina. She had seen medical procedures done with C-human biotech before but always under controlled circumstances. In a hospital, the lab, even on TV, with a lot of preparation, doctors, consent, everything documented and reviewed. But in the moment—a real-world, blood-on-hands, crisis situation where a life was saved? What happened was like magic compared to what Earth could do, and it was hard not to be awed by that. She would never forget that gun pointing at her, but she would also never forget seeing those bullets float up out of the envoy's body.

She rubbed her temples, trying to relieve a headache she hadn't even noticed before. It had been a stressful day, and it was only half over. Tomorrow they would be leaving for Jupiter and, a few days after that, traveling to Sapher, the Society government world located somewhere near the Orion Nebula. Nina knew there were Earthers already out there, living in the Society, but could only imagine what their lives must be like. She closed her eyes for a minute to rest and immediately drifted off to sleep.

4

While he walked down the corridor, Marcus watched through the shiplink as *Fulcrum's Light* slid into standard space a full light-minute's distance from the fourth planet in the Travanis system. It'd taken some practice to get used to "seeing" something in his mind's eye while moving about in the physical, but after some time, it was even easier than walking around using a cell phone. The floors were flat, but the light gray walls of the bioship's corridor curved outward slightly, and they always gave Marcus the impression that he was walking down tunnels dug out by a giant worm. But they didn't come off as ominous or dark; the ceilings were bioluminescent and cast enough soft light to give the feeling of a clear afternoon day.

"Marcus," a voice said.

He let go of the external image and turned to see Dr. Sumiko Ueda approaching him from a side corridor. The Japanese astrobiologist was average height, with bangs that accented her face, and long black hair that fell past the shoulders of her ship suit. Marcus picked up waves of frustration coming off her, through his bioweb. There had been some debate over the Earthers being part of the mission, given what had happened on Earth. Envoy Rahel tended to be a little overprotective, but he knew she meant well. Marcus had been the only one to suffer any disorientation during the terrorist attack on the Earth delegates; his bioweb and Rahel's were the only ones with no restrictions, but for the other Earthers, filtering protocols limited the amount of emotion coming through, so they hadn't been affected like him. Lead Dr. Leikeema had run a check on him to make sure he didn't suffer any unexpected effects after the incident in the Nexus, and now he was on his way to join the recon team headed to the moon's surface.

"Hey," he said. "I was just in medbay but didn't see you."

"I was running errands. Can you believe this?" she asked, coming alongside him. "I'm right here, and they won't even let me study them. They won't even let me access a visual of them!"

"You mean the natives of the planet?" Marcus asked, confused about what that had to do with what happened on Earth.

"Well, yeah," she said. "What else would I be talking about?"

"Uh, the attack back home." Marcus immediately felt her shame and embarrassment, which in turn made him feel the same for calling her out like that, which he hadn't meant to do.

"God, I didn't..." Sumiko shook her head, at a loss for words. Marcus didn't try to block out her flood of emotions but instead acknowledged them and let them flow over him without getting caught up and losing himself in experiencing them. He hadn't realized how different some of his training had been from other Earthers until he had come on board.

"We've just seen that type of thing so much that..." Sumiko started again, and paused sighing.

"You get desensitized to it." Marcus understood how she felt.

"I guess," she agreed. "And then perceiving it through the Nexus just made it all the more surreal. Even with being able to feel some emotions." She looked at him, but Marcus didn't know if she was picking up his feelings or just reading body language. "But it must've been even worse for you with full access."

"I'm still getting used to it." Marcus had barely had time to get to know any of the other Earthers over the past week because Sarjah had immediately given him an intense training schedule. The few times he had been able to speak to Sumiko, they had gotten along, but he didn't want to get into a discussion now about how much it had bothered him.

"You headed to the portal chamber?" he asked.

"Yeah, somebody from Medical has to be there for missions," she said.

As Earth moved into NHC status, select Earthers were assigned to study with C-humans in specific areas, usually involving medicine or engineering, but there were also some military personnel. Marcus guessed the last was done to appease nations back home who still had fears of alien invasion. The five Earth humans on board were a diverse group, and Marcus suspected one reason the Society chose a wide mix of people from Earth was so they could observe how they interacted with each other as well as with C-humans. His own training would take him all over the Society, so he would only be on *Fulcrum's Light* for a few months before moving on.

"It just seems like busy work," Sumiko continued. "Since the recon team can be monitored from anywhere on the ship. I think Dr. Leikeema was just trying to get me out of her hair."

Marcus felt that strong wave of frustration again, but it had nothing to do with Earth. He looked at the wall and sent a data request with his bioweb. An image of the planet and its moons appeared in the chromatophores of the corridor's wallskin and moved with them as they walked. The planet's second moon was a rough, irregular-formed object, twelve and a half kilometers in diameter. It's potato-like shape was more reminiscent of an asteroid than a moon and it had no doubt been captured by Travanis 4's gravity, similar to the way some astronomers believed Mars got its moons.

"So, what were you saying about the planet?" he asked. "I thought they were also C-human but at some preindustrial level—"

"They are, but their race is silicon-based," she said, relieved to get back to her original point. "I didn't even think that was possible. It's like something out of"—she rolled her eyes and waved her hand, taking in the spaceship around them, the other C-humans going about their duties, and the image on the wallskin keeping pace with them—"science fiction."

Marcus's blank stare no doubt gave away that he had no idea what she was talking about.

"Are you kidding me?" she asked. "What do they teach you Americans in school?"

"Probably the same thing they teach you Japanese folk, just in a different language."

Sumiko gave him a sidelong glance but couldn't suppress her smile. "Ha-ha."

"Sumiko, I'm into VFX and programming, not biology. I know Earth humans are carbon-based organisms, but aren't there a bunch of different types in the Society?"

"Not really. Carbon based are by far the most common, and then there are some carbon-silicon based, like the Fent'ri." She nodded her head toward a four-foot yellow C-human walking past them in the other direction. "But silicon-based hominins are rare. I looked it up, and there have only been three in the entire history of the Society. And these are currently the only known living race that is."

She had a faraway, look in her eyes. "The papers I could write if they just let me see..." The dreamy look in her eyes turned conspiratorial as she stared at Marcus.

"Nope," he said, stopping at the transit vein entrance, mentally sending the open code with his bioweb. The door dilated, its surface opening like a pupil in the dark, and they stepped inside the slightly rounded elevator. Usually, it was easier to portal wherever you wanted to go inside the ship, but with the current mission status, that was restricted to emergencies.

"Oh, come on, please," she said, pointing to the image that flowed around the corridor wall and displayed on the elevator wallskin now. "You're the Nexus guru. Just give me an image of what they look like."

"And get portaled back to Earth?" Once the door closed, there was no sense of movement, but through the shiplink, Marcus could track their location easy. "And most likely start some interstellar incident. Nope. Uh-uh. Not me."

"You're exaggerating." The halfhearted way she said it let Marcus know she knew the truth but was just frustrated.

"Look, I get it," he said. "Kind of. But you know I couldn't access that data even if I wanted to. As open as they are about letting us do things, they're serious about guarding their tech and how it's used. Especially when it comes to uncontacted human cultures."

"Yeah." She sighed in defeat. The door dilated, and they got out on the portal deck. The image of the planet continued to follow them until Sumiko waved it away. "And I know it's silly. I'm an astrobiologist who gets to live in a closed environment, long-term, with more different C-humans than people on Earth even know exist. On a freaking living ship!"

He was still sensing a jumble of emotions from her, but as he had come to learn in his months of training, being able to feel someone's emotions and knowing what caused them wasn't the same thing.

"Then what's really bothering you?"

They walked in silence for a moment before she sighed and answered. "I guess I'm trying too hard not to be like Anime Guy."

"Who?"

Another sigh. "Back at the university I worked at, we had this visiting professor from Britain who loved animation. Brilliant man, and nice; he just couldn't seem to understand that not all Japanese people watch anime and read manga. It really got annoying after a while."

"And you don't want to come off here like everyone is just a science experiment?"

"Exactly," she said as they approached the portal chamber door. "And I know we're encouraged to ask questions, but I guess there's still a part of me that holds back."

"I know I don't know you well, but do you think the Nexus might be making you overcompensate?"

"How so?"

"Well, normal people are considerate of others' feelings when they talk to them," Marcus said.

"Uhh..."

"In general, I mean."

"I guess, yeah."

"But with the Nexus, you can actually feel others' emotions," he continued. "And if what you're feeling from someone seems out of place for what you're discussing, it's easy to misinterpret or start to wonder if what you said is the reason for that."

"My group's bioweb instructor used to talk about that," she said.

"Mine too. So, because you remember how this professor made you feel, you don't want to do that to others. Then you start to wonder if this feeling or that feeling is in response to something you've done even before you said anything. Then you just get kinda stuck, afraid to say anything."

"Like when I first came up to you, you thought I was upset about Earth, not realizing it was something else?"

"Right," he said. "I still get confused by it, and honestly... I don't know if Earth is ready for this."

"I hope we are," she said, then rubbed her hands together like a mad scientist. "And I guess the good thing is I get to experiment on all the Earthers as much as I want."

"I feel better already," Marcus deadpanned as they went inside the portal chamber. "And look on the bright side."

"What's that?"

"If you get homesick," he said with an innocent grin and shrug, "I do love talking about anime."

"Oh my God." She gave him another exaggerated mean look. "Only if you promise to teach me about guns. Don't all Americans get one when you're born?"

He laughed. "It's optional."

. . .

THE PORTAL CHAMBER was near the front portion of the ship and took up two levels. Near the area where Marcus and Sumiko entered were control stations where portal technicians worked. Along the side walls were alcove areas where teams prepped. The center of the cavity was a clear area where the portal opened. The chamber had the power to generate one large portal that could open up to thirty light-years away, which was small-scale next to the largest planet-based megaportals that could send things thousands of light-years. Multiple smaller portals could also be operated at the same time and work at distances of many millions of kilometers. That was overseen by the portal technicians, p-tecs, but crew could also use their biowebs to connect to the chamber and have it portal them around the ship.

Marcus walked over to one of the wall alcoves where the others were getting ready, and Sumiko went to confer with the p-tecs. There was a six-person recon team going to the surface. US Navy Lieutenant Scott Grayson, the only other Earther there, was off to the side with Lead Security Officer Tuhzo, another Xindari, and Kleedak Pah, a roughly eight-foot-tall blue reptilian C-human, going over some equipment tests.

Tuhzo had many streaks of gray in the mane of black hair that circled his shoulders, so Marcus assumed he was older, although he couldn't tell by facial features. And the few times he had been around Tuhzo, Marcus had found him to be even more reserved than other Xindari.

Grayson almost looked like a kid next to Kleedak's huge bulk. The hairless blue reptile was one of the largest C-humans Marcus had met, and the Axlons' sleeveless ship suit revealed scaled arms far thicker than Marcus's thighs, making the size difference seem even more unreal. From what Marcus had seen in his short time traveling through the Society, C-humans, while almost all bipedal, ranged in size roughly from four feet to eight feet. There was no one definitive average. Xindari and Netheans were similar to Earthers near six feet, while Axlons like Kleedak were eight and Fent'ri like Dr. Leikeema, Sumiko's boss, were around four feet.

"Greer," Grayson said, seeing him walk up. "They finally letting you out of the classroom to have some real fun?" So far Grayson was the only other American Marcus had met in his time out in the Society.

"I was actually surprised Sarjah wanted me on the recon team so soon," Marcus said, noticing her coming into the chamber and talking to t'Zyah and the p-tecs over where Sumiko was standing.

"You know how reptiles are," Grayson said.

"Yeah, always protecting their little mammal cousins," Kleedak said, zer deep laugh reverberating off the walls.

Tuhzo grunted, maybe in approval, maybe disapproval —it was hard to tell with Xindari—but he never stopped checking equipment.

"Sounds like somebody's still mad I beat their high score." Grayson finished putting together the large rifle he was holding and looked down its sight, aiming at the far wall.

"Ha, don't strain yourself lifting that," Kleedak said, hefting his own gun, which was about the size of Marcus, to his shoulder. Marcus consciously corrected himself, knowing "he" was inaccurate because Axlons were a hermaphroditic race. When Marcus had first started training on the planet Ya'sung, several people in his group, including him, had to let go of the idea that physical size had anything to do with gender. Their first teacher was a Ta Wei, an all-female amphibian race that averaged about seven feet tall. And that unconscious musing started his bioweb bringing up statistical info on the number of sexes different C-human races had.

"I don't know, dude," Grayson said. "Looks like you might be overcompensating."

"How can one overcompensate for such magnificence?" ze asked.

"If possible, I'm sure an Axlon will find a way," Tuhzo said, never looking up from the recon spheres he was now examining.

"Indeed, indeed, little cousin," Kleedak said, zer big blue hand slapping Tuhzo affectionately on the back. "We would find a way!"

"Wait, did you just make a joke, Tuhzo?" Grayson asked. "Is that even possible?"

Kleedak chuckled. "Xindari are stoic, young cousin, but when they laugh, they laugh true."

"What does that even mean?" Grayson asked Marcus.

Marcus shrugged. "Got me, man. But I bet it got something to do with balance."

Tuhzo glanced at Marcus; was that mild surprise in his face? "It seems you do listen to Sarjah," he said, going back to adjusting the equipment. "Perhaps we will be able to teach you Earthers something after all."

"Uh, we got a lot to teach y'all, too," Grayson said.

Kleedak guffawed, zer voice booming, even Tuhzo had a half smile, and Marcus felt a ripple of humor spread out on the shiplink through the C-humans in the portal chamber. It was the type of good-natured laughter you have when you hear a child say something silly. He even saw Sumiko smile.

"Dude," Grayson said, picking up on it. "Did we just get laughed at?"

"We leave in five, people. Let's focus," t'Zyah said as she

walked up to the alcove next to Marcus and stood so close to him that he could feel a tingle from her bioelectric field. After Netheans, the A'Quan were probably the race people on Earth saw the most. t'Zyah was the lead metatech on board and third-in-command of the ship. She was average height for her people, about five feet tall, with purple eyes. The left side of her slightly oblong head had a few spiraling tattoos on the bald sky-blue skin, that occasionally glittered.

"Skins on, everyone," t'Zyah said.

"Copy that," Grayson said, accessing metaspace, and the surface of his ship suit started to shimmer. His feeling of excitement was strong over the shiplink.

Marcus had noticed early on that the Earthers he had met so far had varying degrees of success when it came to keeping their feelings from being transmitted through the Nexus.

"You ready, Ditec Greer?" t'Zyah asked, having to tilt her head to look up at him because of their proximity.

"Uh...yes, sorry," Marcus said, realizing some of his own excitement was probably also seeping out over the shiplink.

The moon was too small to have any real atmosphere, so they had to wear EVA suits to protect them from space. And as with most Society technology, the so-called voidskins were organic.

Marcus opened his perception to metaspace and sent an activation code with his bioweb. Putting on the suit wasn't like the cumbersome task that Earth astronauts had had to endure, with many people helping them fit in the bulky, multilayered material. Voidskins were stored in a pocket dimension tied to the ship. Linked to his personal biosignature, the protective suit materialized around the contours of his body, melding with the organic material of his ship uniform, so it was not necessary to strip down when putting in on. The voidskin effectively became a second epidermis that could withstand the extremes of space. His first instinct was always to hold his breath as it formed over his face, but it wasn't necessary. The voidskin absorbed the carbon dioxide from his expelled breath and fed oxygen directly into his skin and nasal cavity. It absorbed all bodily waste, dry skin, sweat, urine, feces—the last two things, Marcus had never gotten used to in training.

The voidskin was controlled through the bioweb, but it also responded to biochemical reactions from the wearer's body. That way, if the person was unconscious or severely injured, the skin could stabilize them until help arrived. It increased strength, was very durable, and generated a strong bioelectromagnetic field. It also provided a great deal of protection, blocking radiation and temperature, and was able to self-heal, but it could still be damaged by enough energy or physical force. Marcus turned his hands back and forth, looking at the dark covering. The epidermis of the voidskin shone like an oil slick: dark gray and blackish, but depending on how it caught the light, waves of color seemed to slide across its surface, the purples, greens, yellows, and reds giving an added apparent layer of depth. Even though his head was fully enclosed, there was no sense of confinement like with a full-face scuba-diving or gas mask. In fact, it felt perfectly comfortable, as if he were only covering his skin with his hand. The suit's interior really did feel like an extension of his flesh, matching his body temperature and skin texture perfectly.

A pulse alerted him, and Marcus saw t'Zyah had sent an image of a recon sphere to him, a gentle reminder that he acknowledged with a nod. He took a melon-sized spherical object from the alcove before him and synched it to his voidskin, leaving it to hover next to him. It would follow him until deactivated.

System check, t'Zyah said to everyone over the shiplink.

How to run through his systems came to the forefront of Marcus's working memory through his bioweb. The knowledge was there, just like his natural memory of what he had had for breakfast. All of his systems were online, and just by shifting his focus, he could see all around without turning his head, because the voidskin's external surface served as one big sensor, interpreting EM spectra.

"Are we expecting trouble, Lead t'Zyah?" Grayson asked out loud.

All the voidskins looked similar on the exterior, but Grayson's, Kleedak's, and Tuhzo's were the much bulkier ultra-voidskins worn by security. Usually just called ultraskins, they were able to generate a stronger bioelectromagnetic field, giving them more strength and firepower, better shielding, and propulsion.

"Ship scans indicate nothing on the surface but a data portal. No other structures or life," t'Zyah answered. "But this is an illegal operation in clear violation of multiple Society laws, so some type of countermeasures, or boobytraps, are not out of the realm of possibility. Be on your guard."

"Understood," Tuhzo said.

Group, link up, t'Zyah transmitted over the shiplink.

Anyone with a bioweb could access the Nexus from anywhere in Society space. Shiplinks were only a microcosm of that, where everyone on board linked through the ship's lifecore. This gave an ultra-secure line of interaction where the lifecore was analogous to a server. Within that, a grouplink between a few people could also be formed.

Kleedak, you and Lieutenant Grayson will take point, then

myself and Lead Tuhzo, t'Zyah said. *Ditec Sarjah, you and Ditec Greer bring up the rear.*

Everyone acknowledged the order.

Marcus shifted his weight from foot to foot, getting comfortable and covering his excitement. Standing there in a spacesuit, on a biological starship, about to go to an alien moon, was about as far from Atlanta as he could imagine. Until he had actually come out into the Society, he hadn't admitted to himself, on a conscious level at least, how much he had wanted to get away. It'd been years since his parents had died in that car crash and he had moved in with his grandparents. A hard path for a teenager, but they had always been there for him and did the best they could. But they were old, and as he matured, the reality of him starting to have to take care of them was a shadow he hadn't noticed behind him at first. In fact, the only reason he felt comfortable taking this assignment was because he knew his grandparents would be okay from a health point of view, with all of the Society's medical technology being offered on Earth. It didn't mean life problems disappeared—finances had been really hard when he went to college and kind of still were—but his current pay was helping with that, and at least he was free to be there without worrying about their health. Now he was slowly realizing the longer he was out in the Society, doing things like this, the more he found himself enjoying it. The more he wanted to stay. And on some level that made him feel a little guilty, like he was abandoning his grandparents just to have fun. He knew it wasn't that simple, but it still weighed on him. Not so much that he actually called but enough that he sometimes thought about it.

Recon team ready, t'Zyah said to the portal techs.

Marcus and the group moved near the center of the

room. The empty air above the platform before them seemed to spiral in on itself like a swirling heat shimmer, then there was a ripple, and a half-spherical section became a portal, which appeared as a minor air disturbance. Portals provided pathways through metaspace, but they were not wormholes: they were not two specifically linked endpoints which allowed someone to see to the other side like a doorway. But the surface of the moon was clear in his mind's eye from the ship's sensors. While he stared at the surface, Marcus was aware, also through the shiplink, that t'Zyah had notified the captain they were ready and of the captain's response. On a deeper, more subconscious level, he was aware of other crew members accessing the recon group's POVs.

Let's move, people, t'Zyah said.

Tuhzo waited off to the side, suited and ready. Next to the portal, Kleedak's already imposing figure seemed almost ridiculously large in zer ultra-voidskin. Drone spores emerged from Kleedak's suit and flew through the portal. Then ze and Grayson, weapons ready, followed the spores. They took up flanking positions; Marcus could see them through the drone spore's feed as they scanned the area, and he could also see them through their own POVs in the grouplink. t'Zyah and Tuhzo followed when they gave the all-clear.

Our turn, baby culture, Sarjah said as she moved forward. *Stay focused and in this moment, and do exactly as I say.* With that, she stepped through the portal.

Marcus had used a voidskin in space before but only in training, never on an actual mission. He hadn't realized it would feel so...real. He took a breath, calming himself. Then a little thumbs-up icon pulsed in his mind's eye, accompanied by a feeling of confidence. Sumiko had sent it on a private link. He glanced over to where she stood, near the p-tecs, and smiled, letting her access his gratefulness. Then he nodded to himself and stepped forward...

...onto the moon's pockmarked surface. His voidskin automatically compensated for the change in gravity, and as he started to rise, its bioelectromagnetic field pushed him down slightly. He only rose a foot in the air as he glided forward into his next step.

The transition from the bright interior of the portal chamber was jarring as the apparent darkness of space surrounded him. Marcus stood for a moment on the grayish regolith. The small moon's barren landscape was marred with craters and jagged outcroppings. Small rises and valleys blocked much of his view, but between some he could see the unnatural closeness of the horizon. From where he stood, the planet Travanis 4 loomed large before him in the "sky." Swirls of white clouds floated over the planet's yellow-orange landmasses and dark blue oceans. A beautiful sight but dissimilar enough from Earth to drive home how incredible what they were doing was to Marcus.

The people on the planet had no idea that other beings, who also called themselves human, were watching over them. Just like six years earlier, Earth had had no true idea that they were not alone in the galaxy. Living in the comfortable, innocent ignorance of its UHC status, while the Society Protectorate guarded the Solar System's border. An innocence that was shattered when a civilian Society ship had an accident in metaspace and was forced to crash-land. Numerous laws had been broken by choosing Earth, but it had been the only habitable planet within a few light-years that the bioship could reach. And while a Protectorate ship would have sacrificed itself before revealing C-humans to an Uncontacted Human Culture, the civilian ship did not.

When the bioship crashed into Hawaii's Big Island and the few survivors were found by the US government, the Society had no choice but to reveal itself to Earth and try its best to mitigate the panic.

Marcus knew this situation was very different. This was no accident but someone in the Society purposefully interfering with a UHC. And the implications of a civilization as advanced as the Society having people who would do that were frightening.

Stop sightseeing, baby culture, and let's get to work, Sarjah said to Marcus on their private link as she moved, her bioelectromagnetic field allowing her to coast above the surface.

Marcus took one tentative glance over his shoulder at the portal, but it was now closed, and the starkness of the landscape was broken only by some footprints that seemed to start from nowhere. He looked up, seeing *Fulcrum's Light* in a low orbit, then took another breath and followed the others.

The bioship's portal had opened midway up a small rise. About one hundred meters before them, the recon team could see a small object, about the size of a dining table, which seemed to grow from the regolith. Kleedak's larger form was on point and had stopped about forty meters from it, and was monitoring the drone spore data with zer ultra-skin sensors, which Marcus could also access.

Standard dimensional energy signature, Kleedak said.

Ship sensors confirm area is clear, t'Zyah said, moving toward him slowly, more coasting forward in gliding jumps than anything resembling walking. *But I want you and Grayson doing a perimeter sweep.*

Copy that. Kleedak and Grayson split up, circling the target. Marcus lost sight of them as they moved around outcroppings, navigating the landscape. He kept track of them through their ultraskin POV's and also from the sensors of *Fulcrum's Light* overhead.

Tuhzo now took point, and Marcus followed t'Zyah and Sarjah the rest of the way up the rise. The object was about two meters in diameter and looked similar to a coral reef, with protruding appendages that were very treelike. Within its porous surface was a faint glow that pulsed with energy.

Tuhzo stood next to the object, and on the grouplink Marcus observed the results of his in-depth field scans. *Clear,* he said, then glided around the small rise, keeping watch.

What is this? Marcus asked t'Zyah, who knelt by the object. Drone spores from her voidskin floated about to land on its surface.

A data portal, t'Zyah answered. *It collects information and sends it through to wherever its exit point is. It's so small because all the power to generate it comes from the other end.*

If it's just sending data FTL, why not use the Nexus? Wouldn't that be easier?

Anything sent over the Nexus could be potentially tracked, Sarjah answered. *Even if the encryption couldn't be broken, the source and destination could ultimately be found out.*

And since Travanis 4 is a UHC, a dimensional signal coming from here would be flagged instantly, Marcus said, understanding.

Exactly, Sarjah said. *But this is a direct portal from here to the endpoint. The only way to detect it is to actually be close enough to pick up its energy signature. And even then, that's not guaranteed. You did a good job even noticing this from the background spatial flux, even though you didn't follow through.*

Marcus's surprise at the backhanded compliment was clear over their private link.

Don't get cocky, baby culture, she responded without even a glance.

Sarjah activated the recon sphere following Marcus, and it floated up to land on a console-like protrusion of the data portal. Marcus could detect the micro filaments it extended to the panel, then Sarjah put her hand up to the sphere and more micro filaments connected to her voidskin. The sphere served as a buffer to access the portal's interior biomechanics. *Mirror me, Marcus,* she said.

Through their private link Marcus accessed her metaspace presence. A wall of encryption rose before him in his mind's eye. It was similar to some he had faced in simulations while training, but it had subtle differences.

Eternal Balance, she cursed. *t'Zyah, I think this is third-civ encryption.*

My Gods, are you sure? t'Zyah's voice sounded worried as her voidskinned figure floated back around to them from the other side of the data portal.

Stand by. Sarjah's digital presence skimmed the firewall, firing off random packets of code designed to trace energy patterns.

Even though their emotions weren't transmitting, from the way they were talking to each other Marcus could tell something was serious, but he wasn't sure what. He accessed the Nexus to research third-civilization technology. He knew the general big picture of C-human history, but it had never been his focus. He had had enough on his plate with ditec training and learning about the Society. It was only now that he tried to research it that Marcus realized the specifics of the tech were off-limits. He understood the Society withheld certain knowledge from NHCs for fear of cultural contamination, but as a ditec he had access to more than the average person, so if he still couldn't access it, it had to be serious.

He knew the basics: the third C-human mega-civilization had officially been called 011000101110101110, but was usually referred to as the third-civ. It had existed in the ancient past, although the exact dates were restricted to him. It had used mechanical-based dimensional technology, not biological like the Society. The strange thing was that the civilization had disappeared all at once, every single person, which was still one of the biggest mysteries in C-human history. But an old mystery was all he ever considered it, like how the pyramids were really built, or something like that. It just hadn't been relevant to him, because it was so ancient. And he realized that the people of Earth were going to have to rethink their views on time. Earth's recorded history was only about five thousand years old, but the Society itself was almost three times that age. And it was only the most recent—and youngest—of the five human mega-civilizations that had risen and fallen, stretching back to the Hu'ma, the first human civilization.

For Earthers, World War I was little over one hundred years ago, and that might as well be the Dark Ages as far as Marcus's generation was concerned. He knew only the bare bones of the Society's fourteen-thousand-year history. So, it was no surprise he hadn't thought much of something that had happened in far pre-Society history. Although he did think it strange that exact dates of the previous human civs were restricted from NHC people.

As he wondered about the best way to ask Sarjah about it, Marcus became aware of a few others joining their grouplink. There was no visual image, but each person's presence gave as distinctive a feel as different appearances did.

Sarjah, Captain Ahmon said. *Can you determine the destination of the portal signal?*

Possibly, Captain, she answered. *I'm checking.*

Analysis of the portal's receiving signal is standard Society technology, Yeizar of Eleven, the Oodandi ditec on duty in the ship, said. *As far as we can tell, a number of microsatellites in orbit around the planet are collecting data on the indigenous race.*

To what purpose? t'Zyah asked. *They don't have digital entertainment yet.*

Unsure.

We might know, Captain, Dr. Leikeema said over the link from Medical.

Go ahead, Doctor, Captain Ahmon said.

Dr. Ueda's desire to learn about the natives got me thinking, Dr. Leikeema began, and Marcus noticed from a quick wave of embarrassment that Sumiko was also on the link. *Studying the small amount of data Ditec Yeizar was able to pull leads me to believe that the focus is biological information on the flora and fauna of the planet. It might possibly have something to do with this race being silicon-based.*

That sounds ominous, Marcus said.

t'Zyah looked at him. *Occasionally, some bored idiots try to steal broadcast entertainment from UHCs for collectors. It's rare, but it happens. But this hints at intentional active involvement in UHC development. That hasn't happened in over two thousand years.*

If it's old tech, he asked Sarjah privately, *shouldn't we be able to crack it easily?*

Sarjah stopped probing the platform's encryption for a moment and turned to look at Marcus. Her voidskin went transparent around her head so he could see her face. Not necessary, since he could see her in his own HUD, but he realized she was doing it to put a weight of importance on what she said next. *This is serious, Marcus. Anyone running an illegal operation like this with pre-Society tech is not to be taken lightly. The third-civ lasted...a long time. And while the Society has incorporated and adapted knowledge from all the previous human civilizations to perfect our biotechnology, there are fundamental differences in all our tech, which means that each civ was still more and less advanced than us in many ways. Third-civ virus countermeasures can bypass our bioweb safeguards and leave your brain fried. Shadow my link, but don't dive separately this time. Study what I do.*

Marcus was about to say he could handle it, but the expression on her face made him realize she was worried even before he sensed it in their link. Some body language translated across the races, but a lot didn't. And while biowebs could translate body language directly into the user's memory and the Nexus could convey emotional content, knowing something, like an expression, because you recognized it always drove the point home a little clearer for him.

Sarjah's infiltration was beautiful. Data work in the Nexus was interpreted in the mind in various ways. Marcus did not feel like he had a virtual body flying over some digital landscape. It was more of an understanding of something. Like looking at one of those optical-illusion pictures long enough and seeing a pattern emerge. Or when dancing to music—even when you've never heard the song before—and knowing where the beat is going to go next and adjusting your movement to it as it happens.

Sarjah's presence moved around, directing energy patterns and code as Marcus observed through their private link. It wasn't so much that he watched her but that he felt what she did. She traced the dimensional signature the portal used, but in an obscure, roundabout way. Some of her choices were obvious to him, while others weren't at all. He would spend a good deal of time reviewing what she did and why, later. But for now—

The transition from slow movement to being sucked down a well was sudden and jarring—like taking that first drop of a roller coaster, with your eyes closed. Marcus caught the briefest hint of fear from Sarjah, then she was pure focus. Feedback loops cascaded against her consciousness; energy viruses tried to burrow into her bioweb. He was connected only by a thread, seeing everything a millisecond after she faced it, and he realized how much he still had to learn.

Their physical bodies were still there in front of the data portal, but their consciousness navigated metaspace. The direct route the portal used to send data was encrypted. Its D-signature left faint traces that Sarjah homed in on, but metaspace was infinite, and the areas she navigated were like nothing Marcus had experienced before. This was the framework of the third-civ, and it was bleak. It wasn't like the Nexus, which was a community; even when just accessing data and not interacting with others, it felt like a garden. But this, this was a desert, empty and cold. He understood why the issue of the third-civ was so important, and why he had been foolish to think of it as a minor mystery. The entire civilization had vanished in one moment. Hundreds of billions of people. No bodies, no mass destruction, no traces, just gone. And while many of their cities and infrastructure were taken by age now, the framework of their tech still existed in metaspace. And the overpowering presence of that vast emptiness was... deceptive. You could easily lose your way. For a few moments, it felt like he and Sarjah were the only two beings in existence. His awareness shadowed her as she moved, searching, lost, found? He wasn't sure it mattered. It was unending.

Then she was out of the system and breathing hard. Usually, through their private link, Marcus could feel snippets of emotion bleed through, but she had closed off so completely, there was nothing. He didn't think Sarjah realized her faceplate was still transparent, because he could clearly see the fear on her face. He was beginning to get the feeling that she, or maybe even both of them, had almost died.

Sorry, Captain, but I couldn't trace its output, Sarjah finally said. *I recommend we bring in a specialist. I made as certain as I could be that I didn't trigger any alarms, but there's no guarantee I succeeded.*

Okay, people, t'Zyah's voice sounded over the grouplink. *Captain concurs; we're going back to the ship. Let's move out.*

The recon team joined back up and moved to a point to be portaled back to the ship. To Marcus, the technology of the Society was so far beyond Earth that he had begun to take it for granted. Now to be faced with something that could worry even them was a disquieting thought. And it also disturbed him a little that there was so much the C-humans still had not told them, and he hoped the powers that be on Earth were keeping track of things.

5

"Ambassador Isaacs?"

Zachariah Isaacs blinked, realizing that was the second time his name had been called. He turned away from the panoramic window and its view of Sahara City. Peter, one of his aides, was waiting patiently by the large desk in the office space they had been provided. Next to him, the TV was showing the station attack again and reporting the latest news—news that Zachariah himself had just received confirmation of—from the UN Security Council. An extremist group calling themselves True Humans had taken credit for the attack. If it didn't have such frightening implications, Zach would almost be impressed by them. A radical group that ignored all the old dividing lines: racial, religious, political, gender, everything. Its members had one thing in common, and it was the only thing that mattered to them. They were all humans. Earthers. And since they didn't believe the C-humans of the Society were legitimate, they called themselves True Humans. Their goal was the removal of all C-humans from Earth and the solar system.

"Is it time?" Zachariah asked.

"Yes, sir," Peter answered. "Everyone's arrived. And the other Society envoy is on her way down from orbit."

Zachariah took a deep breath as he moved toward the door. He was tired. His whole political career had been spent trying to cross the aisle and bring some bipartisanship back to the government. The world hadn't really had time to find true balance after the growing division of the last few decades, seen in country after country. Then the Crash had happened, and what should have united humanity like never before was turning out to be one of its biggest polarizing events. Indeed, most of the problems were because the "aliens" claimed to be human also. Zachariah shook his head. He was almost ashamed of the thought, but he feared adding more races, given Earth's history, was going to make this an uphill battle. They hadn't even left Earth yet, and he had to wonder if his first official job as Earth's ambassador to the Society would be an attempt to broker peace.

The biggest issue now was that the Society had not made an official statement to the UN General Assembly yet about the attack. With Ambassador As the Gentle Wind and Envoy n'Dala out, the next highest-ranking C-human official on Earth was a Nethean Protectorate officer in the New York UN office. And he would only relay medical information that everyone had been treated and survived the attack, and that the vice ambassador would return from orbit to speak to the UN soon. But nothing about whether this was considered an act of war. The UN Security Council, and all the experts, agreed that the Society would not attack the Earth because of this, but still. At best, it was a terrorist attack; at worst, it was a high-profile assassination attempt. There had been some attacks before, violent protests, even bombings, but nothing like this, with two prominent C-humans targeted successfully. Now it seemed most people in the world were waiting to see what happened next. It was a small blessing that reporters were only being allowed into the city tomorrow to cover the launch.

"Mr. Ambassador." Phai Lin, his other aide, had just answered the phone before he reached the door. "The Russian president is on the line, sir."

"Dammit," Zachariah said.

Since they had arrived at Sahara City, he had been on multiple calls with the UN Secretary-General. He had also talked to the US president, China's president, Britain's prime minister, and a few others. Even though officially Zachariah answered to—and only had to report to—the United Nations, some of the superpowers still felt they deserved personal time. Everyone was a lot more worried than they let on. And he couldn't ignore a call from Russia without causing more political hurdles down the line.

"Okay. Peter, tell the consuls general I'll be right there," he said, taking the phone. "Mr. President, hello."

ZACHARIAH SAW that the conference room was full; twelve people were sitting at the table, while numerous aides and staff sat or stood along the walls. Their delegation was officially an embassy, but because it represented the entire planet, it was set up uniquely. Zachariah was the ambassador and head of the embassy. He answered directly to the United Nations and was authorized to speak on behalf of Earth. Then there were six consuls general who represented the different regions of Earth: North America, South America, Europe, Africa, Asia, and Oceania. They reported to the UN as a whole as well as to all the nations specifically in their region. They could even overrule Zachariah with a five-to-one vote among themselves. And in addition to the embassy having standard offices, like management and political, there were others that stood for Earth as a whole. The consul heads of those five offices—theology, medicine, science, culture, and the arts—made up the rest of the group at the table. And most of these people had had little chance to work together long.

The delegates were an in-your-face representation of the diversity of Earth, something alt-right media and conspiracy theorists had repeatedly criticized. But the Society was dealing with the Earth as a whole, not any single nation. This was why the United Nations was taking point, having suddenly been thrust into a role of influence it had never truly known before. And Earth Embassy was a true global involvement, with staff from every country on the planet, even if a number of those countries were still upset that a North American had been chosen as ambassador—it didn't matter that Zachariah was from Trinidad, not America; it was close enough.

Here, there were just as many women as men, those of different religious beliefs, and every tone of skin color imaginable from the African consul general's dark brown skin to the European consul general's pale cream skin. However, to Zachariah's disappointment, equally in-your-face was how hard it was for everyone to get along. Most of the conversations—arguments?—between the people sitting at the table died down as he took a seat, but not all.

"—so they say, but we have no way of knowing if they are really fourteen thousand years ahead of us," Bakti Saputra, the Indonesian consul general for Asia, said. "That could be a lie."

"It really doesn't matter," Jone Chand, the Fijian consul general for Oceania, said. "One thousand, fourteen, or twenty. Over the last five years, we have seen with our own eyes that their technology, next to ours, is like ours next to ants'. So, it doesn't matter *how* much more, because it *is* sufficiently more advanced than ours. They grew this entire city we're sitting in in about three months. What more do you need?"

"You see this city as impressive," Bakti said. "But I see it as a clear reminder that they could level any city on Earth and then replace it as they see fit. And now, with this attack, they have an excuse."

"To what purpose?" Camila Carrasco, the Chilean consul general for South America, asked. "Whether the superpowers want to acknowledge it or not, it is well accepted that if the Society wanted Earth, they could take it. So, why a pretense?"

"I have no idea why," Bakti continued. "All I'm saying is that we have to be aware of the fact that the assassination attempt could've been done by the Society itself to further its own goals."

"Being aware of the *possibility*"—Astrid Pedersen, the European consul general from Norway, emphasized the last word—"and actively believing it without a shred of proof is counterproductive to this embassy's mission."

"Is it, though?" Bakti had scoffed, but it was Richard Hines, the North American consul general, who asked the question. "I would argue that blindly following the Society is far more dangerous."

"We are not here to investigate the attack," Zachariah said before anyone else could continue. This was the same type of speculation that was going on at the UN, and it wasn't helping. "The Society vice ambassador to Earth is going to the UN to speak, and the investigation into the attack will be handled by the UN Security Council. We will be getting a full update from the Society envoy to the embassy in a few minutes, after which you can finish contacting the governments of your respective regions. I've already given a preliminary report to the UN.

"What's the word on our people who didn't make the train?" Zachariah asked his deputy chief of mission, Xian Xu, who was sitting next to him. The Chinese woman was an ex-mayor, just as Zachariah was, and word was she had been in the running for the Asia consul general seat.

"Everyone injured was taken either to orbit or to a Cairo hospital with a Society biomedical technology section." The embassy's second in charge answered without referring to her notes. "A number had critical injuries, but they are all stable now. Others in the station who got left behind when the train pulled out will arrive on the next train before the orientation."

"Mr. Ambassador," Dr. Aleksei Romashenko, the Earth Medicine consul, said, "we need to schedule psychological counseling with everyone. And that would be best done on Earth. If we could postpone leaving for a few days—"

"That's not possible, Consul Dr. Romashenko," Deputy Chief Xu interrupted. "And all the staff have gone through extensive psych reports over their training period."

"Seeing who was fit to work this type of mission, yes," Aleksei said. "But treating survivors of a terror attack is a very different thing. I guarantee you there will be some people suffering from PTSD."

"I don't take that lightly, Doctor," Zachariah said. "But we have to be at Sapher in time to see the Assemblage's opening session. Postponing is simply not an option."

"But, sir—"

Zachariah held up his hand so he could continue. "Work up a schedule with Deputy Chief Xu to be carried out on the trip to Jupiter, and we will reassess once we reach Galileo City. Worst-case scenario, we will replace anyone you have doubts about."

Zachariah could tell Aleksei wasn't thrilled by the possibility of having to make the choice to end someone's chance at history before they even got to go, but Zachariah was confident he would make the best choice for the embassy. Dr. Romashenko was a world-class psychologist and psychiatrist from Russia who had given up a prominent university position, and practice, to be on the mission. Everyone at the table had successful careers they were leaving behind, for the same reasons people always made such changes: more influence, more power, more prestige, more challenge, and a few, like Zach, who honestly believed they could make a difference.

And there really was no option to change the schedule. The Society's governing body, the Assemblage, was about to have a major vote concerning another Uncontacted Human Culture. And since Earth was recently a UHC itself, it was considered important for the delegates to observe. The main goal of Earth Embassy's mission was not simply diplomatic relations with the C-humans but to actually observe how the Society governed its civilization, how that might affect Earth—and to ultimately give a recommendation on if Earth should eventually join.

"Have you heard any further news on the condition of Envoy n'Dala?" the Earth Theology consul asked.

"I'll be visiting her next," Zachariah said. "I've been told that she's fine and recovering. Also, Consul Dr. Romashenko, I'd like to commend your team member who helped."

"It was a Dr. Rodriguez," Aleksei said, conferring with his aide. "From New Mexico. I'll arrange it."

"She needs to be debriefed," Richard said. "She may have seen or learned something useful."

"She helps save the envoy's life, and you want to drag her in for interrogation?" Aleksei was indignant. "I won't stand for that."

"She's an American citizen," Richard said. "It's not up to you."

"But it is up to me," Zachariah said. "And we are not going to start bringing in our own people for questioning whenever they interact with C-humans."

"Agreed," Jone said, followed by Astrid.

"While I don't agree with the consul general of North America's implied intent," Esi Owusu, the Ghanaian consul general for Africa, said, "we are here to learn about the Society to better inform Earth. So, when opportunities present themselves to learn things that the Society has not told us, that should be explored." She glanced at Richard. "With the understanding that they don't violate our moral beliefs. This doctor is not a criminal."

"I'm not saying she is," Richard said with a cocky shrug. "She's a source of information, as you said."

Zachariah was sure some backroom deals had gone on for the North American consul general to be from the States instead of Canada or Mexico. The Society had final veto on anyone traveling to its worlds—not hard when they had the only means of transport, but they had only ever exercised that power once. Earth chose who spoke for it. Every region picked its own representative for consul general. In fact, the UN itself had gone through much restructuring now that it was officially speaking for the Earth. Nations could still speak for themselves, but no longer did superpowers have final say. Not that most of them acknowledged that fact yet.

Zachariah felt like the whole embassy process was

already designed to take Earth's problems with them. The embassy consuls general had only met as a group once before, and Zachariah could already see the lines they were starting to fall under. North America and Asia didn't trust the Society. Europe and Oceania tended to be pro-Society, while Africa and South America fell in the middle. Even though those last two regions, and Southeast Asia, had received most of the medical aid from the Society, centuries of colonization and foreign interference had ensured that any more technologically advanced power would be scrutinized heavily.

Zachariah's goal was to make the best choices for Earth, not any one nation, and certainly not the Society.

"I do expect Dr. Rodriguez to file a full report for medical," Zachariah said to the Earth Medicine consul. "I leave it to you to follow up with her about any details."

"Understood," Aleksei said.

Peter informed Zachariah that the envoy had arrived, and Zachariah told him to bring her in.

An air of quiet overtook the room as the purple-skinned C-human entered; her wavy black hair was pulled into a professional bun, and her blue business suit was similar to Western fashion without being an exact match. The envoy had a disarming smile and relaxed manner, like all the other Netheans Zachariah had met, and she seemed completely at ease as she took the offered seat near him. He had never asked, and it was hard to judge age, but Zach guessed she was similar in age to his own early forties.

"Everyone, this is Envoy Last Rain in Autumn," Zachariah began. "As you know, she is the envoy assigned to Earth Embassy and will serve as the point person for matters of cultural understanding as we travel in the Society. She wasn't scheduled to meet us until we reached Jupiter, but I asked her here now for further clarity on the situation." Zachariah introduced the rest of the people present.

"First, we want to offer our apologies for the attack on your people and assure you that those responsible will be brought to justice." Zachariah had first met Last Rain in Autumn about six months earlier, not long after his nomination as ambassador had been ratified by the UN and approved by the Society's New Human Culture Division, which oversaw contact. He had come to value her insight on the Society, but due to his schedule, he hadn't been able to get to know her as well as he would've liked.

"I have no doubt of that, Mr. Ambassador," Last Rain in Autumn said. "As we have stipulated, local law takes precedence on crimes committed. That's true whether it is a full Society member world or a New Human Culture–status world."

"Yes, and we've seen that's the case in the past when other minor incidents have happened," Zachariah said. "But you can understand how something on this scale has our governments a little unsure of the Society's response."

Envoy Last Rain in Autumn looked at Zachariah with an expression of curiosity, then at the other council members.

"Cousins," she said. Her smile didn't come across as condescending but rather like a friend telling you whatever stupid thing you had done was okay because you were friends. "Knowing the history of your world, I can understand your fears when faced with a more technologically advanced people. But even if the ambassador and envoy had died, there would be no retaliation against Earth, under any circumstances. Earth's future is for Earthers to decide. NHC status is for your people to study our wider C-human civilization and decide if it's right for you."

"And you still claim you will leave if we decide that we don't want it?" Bakti asked.

"Claim? No, Consul General Saputra," Last Rain in Autumn answered without pause or insult. "Statement of fact, yes. Over our history, a number of NHC worlds have chosen not to join the Society."

"Forgive our colleague's bluntness," the South American consul general said, casting a look at Bakti. "But since most of what your people tell us, we have to take on blind faith, it can cause us to cover the same ground."

"That's perfectly all right, Consul General Carrasco," Last Rain in Autumn said. "Part of my duties is to help you find the answers you need and even the questions you don't know you have yet."

There was more discussion, the different consuls general asking variations of questions they had heard answers to many times and seeking assurances they could pass on to their regional world leaders. Zachariah mostly listened. Even though the room was made up of people who would be representing Earth, they had had very little personal time in dealing with C-humans. Ambassador As the Gentle Wind and Envoy n'Dala were the most well-known C-humans, and the vast majority of interviews and reports were done by them. The Society had very strict contact protocols, and some of their choices were not clear to Earth. They claimed they wanted the Earth Embassy delegates to have an unbiased view of the Society and didn't want overexposure to too many C-humans to cloud Earth's opinions before they reached Sapher and saw firsthand what life was like. Everyone selected for the embassy had personally met C-humans in their training, interviewed with and worked next to them, but the first full social group meeting wouldn't happen until the orientation and reception later that evening.

They were going to have to learn to stand together if the embassy and Earth were to succeed.

AMBASSADOR ISAACS and his aide Peter Donnelly followed the Nethean down the hallway to Envoy n'Dala's room. Peter was a lanky young British man who seemed very enamored with all things Society, and he easily chatted up the C-human. Zachariah was distracted by how this part of the hotel had a more organic feel to its structure. Sahara City was still being built, or grown he supposed was a more accurate term, so it was still fairly empty of people. He had no doubt Consul General Saputra was an alarmist, but Zachariah had to acknowledge he wasn't completely wrong. The Society had no need for Earth's infrastructure. They could grow entire cities wherever they wanted. They stopped in front of a large circular door that dilated to reveal an A'Quan who motioned them into a waiting room.

"Ambassador Isaacs. Mr. Donnelly. I am Envoy n'Dala's personal aide, tuu'Karo." The short blue man shook their hands. Zachariah didn't notice it when he spoke to A'Quan women, but their race averaged about five feet tall, so when he met a male, he always thought of them as short before he could rein in his judgment. At least Zach thought he was a male, but he had to admit that sometimes it was as hard for him to tell the difference between the three A'Quan sexes.

"I appreciate the envoy taking the time to see me, considering."

"No trouble, Mr. Ambassador. The doctor is— Ah, here ze is now." tuu'Karo turned slightly as one of the other doors dilated and another A'Quan came out of a larger room.

"This is Dr. sa'Xeen," the aide introduced them.

"Doctor," Zachariah said. "How is Envoy n'Dala doing?"

"She is recovering quite nicely," sa'Xeen said. "She still needs to take it easy for a bit, so I would ask that you don't talk business. But she's okay for visits and is expecting you."

"Your aide can stay here if you like," tuu'Karo said.

Peter could barely hold back his excitement at the prospect of hanging out with a C-human without his boss, and Zachariah wondered if he might need someone older for the position.

"I'm sure that will be fine," Zachariah said, entering the room the doctor had just come from and nodding to Peter as the door closed behind him.

"Ambassador Isaacs," a voice said. "Welcome. Can I get you something to drink?" Zachariah turned to see Envoy n'Dala sitting on the sofa with her legs resting on an ottoman. She wore a type of light gray linen overwrap that Zachariah assumed must be a bathrobe. The A'Quan's blue skin was not quite as vibrant as normal, and there was just the slightest effort involved when she stood up. Other than that, he would've never guessed she had been shot a few hours earlier.

Zachariah started to walk forward, then had to stop for a moment and orient himself. Was he lighter? He did a small bounce up and down to test himself; the difference was subtle but definitely there. n'Dala looked at him a moment, then smiled understandingly. "Oh, yes, the gravity in here is set to my home planet's norm. That's about point seven of Earth. The doctor said I would rest better, but I can change it if it bothers you."

"No. No, it's fine, Envoy. I'm glad to see it wasn't as serious as I feared," Zachariah said, shaking the offered hand, thinking how the new normal had gone to talking about changing the gravity in your room like you might turn the heat up. A faint tingle went up his arm, and the hairs on his hand rose. The bioelectric field A'Quan subconsciously generated wasn't dangerous to humans, but it still made Zachariah remember that these people, no matter that they called themselves humans, were not from Earth.

"Not serious?" n'Dala seemed to think for a moment. "Oh, you mean because I'm moving about? No, I almost died. No question. If I had gone to a full medical facility, you would never even know I was hurt, but I didn't want to get shipped off-world. I felt the incident had already gotten enough news, especially with the ambassador having to be taken to orbit for surgery. Dr. Endless Green Sky did a fine job on me, and what politician doesn't mind getting a few hours' rest while on the clock?"

She smiled at her own joke and motioned for Zachariah to take a seat. "Tea okay?" She kept talking as she sat down *right* next to him. "I just love Earth's green tea, very similar to hola berry back on A'Qu, my homeworld."

Zachariah adjusted in his seat momentarily at the invasion of personal space but stopped himself before he moved over. A big part of the training for all embassy personnel was about the cultural differences they would face and how to react from knowledge, not bias. A'Quan communicated through their bioelectric field as much as verbally, so their people tended to stand much closer to each other, and the concept of personal space had never arisen on their world. Whenever he saw A'Quan together, they were always close to each other. He tried to imagine an ambassador on Earth being shot and then entertaining political guests in their bathrobe as if nothing was wrong, and found himself smiling at the natural casualness of it all.

"Tea would be fine," he said.

The coffee table in front of them extruded cups, and a spherical fabricator floated over and poured liquid into each —the pungent aroma unmistakably green tea. Zachariah handed n'Dala her cup, and she smiled thanks.

"I wanted to come by and see how you were firsthand, Envoy n'Dala," Zachariah said after he had taken a sip. "And to apologize for what happened."

"I appreciate that, Ambassador—"

"Please, call me Zach."

"Zach," she said nodding. "Please, call me n'Dala. And thank you. Fear isn't something that goes away with advanced technology. The worst part for me was the anticipation. But working with NHCs is dangerous, and I accepted —"

"I'm sorry," Zach interrupted. "Anticipating what?"

n'Dala stopped as she was about to take another drink, a sigh escaping her lips. The hairs on Zachariah's arm closest to her started to rise, and he felt a slight tingling, like goosebumps but mildly pleasurable. He snatched his arm away instantly, looking at n'Dala and trying to keep his mind from making dark assumptions.

n'Dala startled a little at his reaction and then seemed to realize what she had done. "I'm sorry," she said. "It seems the doctor's medicine has me a little more out of it than I realized."

Zachariah rubbed his arm absently as he looked at her, trying to read the situation without reading into it. "What was that?"

"My bioelectric field trying to connect to yours." She saw his body language and held up her hands in a calming gesture. "It wasn't meant to be intimate."

"Intimate!" Zachariah blurted out, standing up quickly. "Envoy—"

"Communication, I mean," she said cutting him off. She started to say something, shook her head, started again, then sighed, leaning back into the couch.

Zachariah wasn't sure what she meant and found himself staring at the trace of the wound on her neck. He cleared his throat and set his cup down. "Perhaps I should let you get some rest."

"You know my race communicates through a bioelectric field as much as verbally, right?" She was looking in her cup. "Much the same way your race subconsciously reads body language."

"Yes," he said slowly.

"It's involuntary. It just happens when we discuss personal things. So, naturally, it's an intimate experience. But not sexual," she continued quickly. "Just personal. And I was unconsciously answering your question that way."

Zachariah wanted to pursue whether a human—Earth human—could actually communicate with an A'Quan human like that but realized that he had gotten distracted from his initial question. "When I asked what you had been anticipating?"

n'Dala nodded her bald, oblong head and took another drink but didn't look at him.

"You knew," he said, his mind racing to all the implications of what the Asia consul general had said earlier. "You knew you were going to be shot."

"We knew they were going to try and kill me and the ambassador, yes," she said, holding her cup out to the fabricator, which poured her more tea. "But we couldn't know if they would succeed or not."

"But the Society planned this?"

"Of course not!" She looked at him, shocked, the blue of her irises fluorescing brightly.

"Then how did you know?"

The look she gave him wasn't quite what a parent gives a child when they ask an obvious question, but it was close. "Ambassador... Zach, the Society is a fourteen-thousand-year-old civilization. And it's the fifth major human civilization, the others having been just as, or more, advanced.

"There is no communication technology you have that we can't crack. No encryption. No firewalls. No code. Nothing. That's not meant as an insult; it's just...science."

Zachariah watched her as she took another drink of her tea. From all his training, Zach knew that A'Quan and Netheans had very similar body language to Earthers. That was one of the reasons they were the C-humans most often dealing with Earth. n'Dala was lost in thought, and he could tell by the way she glanced at the door leading to the area with their aides that she wanted to say something she wasn't sure she should.

"The group that shot me has been planning it for months," n'Dala said finally. "But 'True Human' isn't just a group of angry radicals. It has backing from members of numerous governments and multinational corporations, those who feel that the presence of the Society with its free medicine and magic cure-alls threatens their power and prosperity."

Zachariah found that he was sitting down again, his legs unable to hold him up. The magnitude of what she was saying left him speechless. He had been in numerous meetings with heads of state, intelligence agencies, and top scientists. It was obvious that Society technology was far beyond Earth, and some had even postulated that Earth should assume that, for all practical purposes, the Society knew everything. But countless things had been done to try to ensure private lines of communication. Something that now seemed overly optimistic on Earth's part. And if what she said was true about those backing the terrorist group True Human, he had to report it.

"What governments? Who exactly are you saying was involved?" he asked.

"It's not my place to tell you that. I'm sorry."

"What? If it's true, why wouldn't you tell us?"

"Because you'd never trust us."

"We wouldn't accept it on blind faith, no. Of course not. But something that big leaves trails. And if the evidence is there, we would find it."

n'Dala turned to face him, and he felt the hint of a chill across his hand, but she crossed her arms, and it stopped as quickly as it came. "Do you watch sci-fi movies?"

"Excuse me?"

"The science fiction movies of your planet. You ever watch them?"

"Some, not really," Zachariah admitted, not knowing how it was relevant. "Strange, perhaps, considering I'm going into space, but it was never my thing. Why?"

"Your culture has an inordinate number of movies that show aliens attacking Earth. They come to steal your water, your women, your land, and so on."

"Well, history shows what happens when an advanced civilization meets a less advanced one," he said automatically.

"Earth history," she said.

Zachariah knew the argument she would make. There was even a famous interview with one of the first C-humans to talk to Earth, which had gone viral years before. Assuming that an advanced civilization would take over a less advanced one because it had happened over and over again in Earth's history was a very Earth-centric view. It was what *Earth* humans would do. But they argued aliens, by their very definition, were alien. Different cultures, views, values, and experiences meant that each case would be different.

"The galaxy," she said. "Just this one galaxy, is inconceivably vast. It's over a hundred and fifty thousand light-years across. The Society is barely over eleven thousand. Not only are there many other species out there, but there are older and larger civilizations out there. Some get along, some don't. And we take the responsibility of meeting a new C-human world very seriously, especially when that world is endangered by us. Earth wasn't scheduled to be contacted for another two centuries at least.

"The fact is," she continued, "that Earth's current state of development is the most dangerous time to contact a new race. That centuries-long period where a race is discovering electricity and creating technology. Not hammers and clocks but computers and particle accelerators. When it first gains the ability to accidentally, or negligently, genocide itself and doesn't yet have the maturity to unify."

"I've heard some C-humans say that before," Zachariah responded. "But I'm not sure I agree. We've faced a great many changes in just our first two decades of this century. We can adapt."

"And adapting is one of the things all humans do best," n'Dala said. "But during this phase, even with as much change that is going on, worlds get set in their way of thinking. Their view of the universe and their place in it is like a comfortable blanket. And it takes more than facts to change that; it takes time. Time for it to spread out to the masses and become the next new comfortable truth. So, when a civilization just advanced enough to destroy itself is faced with the sudden realization that their worldview is false, well, I don't have to tell you it's shocking on a global scale that can have catastrophic consequences."

"Like the Long Year?" Zachariah looked at her, but his thoughts were lost in the past. For about a year after the C-human bioship crashed into Hawaii—when the Society decided to reveal its existence—the nations of the world were in a panic, and World War III had been a very real possibility. It seemed like every few days, there was a new controversial news cycle: riots, wars, crashing markets, religious upheavals, just an unending deluge of hopelessness and fear. Nobody had the answer, and it seemed the best people could do was live day to day and hope that tomorrow, humanity wouldn't be remembered like the dinosaurs.

That period had felt like it lasted a lot longer than a year.

"Exactly," she said. "Earth, thankfully, survived that knee-jerk reaction. So, now you find yourself trying to learn to live with some *aliens* coming down here, telling you we're related, while at the same time, you're still trying to learn to deal with each other. And to be honest, a number of races in the Society don't believe you will survive yourselves. That's why the NHC program has been so fast-tracked. Getting you out into the Society so you can see with your own eyes is vital.

"So, yes, we could tell you what we know," she continued. "But it would just reinforce an *us versus them* mentality. You would never be sure that we didn't manufacture the evidence or influence it in some way."

"Some would believe that regardless," he said.

"True," she agreed. "But Society contact procedure has evolved over many, many thousands of years of having done this with hundreds of C-human races. And we've learned to let each new race deal with hate movements, and terrorists, in its own way. In its own time."

"Even when that can cost you your life?" Zachariah asked. "You didn't even protect yourselves."

"The ambassador and I could have used internal force fields or worn voidskins, yes. But imagine how that would look to the world. Us, standing there clean and unharmed in our fancy technology while Earthers lay around us bleeding and dying. Would that really discourage more attacks or just provide one more reason to call us 'other'?"

Zachariah had no way of knowing if everything, or anything, she said was true, but his instincts told him she was sincere. And he had to wonder if he would be willing to make that same level of sacrifice. For Earth, yes, no question, but for aliens?

"Everyone in the Society's New Human Culture Division understands that this is a dangerous assignment and we could die." She glanced out the window. "If we stopped this group, stopped all attacks, or used force in any way, there would always be resistance. But if we let Earth change itself, at its own pace, allowing people to experience the benefits...well, then eventually, you will come around. This, of course, takes generations. That's why NHC status can last hundreds of years."

"So, if the outcome is Earth becomes part of the Society either way, then isn't it still conquered?" Zachariah wasn't sure he knew the answer to that himself. "Does it matter how?"

n'Dala looked at him appraisingly for a moment. She seemed to give his question honest thought. Then she handed him his teacup again and smiled sincerely. "That, cousin," she said, "is what your people are sending you into the Society to find out."

6

"Thank you, Ditec Sarjah," Captain Ahmon said, then looked around at the other officers in the room. "And yes, it has been checked and confirmed, we are dealing with third-civ technology."

After giving a preliminary report to the Protectorate Council, Ahmon had called the staff briefing to go over everything. He was disturbed greatly by the fact that he, of all people, captained another ship that was involved with a UHC incident. But what was, was. He would face the reality of the situation and deal with it in a way that best helped all involved.

As Sarjah took her seat there were one or two murmurs of shock from the others at the table but mostly stunned silence. Instead of meeting via shiplink they were all physically present in the briefing cavity which was connected to the bridge, like the ditec and captain's cavity. Sitting around the table were Commander Ja Xe 75 05 his Lead Officer, one of the few Zin Ku Lai in the Protectorate; Lead Metatech t'Zyah; Lead Bioneer Jahnas; Lead Doctor Haxi Leikeema; Lead Security Tuhzo; and Ditec Sarjah, who had just finished her report of what she experienced while connected to the data portal.

"And its truly believed that this is some group in the Society responsible for this?" Dr. Leikeema asked. She shifted her four-foot yellow body in the chair as her purple eyes looked around at the others.

"That can't be," Jahnas said.

"It seems most likely," Tuhzo said at the same time.

"The last time something like this happened was over two thousand years ago," Jahnas said shaking her head. The reddish-orange carapace of her facial plates made it impossible to read expressions, but to Ahmon her scent revealed she was worried the security lead was right.

"Things happen when they happen," Tuhzo said, quoting an old Xindari saying.

"And what happens once, happens again," Jahnas finished the saying. "That doesn't mean this isn't an outside influence."

"And why would C-humans do this?" Dr. Leikeema said before Tuhzo could respond. "Everyone knows how dangerous pre-Society technology can be."

"That is truth, Doctor," Ahmon said. He knew the lead doctor was one of the only people on board who had seen firsthand the horrific effects third-civ tech could inflict. He also knew that could cloud someone's judgment. "And speculating who is behind this will not help our current mission."

Ahmon looked to Jahnas and t'Zyah. "Is everything set for the transfer?"

"We're still fabricating the host shell, but it should be ready within the hour," Jahnas said. "I have a few bioneers who've done this before and don't anticipate any problems."

"And I spoke to Director Golamee before the briefing,"

t'Zyah said. "Her team is ready to transmit when we give the signal."

"Good," Ahmon said. "Lead Tuhzo, I want all security updated with current combat memories. Commander Ja Xe, make sure the ship is ready for hostilities."

"Do you really think we'll see a battle, sir?" Ja Xe 75 05 asked. Even though no one was sharing emotions over the Nexus, his silver scaled skin unconsciously displayed some yellow and orange patterns, which Ahmon knew was an indication of anxiety and frustration.

"Most likely we will be stationed in this system," Ahmon said. "Active defense ships will be sent to the location of the data portal once we find it. But I still want us prepared.

"I informed the Protectorate Council of the situation." Ahmon glanced around the room. "For now our orders are to prepare for the arrival of the third-civ specialist Golamee Asa, director of the Third-Civ Institute in border space. This has the potential to be another UHC changing event, so there is a great deal of discussion at the highest levels."

"With what is happening on Earth right now and with so many Earthers on board, emotions will be running high," Dr. Leikeema said.

"Agreed. But this is a very different situation than what happened on Earth," Ahmon said. Since the *Fulcrum's Light* was on a routine patrol, which included trainees from an NHC, the ship only had a few crewmembers who had experience in border space. In fact, Ahmon was the only crew that had ever been to Earth, although that trip had disturbed him more than anything else in his life. "I don't want the crew overcompensating and making bad choices in a vain attempt to prove something."

"I'll keep people focused on work," Ja Xe 75 05 said.

"Once I have final orders from the Council we will

reconvene," Ahmon said. "But for now we will continue with preparations. Dismissed.

"Sarjah, stay a moment," Ahmon said to her as the others began leaving.

"Captain," Sarjah said.

"t'Zyah told me you requested to have Ditec Greer assist you with the consciousness transfer," Ahmon said. "You believe he is ready for that?"

"That is truth," Sarjah said, and her shoulder and head angle displayed resolution of purpose. She knew she had made an unpopular decision but was determined to stand by.

"That seems premature," Ahmon said, his own posture open, waiting. "Elaborate your reasoning."

"Earthers' innate intuitive nature is well documented," Sarjah said. "And I have found Ditec Greer to be an exceptional example of this, even though he doesn't fully realize that himself. I believe that his reaction to the assassination attempt on Earth may have shaken his confidence and that this will help bring it back into balance."

Ahmon wasn't concerned about the trouble Ditec Greer had had with the Nexus. It was a natural misstep for someone early in their training. Ahmon's reluctance was about having Earthers involved in this mission at all. The Society's accidental exposure to Earth had almost resulted in a global war, and he had seen little evidence in the years since to believe that Earth's leaders had learned from their mistakes. So, Ahmon felt the Society had an extra level of responsibility to Earthers *because* their culture was so immature.

"It may help him. It may not," Ahmon said. "Transitions are delicate procedures. If his way is so easily lost, it seems he would benefit more from refreshing basic techniques."

"I agree with that assessment and have already revised his training schedule," Sarjah said, the subtle shift in her posture showing acquiescence yet still resolution of purpose. "And I also believe that observing more advanced things will help broaden his understanding of metatech and strengthen his core skills. Whether or not he can accomplish it will depend on him."

There was merit to her argument, but Ahmon was still not convinced that Earthers would succeed as dimensional technicians. The entire speed with which the New Human Culture Division was operating with Earth disturbed him. But Sarjah was an excellent ditec, and he trusted her judgment.

"Very well. He may assist with the transfer," Ahmon said, "But I don't want him to go back to the moon's surface. In addition to helping those of Travanis 4 we have to protect the Earthers as well."

"Understood, Captain."

7

M arcus and Envoy Rahel Ashenafi exited the transit vein at the bioneering level. Their continuing argument had been going on for three decks since she had caught up to him coming from the medical bay.

"I'm not saying that you don't have the ability, Marcus." The tiredness in Rahel's voice was overshadowed by the wave of exasperation that flowed from her. "I'm saying this isn't something you should be jumping into right now. You're here to learn and—"

"What better way to learn than by doing?"

"Doing and rushing to do don't necessarily produce the same results."

Marcus had only known Rahel for a month, but he liked her and had come to respect her. She was from Ethiopia, had the same dark complexion as him, and wore her curly, black hair pulled back in a ponytail. He guessed she was late thirties, not quite old enough to be his mother, but the older sister/auntie vibe had definitely crept into their relationship.

Fulcrum's Light was still in orbit of Travanis 4's moon. For now, Captain Ahmon still had the ship on alert status, even though the chances of the incursionists' showing up there were remote. As they moved down the corridor, Rahel casually spoke to many of the C-humans they passed, either verbally or through the shiplink. She had been using a bioweb long enough that she was obviously more comfortable with it than the other Earthers on board, even himself, and while Marcus didn't always agree with her, he acknowledged that she knew Society culture better than he did. She was one of the First Six Hundred, and it hadn't occurred to him before that she could have written her own ticket to any job she wanted on Earth.

"Do you regret having to babysit me?" he asked.

"What?" she asked, confused, as they turned at an intersection into another corridor.

"Well, a lot of the first envoys went back to Earth," Marcus said while pulsing an apology to someone he had bumped into, at first mistaking the four-foot Koroukh for a child. "But with the new ditec program and Earth Embassy finally coming out here, I know some envoys were tasked with serving as guides, helping us acclimate to...all this"— he waved his hand, taking in the bioship and C-humans —"when you could be living the good life back home, doing the talk show circuit and lectures, making a lot of money."

Rahel was quiet for a moment, and Marcus wondered if he was right. She was the only person, beside Sarjah, with whom he had a continuous private link, but he couldn't detect a shadow of emotion coming from her when she didn't want him to—a testament to her skill. After the bioship crashed on Earth, it had taken the world a while to stop freaking out. Then about two years after the Crash, the Society allowed every single country to send three people out to travel around the different planets and see firsthand that they were not bug-eyed, rat eating monsters with ulterior motives. These three envoys were always one law-enforcement/military person, one scientist, and one average citizen. Rahel was the citizen from her country.

"Do you remember what happened to that North Korean envoy?" she asked.

Marcus was taken aback. Those first envoys from Earth had spent a year traveling the Society and sending reports back to Earth. Once they returned, their lives were irrevocably changed into celebrity status: talk shows, book deals, followers, the works. It also became apparent that many governments were not content to just take the word of what their envoys said, and stories of torture-level interrogations surfaced. "Was he one of the ones that had to get asylum?" he asked.

"The first of many," Rahel said. "One minute, the UN General Assembly is in normal session; the next, a bleeding, half-naked man tied to a chair is portaled onto the main floor."

"Yeah, that was when Earth first learned how invasive portal technology was," Marcus said, remembering the crazy news cycles and seeing videos of numerous envoys appearing from thin air in the UN.

"Wait, your government—"

"No, no, as far as I know, that never happened with our envoys. But that was just another wake-up call to how things had changed," Rahel said. "People realized that for good or bad, there was always someone watching us, judging us— even though the Society wouldn't admit that. But they didn't try to hide it, the way more cynical people expect governments to do. And they didn't try to punish us for things. North Korea still got medical aid."

At first, some countries had refused to send people from

certain groups, like Afghanistan, who didn't pick any women. But the Society had final say on who went, and they only accepted a true representation of Earth's population. Countries that didn't want to abide by that were simply not allowed to send envoys. And as more and more countries did, most of those left out relented. And as envoys came back, it became obvious that the Society protected them, and any that were in danger were portaled to the UN, where other countries were more than happy to offer them asylum. They were probably thinking they could keep any information learned, but the Society shared all envoy reports with every nation.

"I guess I'm just saying the Society gave us a lot more transparency than we expected, maybe even deserved, but they still have secrets. And rightly so; there are some things that we as a civilization haven't really...learned to come to terms with."

Marcus felt the briefest wave of what might have been awe from Rahel, but he wasn't aware of the context, or even the feeling, before it was gone. This wasn't the first time she had been lost in thought and completely closed herself off from sharing over the Nexus.

"So, I don't feel like I'm babysitting," she continued. "I'm helping other Earthers face this new world. None of those envoys knew that the luck they felt for being picked to explore the Society would cause them to lose their homes, even their countries, when they got back to Earth. And from everything I've seen whenever previous C-human civilization technology is involved, the Society takes it very seriously. You have to be ready for how it affects your life out here as well as how it can change it back home."

Marcus thought she was being overly cautious, but he had to admit he hadn't considered what things would be like after he returned. Would he just be able to pick up his life? Would he want to? Working on a movie was nothing compared to this. Of course, he had seen some of the horror stories about people returning, but he didn't think it had anything to do with him. He wasn't just going out to explore the Society; he was more exploring how it could work for Earth. And he liked that what he was doing was important.

The simple fact was that not all C-human races were as comfortable with dimensional technology as others. Sometimes, the reasons were cultural or spiritual, sometimes psychological or biological. Being able to mentally perceive and then interpret multiple dimensions was not easy, yet races that were very intuitive, like Earthers, usually did very well. A number of the people from Earth he trained with had been artists, cops, story tellers, programmers, analysts, and even athletes. Imaginative people who often trusted their gut in everyday life and/or were good at pattern recognition.

"I understand that there are some risks, I really do. But unexpected situations are exactly what we need to know about. Besides, when you asked the Ditec Council, they agreed with me, didn't they?"

From the look on her face—and the wave of annoyance she let slip—he knew he had guessed right and she had already voiced her concerns to the Dimensional Technology Council.

"Yes," she said grudgingly. "They assured me that as long as you personally didn't try to use the third-civ technology, the risks were minimal but not nonexistent."

"Rahel, the whole purpose behind allowing some Earthers into the dimensional technician program was to fully understand how we would adapt to the technology," Marcus said. He knew it could be argued that they were guinea pigs, but he had learned enough about Society medical technology firsthand to trust that he wasn't at any health risk. He had been in high school when the Society arrived, and his generation didn't see things the same as Rahel's. He was old enough to know people whose families had been faced with cancer or other terminal illnesses, before the new medical tech changed that. Sickness as a part of the human experience was still real, but to Marcus, a world without disease had become the norm. The Society had assured them a bioweb, or being a ditec, wasn't addictive, but if for any reason they couldn't reacclimate to life on Earth, they would be allowed to live in the Society. And that was something that appealed to him more than he cared to admit.

They reached the main entrance to bioneering, and Rahel looked at him for a moment. "Okay," she finally said. "I just want to make sure you are going into this with your eyes open. It's only natural for us to get distracted by personal stuff and miss the bigger picture. Majid is an engineer, so a ship is the perfect place for him. Sumiko is an astrobiologist on a living ship, and Grayson is military on a military ship. I know." She held up her hand forestalling Marcus. "They say the Society's Protectorate isn't military but..." She shrugged and gave Marcus a look. He had to agree. While its primary duty may be called protecting, he knew this one ship had enough firepower to level a planet, and it was only a midsized Protectorate ship. When he had come on board at Sapher, *Fulcrum's Light* had been parked near a capital-class Protectorate ship. And while he was restricted from a lot of data about it, he had picked up from idle conversation that it had the ability to destroy a star.

"It's easy to get blinded by the shine of the Society and forget that they can also make mistakes," she finished.

"Which is why I am glad I got you." He smiled with a mock bow while pulsing an image to her of an old woman sitting in a rocking chair. "For all your many, *many* years of wisdom."

The expression on Rahel's face was completely blank and didn't emote at all. But the image she pulsed back to him was of her giving him an exaggerated side-eye, pursed-mouth look, while at the same time the emotion he felt through their private link was pure joy, like seeing your child walk for the first time. Her physical body language, her sent image, and her emotion were so different that for a moment, he froze in confusion unable to figure out what to respond to. He had no idea how she did that or that you even could do that.

"You also got me because you haven't learned you don't know everything yet," she said, turning and going into bioneering with a trace of smugness. "Come on, young'un."

THE BIONEERING CHAMBER was shaped like a huge torus, over two levels high. When Marcus had first seen it on his arrival tour, he felt like he was walking around the interior of a giant doughnut that had a number of alcoves and other connecting cavities along its outer circumference. There were multiple different C-humans moving around and working on various things. Absent were the sounds of machines: whirring motors, electric whines, clanking pistons, or the hum of reactors. What he heard was more akin to whale song and heartbeats. Resonating, melodious sounds, the deepest of which he could feel vibrating through his body. No one coming into this room could doubt that the ship was a living organism. And the source of that was the lifecore.

The lifecore formed the entire center of the torus and was the engine and main computer—the heart and brain—of the bioship. It maintained a stable point between standard space and multidimensional space, or metaspace, allowing it to draw power from other dimensions. Thus, it provided all the energy for the grav fields and to move the ship into, and manipulate, metaspace. But the bioship itself wasn't a sentient being that thought. The brain aspect of the lifecore was more analogous to an auxiliary neural network that everyone could tap into to access data and adjust their conscious perception to supercomputer speeds.

Marcus and his parents had visited the redwoods on one of their last family vacations before they were killed. The circumference of the lifecore dwarfed even those massive trees. Along the lifecore's surface were clear patches that glowed softly with their own purplish light set off by flashes seemingly from within multiple translucent layers. A multitude of patterns, looking like veins embedded in the floor and ceiling, snaked from the lifecore and spread throughout the entire cavity. These merged into workstation consoles that appeared to have grown from the floors and walls. A few bioneers were at different consoles, their hands immersed inside or moving across the panel-like surfaces, apparently manipulating controls.

Marcus saw Sarjah across the chamber, talking to the lead bioneer. Jahnas was a Koroukh; a four-foot-tall race of C-humans that had a reddish-orange carapace that covered much of their thin body and extremities, which reminded Marcus of insects even though he knew they were mammals. Jahnas was wearing a variation of a voidskin to allow her to comfortably move about in the ship's gravity. Lifecores generated enough biogravitic power to manipulate gravity across the ship, either localized in one room, forming the ship's shields, or powering the grav drive. But just like the atmosphere was averaged out on board the ship —because different races home planets had different levels of oxygen—so was the gravity, and races like the Koroukh, who evolved in 0.5 g, needed the boost of a voidskin in the ship's 1.13 g.

"Ditec Greer," Sarjah said, noticing him. "Normally, this wouldn't be a part of your training yet, but please join us."

"Honestly, is it just me or do Xindari not really like humans that much?" he asked Rahel quietly.

"It's not that they don't like us; it's just they think we're too violent to be given NHC status so quickly. And I promise you Sarjah is easier to get along with than the captain," she said. "Could also be the fact that you just said *humans* meaning us from Earth and not them."

"You know what I mean," Marcus said even though he had realized it himself right after he said it.

"Look, every new race we meet out here is different in some way," she continued. "Just like we are to them. Xindari actually have a strong sense of compassion, but it gives them a strange sense of responsibility. That's often mistaken for arrogance, and yeah, they can be a pain in the ass to us, but I've yet to meet a race as straightforward and honest as them. It's well known they don't lie."

Marcus looked skeptical. "I think anybody can lie."

"Can? Probably. But as I understand it, they just don't. Really listen next time you talk to her."

"Oh, I do. That's why I don't miss the insults and snide comments."

"But has she ever not given honest praise when it was due?"

Marcus started to automatically respond but stopped

himself. He grudgingly had to admit Rahel was right about that. "I suppose not."

Ditec Greer, should I have everybody go to lunch while you finish your conversation? Sarjah said over the shiplink, ensuring everyone in bioneering heard. A couple of bioneers nearby glanced at him, smiling.

Marcus gave Rahel an *I told you so* look, and she suppressed a laugh as they walked over to the others.

Lead Jahnas guided Marcus and the others into a cavity adjacent to the main torus chamber. The space was about ten meters across, and a large fabricator took up one wall. Majid Ebrahimian, the Iraqi electrical engineer, was off to one side with his hands manipulating a panel of the fabricator. He looked to be in deep concentration. Bioneer Sinju stood next to him. The four-and-a-half-foot-tall, white furred Yotara watched Majid's progress, his thin catlike tail swaying back and forth. When Marcus accessed the shiplink, he could see that Majid was examining the energy flow of the fabrication process and making minor changes.

Sumiko was also there with Lead Doctor Leikeema. Sumiko wasn't tall but she seemed big when standing next to the four-foot-tall Fent'r. The yellow-skinned doctor had long purple hair, braided in a ponytail, and her purple eyes studied Majid carefully.

"I didn't know you would be here too," Marcus said quietly, walking up to Sumiko.

"I just found out," Sumiko said. "Since the transferee is sentient, we have to be on hand."

Marcus was usually so focused on his own training, which was more specialized, that he glossed over the fact that they were all there learning. Protectorate ships had two divisions: bioneering and metatech. And Dr. Ueda's field, astrobiology, fell under medical, which was a subdivision of bioneering just as dimensional techs and portal techs fell under metatech.

Sumiko glanced at the C-human who was her boss. *Or maybe I just bugged her enough about seeing the natives that this is a concession,* she continued on a private link. *I'll take it.*

Ha, maybe. He shared in her feeling of humor.

"You know, I assumed the tech specialist would arrive by portal or another ship," Sumiko said aloud.

"Yeah, I'm still trying to wrap my head around their consciousness being transferred into an organic shell." Marcus knew specialists in third-civ tech had been dispatched to their location. But given the time-sensitive nature of the situation, Golamee Asa, head of the Third-Civ Institute, had been requested to transfer in immediately.

I can't wait to see. Sumiko's feeling of excitement washed over him.

In some ways, the fabricator reminded Marcus of a giant oven, one big enough to fit a car. Through its transparent door membrane, he watched biomass that was extruded from the interior walls form a biosphere. The beach ball–sized object floated in the center while grav and magnetic fields manipulated the secreted matter to mold and shape its form, like invisible hands shaping clay. It had a tough, leathery hide with a fine trace of veins.

"Do you think it's ready?" Jahnas asked Majid, and Marcus realized it was a test. Apparently, he and Sumiko weren't the only ones getting training today.

Marcus observed Majid trace the routes of several veins within the sphere and analyze them against a template in the bioneering base file. It was similar to when he had shadowed Sarjah through their private link, but since Majid was working on the shiplink, anyone could have access. Majid checked a number of other things that dealt with chemical connections and bioelectrical flow before he stepped back and nodded to Jahnas.

"Yes, it's perfectly healthy." Majid couldn't quite mask his smile as he received a couple of congratulatory pulses from Sinju and some other bioneers in the room.

"So, this is alive?" Marcus asked because of Majid's use of the word *healthy*.

"Basically," Jahnas explained. "It's entirely biological, but not intelligent. Think of it like... On your world they've started growing organs in labs, correct? It's like that. This is a mobile organ that will house the transferee's consciousness."

"That's amazing," Sumiko said, looking like she wanted to dissect the sphere right there on the spot. "And the transferee will have full sensory perception?"

"Yes," Jahnas said. "The sphere has full-spectrum sense: optical, olfactory, audio, tactile, and taste abilities."

"It can consume food?" Sumiko gasped.

"No, but it has taste receptors to identify a wide range of things,"

"Impressive," Sumiko said.

The clear membrane of the fabricator pulled open, and Majid and Sinju stepped inside to make some final adjustment to the sphere.

"But why couldn't this expert just portal to the ship?" Marcus asked.

"That was covered in the briefing I sent you," Sarjah said. "Do you have no better questions Ditec Greer?"

Admittedly, Marcus had only skimmed the message Sarjah had sent him about reporting to bioneering because he had been so involved in his discussion with Rahel at the time. But her response still annoyed him. "So, now I can only ask questions you approve of?"

"I petitioned for that right but was refused," she said.

"Huh?"

"Twice."

Marcus could feel Rahel's amusement over their private link, but he refused to give her the satisfaction of looking at her.

"Because they are on the far side of the Society from us, in the borderland area where there are no megaportals," Jahnas answered him. "So, it would take a few days,"

A few days to cross twelve or so thousand light-years. Marcus just shook his head at the casual way C-humans talked about certain concepts that, to him, were still barely conceivable.

"Let's get ready," Dr. Leikeema said. "The transferee needs to link with the sphere soon."

Majid and Sinju moved the biosphere from the fabricator into the main bioneering cavity. It floated about a meter off the floor as they gradually pushed it. In a clear section of the main chamber, surrounded by workstations, the floor started to bubble and warp. A plinth grew up to about a meter in height, and the biosphere was maneuvered over to hover above the stand. Marcus could see faint traces of energy veins going from the base to the lifecore's central trunk.

Sarjah stood on one side of the sphere and directed Marcus to the opposite side.

Now you're just going to mirror me, Ditec Greer, she said in his mind. *Observe the dimensional paths I take and how I guide the pattern to the link point. Don't attempt to interact with the transferee.*

"Got it," Marcus said. Sarjah looked at him a moment, then turned her focus on the sphere.

Marcus closed his eyes and let his conscious perception

of the physical world drift into the background. His breathing, the sounds of bioneering, random people talking, how he was standing, smells, he let it all go. He drifted past the shiplink where local info was available with a thought: bioneering's files on the biosphere, the doctor's review of the sphere's physiology, and other departments on board going about their business. He mirrored Sarjah as her perception moved into the Nexus, where all the knowledge of the Society was available. Where anyone could connect with anyone else.

This simple shifting of his awareness was what most of his training had been like over the past six months. When Marcus had first left Earth, he had been so excited, he could barely sleep for days. And seeing Galileo City and Jupiter was almost like a dream. All the different C-humans, the ships in orbit, the portal, it was everything he imagined. Then he'd gone through the portal to Ya'sung, the world he trained on, and the boringness of his immediate future became apparent to him.

Ya'sung was a pastoral world that looked nothing like the sci-fi utopias he saw in movies. No skyscrapers or flying cars, just single-story homes and people who walked everywhere. After getting his bioweb, he had spent days practicing breathing. Breathing! For a while, it felt like a bad New Age nightmare. Then, one morning, he had awoken to such a strong feeling of contentment and love for his wife that he rolled over to kiss her awake, only to realize he was alone and not married.

He wasn't feeling the emotions of someone in the dorm he was staying at, not even someone from the planet. Distance was meaningless to the Nexus. The thoughts and feelings of someone next to you were just as strong as someone thousands of light-years away. Learning how to balance that and incorporate it into normal, everyday life took practice. And that was just basic bioweb ability; it was months before he was allowed to touch on the concepts of ditec biowebs. Now he and all the other Earthers in the program were in the practical part of training, where they were partnered with an actual ditec.

Sarjah's first connections seemed to be a standard communication, but soon enough she moved from the Nexus into a different dimension of metaspace. When Marcus had first started training as a dimensional technician, it had been difficult for him not to think numerically when dealing with other dimensions. Concepts like the fourth or fifth dimension were ingrained in everyday thinking on Earth. So, it had taken a while for him to understand there was no hierarchy. Normal space was length, height, and width—one, two, three. But to a person, they are all the same: he could walk straight, jump up and down, or move to the side in any combo he wanted. There was no law that length had to be first or third; it was simply a part of space. Other dimensions were no different. When he mentally moved into one, he discovered different ways to move that not only could he not perceive before but that his mind *couldn't* even conceive of. So instead of only being able to go straight, he could go @$%-straight, or #&!-straight. A right turn wasn't his only option when he could turn @#&-right, or %!*-left, or $!^-down, or any of the other infinite directions that he had no concept for when in standard space. His three-dimensional mind could only remember metaspace in analogies because something like moving @? &-up was only possible there. And metaspace wasn't just made up of other spatial dimensions but other conceptual dimensions like emotion, communication, awareness, and more that he hadn't even learned a name for yet. It was in one of these dimensions that his consciousness now resided, just as he knew his physical body was still standing in front of the sphere in bioneering.

In one sense, he was always aware of his physical body, the same way someone was aware of their body while watching TV: it's there but the person's focus—their conscious awareness—is on the TV show. They might shift positions, rub their eye, scratch, or cough, and still never give conscious thought to the movement. Mentally, emotionally, their awareness was focused on the show. Yet no matter how good the TV show, a normal person couldn't lose their sense of self to it and not "find" their body again. But that was a very real possibility in metaspace. Only a part of Marcus's consciousness was in his body currently, and if that connection were severed, at best he would be severely brain-damaged; at worst he would be not dead but a comatose, empty shell, while the last parts of his conscious-ness lost cohesion and dissipated across multiple dimen-sions. True oblivion.

It was there in the vast nothingness of a dimension of metaspace that Marcus's primary awareness now resided. He had never been this deep before. He wasn't even sure emotions were the same there because he wasn't scared at all, even though all of existence seemed to be only his consciousness and Sarjah's.

Gradually, he became aware of another presence, another mind near them, even though there was no distance. It was fuller, more solid than when he connected to someone in the Nexus. It wasn't simply a specific thought of a person, like words or images when talking to someone over a link. This was the entirety of a person—every thought there just under the surface, everything that made them a person—the essence of their being. Their consciousness? It felt like the difference between talking to someone standing close to you while your eyes were closed or talking to someone on the phone. You could feel their actual presence.

Sarjah guided this essence to the biosphere, where it housed itself and the neural patterns that were in metaspace now imprinted in the synapses of this new physical shell. As they came back to real time, Marcus realized that if he wasn't looking at the sphere, he couldn't tell from its D-signature that there wasn't an actual person standing there with them.

Whew, a distinct, feminine voice said over the shiplink. *That's always disconcerting.* The sphere manipulated magnetic fields and rose higher into the air as its skin pigmentation shifted slightly as the trace of veins glowed and pulsed slowly. It vaguely reminded Marcus of the alien Nui but without all the tentacles.

"Welcome aboard, Director Golamee," Sarjah said. "I'm Ditec Sarjah, and this is Ditec Greer. We look forward to working with you."

A feeling of pleasure and gratitude filled the shiplink. *Thank you,* the biosphere said. *I was amazed by the report I got on the device. Nothing like this has been found in centuries. When can we get started?*

"First, we have to make sure the transfer and shell are stable," Jahnas said, with Sumiko beaming at her side, looking like she couldn't wait to start poking and prodding. "It shouldn't take long."

"The captain will call a meeting in a few hours, Director Golamee," Sarjah said. "And we'll work out the specifics then."

"Very well," Golamee said as Dr. Leikeema, Majid, and others began some tests.

8

Nina felt the orientation held in the auditorium of the hotel was more of a formality than anything else. Aside from an update about the ambassador and envoy, they hadn't really learned anything that had not been drilled into them over and over since everyone had been notified of their post one year earlier. Thankfully her headache was gone; Nina had looked for Manaia but had not seen her, which wasn't surprising, considering how fast she seemed to make friends.

Now that the basics were out of the way and evening had come, everyone was moving into a ballroom down the hall for the reception. The hallway itself was massive, easily as wide as a city street. The outside wall was entirely a window that looked out onto the city. The setting sun shining through the numerous crystal-like skyscrapers cast a magical reddish-orange glow across the city, that was quite beautiful.

Nina moved inside the ballroom, which was spacious and elegant without tipping over into extravagance. Around the edges were numerous columns that stretched to the ceiling, patterns of light flowing within their surfaces, and they were surrounded by an abundance of lounge seating. The floor was full of narrow, high tables where people could stand, drink, and socialize.

There were some C-humans dressed as waiters who moved around with trays of drinks and snacks, but Nina noticed many of the Earthers were enjoying the novelty of getting their drinks from fabricators. The baseball-sized spheres, similar to the one Dr. Endless Green Sky used, floated around the room, pouring drinks seemingly directly from their shimmering porcelain-like surfaces. How they produced the liquids and foods she had no idea, and it was the subject of many conspiracy theories she had come across on the web one day.

The orientation was now a social mixer where the Earther delegation could mingle and talk to C-humans in a casual setting, something they had never truly been able to do before today. Nina had met many C-humans, of course, just as all the staff had once they'd been picked. Millions of people had applied for Earth Embassy positions, but only about three hundred were chosen. And a major part of the selection process was weeding out those people who wouldn't be able to adapt to working with aliens. This meant that the majority of settings where candidates met C-humans were highly monitored and always felt like part of a test; even if it seemed like a casual meeting, everyone knew they were still being interviewed. This was the first time people could just relax and be themselves while getting to know their alien cousins. But Nina had no doubt this was being monitored as heavily as every other meeting.

"Dr. Rodriguez." A well-dressed man in his early thirties approached her as she navigated the crowd.

"Hello," she said, taking the offered hand.

"I'm Bradley," he said. "Chief aide for Richard Hines, the consul general of North America. We wanted to congratulate you on your quick thinking during the attack," he continued, with a politician's smile that immediately made her feel this was more than social. "We also want to talk to you about what happened and what you saw."

"Um, of course," Nina said. She had figured she would have to talk to numerous bigwigs about what happened. "I did tell everything to the UN security, though, right after it happened."

"Which was exactly what you should've done, Doctor," another voice said.

Nina looked to see her boss, Dr. Aleksei Romashenko, walking up to join them. He was accompanied by a Nethean woman she didn't recognize at first as the one who had helped her to her room.

"Consul Dr. Romashenko," Bradley said, obviously a little taken aback. "I was—"

"Please inform Consul General Hines that I'll speak with him soon," Aleksei said, cutting him off. "As well as Ambassador Isaacs."

"Of course, sir," Bradley said with a tight nod. "Dr. Rodriguez." Then he turned and merged into the crowd.

"What was that?" Nina asked. She had liked Aleksei from the moment she first met him during training. He'd always come across as no-nonsense and straightforward, and never failed to recognize the accomplishments of those who worked under him.

"Is politics." He frowned after the aide, then collected himself. "I'll fill you in later. And excuse my manners. This is Fresh Snowfall on the Lake. She's a—"

"Cultural historian," Nina finished, taking the woman's

hand and smiling. "She was kind enough to help me find my room earlier."

"Hello again," the Nethean said. "I was just telling Consul Dr. Romashenko about Jupiter and happened to see you."

"Which reminds me, I did want to give you a warning, Nina," Aleksei said. "There is some talk of having you on stage tomorrow for the departure ceremony."

"Are you kidding me?" She just wanted to get to work and leave all the drama behind.

"I know." He shook his head. "But part of being able to go into Society means we occasionally have to play ball, yes. Speaking of which, there's Deputy Chief Xu; if you'll excuse me, I need to speak with her."

"Please, take your time," Fresh Snowfall on the Lake said. "The doctor and I can catch up."

"Do you know what's going on?" Nina asked her once Aleksei left.

"My guess is that you'll be in the center of some political maneuvering for the next few days," Fresh Snowfall on the Lake said, "as people try to carve out their place."

"I'd much rather be scanning brains," Nina said.

Fresh Snowfall on the Lake laughed. "That's why I'm a historian. All the crazy people I deal with are long gone." She smiled. "But tell me, how are *you*? Have you had a chance to let your family know you're okay?"

"I did, yeah," Nina answered, lost in thought.

The Nethean's gold eyes looked at Nina closely, and the overly large irises seemed more emotive. "But it didn't turn out well?"

"No, not..." Nina started. "Not exactly. They're just acting like normal parents. I was just thinking of everything that happened today and now this ceremony tomorrow. I just don't want political drama to overshadow the importance of the human side of things. Or the C-human side of things, I guess I should say."

"That's always a danger." Fresh Snowfall on the Lake smiled. "But from the Earthers I've been able to speak with so far, I think many of you feel that way."

Nina appreciated the sentiment and hoped she was right. Nina had never been such a workaholic that she neglected family; the two things were linked in her mind. It was all about family, and if she could keep others from going through similar hardships, that was worth fighting some stupid politics.

"Can I ask"—Nina wasn't sure how to phrase her question—"how do people in the Society feel about it? I don't mean the official response but regular people; what do they think about the attack? Are we just perceived as...I don't know, backward?"

"No, no, not at all." Fresh Snowfall on the Lake reached out and squeezed Nina's hand. "Most planets go through some type of phase like this. Context matters. Not only does the history of the Society show this—and I can tell you some stories, believe me—but the history of C-humanity as a whole is full of examples of how difficult first contact can be."

"But isn't that just ancient history to you?" Nina asked.

"Not in the way you mean, I think," Fresh Snowfall on the Lake said. "Yes, our civilization has been around a lot longer, but we are well-versed in our history. When the Society started, there was, of course, a lot of disagreements and conflict, even some wars in the very beginning. But we were also able to see how some things had gone bad for previous C-human civs and fortunately could avoid the same paths."

"Actually learning from past mistakes," Nina mused. "We could do with some of that."

"I think the existence of Earth Embassy itself, when just five years ago global conflict was so close to breaking out, shows that you all have learned a lot. It's an ongoing process, and like anything else, it can take time."

She and Fresh Snowfall on the Lake talked for a long while, and the mood of the ballroom seemed to get more relaxed as Earthers got more comfortable and in some cases tipsy. With so much mingling, Nina eventually got separated from the historian. She also ran into Manaia twice, each time talking to a different handsome C-human. Eventually, Nina stepped out into the hallway to get some air. She had started to feel a little anxious and wasn't sure if the crowd was reminding her of what had happened at the station or if she was just tired and worried about tomorrow's departure ceremony.

"As much as your face is all over the net, you're a hard person to catch up to," a voice said behind her.

Nina turned to see a dark-skinned woman with short, natural hair. "Omoni!" she said, hugging her friend, happy to see a familiar face. "Wow. I haven't seen you since—"

"The Paris conference," Omoni finished.

Dr. Omoni Akande was an astrobiologist from Nigeria working with the science contingent. They had met at some of the joint training seminars and hit it off. The UN did its best to manage the selection and training process, but it was an uphill battle. Nothing like Earth Embassy had ever been done before, and trying to get every nation to agree on formats had started to take too long. So, each country trained its own people, and there were occasional larger meetings where embassy officers with overlapping fields could meet.

"I saw you on TV, being the badass doctor," Omoni said.

"God, that's been totally blown out of proportion."

"That's politics, hon," Omoni said, taking a good look at Nina. "I can't even imagine what it was like. How are you holding up? Can I do anything?"

"I'm... I'm probably better than I should be," Nina admitted. "Given what happened. But at the same time, that's just it. The way that doctor healed her. And all this."

"It's hard to believe that was just this morning."

"Right," Nina agreed. "And tomorrow we're leaving Earth. Don't get me wrong: I was scared as hell, but I don't know that it was crazier than any of the other stuff going on."

"It could take a while to process," Omoni said. "Just know that if you need anybody to talk to, I'm here."

"I appreciate that. Really," Nina said as they started to walk back into the ballroom. "So, otherwise, how are you?"

"Excited. Nervous. And everything else."

"Sounds about right." Nina took two drinks from a passing waiter and thanked him, handing one to Omoni. The C-human waiter was a hominin that she had never seen before, unbelievably slender and covered in short greenish and orange feathers. Nina looked at him as he walked away and shook her head.

"This will take some getting used to," Nina said, moving to stand next to one of the unoccupied high tables in the crowded room. "I can't put my finger on it, but I always thought the C-humans, Netheans and A'Quan at least, kinda looked like people in body paint and costumes at first glance, but now that I'm seeing so many different C-humans at the same time, I feel like there's something off."

"It's the bodies," Omoni said. At Nina's unsure look, she

continued. "A lot of C-humans' bodies are shaped differently, bipedal and humanoid, yes, but subtly different. Something you might not fully notice at first. Maybe their neck or arms are a bit longer than normal, or their waist a tad too narrow, eyes slightly too big or small, different-jointed legs, their torso or limbs too thin, too squat, whatever. Subconsciously, you know a regular hu... Earth human's body doesn't quite look like that—so they couldn't just be people in costumes but something else."

As soon as she said it, Nina knew she was right and wondered how she had never noticed that before. There must've been half as many C-humans in the room as there were delegates, and everyone was mingling. While most were Netheans and A'Quan, Nina had counted at least six other C-human races she had not seen before. Never had it been more obvious to her that humans, Earth humans, were all one color, just different tones. The dark skin of somebody from Kenya next to the pale skin of somebody from Norway didn't seem all that different when seen next to purple, green, or orange skin—and especially not next to the C-humans with feathers, scales, or fur.

"I was glad to hear that the envoy would be okay," Omoni said. "I was feeling a little guilty."

"Why?"

Omoni glanced around, a little embarrassed. "Well, after watching the clip, and the shock of seeing you and the violence of what happened...I couldn't stop looking at her blood."

Nina stopped, drink halfway to her mouth, and leaned closer. "I was shocked by that too."

"They've been here for years, and there're still so many basic things they leave us in the dark about."

"Basic to us," Nina said. "But there could be a million

reasons for that. And we have been allowed to study Nethean biology thoroughly."

"Whose blood is red," Omoni said. "But maybe it was just so we wouldn't focus on the difference. I know I couldn't stop wondering if it was some analog of hemocyanin, the copper-rich protein that makes octopuses' blood blue, or—"

"Octopuses have blue blood?"

"Yeah, but A'Quan are vertebrates, so they're not something from an analogous mollusk tree, like octopuses." Omoni said. "And of course, they're mammals."

"That's still a hot topic though, right?"

"Oh my God, is it. Obviously, they're humanoid," Omoni said, glancing around the room at some of the non-mammal C-humans, like the feathered man they had gotten their drinks from. "But the debate about how amphibians, reptiles, avians, or aquatics can actually be hominin isn't gonna be solved until we get out there and the Society allows us more access."

"Dr. Rodriguez," a voice said before Nina could consider this. She turned and saw Dr. Endless Green Sky approaching them. "It's a pleasure to see you again. How are you?"

The doctor was wearing a gray, single breasted fitted suit, not too dissimilar in style from something men on Earth wore. And, Nina had to admit, he wore it well. Nethean bodies were proportioned the same as Earthers—and the doctor was fit.

"Um, hi." She faltered for a moment when she realized she was staring. "I'm good. Good. And this, this is my friend Dr. Omoni Akande."

"Hello," Omoni said, shaking his hand, but not before casting Nina an amused *I know what you were thinking* look.

"An astrobiologist," Endless Green Sky said. "I look forward to working with you, Dr. Akande."

"You know who I am?" Omoni asked.

"Of course," he responded. "You know we can look up information through the Nexus. No different than when you Google something; we just don't need an external device to do it."

"I think they said we get introduced to that technology on our trip to Jupiter," Omoni said, glancing at Nina for confirmation. "Now, that will take some getting used to."

"If it's one thing we humans are, it's adaptable," the purple Nethean said. "You'll be mastering tech and meeting C-humans way weirder-looking than me and not batting an eye before you know it." Then he got a thoughtful look on his face. "Not batting an eye; this is the correct context, yes?"

"Uh, actually, yeah." Nina finally found her voice.

Endless Green Sky sighed, relieved—at least, that's what Nina read into the movement. "Oh, that's good." He leaned in a little to whisper. "This is my first assignment with an NHC, and I admit I'm still a little nervous with your language. Just the other day, I told an Earth human it was just like riding a bike."

"What's wrong with that?" Nina asked.

"We were talking about Earth divorce customs," he said.

Nina laughed as naturally as if she were talking to anyone. Which she knew was the whole reason for this mixer, to help her and the other delegates feel comfortable with the whole situation of meeting aliens.

"I thought you had some type of translation ability?" Omoni asked.

"Oh, we do, we do; there are so many languages in the Society, it would be impossible to learn them all, unless you're Galezian, but they're a whole other story. My bioweb would allow me to understand you, but since you don't have one, it's best to actually learn your language."

"Well, your fluency is impressive," Omoni said. "Is your race especially gifted with linguistics?"

"No, that would be the Ta Wei." Endless Green Sky pointed to a tall, orange amphibian C-human a couple of tables away. "They can imitate almost any sound."

"But what about Netheans' eidetic memory? Surely, you wouldn't need a bioweb to remember a foreign language, would you?" Nina asked. After an incident at the hospital she worked at, Nina had left to go to a facility focused on learning to incorporate Society biotech. There she had begun to focus more on neuroscience than neurology and had even co-authored a few well-received papers on memory and how biowebs affected Earther brains. Work she believed was influential in her being accepted to the embassy. It was also when she learned that Netheans had perfect memory retrieval and that the bone ridges along the sides of their heads helped radiate heat away from their brains.

"That's true for Netheans and some other C-human races," Endless Green Sky said. "I can remember all the rules and pronunciation of English or Hausa"—he nodded to Omoni—"but idioms can be such a culturally specific thing that you can use them incorrectly even if you know the grammar and vocabulary of the language."

"And, of course, physiology is important," Omoni added. "If our races didn't have similar vocal cords, we wouldn't be able to speak your language even though we could understand it."

This led them to talking about the physiology of vocal ability and how it varied in the different C-human races. The Society encouraged local science on any NHC world.

Their goal was not to stagnate or hinder scientific discovery but to supplement it as the planet matured to a higher level of technology on its own. So, while the Society had no problem providing the cure for diseases like cancer, they would not provide the formula. They only pointed to the path and let local science come to discoveries in its own time. Nina and Omoni joked about having learned enough to co-author a new medical paper.

"I understand that language is one of the reasons Netheans were chosen as our mentor race," Nina said. "But I've also heard some people mention sense of humor?"

Endless Green Sky held in a chuckle, and Nina found herself smiling also. He said, "It may seem trivial on the surface, but the ability to laugh and find humor in the same thing really goes a long way to fostering trust. Who doesn't love to see a video of some old person trying to walk on ice, yet they keep falling on their butt?"

Nina and Omoni stared at him in surprise, glancing between each other at a loss for words.

His smile grew even brighter. "I'm messing with you, of course."

"Oh my God," Nina said, smacking his arm reflexively. "You had me going."

Endless Green Sky put his hand to his arm where she hit him and looked confused.

"I'm sorry," she said, fearing she must've crossed some cultural taboo line. "I wasn't thinking. It's just something friends..."

He smiled broadly and patted her arm. "Sorry, couldn't resist getting you again."

Omoni burst out laughing at that, and Nina glared at them in mock anger. Then she tipped her glass to his. "Payback is coming, Dr. Sky."

"Oh, no titles among friends, just Endless Green Sky," he said, still smiling.

"Nina," she said, their eyes holding each other for a moment.

"Is it true your full names are even longer?" Omoni asked.

"It is," he said, large green eyes leaving Nina, but not quickly. "We don't name our children until they're born. I don't have kids myself, but it's that moment when parents see their child for the first time and try to put into words all the emotions they are experiencing. For a race that doesn't forget anything, the names are often analogous of what the parents were doing or feeling at an important moment in their lives or when they first decided to have a family."

"That's beautiful," Omoni said.

"I think so," Endless Green Sky said. "But it also makes for some long names; not a problem for us, but we usually use a shorter version when talking to other C-humans. You've heard of Ambassador As the Gentle Wind, of course. But his full name is Remember That Night We Sailed Under the Stars as the Gentle Wind Carried Us Down the River."

"Really?" Nina asked, she and Omoni glancing at each other, expecting another joke.

"Really," he said.

"So what's your full name?" Nina asked.

"Well, nothing I'm ashamed of." He looked at both of them. "But given some of the cultural differences, and this being an official function, I'm not sure I should say in public."

"Now, that sounds like a juicy name," Omoni said.

"No, that's my nephew, 'First Cup of Juice in the Morning.'"

"Now I know you're messing with us," Nina laughed.

"No, I swear," Endless Green Sky said, holding his hand to his chest in a gesture she wasn't familiar with.

"Greetings, cousins," a voice seemed to say from everywhere, distracting Nina before she could respond.

A large image of a Nethean's head and torso floated in the air above one of the main doors. The speaker was standing underneath the image. "I want to say how much of a pleasure it is for us to get to talk to you like this. New human races entering the Society rarely happen in the lifetime of most citizens, so believe me when I tell you that we are truly honored. And whether Earth ultimately decides to join the Society or not, know that you always have family in the galaxy."

Nina thought it was going to be another boring speech, but something about Endless Green Sky's expression told her there was more to this.

"Now, up until this point," the speaker's smiling image went on, "Earth has only seen a few of the other C-human races that make up the Society, and I know you still think of us as aliens, not really as humans. And that's completely natural," he said, raising his hands in a very human gesture. He pointed to some people in the crowd as he talked. "I mean, this guy here is green, she's orange, her, she has feathers, and that guy has blue scales, for heaven's sake."

"Don't be jealous, mammal," the reptilian C-human said, running his hand down his blue scaled arm.

Nina laughed along with everyone else. The Nethean speaker's casual manner and jokes relaxed everyone, and Nina could see the importance of what Endless Green Sky meant about humor.

The speaker smiled and continued. "The history of all our races has shown that we all reacted the same way when we first discovered we were not alone in the Milky Way, much less the only hominins. So, I get it.

"But now that you're actually going out into the galaxy, there will be times when you meet non-C-human species. The Society is over eleven thousand light-years wide, after all, that's over sixty quadrillion miles, and while the Hu'ma —the original human civilization—spread their DNA across a vast stretch of space before they moved on, it didn't take everywhere. And not every planet within C-human space gave rise to hominin intelligent life. There are a few non-hominin species that naturally evolved within our space, and some have even joined the Society."

There were some murmurs in the crowd as people started to realize where this was going. Nina felt a bit anxious herself, and Omoni had stopped, glass half-raised to her mouth, glancing questioningly at Endless Green Sky, who gave her a knowing nod.

"I want to take this time to introduce you to two of those species," the speaker said, and turned toward the opening door.

Several gasps, and at least one scream, spread through the crowd as what appeared at first to be two giant spiders walked into the room. Nina instinctively took a step back and realized she had reached out to grab Endless Green Sky's arm.

"Everyone, please. These are Society citizens just like us. There's no need for alarm. This is Envoy Q'za who is a Z'tainian," the image of the speaker said calmly, but loud enough to drown out the shocked noise.

Nina saw that they weren't spiders at all; they had four legs. Their movement was similar to a crab, but they stood about as high as a horse's body. They had a leathery bluish oval midsection with four multi-jointed legs that came out from their core. Their upper side and legs were covered in milky crystal-like orbs that, Endless Green Sky whispered to them, were sensory organs.

"And this is Envoy Mywah, a Nui," the speaker said as two other, just as weird-looking aliens entered the room. At first, Nina thought they were like large squids. But their greenish bodies were completely spherical, and sprouting from them were several tentacles at least two meters long. They moved by rolling, multiple tentacles touching the ground and pushing them forward as their body rotated. The tips of the tentacles tapered into numerous cilia longer than her fingers.

The image of one of the crablike aliens appeared next to the head of the Nethean speaker. Nina could see that most of the people who were close to the door had stepped back. She also noticed that every group of Earth humans had at least one C-human standing with them.

The crablike alien spoke. She could see no mouth, but the purple Nethean's image wasn't talking, so it had to be it. He? She? Nina wasn't sure.

"Greetings hello," it said. "We apologize for any shock caused you. Always pleasure to meet new human culture. And believe it or not, you look just as weird to us."

After a moment, what it said sank in and people started to chuckle.

"We hope you enjoy the rest of your night, everyone," the speaker said as his image disappeared. And the rest of the evening was interesting as people worked up the nerve to talk to the four *true* aliens.

"That was well played," Nina said to Endless Green Sky.

"Hmmm?" he said.

"Get everybody relaxed and comfortable talking to...C-humans. And then let us know the galaxy is a lot stranger than we realized."

He just smiled.

As the evening wore on, Endless Green Sky was lured away to talk to other groups, and Omoni, with Nina firmly in tow, was easing closer and closer to two of the new alien envoys. Nina had to admit that she was as fascinated to learn about their neural structure as Omoni was about their biology. Glancing around at the people nearest them Nina couldn't help but smile.

"What's so funny?" Omoni asked.

"Look at us." Nina nodded, taking in the groups of people who were milling around talking, yet obviously waiting for their turn to talk to the aliens. "I feel like we're the guys in a bar waiting for our turn to talk to the hot woman that's been shooting everyone down."

Omoni laughed. "True. But this answers so many questions. I know the Society never hid the fact that there were other alien species, but they've never given details on them. And now—"

"Greetings hello." Nina and Omoni both startled when they realize the Z'tainian was now talking to them.

"Hey... Hi, sorry, hello," Omoni said while Nina echoed her.

"Researching, correct? Files indicate you are astrobiologist and neurologist/neuroscientist," The alien's voice came from a fist-sized disk attached to its body. Nina couldn't see anything that looked like a mouth. It wasn't wearing clothes but had a few buckles and straps with pockets on its arms (legs?) and body. It was also physically intimidating up close, the central body about six feet high. Its legs were thicker than her thighs and looked to be longer than her whole body if fully extended. The Z'tainian's skin was tough and leathery like a rhino, but the color was a bluish green, with darker stripes around its core. The numerous crystal-like orbs that grew out of its body had the faintest glint to them. Endless Green Sky had said they were sensory organs, but she didn't know if it was polite to only stare at one while talking.

This was a real alien. Nina understood how true what she had said to Endless Green Sky was. C-humans were scary to a lot of people, but overall, they presented a comfortable view of the universe. People on Earth had become so used to seeing humanoid aliens on TV that it was almost what was expected by the layperson. But this being, this was more what scientists like Omoni truly expected. Nina wouldn't have known it was sentient without being introduced to it—her? Him?

Even as she and Omoni talked to the obviously intelligent alien, Nina could feel that primal gut reaction to something so *other*. But she wanted to learn about them. Although, she knew some people, like her ex, who would see these beings as monsters not sentients. She hoped Fresh Snowfall on the Lake was right and that most people would see the truth in time.

WHEN NINA finally got back to her room, she just sat on the edge of the bed for a while, staring out the window at the city. Her headache was back again, and stronger, but she wouldn't let it spoil her mood. Tomorrow, she would be leaving Earth to live and work with C-humans and possibly true aliens like the Z'tainians and Nui. Was that just this morning when the envoy had been shot and she was marveling at *her* alienness? A hell of a Monday.

She jumped a little when the phone rang, and rose on her elbows, only now realizing she had started to doze off. She rubbed her eyes, squinting at the bright screen in the dark room, and her heart sank. It was her ex. She just looked at the phone for a moment, not sure if she wanted to be bothered. Ultimately, she decided not to put it off.

"Hi."

"Hey," Tony's voice said.

Only two words, but there was a weight of history from past arguments that made it feel like they had already been talking much longer.

"I was gonna call you before I left tomorrow," Nina finally said.

"I'm glad you're okay," he said. Another pause, then he continued. "I spoke to your parents earlier. They told me you were fine."

Meaning she hadn't bothered to call and tell him. A point she had to concede.

"Sorry," she said. "It's been a crazy day. I—"

"Nina." He seemed to look for the words before he continued. "It's not too late to come back. I love you. Your parents love you."

"That has nothing to do with why I'm going, Tony, and you know it."

"Doesn't it? There's nothing they can teach you that will bring your grandparents back."

"Are you kidding me with this shit?" Nina said. "You don't think I know that? And you just conveniently ignore all the people who can be helped."

"Maybe because you conveniently ignore how many people they hurt. They are tearing this country apart."

"Stupidity was doing that long before the Society came along." They were on old, comfortable ground now. "People want to look everywhere else for the problems in their life except themselves."

"And some people want to look outside themselves to be saved."

"Tony." She was tired and beginning to think the real reason she hadn't called was because there was nothing new to say. "Some crazy people tried to murder a bunch of civilians. It's just luck nobody was killed. The ambassador barely survived."

"Maybe that was the bad luck," he said. It was one of those heat-of-the-moment things that couldn't be taken back.

Nina half-pulled the phone away to stare at it open-mouthed. Tony had said those words, but she couldn't stop hearing that terrorist scream "fake human" when he shot the envoy. That hatred, anger, and fear that people let eat away at them until they were hollowed out. She didn't want that in her life.

"I guess it was also bad luck for all the other people caught in the explosion, huh? People like me?"

"You know I didn't mean it like—"

"I know that I'm done," she yelled, hanging up and throwing the phone on the bed. She paced back and forth not so much in anger but in weary frustration. And she knew from long experience she wouldn't be falling asleep soon. Not to mention that the headache was even worse now.

She was about to turn the lamp on when she caught a glance at the time on her phone and froze. It was eleven fifty-seven, which wasn't the issue. It was that the number seven appeared red and the five was purple. She unlocked the phone, thinking it was just a trick of the light, but the small numbers on the top of the screen were also colored and the battery percentage was colored also. Seventy-three percent, with another red seven and an orange three. Nina blinked and rubbed her eyes, a frightening feeling crawling up her spine. She grabbed a scrap of paper and a black pen, fiercely scribbling some numbers down without looking. Turning the lights on, she took a moment to calm herself before she looked at what she had written. The numbers on the paper were colored also.

Nina stepped back in horror, hands coming to her mouth. She was experiencing synesthesia, when people's senses became mixed up and what triggered one sensory pathway might also trigger another. A person hearing everyday sounds may see colors at the same time, so car horns could sound orange or blue, or someone who smelled odors may see colors. Some people tasted a specific food whenever they heard certain words. Synesthesia could affect any of the senses—a sensation in one causing an unrelated sensation in another. Its most usual form was grapheme-color synesthesia, in which individual letters and numbers appeared colored even though they weren't. It wasn't a common phenomenon; only a small percent of the population had it. But almost everyone was born that way; it didn't just pop up later in life. And that was the source of her fear and confusion.

The only time she had seen it happen spontaneously was when she was doing research on bioweb and exosensory device technology. And while the Society didn't let Earth study the technology, they had allowed neuroscientists all over the world to study the effects of these devices on Earther brains. Over the last few years, hundreds of people from Earth had been given this tech, and all the testing had shown that it was safe. But it was also noticed that some of the biotech used for accessing memory left residual traces in the brain. Those traces could manifest through various side effects, including temporary episodes of synesthesia. That could only mean that one of the C-humans she had met had used such a device on her without her knowledge.

That didn't just go against everything she believed about the Society but everything she wanted to believe about them. So many lives had been saved by their advanced medicine, so many families given a second chance, that that type of betrayal was too much to casually accept. There had to be another explanation, something she was overlooking. But as she thought back on her day, she realized the headache she had earlier was the first sign of it, even though she hadn't noticed colors. And the cold truth was the only C-humans she had been around long enough to do it were Endless Green Sky and Fresh Snowfall on the Lake. Two people she had genuinely liked. Nina slumped onto the bed as she tried to accept the emotional flood of what that meant.

One of them had copied her memories.

9

After helping guide Golamee, Marcus was supposed to be resting to get ready for their mission back to the moon. But while he was in his quarters, he'd gotten sucked down the social-media black hole.

Since their discovery of the incursion, Marcus had been picking up a lot of strong feelings of solidarity, compassion, comfort, and regret. At first, he thought it was spillover from the crew on the shiplink, but he soon realized it was from people all across the Society. It was *Fulcrum's Light*'s day cycle, but it was the middle of the night where Earth Embassy was, and day/night cycles were different across the Society depending on what planet you were on, so there were entire Nexus groups still trending the story.

Just about every C-human in Sahara City had been sharing their views of what was happening with the embassy Earthers, and he had gotten fascinated watching the orientation mixer. The Society didn't have serving staff like on Earth, but in dealing with NHCs, they would often emulate the culture to help ease relations. So, all the C-human waiters were actually highly trained members of the New Human Culture Division. But one of the most popular feeds was from a C-human who wasn't part of the NHCD. He had won a lottery which allowed him to come to Earth and be a waiter at the mixer. It sounded like a strange reward at first, but given how C-humans viewed NHCs the guy was considered lucky. He was a young Nethean whose commentary on the evening was quite funny. Marcus got caught up watching when he saw the Earthers' reaction to meeting the non-C-human sentients, which was pretty much the same as Marcus and the other ditec trainees had had when they had first met them. The young Nethean's good-natured laughter at the Earthers' reactions was punctuated with the feelings of his own experience the first time the Nethean had met a Kula'ka—a triped C-human race Marcus had only seen images of—and how he reacted. The self-deprecation helped to convey the feelings of solidarity he had with the Earthers' reactions.

To Marcus, it was that emotional aspect that made the Nexus so much more than just "social media." It was easier to relate to each other, not just in beliefs or humor but also in the sharing of grief and empathy. Support that gave comfort not in words or platitudes but in a shared understanding and acknowledgment of the experience and how it affected you on a personal level. That level of openness was something he believed the Earthers at the mixer didn't fully understand yet. Marcus knew that his generation's concept of privacy was very different from his grandparents'. In fact, it was the Nexus that allowed him to better understand older people's views on privacy.

There were plenty of people on Earth who lived their lives through the lens of social media and their phones, constantly taking pictures and video of whatever they were doing at the moment. Not just famous influencers but regular people posting about an experience they were having: taking a pic of a landmark they were visiting, showing a pic of a new outfit they just got, sharing a bad experience they just had, commenting on something trending or on what a friend just posted, or a hundred other things. It was the new norm of modern life, at least in more-developed countries. But because they lacked the firsthand experience, Earthers didn't realize how profoundly more pervasive and subtle that sharing was with a bioweb. Someone else's entire perception could be experienced. Everything that every C-human saw, heard, and felt was available (if they shared it) to anyone connected to the Nexus who cared to look.

Nobody shared private conversations without the other person's knowledge—for all the lack of privacy with Society tech, they had a deep respect for privacy, something else he wasn't sure Earth was really ready for. But the sheer amount of data available from everyday life would astound most Earthers, young and old.

There were entire Nexus groups with hundreds of millions of people just talking about different aspects of the embassy. Earth, as with any new human culture, was almost always one of the biggest trending stories across the Nexus, but since the attack at the train station, there were countless subgroups that popped up to discuss, console, and share about what happened.

His mind drifted around the Nexus, one group leading him to another. Some stuff he focused on; other things he shifted to memory cells for later absorption and reflection. Once, he sensed another Earther ditec in a group he was perceiving. Since there were only one hundred Earther trainees randomly coming across another one in the Nexus was practically impossible. But given so much focus on the attack and how the subconscious and stray thoughts could affect ones search he wasn't surprised. He stopped himself just before he contacted them. His class had been encouraged, not ordered but repeatedly encouraged, not to contact each other while still in the six-month training period after they left Ya'sung. They were told it would slow them from fully integrating with the dimensional technician bioweb because they would get stuck with each other's bad habits. He understood, but there was often the temptation of talking to someone who could really understand his situation.

Or maybe he just needed to talk to someone more down-to-earth. He considered calling some of his friends back home, but that usually ended up with him doing most of the talking because everyone wanted to hear about his adventures. Should he call his ex-girlfriend? They had ended things amicably, neither of them wanting a long-distance relationship, and him being in space was "long distance" on another level. But they were still good friends, and he missed talking to her sometimes. He was still debating when Sarjah contacted him, not strictly with words, but he felt that she was ready to discuss the mission and where he should report to. He'd have to call home later. It wasn't until he was leaving that he guiltily realized he still hadn't called his grandparents.

THE RECON TEAM and support were in a separate chamber on the same level as the portal chamber. Sarjah was running Marcus through some practice simulations while Golamee was using the Nexus to confer with some specialists from across the Society. He could perceive Rahel and t'Zyah with her, though physically t'Zyah was on duty in the ditec cavity and Rahel was in her quarters. Golamee's transfer sphere floated off to one side. So, while her temporary physical shell was here, mentally she was meeting with people thousands of light-years away through the Nexus. Of course, that was while her real body was tens of thousands of light-years away, on the far fringe of Society space.

"You're losing focus, baby culture," Sarjah said to him as she mentally observed his progress in a training maze she constructed in the Nexus.

"You know, for such an enlightened race, Xindari sure love to throw in some insults."

"Don't be insulted by truth, and you will find more peace in your life."

"What is that, from a fortune cookie?"

"If baking truisms into food will help you learn, then I will share some of my raise-sibling's recipes with you."

There hadn't been a trace of humor over the shiplink, but Marcus was beginning to note a certain absence of emotional content in some of Sarjah's comments that he suspected meant she was consciously keeping him from feeling her amusement. If she was even capable of amusement.

Her head shift, which his bioweb automatically translated as a raised eyebrow for Earthers, hinted that she had picked up on what he was feeling even though he hadn't said it. But before she could say anything, she received a pulse over the Nexus from Golamee, asking her to join the meeting.

"Keep practicing, Ditec Greer," she said to him as the floor of the chamber morphed upward to form a stool that she sat on, and she closed her eyes.

Through their private link Marcus could perceive Sarjah

conversing with Golamee and some others, but without joining their meeting, he couldn't tell who was speaking or what was being said. He also perceived that Rahel and the captain were now in a Nexus meeting with the Protectorate Council.

Marcus looked around before he tried the training maze again. On the other side of the chamber was the security team, going over their plans for the mission. Lead Security Tuhzo, Kleedak, and Grayson were standing still with a distant look that told Marcus they were working via the shiplink. A small-scale projection of the data portal and its surrounding landscape hovered nearby as the bioneer Sinju and a couple of others talked and made minor changes to the image.

Marcus listened for a moment as Sinju started explaining some point to the security group via the shiplink. In the back of his mind, on an unconscious level, Marcus could feel a connection to everyone aboard the ship, and with the slightest concentration on any one person or persons, he could open a private conversation, verbal or virtual. But the shiplink was local to the vessel—no one outside the ship could connect that way. If he wanted to communicate with people beyond the ship, it was through the Nexus, which connected the entire Society.

Letting his perception expand, Marcus focused on the Nexus again. Instead of training, Marcus took a moment to try to track down more information on the third-civ. The Nexus Index opened in his awareness. It wasn't a separate place but an aspect of the Nexus that would search it for the data he wanted. And there were massive amounts of data in the form of histories, research, chat groups, and more, but again he found that anything but the most basic overview was restricted. Almost no knowledge was forbidden in the

Society, although there were some things people from NHCs were restricted from accessing. The fact that this information existed wasn't hidden, but for want of a better term, it was blocked. This usually came in the form of a feeling that whatever he was trying to access was...*off-limits* was the wrong phrase, but more the understanding that there were other things Earthers had to be exposed to first before they were ready.

What are you doing?

Rahel's voice startled Marcus as he was trying to figure out a way around the data blocks. She was still in her quarters, speaking to him through the Nexus.

"I thought you were in a meeting," he said out loud but still letting it transmit to her. With his eyes closed, he wasn't "seeing" the Nexus as any type of visual image; the knowledge just flowed through his mind. "And what is the big deal about the third-civ? Why would—"

That's what I was meeting with the council about, she said. *There are some things we need to discuss.*

"That don't sound good," he said, looking at her image as he let the Nexus Index go.

It's political, she said. *As far as anything is in the Society.* At his questioning look, she continued. *Once Earth Embassy reached the Orion Molecular Cloud Complex and got settled in the capital, there were certain things they planned on revealing to Earth's ambassador first. And facts about previous civilizations is one of them.*

"Okay. Why?"

NHCD protocol, which to me means they just wanted to put it off. But for now, you have been cleared for access to previously restricted data on the third-civ.

"But it's something you already know about?"

Marcus felt the barest trace of emotion from her, but it

passed too quickly for him to really understand. It felt like...
fear, on some level, or a healthy respect for something you
should be afraid of, but there was also the feeling of...awe,
reverence maybe. He couldn't be sure. Whatever had
happened to her in the Society had left a mark.

Yes, she answered him after a moment. *But not directly.
We... I...* She shook her head, unsure how to go on.

*Near the end of one of my missions as an envoy, on one of my
trips around the Society, my ship was... It encountered previous
C-human civ tech,* Rahel said. *Which isn't relevant to the
current situation. But since I've had the experience, I was
included in the talks about this and you.*

"But what does—"

*Listen, just access the data on the third-civ available to
you now.*

Rahel was genuinely worried about him. She let that
feeling show. That stalled the further questions he was
going to ask. So, he closed his eyes and encompassed the
Nexus Index again, and he realized the blocks were gone.
His subconscious was already guiding the search parameters, so information opened in his mind almost before he
had formed a thought to retrieve it.

Knowledge of the third human civilization poured into
his bioweb's memory cells. He knew about it as if he had
studied it his entire life. A general understanding that was a
part of his memory the same way he knew about the Great
Wall of China or the Civil War in America. But as Marcus
sank into the memories, letting his conscious mind focus on
certain points, he began to realize something that he had
trouble accepting into his general framework of how the
world worked. The third-civ was ancient.

The fact that the Society was the fifth hominin mega-
civilization was never hidden from Earthers. Everyone knew

it was almost fourteen thousand years old—thirteen thousand nine hundred and ninety-eight, to be exact, so the Society claimed—and that other hominin civilizations had risen and fallen in the past. This had started when the first hominins—who were called the Hu'ma—had evolved advanced technology and spread their genetic code across this region of the Milky Way. The Society was the latest example of this natural cycle of intelligent life.

The Society didn't try to come off like they were the epitome of hominin evolution or morally superior to previous C-human cultures, although at times, Marcus did feel like some of the C-humans he met had a "fifth time is the charm" mentality. The Society presented itself to Earth as honestly as it knew how. It was modern C-humanity, and in time, like any civilization, it could rise, thrive, and fall just like anything else. It was that "in time" that Marcus was now trying to come to terms with.

Marcus, like most people he had talked to, thought of the previous C-human civs the same way he thought of previous ancient civilizations on Earth like the Sumerians, the Romans, or the Egyptians. Civilizations that had lasted hundreds of years and had influenced the world long after they were gone. Rome was one of the longest-lasting empires in recorded human history, and if you included the Byzantine reign it had lasted over a thousand years.

That was nothing compared to the Society, which he believed was one of the reasons many Earthers had a hard time accepting the C-humans' claims. But much like Sarjah always said of Earth, the Society was just a baby civilization compared to its predecessors.

The third C-human civilization had lasted 1.3 million years.

One million, three hundred thirty-seven thousand, eight

hundred and twenty-three years specifically. Marcus shook his head in disbelief, as if that would clear his mind. As if he could rearrange the numbers into something more manageable. It just seemed unreal; he didn't doubt that it was true as he stood there in a custom-grown room of a living spaceship, thousands of light-years from Earth, surrounded by cousin species to his own *Homo sapiens*, using technology to basically talk telepathically. No, he didn't doubt it. He just couldn't easily wrap his head around it. Not even counting the arrival of the Society, Earth civilization had grown and changed so much in the last few hundred years. Most people just didn't grasp the concept of time if it was longer than a decade or so. Smartphones hadn't even been around for a generation yet; hell, he knew people that acted like the nineties were just about a decade ago and not last century. And the third-civ was a million-plus years old.

Some aspects of the Society seemed utterly alien to him —as young as he knew it was—but a million years? How did they even stay human? How was it recognizable? If you took a thousand Roman Empires and lived them back-to-back, the third-civ was still older.

He perceived Rahel, who pulsed him a nod of understanding.

"I..." He couldn't find the words, didn't even know what he wanted to say. America was four hundred long years old, the pyramids were over four thousand years old, some Aboriginal culture maybe went back tens of thousands of years, but all that was just the humidity on the dew on a drop in a bucket in the ocean. He could feel that Rahel had gone through the same realizations, the same feelings of insignificance...no, she had experienced it to an even greater degree than him. And that's when the other shoe dropped.

For as long as the third-civ had lasted, he just consciously realized how long ago it had *ended*.

Six hundred and eighty-seven million years ago.

Marcus had to check that fact multiple times to be certain. He had assumed that previous C-human civilizations were old like Neanderthals, not so old they made dinosaurs look young. What did that mean for the age of the first and second C-human civilizations? Billions of years? On some level he knew he still couldn't access that information, but he was too focused on what he could access to care.

The cataclysm that had ended the third-civ hadn't been some long, drawn-out war or a sickness that ravaged them for generations. It had happened all at once. Instantaneously. Across the entire civilization. And no one in the Society had ever figured out why or how.

There were a multitude of theories across the Nexus, but no one truly knew. The prevailing belief was that they had done it to themselves. Whatever the case, every living being had vanished from one moment to the next. And all technology glitched for a few seconds, so even what had survived to the Society's day could offer no real answer. And that was when he really grasped the caution Rahel tried to instill in him. As advanced and enduring as the third-civ had been, it still ended, and the smartest people alive today had no idea why or how. It was so easy to get swept up in the glamour that was this super advanced civilization coming down to Earth—curing disease, inspiring the planet with their magic-like technology—that it was easy to forget they were still human. And fallible.

"But how can nobody know what happened to them?" Even as he asked Rahel, Marcus's bioweb opened expanded memory clusters, and he could see (remember) all the research and resources that had been poured into trying to find the answer for the last thirteen thousand years when a young Society had first discovered the horrific mystery.

He felt Rahel shrug. *You know as much as I do now.*

"In that mission you were on, you encountered something ancient like this?"

She sighed before she answered him, but her emotions were locked tight, and he couldn't feel anything. *Older*, was all she said.

"Older! But you won't tell me what?"

It's not that I don't want to talk about it, but...some stuff I can't, not yet, and other stuff I'm not allowed to. The UN classified it, but the specifics aren't similar or relevant to this, she answered. *What is, is the experience. Not everybody came back from my mission. I just want you to understand that dealing with pre-Society tech isn't something you should take lightly.*

"Then why are they even letting me go?"

I'm not fully certain, Marcus. I believe they're trying to not scare Earth, Rahel's perception focused on the others. Sarjah was out of the Nexus meeting and talking to Kleedak about mission details. *Since this all started, the Assemblage has had some high-level meetings with the Protectorate Council. Interfering with a UHC is one of the few things their government gets worked up about. All I know for certain is that after my mission, the Society made a lot of promises to the United Nations about sharing information on anything that happens to Earthers. I think they wanted to reveal some things to the embassy personnel after they were living on another planet in the hopes that Earthers would accept the truth easier when living surrounded by it every day. The Society is genuinely worried about accidentally harming Earth, I know that's true. Unintentional contact with UHCs rarely goes well, and from my dealings with different C-human cultures, I've found that some of them believe allowing us to see everything, unfiltered, is the only real way to save us.*

Others feel the opposite. They truly believe too much information will lead to us destroying ourselves. I really don't know what's best; just be careful.

"Ditec Greer," Sarjah called him. "We need to review some points."

We'll talk later, Rahel said to him. *For now, I have to report to the UN Security Council.* And her presence disappeared from the Nexus.

Marcus rubbed his face as he walked toward Sarjah. Now that he was paying attention, he noticed there was a seriousness to all the C-humans present. And just under the surface, there was a sense of protectiveness they felt not only for the planet's inhabitants but also for the Earthers aboard. They were taking this seriously. It also wasn't lost on Marcus how completely the Society controlled the Nexus and what was allowed to be seen.

10

Physically, Ahmon was in his captain's cavity, but mentally, he was completely immersed in a Nexus meeting. He didn't waste effort visualizing a specific environment; he simply allowed himself to be aware of the presence of the members who were all linked in a secure communication. The meeting had two speakers from the Assemblage, the governing body of the Society, and also councilors from the Society Protectorate Council and the director of the Metatech Research Agency.

And you are certain of this? Ahmon asked. He was still surprised that Envoy Rahel Ashenafi had been called to speak at the meeting. And even more surprised that he had been excluded from hearing some of her discussion. Undoubtedly the stories he heard about her had been true.

Captain, having Earth become an NHC this quickly is new to everyone, Speaker O'gon said. *And we have made promises to the Earth's United Nations that we will not hide from them information regarding ancient humans. True, NHCD contact protocols have been carefully crafted to cause as little stress to NHCs as possible, and we are aware of the disaster that can result from giving too much knowledge before a race is ready. That must be balanced with trust. And it is the decision of this body that trying to hide this info will not help in the long run.*

That does not mean they need to be an actual part of the mission, Ahmon said. *Earthers are not ready—*

We are aware of the Xindari position on Earthers, Captain, Speaker Zuka said. *But there are precedents.*

For this? Ahmon asked.

Earthers have already been exposed to pre-Society tech, Speaker O'gon said.

Also, Captain, as I'm sure you know from your own experi-ence, the metatech director said, *everyone in the Society knows about previous civs. We grow up with this knowledge. The Earth-ers, however, will present an unbiased view of what we face. We are not asking you to put the Earthers into harm's way, but our training analysis has been thorough. We are certain that many of the Earther ditecs would be able to handle this, and that Ditec Greer is one of them.*

We must prepare for what Ditec Golamee finds, the Protec-torate Galactic South Councilor said. *I move that we begin mobilizing ships to go to the target system once it's found.*

I agree we should dedicate ships to this, the Protectorate Coreward Councilor said. *But I don't think we should pull most ships from their current missions.*

Agreed, the Protectorate Rimward Councilor said. *The receiving portal could be far outside of even Society border space. But—*he continued, focusing on the other meeting members *—we can't overlook the possibility that the receiving signal could also be within Society space, however unlikely that may be.*

The aspect of the simulated environment changed, and a map of Society space became the primary focus of every-one's attention. Ahmon perceived the eleven-thousand-light-year-wide volume of space that made up the Society member worlds and the even-larger volume that it was surrounded by, the borderland that was the old boundary of the third and fourth human civilizations, which reached close to the core of the Milky Way and also into the galactic halo. The Protectorate mostly operated in the borderland areas. While there were no Society worlds there, there were still many dozens of UHCs in various stages of development.

Presently, there have been two areas with old civilization activity, the Protectorate Coreward councilor said. *But they were believed to be random, isolated occurrences. They're being reevaluated now.*

A few highlighted areas had active, working third-civilization tech that the Society still hadn't been able to safely shut down, even after millennia of trying, so they were quarantined. A large volume of the map was marked as the Divinity Cascade, where the final wars that ended the fourth civilization happened. Those atrocities led to multiple areas of space, stretching many hundreds of light-years, that had been scoured of life down to the microbial level.

Cleaning up those areas and protecting UHCs was the Protectorate's main goal. It wasn't a single-minded obsession, but Ahmon did feel that the Protectorate, and by extension the Assemblage, was overcompensating when it came to Earth. In the last eleven thousand years, there had only been five instances of unapproved exposure to UHCs. Three were accidental, like with Earth, and two were intentional, the last being about two thousand years ago. Unfortunately, in all of these instances, except one, the UHC races had been unable to adjust to a new worldview, and all had ended up destroying themselves. So, now a different approach was being tried, by giving Earth a great deal more access to knowledge in the hopes that they would be able to adapt. He honestly didn't believe they could.

We'll dispatch ships to a few of the more obvious areas, but until Director Golamee determines the location, we can only prepare, Speaker O'gon said. *We will brief the Assemblage Action Council after this meeting. Captain Ahmon, please continue with your mission to determine the location of the target system.*

Understood, Ahmon said.

Ahmon let his consciousness flow from the Nexus meeting, and he became aware of his physical surroundings again. The plain interior of his captain's cavity allowed no distractions when he needed to clear his mind. He felt the mood of the ship; if anything, having Earthers on board seemed to give everyone an added sense of resolve. Everyone except him, perhaps. This was a path he did not want to walk again. Over the Nexus he felt the presence of some of his raise-siblings and a birth-brother, but he didn't feel like communicating.

Speaker O'gon's statement that Earthers had encountered pre-Society tech before was not a complete surprise to Ahmon. A couple of years ago, Rahel had been in one of the first Earther groups stationed on a Protectorate ship. That mission had ended in several deaths, a scuttled ship, and a classified rating far higher than he had access to. Another interesting point was that aside from Rahel, the only other Earther to survive was Victor Stanley, who was now captain of Earth's emergence vessel. Xindari weren't curious by nature or susceptible to gossip, but enough facts leaked out to indicate Rahel's ship had had some dealing with pre-Society C-human tech. Most likely second-civ, not third, so he could understand how it could cloud her judgment.

He breathed deep, centering himself. The reasoning of

the Protectorate Council troubled him not because he didn't see the logic in it but because he did. He had even considered sending Ditec Greer back to the surface with the third-civ specialist. As a former ditec himself, Ahmon understood how the subconscious mind could affect one's perception of metaspace, and that a ditec without preconceived bias might provide a deeper insight into whatever was found. But he had disregarded that thought. Now Ahmon had to question whether he had done that because he wanted to protect the Earther, or because on some level he let his view that Earth was not ready, as a whole, cloud his judgment. Because he had seen firsthand what horrors Earthers were capable of.

Ahmon allowed Earthers to frustrate him more than he cared to admit, but he could not ignore his own truth. Given his history with Earth, it was unfortunate that the ship he captained was the one to discover an incursion in a UHC system—although his birth-sibling, Naqah, would no doubt tell him it was the universe's way of bringing him back to true balance. Nevertheless, it was a coincidence that couldn't be overlooked because it did have a possibility of affecting the mission. And while he was focused in general, Ahmon had to concede that his concentration was off. Since this type of incident had not happened in thousands of years, deep feelings about it were normal but it was a fine line, and he knew he could easily tip over into either trying too hard to suppress his feelings or being overly guided by them. Only in the center of that would he find balance.

Earthers were not ready for NHC status. Of that he was certain. Many C-human races believed that, but not enough to stop a consensus being reached in the Assemblage to grant Earth NHC status. Ahmon felt the best way to guide a young culture was through slow teaching and letting them gain wisdom. Balance would come in time. If they survived as a race. But Xindari and several others believed that the Society's true role was to help ease as much suffering as possible as Earthers inevitably destroyed themselves. To be there to comfort them as they chose their path, not force them to walk a different path.

11

Nina looked around the crowded lobby of the hotel but didn't see the Earth Medicine consul anywhere. She liked Dr. Aleksei Romashenko, but he did strike her as a little more politician than doctor. Although that was true of a lot of high-level medical staff once they reached a certain stage in their career. But he seemed like an honest man to her, which was most important.

Last night, she had been tempted to call him and report everything. A good part of their delegate training had focused on reporting anything unusual during their term—more unusual than being stationed on an alien planet. The only thing that stopped her was that the synesthesia episode had only lasted a few minutes, and the logical first response of anyone would be to question if she had imagined it or dreamed it. Nina couldn't discount that possibility even if she was sure it had happened. The simple facts were there was no proof, it had been late, she *had* been drinking, she had just had an argument with Tony (who had a mad hard-on for C-humans), and, if nothing else, that very morning she had survived a terrorist attack. Most people's first thought would be that the pressure had gotten to her, and she knew she would think the same thing if it happened to someone else. So, she had decided to sleep on it before she made any final decision.

This morning, she had felt surprisingly rested and even enjoyed a blissful couple of minutes lying in bed before she remembered what happened. Now Nina put her hand in her pocket and pulled out the crumpled piece of paper she had written the numbers on last night. The writing only appeared as normal black ink now, of course, but it did happen—she was sure if it. Mostly. She had been so angry at Tony...and it had been a stressful day. She stared at the black numbers on the paper again. The seven really had been red...hadn't it?

She didn't think the Society as a whole was responsible, but some C-human was definitely—if it had really happened—and she had to report her suspicions at least.

"There you are," an accented voice said.

Nina turned to see Aleksei and an aide approaching. "I was just looking for you," she said.

"Is good, I'm here," the medical consul said, walking past, barely slowing down. "Come with me, please; we don't have much time."

"Um, time for what?" Nina asked, wondering for a crazy moment if he already knew.

"I have to apologize for the politics, Dr. Rodriguez," Aleksei said as he led her into a room. "But the ambassador was insistent."

"Excuse me?" Nina asked, confused. Then she realized that most of the people in the room were the big shots. Ambassador Isaacs and Deputy Chief Xu were there, talking to Envoy n'Dala. And all the other consuls general and consuls were present as well.

"I know you don't like politics," Aleksei said. "But apparently, it was decided at the highest levels that you should be on stage for the sendoff ceremony."

"What?"

"This came from the UN itself a few minutes ago," he said. "They feel it adds a human-relatable story to the embassy. And I did warn you, but don't worry; you don't have to speak or anything."

"Dr. Romashenko, we have to talk," Nina said, glancing around at all the people. She squeezed the piece of paper still in her hand.

"It will have to wait," he said.

"It's very important, sir." Nina touched his arm to get his attention. When he saw her face, he realized how serious she was.

"What's wrong?"

Nina started to speak, then paused, the reality of where she was breaking through for a moment. There were just too many people around, and she didn't want to risk it being overheard.

"Did Consul General Hines's aide bother you again?" He was genuinely concerned.

"Huh? No, no," she said just as the call came for people to go on stage. Aides and C-humans began directing the consuls general to the entrance. If she tried to pull him aside now, it would draw attention.

"I'll tell you after; don't worry," she said.

NINA ADJUSTED herself in her seat for the third time in as many minutes. Sitting on the stage with the ambassador, consuls general, and the consuls was more annoying than intimidating, but at least she didn't have to speak or answer questions. The room was packed with reporters from all over the world, all of whom had arrived in Sahara City that morning. Afterward, the reporters would be given a tour of the city and a great vantage to watch the launch of the ship taking the embassy personnel to Io.

There had been talks of parades and a huge sendoff ceremony, but ultimately it was decided to save that for the official opening of Sahara City and the launch of the emergence vessel *New Gaia* in six weeks. Since that ship would have mostly civilians and serve as a mobile piece of Earth culture, it had more relevance to the average person than a group of politicians and scientists. Yet Nina had no doubt this would be widely watched around the world. And here she was sitting on stage—feeling like crap.

As Nina looked out on the crowd of reporters, she started to feel anxious; the flash of photography, the noise, the faceless people pointing TV cameras, it all reminded her of the train station. She shifted in her seat again, trying to keep her face blank, knowing that pundits would drag this through the news cycle for weeks. What damn suit had thought it was a good idea to stick her on stage? Nina was so focused on trying to look normal that she was mildly surprised to see that Ambassador Isaacs was already at the podium, speaking. She hadn't even heard him introduced.

Nina only half-listened to the ambassador as she played the night's events over in her mind again and compared them to the times she had noticed the synesthesia phenomenon in the lab. She didn't know if the medical consul was even aware of the reports on it, because there was so much data being compiled on all aspects of the Society's medical technology. She herself had seen reports of mild allergic reactions, memory flashes, cramps, tinnitus, and dozens of other things—meaning that temporary synesthesia would be seen as just another side effect. But the specifics of it only occurring with certain types of neural activity were the problem. It had to have been some type of memory read, hadn't it?

After the ceremony, she would tell Dr. Romashenko. She glanced at him and couldn't help but notice Consul General Hines, the man whose aide had been chased off. She still hadn't learned what that was all about. She just wanted to study brains and help bring new treatments to the masses of people who needed it—not deal with political maneuvering. Aleksei's first act would be to report it to the ambassador, and as she sat there, hearing the ambassador talk about a new age and other catchphrases, she realized she had no idea what type of man he really was. Of course, she had seen his now-famous speech at the UN that finally put him over the top of the other candidates, and he seemed like a genuinely good person, and bipartisan to a fault. But that didn't mean that anything he said was true or even something he believed.

And as she sat there staring at the crowd—cameras flashing, reporters fiercely writing, everything being seen by the world—Nina had the sudden realization how it would be received when the news came out of the Society having the ability to invade and read someone's mind without their knowledge. If there was a simple explanation for what happened to her, or it ended up not being true, it wouldn't really matter. Not in today's world of social media. The accusation alone would always be in people's minds. All it would take was one opportunistic politician trying to make a name for themselves, and it would polarize people's views even more, not to mention making hate groups like True Human feel justified and maybe even legitimized. The chance that she might contribute to some terrorist ideology, in any way, sickened her stomach.

And the shadow of a thought she wanted to ignore was gaining dangerous cohesion in her mind. People were already polarized—not as bad as it was during the Long Year, but still—and something like this could tip the balance. People like her mother and Tony may only be reacting out of misunderstanding and misinformation, but their fears couldn't be ignored or trivialized. They had to be allowed to see the truth for themselves. Nina didn't gloss over the fact that part of that truth was what had happened to her. But she seriously doubted that was the Society as a whole, because a bigger part of the truth was that there were children alive today who would grow up in a world that didn't know disease or the devastation it could bring to a family. And while what happened to her wouldn't stop relations, it might slow things down, might add more layers of bureaucracy. And how many people would suffer and die in that time? Then she remembered her grandmother's last days, and she knew they needed the Society. Earth had to change. But she was too good a researcher, too good a scientist, to ignore facts simply to feel more comfortable with her desired theories. So, if she was going to accuse some C-humans, or the Society itself, she needed to be certain. She had to be. And the only way she could do that was using Society technology.

Envoy n'Dala was speaking now. She still looked to be recovering, but to Nina, to be able to get up and give a speech after being shot twice the previous day was the type of miracle she had come to expect from the Society. Even though no questions were being allowed, a few were shouted out, asking if she resented Earth, the Society's response, and even Nina's role in what happened. n'Dala navigated them all quickly and inoffensively.

The rest of the ceremony went by in a blur to Nina. After they were allowed to leave, she found herself speaking to Ambassador Isaacs and Envoy n'Dala. There were praises and thank-yous given, but as Nina spoke to them, she couldn't get out of her head that this was a career-ending decision whether she was right, or wrong, about what happened. The fact that she waited to report it wouldn't be overlooked, but she believed Earth's relation with the Society was worth the risk of being sure.

When Aleksei told her the medical contingent would get a tour of the medical bay on the ship and a chance to examine equipment she finally decided. She figured she would be able to use the lab to verify her conclusions one way or the other. Surely, delaying for another day wouldn't hurt. She managed to gloss over Aleksei's questions and passed it off that she just hadn't wanted to go on stage. He had no reason to doubt her, and she felt bad for lying to him —and even now was still tempted to tell him.

THE LOBBY WAS AS CROWDED as it had been yesterday, but now people were leaving. She stood at the hotel's train platform where they had first arrived. From there it would take them to the starport. As she waited, she scrolled through her phone. Social media was still far too flooded for her to make a dent in, but she stopped when she saw a text from two of her cousins. They had gone up to Taos for the weekend, and it was a picture of them skiing. She would miss that and them.

"Nina." Nina stiffened at the sound of the familiar voice

but tried not to let anything show on her face when she looked up to see Endless Green Sky.

"Doctor," she said, knowing it was too stiff and formal. "How are you?"

"Excellent," he said glancing down at the phone she was still holding up in her hand. "Skiing?"

"Huh? Oh, yes." She put her phone away. Nina didn't want to talk to him, yet at the same time she wanted to come out and ask him. She didn't want Endless Green Sky or Fresh Snowfall on the Lake to be guilty, but she was sure it had to be one of them. "My cousins and I would go all the time, but this year I guess I'll miss out."

Endless Green Sky got a thoughtful look on his face. "You know, I'd like to show you something when we get to Io. But I want to keep it as a surprise."

"Sure," she said. She hadn't seen Fresh Snowfall on the Lake today, so if she had another synesthesia episode, she would know it was Endless Green Sky and not her. But Nina didn't think this brief talk was enough time. And he hadn't touched her. "I look forward to it."

"Are you feeling okay?" he asked. "I haven't committed a cultural faux pas, have I?"

"No, no," she deflected. "I'm just anxious about the trip."

The train came up then, and they said their goodbyes.

THE PEOPLE of Earth had only seen a couple of different types of Society ships. The one that had crashed in Hawaii, startling Earth out of its me-centric adolescence, had been shaped like an ellipsoid. The ship they were riding to Jupiter's moon Io was basically a long cylinder with a smooth, unbroken surface that Nina swore look like polished bone. But she knew the organic technology they used wasn't like any material from Earth.

At the starport, on the edge of the city, the train pulled up to a stop a few hundred meters away from the ship, then, with a smooth transition, traveled sideways until it glided to a halt next to the vessel. The walls of the train dilated open, and Nina could see some C-humans standing next to large doors on the ship. As she stepped out, she looked up and down the train and could see the same thing. Across from every train car, there were rows of doors all down the side of the ship with a couple of C-humans next to them all.

"Welcome, cousins." One of the C-humans near them smiled. "I'm Weda. If you follow us, we'll take the elevator to the concourse level, where you'll be able to watch the launch in the park or go to your apartments." Then the doors opened, and he motioned for them to enter an elevator that could easily fit a car.

Nina could see her own expression mirrored on the faces around her as they walked into the elevator. They had all seen the ship and been given information on its layout. But there was a big difference between knowing something academically and stepping on board knowing you were about to fly to another planet. People glanced at each other as the doors closed, but before anyone could really figure out how to express what they were thinking, the elevator doors opened...on what looked like a nice-size city park.

"Damn," someone said.

"I didn't even feel it move," another added.

The park was about the length of a city block, and it was completely encircled by a street-wide walkway and beautifully structured buildings that looked like a cross between bungalows and seashells. Above them, the roof of the ship was a clear dome—although she was sure it hadn't been transparent on the outside—which allowed them to see the sky.

Nina had been expecting to go through all types of procedures: decontamination, airlocks, spacesuits, everything. Not walking off an elevator into a park where she was going to lie on the grass and watch them leave the planet. No crash couches or seatbelts but ice cream and drinks.

"Can you believe this?" Nina asked to no one in particular, looking around.

"No," a woman answered.

Everyone wandered around and gradually found spots to sit down and relax. The casualness of some Society methods was still a little surprising even after so many years, but people were getting more used to it. She saw a few people being led to the various bungalows, but most stayed in the park for lunch. Spherical fabricators floated around, providing whatever people wanted—blankets, cold drinks, food. Nina swore to God she smelled someone smoking a joint.

"Hello, cousins, this is the captain." The voice seemed to emanate from the ground beneath them. It wasn't loud or obtrusive but calming. "We will be taking off in a minute. Once in orbit, the ship will turn so that you can get a good view of the Earth. Then we will proceed to Io at a leisurely speed, arriving in about two days. Enjoy."

Nina wasn't knowledgeable about astronomy, but she had learned that with modern human technology, a trip to Jupiter would take about five years. And they were going in a "leisurely two days."

When the ship rose, there was no sense of acceleration. The only way she knew they were moving was because the clouds seemed to come down toward them. People talked animatedly once they realized they were flying. Reality took hold in a way that even meeting aliens like the Nui hadn't accomplished. They were leaving Earth. This was happening. Then there was a moment where everything outside the dome was white as they passed through clouds, only to emerge moments later into clear blue sky. And as their ship continued to rise, the blue overhead gradually gave way to black.

"Cousins," the captain's voice came again. "If you look up and off to the starboard side, you can see we are about to pass your world's emergence vessel."

Nina and everyone else looked up. Every world in the Society had a spaceship known as an emergence vessel, given to them when they first achieved New Human Culture status. The ships were crewed mostly by the natives of whichever planet it was from and were large enough to easily house many hundreds of thousands of residents and millions of tourist. An emergence vessel's only purpose was to travel around the Society and allow the different worlds to get a firsthand taste of each other's culture. Contact protocols wouldn't let nonofficial people travel to NHCs for decades because the sheer amount of tourism might seem like an invasion. This way, C-humans could visit "a piece" of Earth.

The emergence vessel's six-mile-wide body was shaped like a starfish with stumpy arms, a standard for that class of bioship. The interior had been designed by an international team of landscapers, architects, city planners, and artists working with C-human bioneers. The top and bottom of the ship were transparent domes, while the middle strip was an opaque, solid surface. The thing that amazed Nina the most, which she had seen in countless videos on Earth, was that the ship was double-sided, its artificial gravity allowing that; the dome on the bottom wasn't a floor but a ceiling.

As their ship rose higher, the interior of the "bottom" of *New Gaia* came into view. From her point of view, it was an upside-down landscape that portrayed a wide variety of Earth's ecosphere. In the center was a small mountain with tree-lined slopes that led down into the different environments in each two-mile-long arm—grassy plains around a lake in one, while other arms held lush jungles, deserts, beaches, and more. It was a miniature ecosystem designed to give visitors a taste of Earth's natural beauty.

Once their ship passed above the emergence vessel, the top half came into view. This side held a city, right-side up, of course. The two-mile-wide central section had many skyscrapers, and the city blended into different architectural areas in each of the five starfish-like arms. One held a massive stadium surrounded by streets and stores like you would find in any major city. Another had several residential blocks with various-style homes and apartment buildings. One had multiple religious buildings like temples, churches, synagogues, and mosques. The designs were a mix from all over Earth.

The ship was a city in space that would initially house roughly fifty thousand Earthers in comfort. In less than two months, it would have its maiden voyage, touring the solar system and, eventually, making its way to the Society's capital world, Sapher, fifteen hundred light-years away in the Orion Molecular Cloud Complex.

Soon the stars above them seemed to rotate. It reminded Nina of being in a planetarium when she was young, the lecturer scrolling through the night's cycle like a time lapse. Only, this was the real thing. A bluish glow seemed to rise to her left, and she watched in speechless awe as the Earth in all its picturesque, cinematic, documentary glory seemed to cross the sky and stopped almost directly overhead. For a few seconds, the park was utterly silent as people from a multitude of countries, races, religions, and cultures looked at the one place they all had a common concept for—home.

Nina tried to find words but could only glance at the others around her as they looked back and forth from each other to the planet.

"We're upside down," someone whispered, but everything was so quiet, many heard it clearly.

She hadn't even given thought to the artificial gravity before hearing that. In fact, when the sky had seemed to rotate, she realized it was the ship turning over, allowing everyone to see Earth. And as the planet started to get smaller, Nina realized they were slowly flying away from it. There was now sporadic talking all around, but mostly in quiet tones as everyone watched that pale blue dot shrink until it seemed to be no more than another star in the vastness of space.

Earth Embassy was officially on its way. And Nina hoped again that she was wrong about her suspicions. She just didn't want to believe that anyone from the Society could have dark ulterior motives.

12

Marcus's voidskinned figure emerged from the portal onto the surface of the alien moon for the second time in as many days. Ultraskinned Kleedak and Grayson had gone first, and now Marcus, Sarjah, and the floating sphere that was Golamee traveled over the surface to the mini portal. t'Zyah had stayed behind to coordinate from the ditec cavity, so Sarjah was in charge. Dimensional technicians, like everyone, tended to have areas where they excelled. t'Zyah was better at ship operations, so with Golamee there, t'Zyah felt her presence on the surface would be redundant.

Marcus had gotten to know Golamee some in the training chamber as the team formalized its plan. She had heard of Earth, of course, but had never met Earth humans before. From everything Marcus had seen, he knew the Society was as information-obsessed as any gen-Zer, and since NHCs were not common, Earth's status was big news across the entire civilization. But Golamee's interest in Earth humans was only a passing curiosity. Even watching the launch of Earth's embassy into space over the Nexus with

Marcus and Sumiko was only mildly interesting to her. In true nerd fashion, she was focused on her field to the exclusion of almost everything. She had been stationed on one of the border worlds, studying third-civ ruins, when the Protectorate had contacted her, and Marcus was fairly certain that only a working piece of third-civ tech could've torn her away from her passion.

This is amazing, Golamee said as they reached the portal and the biosphere slowly floated around it. *The dimensional flux rate is the same as the artifact discovered on Zit'Ku-beta.*

As far as I can tell, so is the dispersion, Sarjah said.

You're right! Golamee's excitement, although not visible in the sphere, was obvious over the grouplink.

As she and Sarjah exchanged more technobabble that generally went over his head, Marcus imagined his expression must be like the one his pop-pop always had when his buddies came over and they talked coding and video games. Even with a bioweb, he couldn't learn everything at once, and the practical experience of doing was invaluable. Sarjah had made it clear to Marcus that he was to observe only, because he hadn't had enough training, then t'Zyah had made it clear to him again before they left. And while Rahel didn't bring it up again, he could tell she was still worried.

Can you back track it to its source? t'Zyah asked from the ship, bringing the mission back on focus.

Golamee didn't answer for a moment, but Marcus could sense that she was intently studying the device. When she finally did answer, the excitement she had first shown was now underscored with a wave of caution.

I believe I can, she said. *But I must stress again, Captain, that it would be better if we had more time.*

Agreed, Director Golamee, Captain Ahmon answered from the bridge. *But the Protectorate Council feels this is important, and I concur. Our first attempt probably alerted whoever placed this here, and we need to find the target system fast.*

Okay, she said in such a way that Marcus realized even in the Society, politics could take precedence over academic, or scientific, common sense.

Director Golamee, Sarjah said. *I will mirror you and provide backup. Ditec Greer, shadow us both for anchor support.*

Marcus knew Rahel would be happy with that. Mirroring meant that Sarjah would be fully immersed in metaspace with Golamee. And while Golamee was the lead, Sarjah would be copying her moves exactly. Marcus, on the other hand, would only shadow them. That meant he wasn't fully in metaspace but linked to someone who was. His presence would serve as a beacon for them to find their way back. Technically, he wouldn't be hurt by anything that hurt them.

Copy that, Golamee answered. *Setting up now.*

Even though there were only a few of them on the surface of the moon, the shiplink gave access to all. Marcus could sense others watching in bioneering and the rest of the ship. None of the C-humans were allowing emotions to enter the link and be a distraction, but Sumiko and Majid were both leaking their emotional states as they monitored Golamee's biosphere data. All three of them got a warning pulse from t'Zyah to focus, and Marcus could perceive her in the ditec cavity, following their progress. He acknowledged, making sure his own emotions weren't projecting.

Proceed when ready, Captain Ahmon announced.

Golamee began the same way Sarjah had before, and he followed their consciousnesses' transition as they entered metaspace. A step removed from the equation, Marcus's shadowed presence did not perceive the other dimensions as clear as normally. Very soon, Golamee started taking paths that at first seemed nonsensical. The third-civ technology was still as mentally daunting as when Sarjah had accessed it, yet Golamee's movements opened up new perceptions, and Marcus wondered how they could have missed the obvious entrance. He discounted the thought immediately as being no different from a two-dimensional person not realizing they could move in another direction until they were brought into a three-dimensional world.

It was a similar concept there. Yes, the third civilization of humanity had used dimensional technology just as the Society, but there were fundamental differences. The Society's technology was all biology-based, whereas the third civilization was mostly mechanical-based, with only about a fourth of it being biotechnology. Marcus didn't pretend to understand all the differences caused by these two techs working together, but he understood that while in metaspace—where their consciousness was separate from the physical—the blending of those two technologies could wreak catastrophic results.

Marcus wasn't sure if it was his imagination, but metaspace seemed to feel different also. The data portal was connected to another point somewhere in standard space, but the dimensional route it took to get there felt...wrong somehow—artificial. Like he was looking at an unfinished simulation of multidimensional planes. When he navigated metaspace with Society tech, there wasn't a mental strain. There was a natural flow to the way humans perceived it. But this was disturbing. Their awareness followed the path of the third-civ tech through what felt like manufactured components of metaspace. Then he saw the other data portal, and the exact location was there in his mind. Success.

Perhaps that was why Golamee let her guard down.

There was no warning when the alarm was tripped, just intense disorientation. Marcus felt like he had been punched in the head, and it took a moment for his perceptions to make sense. Golamee and Sarjah were trapped on another...level—as good a word as any—and he could perceive them but not talk to them.

Dimensions switched and changed. Time felt like it stretched out in standard space. Their physical bodies seemed to be cross-sections of various biological parts, like seeing them from a lower dimension. Their consciousness was battered in a maelstrom of energy. Marcus was going to pull out, but he had a gut feeling and dove in. He followed up after the breach and became an anchor for Sarjah. She in turn was trying to hold on to Golamee.

He wasn't seeing a physical image of Golamee, but he was fully aware of her, and she was terrified. It felt like a tornado trying to suck her up and pull Sarjah with it. And him. He was no longer shadowing them but had shifted his awareness into metaspace to hold them, and now he was in danger also. Sarjah encapsulated her consciousness except for two small parts, each connecting to Golamee and Marcus. She was trying to establish a stable point to give Golamee a reference to find her way back.

Marcus didn't think that would work, but he wasn't sure why. His months of training hadn't taught him this, but instinctually he knew it was true. There were standard procedures for ditecs, but there was no single way to interact with metaspace. How the mind interpreted what it perceived varied between C-human races and also between individuals, regardless of race. One of the other Earthers Marcus had trained with had been a painter, and she often saw things in terms of color and light. Marcus approached metaspace in terms of programming and compositing.

He saw the path to Sarjah and Golamee as a sequence, almost like combining multiple points together to create a unified whole. The same way it took twenty-four static images to make one second of standard moving film. A common problem in visual effects compositing was when a shot didn't blend with the preceding and following sequence of images. A subtle difference in lighting or color was enough to make a scene feel fake, even though the average layperson may only notice it subconsciously and not know why it looked wrong. And to Marcus there was a disconnect between the three of them.

Whatever part of metaspace they were in was structured by a framework of the third-civ. It was counterintuitive, and a chaotic maelstrom pounded against his sense of self. And Marcus felt a part of him was being shorn away. He could barely perceive Golamee now as any more than a strand of emotion—fear—linked through Sarjah. But he should be able to; he didn't have to stay with this sequence. Metaspace was the totality of all dimensions, and if he went "deep" enough, he knew (believed) he could find another route.

He stepped off the path. He was in a forest, until he blinked and found himself a particle in the void of space. *Blink.* He was drowning in something too thick to be water but too thin to be emotion. *Cough.* He stumbled forward across a desolate landscape as multiple suns shined down on him. There were colors he couldn't name but knew were true as they swirled around him in...the empty room he stood in. Nausea doubled him over, and he stumbled, catching himself on the star next to him, stumbled again, even though he had no legs, and with an armless arm reached for the object before him.

He knew it was Golamee, knew that even though a part of him still held Sarjah, another part had found a back door closer to Golamee. And he reached for her, his mental fingers like patterns of quarks. She was so close. Around them there was nothing but an empty white void. Marcus couldn't see himself, or her—they were just concepts waiting to be realized into flesh. Her hold on Sarjah was disintegrating. He was so close. But there was no distance. He almost had her; they almost manifested a way they could link.

Then the last tenuous connection broke, and Golamee's mind was sucked away into higher dimensional space, leaving behind only the feeling of an empty, barren shell. A small part of Marcus's mind felt panic, but he couldn't understand why. The utter blankness of the plane he was on felt totally blissful now. He could just rest there as his troubles melted away. Then he felt a sharp pain through his private link as Sarjah pulled his mind back, saving them both from the same fate as Golamee.

They fell to the surface, their sense of balance gone, and dust slowly drifted about them in the low g. No longer connected to the portal, the real world flooded back in, and Marcus heard the yelling as the bridge crew tried to save them. Before he could fully get his bearings, he felt another pull, not his mind but his body, and he was suddenly on the portal chamber floor of *Fulcrum's Light*.

Then the moon exploded.

MARCUS LAY on the portal chamber floor in stunned silence as the view from the ship sensors fed into his mind. The silent flash of the explosion was so bright, it drowned out everything. And the resulting force burned some of *Fulcrum's Light*'s hullskin as it was bombarded by heat and debris. A good chunk of the moon was vaporized, and the remaining part cracked into three large pieces. All headed toward the planet.

Over the shiplink Marcus perceived Sensor Tech Ujexus analyze the data that showed the explosion was shaped in such a way that the remaining pieces would fall onto the planet below. He barely noticed the portal technicians helping him and Sarjah to their feet as his bioweb absorbed the shiplink's memory of what happened.

As soon as Golamee had sprung the booby trap, the portal device triggered. What he had perceived as minutes while trying to save her and Sarjah had barely been seconds. The p-tecs had gotten the others off the surface but couldn't transport Marcus and Sarjah until they had disconnected from the device. They had made it out with only fractions of a second to spare. Sarjah was looking at him strangely, then she simply said, "Good work, ditec."

He acknowledged with a shocked nod, then the still blaring alarms of the ship spurred them into action. Sarjah ordered the p-tecs to portal them directly to the ditec cavity, as Marcus tried to focus on what was happening outside and what the orders were. The entire crew was connected by the shiplink, but it wasn't a hive mind. He could still make individual choices and even choose to go against the whole if he wanted to. The shiplink was like a real-time conference / social media group with everyone on board as ever-present in his subconscious. If he focused on Bioneering or Medical, he knew what was happening, like clicking a hyperlink on a webpage. And time was subjective, as the shiplink worked on speeds like a computer. The bridge crew was operating at even higher speeds, able to do things in picoseconds.

They appeared in the ditec cavity a moment later, and he and Sarjah took their stations next to t'Zyah. He was vaguely aware that Medical was calling for her to be checked out and that she was ignoring it. He could even feel the other ditecs, who were not on duty, on the shiplink, ready to help from wherever they were.

The explosion had caused a ripple in dimensional space that was disrupting *Fulcrum's Light*'s D-field, and that was the main focus for the ditecs to fix. He joined the group as they adjusted the ship's dimensional signature, but he couldn't fully focus. He kept seeing Golamee and hearing that last shriek of terror as her mind slipped away into effective nothingness. And how the same thing had almost happened to him. He knew he wasn't pulling his weight, but instead of Sarjah criticizing him, she allowed a wave of understanding to filter through their private link. What happened to Golamee had affected her as well. He tried his best to let go, calm his mind, and focus on the moment— remember his training. In a battle, ditecs focused more on trying to disorient the enemy's connection to metaspace, but they also preserved the flow of the dimensional technology. As the D-field balanced out, Marcus's conscious perception also took notice of the bridge data.

Two of the remaining chunks of the moon were on a direct course for the planet. The smallest and third chunk was at an angle that might—might—still clear the atmosphere, but the planet's gravity would probably pull it down. Sensors and tactical analysis showed that the two chunks, while not too large to destroy with weapons, were big enough that *Fulcrum's Light* would not be able to stop all the resulting debris. Enough would rain down on the planet to cause a major ecological disaster, if not outright extinction. And the fragments were also too big for the grav net.

The presence of Captain Ahmon was there, almost like a focal point for the whole shiplink. Marcus could feel the flow of data from Bioneering and Metatech all centered on the captain as if he were the conductor of this celestial orchestra. He made the decision within moments. *Fulcrum's Light* was going to maneuver between the two chunks and use its D-field to alter their course. The chance of success was only seventy-three percent, which was better than the chance of blowing out the lifecore, which was about thirty-nine percent. While Bioneering worked to boost the energy of the lifecore, Medical would deal with interior damage, and the dimensional technicians would consolidate and control the D-field energy.

Fulcrum's Light used its grav drive for short, precise maneuvers, and Marcus had a moment to be impressed by Ky'Gima's skill as she flew the ship. The area around the two moon fragments was scattered with smaller pieces of debris. *Fulcrum's Light*'s gravitic shield deflected them as it glided forward. The two large chunks were less than three hundred meters apart, and *Fulcrum's Light* eased into their shadow.

Bioneering had stroked every extra bit of power out of the lifecore. Marcus and the other ditecs gave their full attention to the D-field that the ship generated. Normally, it only enveloped the ship, allowing it to shift into and through multidimensional space. But the field could be expanded. It was dependent on the power output of the ship, not physical size. The problem was whether *Fulcrum's Light* could produce enough power to maintain a large-enough dimensional field.

Objectively, Marcus knew his perception was running at hyper-fast speeds, but to his subjective mind, he didn't notice a difference. No one talked or even moved as they directed everything mentally through the shiplink. t'Zyah had the ditecs operate in two groups—each subtly shifting the D-field outward on either side of the ship. To Marcus it was like working with clay in his imagination. He visualized

shaping and molding the dimensional field, manipulating
the source code to expand or bend when needed. At first,
there were patches and weak spots, then slowly the D-field
coalesced. When both chunks of rock were encompassed by
the field, the ditecs stabilized the energies and locked their
phase into place. Once the field was as strong as it could be,
the captain ordered the move.

Ky'Gima navigated *Fulcrum's Light* into metaspace,
focusing on rising. Space outside the D-field seemed to
compress and stretch in different ways. The planet seemed
to fall away below them slowly, like a flat plate. The ship
buckled and shook as the expanded D-field caused drag in
metaspace. Bioneering rerouted energy as power arteries on
multiple decks ruptured from the overflow. Vein conduits in
numerous areas burst, spraying rooms in ichor and biomass.
Neural nodes throughout the ship burned out and died
under the strain. The lifecore hummed and pulsed as it
tried to maintain the flow of power and reroute areas that
suffered a stroke. Marcus felt himself grow lighter, then
heavier as the gravity fluctuated. The lights flickered. Venti-
lation shut down until backups could reboot. Entire decks
lost power. The stress on the hullskin was approaching critical, and even though Marcus knew the ship wasn't sentient,
the whine of the ship's structure sounded like an animal in
pain. There was a real possibility of *Fulcrum's Light* itself
being lost in metaspace just as Golamee had been.

Then the stars seemed to snap back into their position
as the ship emerged back into standard space. They had
risen only two thousand kilometers, but enough to clear the
planet. A sense of accomplishment spread across the
shiplink as everyone acknowledged the ditec and
bioneering teams. But the ship was already moving again.
Fulcrum's Light sped out from between the two moon frag-

ments, remnants of debris trailing in its gravitic wake, and down toward the third piece, which was indeed now headed toward the planet.

Marcus watched in fear. The fragment already glowed red from friction as it barreled into the planet's atmosphere. There was no chance to reach it and move it with the D-field even if the ship could survive another attempt. The gravity lance and ZPE main gun were inactive because of damage to the lifecore from the strain of moving the other chunks. And the gamma cannons didn't have the range. Only one option remained. The soft whoop of sound reverberated through the ship as missile after missile fired, their grav drives accelerating them to a small fraction of the speed of light. Fifteen, twenty, they kept launching until a full thirty missiles closed in on the fragment. Marcus perceived Zeinon, the tactical tech, recalculating the warhead yields on the fly—too powerful and they would irradiate the atmosphere; too weak and they might not destroy enough chunks in time. When the first salvo hit, the explosions ripped the rock apart, spewing more fragments as other missiles and their submunitions destroyed those, on and on. From the surface of the planet, it must look like miniature suns winking in and out of existence. The entire shiplink seemed to collectively hold its breath as they watched. There was no way to get all the debris. It was simply a race to destroy enough of the larger pieces to avoid being witness to genocide. Missile after missile closed in on large fragments and destroyed them.

Two final missiles raced after a skyscraper-sized chunk, their passage through the atmosphere a flaming line of hope in the sky. Then, just as it seemed the friction would destroy the missiles, the first one struck, the explosion sending rock flying, and a second later, the last missile vaporized the biggest of those chunks. There was still a rain of pieces that streaked through the sky, trails of fire burning behind them. But nothing larger than a fraction of a meter remained. Sonic booms reverberated in the atmosphere. Vast tracts of one continent's surface were on fire. But most of what was left landed in the ocean. And the resulting tsunami would hit an unpopulated coast. It was over.

The cheer that broke out on board was loud and long. They had saved the planet.

13

After destroying the last moon fragment and ensuring there was no more immediate danger to the planet, Captain Ahmon had moved *Fulcrum's Light* to the star system's Kuiper Belt. The bioship was now latched to a small asteroid, the tentacles on its aft extended to grip the rock. Special glands in the hullskin excreted enzymes to break down the asteroid's mineral deposits, while the ships grav field manipulated this material into external maws to be consumed so the mass could be used in repairs.

While the Society Assemblage was headquartered on a physical planet, most of its leadership were often working spread out across the entire Society. Ahmon had spent the past three hours immersed in the Nexus, in another meeting, this time with the Assemblage Action Council and the entire Protectorate Council, about the situation at Travanis 4. And after all that time, he was ordered to do exactly what he had wanted to avoid from the beginning: go to the location the data was sent to and retrieve it.

As he emerged from the Nexus, Ahmon stood straighter

and took a moment to compose himself. The captain's cavity, situated off the bridge, was a smooth, circular room, light gray and completely empty. The bare physical space allowed him to cultivate mental balance. He had no need for consoles or furniture since all ship business was handled with his bioweb. Ahmon started to access the shiplink to review the status of the repairs, then paused. His mind was not at ease.

It wasn't just the dragged-out politicking of the Council meeting but the entire situation. He was starting to feel the universe itself was unbalanced because of the things happening lately. The Society was one of the most stable civilizations in this section of the galaxy, and it wasn't uncommon to go centuries without problems. It had been over two thousand years since the last malicious involve-ment with an Uncontacted Human Culture, and that was in far border space. But attempted genocide...that was unheard-of. Not to mention that this had been the second major incident in a UHC system in less than a decade.

And he had been at both.

Something that had been pointed out more than once during the Council meeting. Not in a malicious way, but the simple fact was Ahmon had captained one of the first crews to respond to the distress signal of the ship that crashed into Earth. And he felt the underlying concern from some council members as to whether being at two events like this would compromise his judgment. Ahmon wasn't offended by this; it was a legitimate concern. That fact, coupled with having inexperienced NHC crew on board, meant that Ahmon himself was reluctant to go, but *Fulcrum's Light* was the closest ship.

Surprisingly, the target system the data was being sent to was deep within the heart of Society space, not on some border world. About a thirty-nine-hour trip away from their current position. The most troubling thing was that the location within the Society and the use of third-civ tech meant that it couldn't be an alien civilization involved but was some group within the Society. The location also presented a problem for fast response. Portals were the most frequent form of interstellar travel, but starships were not uncommon, although usually they were civilian. The main job of Protectorate ships within Society space was monitoring uncontacted human cultures. Yet most Protectorate ships weren't actually in the Society proper. The Protectorate had started as a mega cleanup project, to safely get rid of dangerous pre-Society tech left over from the third and fourth civs, so that mostly uninhabited area of space was where the vast majority of its ships operated.

The third C-human civilization had been larger than the Society in population, *and* astrographically, it had reached almost to the galactic core and was over thirty-one thousand light-years across, while sometimes stretching hundreds or thousands of light-years above and below the plane of the galaxy. And while the fourth civilization, which was commonly known as the Divinity Cascade, had not been bigger population-wise, it had also been spread out over a wider scale than the Society. But the end of those two mega-civilizations had also ended most C-human life over many thousands of light-years, and the surviving or newly evolved UHCs in those areas were mostly millennia away from industrial revolutions and being ready for contact. So, while it considered the third- and fourth-civ territory part of C-human space, the Society proper only covered about eleven thousand light-years of that area.

It took many millions of years after the Divinity Cascade for C-humanity to recover and start to rise technologically again. Over time as planet-based hominin civilizations developed technologically, some naturally destroyed themselves while others survived to become spacefaring civilizations. As these new interstellar hominin civilizations spread farther into space, they eventually discovered each other and the remains of the previous mega-civilizations, thus uncovering the galactic scale history of C-humanity. Over the next several thousand years conflict and peace ebbed and flowed until the surviving interstellar C-human civilizations came together to form the fifth mega C-human civilization, the Society. And the newest C-human civ learned from the mistakes of its recent ancestors and focused more on stability and culture rather than expansion.

While it had had some major events over its history, in the last millennia or so the Society had generally faced few problems internally—at least before the Earth incident. Simple probability meant Ahmon should go the rest of his life without being involved in something else like that, and yet here he was—again. No sooner had he had the thought than, across the Nexus, Ahmon felt the unvoiced support of one of his raise-siblings. No need for words, or even explanations, just the comforting presence of one in balance.

Ahmon exhaled long and slow, letting the stress and pressures of the external world leave his internal world. He stood point. He was the center that moved. He allowed the focusing technique to calm him. The truth would present itself in time, and whether Earthers could adapt and survive was not in his power to change, only to help.

Ahmon allowed himself to merge with the shiplink again. While emotional sharing over the Nexus was muted when on duty, Ahmon could still detect the undercurrent of feelings about their situation. With so many different C-humans from different cultures on board, balance, as always, was a malleable thing. There was more anger than he thought was helpful—he sent a pulse to Dr. Leikeema about counseling—and some shock, fear, even excitement, but mostly determination. This was another reason the Action Council wanted *Fulcrum's Light* to go. Having Earthers on board was a stark reminder to everyone of what they were fighting for, and a strong motivator.

He partitioned his mind, simultaneously checking status reports, answering specific questions where needed, and reviewing the most recent data on the planet. Golamee had been able to locate the system the data was being sent to, but at the cost of her life. She was the only fatality, but it was unlikely she would be the last. He knew that any group willing to go to the extreme measure of blowing up a moon would not be stopped without a price. When the mission was over, he would have to make a journey to her home-world, as her acting captain and per her people's customs, but until then, nothing could be done, not even an official funeral.

Captain. Tuhzo, the security lead's presence, pulsed him.

Ahmon added one more partition level to his mind and acknowledged him.

Sir, Tuhzo said. *About our weapon stores. Mass isn't a problem, this asteroid has some rich deposits of minerals, but I'm concerned about having enough time to fabricate exotic warheads for new missiles. I would recommend we hold off going to the target system until we are fully combat-ready.*

Ahmon didn't want to go into a possible fight without being one hundred percent, but *Fulcrum's Light* was still the closest ship. *Unfortunately,* Ahmon said, *we must presume the booby trap alerted the perpetrators in some way. So, we can't afford to wait. After major repairs, munition will take precedent.*

Tuhzo seemed like he was going to argue the point, then

simply said, *Yes, sir,* and went about his job as his presence disconnected from the link.

Captain, Ja Xe 75 05, his lead officer, said over the shiplink. *Bioneering reports critical damage has been fixed, and we can do the rest of the repairs in transit. We should be ready to travel in one hour.*

Very good, Ahmon replied. He had seen some of those reports on the shiplink, but his lead officer was conscientious and protocol-driven. Ja Xe 75 05 was also the other reason *Fulcrum's Light* had gotten Earther crew. Zin Ku Lai were the most recent C-human race to fully join the Society, having only come out of New Human Culture status one hundred and twenty-three years ago. But unlike Earth, their world had been unified and at peace even before contact, and they were a deeply religious culture, not violent or warlike. The silver-skinned reptiles usually stayed on their planet, and as far as Ahmon knew, Ja Xe 75 05 was one of still only a handful of Zin Ku Lai in the Protectorate. It was believed that he would be able to relate to, and help, the Earthers understand the Society because his people had so recently joined. Ahmon doubted that would be the case.

And there are really no other ships closer than us? Ja Xe 75 05 asked. He was reviewing the meeting summary Ahmon had sent him. *It's almost a two-day trip to the target system.*

No. The next closest ship will arrive about seven hours after us.

By which time anything could happen.

There are four other ships en route, but they are even farther away, and they won't take a direct course in case anyone is monitoring ship traffic, Ahmon said.

I also just received word that the recon spheres to be sent from the closest inhabited planet are on standby until we get closer to the target system, Ja Xe 75 05 said. *They will be portaled just outside the system, to minimize discovery.*

I don't like taking the risk of sending them at all, but the Council saw differently, Ahmon said. Ships couldn't be sent through portals—at least, not without fully disabling their lifecores—but the target system was close enough to some inhabited worlds that recon spheres could be portaled there, to reach it sooner than *Fulcrum's Light. The chance that they might be detected before we even arrive isn't worth it. Whoever is doing this is careful. Did you note where the target system is?*

You mean how it's suspiciously located in an area equally distant from surrounding Protectorate patrol routes. Yes, I find that disturbing.

Agreed, Ahmon said. *The general feeling of the Action Council is that these are internal agents working toward some personal goal.*

That bothers me more than if it was an alien civilization, Ja Xe 75 05 said. *Someone in the Society intentionally putting an entire race in danger.*

Ahmon could feel the commander's disquiet over the situation. Zen Ku Lai rarely had physical conflict on their world, and the destruction of the moon was troubling him. Ahmon knew Ja Xe 75 05 was averse to violence, but having served with him in crises before he was confident of his lead officer's abilities. He had to be because Ahmon also knew it was likely they would see combat before the mission was over.

Have they made a decision about Travanis 4 yet? Ja Xe 75 05 asked.

The Protectorate Council is sending a survey ship out here to access the cultural impact and make a formal recommendation to the Assemblage.

They can't be considering another contact initiation.

I certainly hope not. It was premature to allow Earth humans into the Society. Doing the same here would be insane.

Speaking of which. His lead officer pulsed Ahmon his view of Envoy Ashenafi walking onto the bridge.

Send her in, Ahmon said, carefully aware not to let his feelings filter through the shiplink.

The wall dilated, allowing the Earther envoy to enter the captain's cavity. Ahmon felt the briefest wave of surprise from her as she glanced over the empty room, but it was gone in an instant.

"I know you're busy, Captain. I won't take much time." Rahel seemed unsure how to proceed, but it was clear she had something bothering her.

"Speak your heart," he said, the traditional saying coming naturally. "You will find no judgment here."

"Okay. I don't think Ditec Greer should go on any more external missions until he's had more training," she said. "He's not a soldier."

"No," Ahmon said. "He's a ditec. Which carries even more responsibility."

Ahmon wasn't surprised by her request. Ja Xe 75 05 and some other officers had voiced the same concerns—until Marcus had saved Sarjah's life. Ahmon had reviewed the data logs himself. He knew fully trained ditecs who wouldn't have been able to anchor Sarjah, much less almost reach Golamee at the same time. No matter how he felt about Earth humans, he acknowledged that their innate intuitive ability made them excellent candidates for dimensional technicians. And Ditec Greer had proven that.

"Captain, Marcus is young," Rahel said. "While part of my role is to help judge how dimensional technology is for Earthers it's also to monitor his state of mind. Marcus simply hasn't had the training yet to prepare him for something like what happened on that moon."

"Fortunately for Ditec Sarjah, he was up to the task."

"Couldn't that have just been luck?"

"Envoy Ashenafi," Ahmon said. "I understand that Ditec Greer is still training. But he is a member of this crew with a job to do. And whoever was responsible for that portal, and bomb, in addition to having advanced resources also has a willingness to commit mass murder. We have a limited time-frame to catch them. In an hour, we will be heading out to track the receiving station since we are still the closest ship, and Ditec Greer will be a part of that mission. That's not open to debate. Earth Embassy should arrive at the Orion Complex in a few days. Once we are back there, you can give a full report, and grievance, to your ambassador."

"Very well, Captain," she said.

Ahmon didn't know Earthers well enough to distinguish between all their facial expressions—Xindari body language was more gestural—but he could tell from the change in her scent that she was upset. Although, surprisingly, she kept any emotions from leaking into the Nexus. His stance shifted subtly to acknowledge her skill. He suspected that she would make a capable ditec herself if she wanted to.

"I will not put any members of this crew in unnecessary danger." Ahmon paused, suspecting what the real cause of her concern was. "I have limited knowledge of your previous mission, Envoy, but if you have specific reasons for alarm, I *will* listen."

Still no leak of emotion, but his bioweb noted her facial expression as a subtle sign of relief. When Envoy Ashenafi had first been assigned to *Fulcrum's Light*, Ahmon had heard some talk of her past experiences. But gossip never led to

wisdom. Only truth and facts could bring real understanding.

"Thank you, Captain, but no, nothing specific." Rahel
stared at the blank wall, lost in thought. Ahmon said nothing, waiting. He thought she would say more about that
mission, but she just shook her head, more to herself, then
asked, "Were there many casualties on the planet?"

"The location where most of the surviving meteorites
fell was outside any inhabited area, as far as we could tell."

"That's good." She paused, lost in thought again, then
continued. "I couldn't help but think: what if something like
this had happened when the Society came to Earth?"

Ahmon nodded. "That would have been catastrophic.
Thankfully, the C-human civilization on Travanis 4 is mid–
Bronze Age–equivalent. They would have no means to
detect *Fulcrum's Light* in orbit but enough understanding to
know about moons, comets, and meteors. And one of their
moons falling out of the sky will be a celestial mystery that
plagues them for centuries, but the real danger is that it will
turn into a legend that alters their core beliefs or changes
their natural development. In the long run, that's always
disastrous."

"That's why the Society is so cautious about contacting
non-advanced C-humans," she said.

"Exactly."

"And part of the reason you're bothered by Earth
humans in the Society?" she asked.

That surprised him. He wasn't aware of how well she
could read him. He thought he had been completely unbiased in his interactions with Earthers so far. So, either she
was more intuitive than he gave her credit for, or he was
even more unbalanced than he realized.

"We all have history, cousin," Ahmon said. "How much

do you know about the events when the ship crashed on your planet six years ago?"

"What I, and everybody, saw on TV as it was happening, of course." Rahel paced a little around the empty room. "I think it was always admitted that a civilian ship had crashed, but it wasn't until I became an envoy that I heard more specifics. How what was originally a leisure trip for a few dozen friends turned into a nightmare when their bioship crash-landed on Earth. I imagine everybody in the Society was watching just as everybody on Earth was?"

"Yes. As the crew and passengers sent out calls for help, the crash instantly became the most-watched event on the Nexus in over a millennium. I was the captain of a smaller-class vessel that was in the galactic vicinity when the crash happened, and we were immediately rerouted to help. The Assemblage called an emergency session as soon as the distress call was received, but the damage was done. The civilian ship had crashed on an island off the coast of one of your major nations."

"Yeah, Hawaii."

"Most on board died on impact; the few who survived were injured, disoriented, and scared. The empathy of our entire civilization—which had tried to comfort them and share their fear as the ship went down and grieved as they died—had to be turned off."

"Turned off? But why? Isn't that exactly the type of situation where people need the emotional support?"

"The survivors were cut off from the Nexus because contact protocols strictly forbade any unauthorized contact with a UHC, so they could only communicate with the Protectorate."

"I'm guessing that caused even more people throughout the Society to talk about it."

"It's not a perfect system because we're not a perfect people. But it has been shown to cause the least amount of long-term damage," Ahmon said. Even all these years later, it could still affect his peace of mind. This time Naqah, one of his birth-siblings pulsed him over the Nexus. She was one of the most balanced people he knew, and he let her feel his gratitude. Her comforting presence was perhaps why he went on talking.

"We were the second Protectorate ship to arrive in the Sol System. My crew and I had to watch as the few survivors were taken captive."

"My God, I had no idea. That's horrible." She let him feel her genuine honesty.

That was when Ahmon first saw how unready Earthers were to join the Society. The Earth hadn't even developed enough to have a unified world system. They fought and squabbled over their pieces of the surface as if what happened to the rest of the planet would magically not affect them also. And as with any culture so fragmented, their response to the Society was a variety of extremes that led to conflict among themselves rather than a unity to face the unknown.

"And the Protectorate wouldn't let you rescue them?"

"No," Ahmon said after a long pause. "We orbited the Earth undetected and impotent to intervene for two days while the Assemblage debated what to do. We had to sit and watch as C-humans were mistreated and imprisoned by the Earthers' knee-jerk fear response."

"I can remember watching that on the news at the school with some of my students." Rahel said. "The whole city was coming to a standstill. Businesses were being closed; everybody was in a panic; no one knew what to think."

"Neither did we. The captain of the other ship had simply wanted to portal all the survivors to safety, but even that wasn't allowed. Any further exposure to Society tech was forbidden. In the past, entire cultures have been irreparably damaged from mishandled contact. So those of us in orbit could only provide moral and emotional support." Ahmon hadn't talked about this with anyone other than family in a long time. "By time the decision was made for official contact, one of the C-human passengers had died from their *questioning*."

Rahel didn't try to justify what had happened—he could feel she was honestly horrified by it—she simply let him feel her empathy.

Over the next few years, Ahmon had been vocal in his opinion that Earth should not be given NHC status. Xindari had a bloody, violent past before their Great Accepting, and he saw much of that same level of violence in Earthers. He grieved but did not regret not saving the C-human who died; the contact laws protected entire planetary cultures, and he knew they were right. But it still disturbed him, and he had spent a few years regaining his center. It wasn't until he got his new command, *Fulcrum's Light*, that he started to feel balanced again. Then he had been told his ship was one of the few chosen to have Earthers on board. One of the official reasons was that he would provide an unsympathetic review of Earthers' potential. But to Ahmon, it was hard not to think that the Balance itself was testing him, allowing him to face his feelings by having Earthers on his ship.

"I bear no ill will toward you or your people, cousin," he said. It was rare that he would let his emotions be felt by the crew, but he allowed her to feel his sincerity. In the short time Rahel had been on board, he had come to believe she was an honest person. "I think you are a fine example of your race." While she didn't let any emotion slip, Ahmon's bioweb did note her facial expression was bothered, and he realized even a compliment like that would cause problems on her world because it would be interpreted through skin tone. Just another example of Earther shortcomings. "I meant Earthers when I said race."

"I realized that," she said. "I know every C-human race has had its growth and maturity phase where it had to overcome its own juvenile personal biases."

"That is truth. In general, mammal and avian races do seem to have more issues with surface color, but it still varies widely. On Xindar, it was warm- and cold-blooded that caused division."

"You could see that by looking at each other?" She was mildly surprised.

"No, visually there is very little change across skin tone for us. But by smell it was obvious. A difference an Earther would probably consider trivial and ridiculous." Ahmon's posture denoted shame. "But the horrors that led to on my planet were no less barbaric than the horrors skin tone led to on yours.

"I sense you are a true person and only mean well," he continued. "But your culture is young, and introducing things to races before they have outgrown their own tendency for self-destruction has only ever worked once in the *entire* history of the Society."

"Well, I hope now it will be twice," she said.

"So do I, Rahel," he said. "So do I."

14

Marcus drifted through the corridors of *Fulcrum's Light* in a haze. After saving the planet, there had been so much to do that he was able to lose himself in the work. The neuron clusters that had blown out around the bioship had to be replaced, and the newly grown ones had to be calibrated by the bioneers and ditecs. Some systems developed malignant tumors that had to be cleansed before the cancer could spread. He had to store a lot of new memories in his bioweb just to help out with work in various departments. After major repairs were completed and things started to slow down, the reality of what happened to Golamee started to seep into his conscious attention, and when he got off duty, full realization struck hard.

He took a transit vein down to the crew quarters deck as he started to access the Nexus, then cursed. He was finally going to call his grandparents, only to find that now the ship was at dark mission status and only official communications were allowed. That was when it suddenly occurred to him that not only could he have died without speaking to them but that he still might. He might never get to speak to his grandparents again.

He spent so much time brushing off calling them because he said he was too busy, even though he wasn't, and now it might be too late. That obvious truth startled him so hard, he stopped in the middle of the corridor, dazed. It wasn't fear so much that got him but a profound feeling that that was how life was sometimes. When his parents got in the car that day, he had had no idea he would never see them again. No idea that some random drunk would cause him to go from loving home to instant statistic—another youth with no parents, being raised by grandparents. No idea what loss truly was, what type of hole it left in you. And his grandparents put up with him every step of the way, through the denial, sadness, and acting out. Even when he retreated into himself and focused on programming. On some level, he may have even resented their unconditional love, wanted something to be mad at. It was years before he understood that, yes, he had lost parents, but they had also lost a child *and* gained one.

If he died suddenly like his mother, their daughter, it would destroy them. Bad enough if that happened on Earth, but in space? Where they may never even get his body? Or even worse, if they had to care for his brain-dead body like Golamee's family would? He started to give serious thought to going back home. That might be best. He didn't know what to do.

He began to wonder if he had gotten so used to controlling his emotions—first because of his parents' loss, then because of the Nexus, and his private link with Sarjah—that maybe he was starting to hide them from himself. Marcus knew none of the other crew from Earth fully understood what happened to Golamee. He didn't need to spy on them;

the shiplink made their presences known with an afterthought, and from the emotions he could feel coming from them, it was clear. They were still elated over saving the planet. Even Sumiko, who had met and talked with Golamee, didn't seem overly broken up about it. He couldn't hate on them for that, though; he got it. A floating sphere made of organic parts wasn't really sympathy-inducing. But Marcus had been there in her mind and had faced the storm of emotions that surged from her as she fought for her life— not just the fear but her love for her husband. She had had a life, an existence, with friends, family, drama, regret, hope, and everything else that made people...C-human.

Rahel, the one Earther who might get it, had tried to talk to him in person and through their link, but he had avoided her. She meant well, but he couldn't handle a comforting talk that was really a veiled lecture. Sarjah might be able to relate, but Medical had had her stay for some test. When he exited the transit vein, only a few people were about, either coming on or going off duty. The crew deck was the only area of the ship with lighting that followed a day-night cycle. It wasn't dark, but since it was the middle of night shift, the corridor ceiling showed a star-filled sky. However, looking at them as he walked had the opposite effect of feeling at home.

What he really wanted was to access the Nexus. There were so many communities there that a person would have to make an effort *not* to find a group that could relate to what they were going through. On some level, that was the problem: being connected to Golamee, feeling her emotions, and now, as a way to help deal with that, he wanted to connect with others and feel different emotions. It reminded him of a friend back home who would drink a beer for a hangover. Marcus didn't think the Nexus was addictive, but it could be one hell of a crutch. And as things stood, he didn't think Earth was nearly ready for it. People back home still lost their shit over regular social-media apps. But add being able to feel emotions to the mix—no, Earth wasn't ready for that, which meant he probably wasn't either.

MARCUS LOOKED out over Atlanta from the rooftop of the building. It was a clear, sunny day, and he tried to take a moment to enjoy the cool breeze on his skin, but ultimately, it didn't help. It wasn't that he could tell it wasn't real—the mindscape created with his bioweb activated all the same neurons in his brain as external stimuli did—he just knew that it wasn't, which made him think of his family even more. With a sigh, he closed the mindscape and opened his eyes. Marcus sat on the floor of his room with his back against the wall. The personal cabins on *Fulcrum's Light* weren't big, but they were comfortable. A separate sleeping area that could hold a double-sized bed, a bathroom with a standing shower, and a small living room with malleable chairs and desks. One wall was mostly empty, and with a thought, he transferred the view of the city there. The scene even shifted subtly, depending on where it was being viewed from, making it indistinguishable from a window.

He had a few photos of his parents and friends on his desk, but it was the picture of him and his grandparents that his eyes kept drifting to. They had given up so much for him that it broke his heart to think of causing them pain. Yet Marcus couldn't ignore the fact that being out here was the first time he had really felt... *Free* was the first word that came to mind, but he felt ashamed for thinking it. Still, he had loved being out here until today. Until Golamee's mind had been sucked away into nothingness. Until it almost happened to him.

Now the mission continued. The ship had had a mourning silence to recognize their loss, but because of Golamee's race's funeral rites, nothing more formal was done. To her people, it was disrespectful to even acknowledge the death until the family had been notified. So, no actual funeral. Hell, they didn't even have a body, and the transfer sphere had been lost in the explosion. And that was partly what made the experience so surreal. It was difficult to accept that she was dead, or worse, and that he had almost died. But he couldn't deny it either. Golamee's last struggle was burned into his mind.

An access chime interrupted his thoughts—Grayson's request for entry as clear in Marcus's head as if he had called out. Marcus ordered the door to open. Grayson stepped in, saw Marcus sitting still on the floor, nodded once, and walked over to the fabricator console. He ordered something Marcus couldn't hear, then came over and sat down near him with a bottle of brown liquid in hand and two glasses. He poured two drinks, then held his glass up and looked at Marcus patiently, waiting. He wasn't much of a drinker, but Marcus took his glass and did the same.

"To Golamee," Grayson said. "I didn't get to know her, but she was part of our crew, no matter how short."

They drank deeply.

They poured and drank once more before Marcus was confident he could speak without his voice cracking.

"I can't stop hearing her scream." His voice was barely a whisper. "It was... It..." Marcus shook his head, at a loss for words.

"Dude." Grayson had to say it twice before Marcus pulled himself out of his thoughts enough to look at him.

They weren't friends. Marcus didn't dislike Grayson, but he had been so busy training with Sarjah since he and Rahel had come on board that he hadn't had much free time. He knew Grayson was the same age, twenty-three, and was from Kentucky, but he had done military instead of college like Marcus. On the surface, they didn't have much in common. Black, White; big city, small town; programming, military—but none of that meant the same out there.

"This is a hard truth, Greer," Grayson said, "but you're never really going to *not* hear that scream. You'll always wonder: could you have done something different, reacted faster, fought harder? And I tell you, man, that shit'll eat you up if you let it."

"Did you ever..." Marcus stopped himself from asking the obvious and stupid question. Besides, he could see in Grayson's eyes that he spoke from experience. He nodded his understanding and poured them another drink.

"I want to say I've never seen anybody die before," Marcus said after a minute of companionable silence. "But that's the crazy thing. I still haven't, not physically. Her body's still out there somewhere, thousands of light-years away. An empty shell, just...erased." He couldn't think of a better word.

"I get it," Grayson said. "That's why I didn't stop by at first. It never occurred to me, because I only saw her as that sphere. Then I heard some people talking, and I realized what it must have been like for you."

"You know, during the mission, when we talked, I never saw an image of her actual body," Marcus said. "It was only the sounds and feelings in my mind. But remembering it... it's like my mind fills in an image of her being sucked away into this whiteness. And I felt myself being pulled in also, but I didn't even care at that point. I..." He sighed, not wanting to see the image again. "You ever think about your family? When you're in the middle of something like that?"

"Stuff like that will get you killed," Grayson said, but then nodded slowly. "But yeah, I'm human, it can happen. More so after the fact, though."

Marcus took another drink while watching the scene of Atlanta play out on his wall. It wasn't a live view, of course, but before he left Earth, he had gotten hundreds of hours of footage. From the aerial view, the cars looked like miniatures, and it reminded him of a toy set he had found in the attic that used to belong to his dad. This made him think of his grandparents again.

"Part of me feels like I'm being selfish," Marcus said. "Like, how could I put my grandparents through that again? They already lost a child, and it nearly destroyed them. But still, I don't want to go back, you know. Not yet."

"I hear you on that."

"What brought you out here? Their big-ass guns?"

Grayson laughed at himself. "Money, actually."

"Really?"

"Yeah. My parents were in danger of losing the farm. You know how it is; it seemed like one policy after another helped big corporations while punching average people in the face. Things have been hard for a while." Grayson took a long drink. "My dad wasn't even pissed when I decided to enlist instead of working the farm. Guess they figured the paycheck would help out."

"Did your dad start the farm?"

"No, my grandfather," Grayson answered. "And my older brother was following in their footsteps so it would stay in the family. If we could stay afloat. And then I found out that any military people who got accepted for a Society mission got a big bonus. Enough to make a difference, you know."

"And since the Society doesn't use money..." Marcus said.

"Exactly. My regular checks could keep going to my parents, since I don't need it out here."

"And I thought it was just me," Marcus said.

"Huh?"

"Out here for money. That's the main reason I joined."

"No shit?"

"Yeah. I was just a teenager when my parents died, and I had to go live with my grandparents."

"That's rough, man."

Marcus nodded. "You adapt. You know. And they gave me everything, of course. Did the best they could. But they were older when they had my mom. Meaning by the time I came along, they were...old, old—and I just wasn't prepared for how much I would have to do for them. They were retired, ready to enjoy life, and yet here they are, having to raise a teenager and pay for college again. And I'm living in my bubble of self-centeredness, and I just didn't realize how tight money had gotten. They had to remortgage their house. Cut back to one car. I mean, I wasn't totally oblivious, but almost all of my focus was on their health. That was completely new to me. Having to take them to doctors' appointments, following up on treatments, medicine, helping my nana with physical therapy after she fell.

"So, then the Society comes along, and medical wonders, ya know. I think that worry is over. Their health is gonna be straight from now on. So, it's all good. Then one day in college, I stopped by Walmart with some friends, and I see my grandpop working there!"

"Damn."

"Right. And he's in that freaking blue vest, walking slightly hunched over 'cause his back was hurting him again. He came out of retirement to work so I could have something like a normal life. That hit me hard. Real hard. And that's when I really noticed the money issues and bills piling up. I moved back home then and commuted. I dropped my unpaid internship and got a part-time job to help out."

"Dude, I don't know how I would react if I saw something like that." Grayson took a big drink. "When I was in high school me and some buddies went through the drive through at the local fast food spot, and when we drove around another friend's grandmother was the cashier. God, we gave him shit for weeks after that. You know kids. Then about a year later my mom had to get a second job, and I realized how hard that stuff was on families."

"Ain't that the truth."

Grayson poured them another drink. "Did you finish school or start working?"

"No, I finished. But even once I graduated, I wasn't making that much. So, when the Society position came up, I just applied on a whim, didn't really think I'd get accepted, but I passed the first round, then the second. And since the Society was only accepting a hundred people from Earth to be dimensional technicians, the government, ours, was offering hella salary to anyone who got accepted. And like you, all that money goes straight to my peeps, so we can keep the house. Problem solved, I thought.

"But then I get out here. My first time really being able to live away from home—"

"And you love it," Grayson said.

Marcus looked at him and nodded almost reluctantly. "I do. I really do. But recently I can't help but feel guilty about that. Especially when something like that booby trap happens, and I realize how close they came to losing me."

"But still, you're not ready to go back," Grayson said.

"Not yet."

"Yeah, being deployed overseas can be tough," Grayson said. "And if shit goes sideways, you know, you just hope they can send your body back. But out here with black holes, and dimensional rifts, and shit, who knows. To be honest, I never took what you did that seriously. I just figured it was some egghead crap that real people would never care about."

"Well, damn, bruh," Marcus laughed, taking another drink.

"You know what I mean." Grayson poured them some more. "But then that freakin' moon blew up, and damn. I could follow what people were doing through the shiplink, but I was useless. Just sitting there, hoping I wasn't about to see billions of people die. Almost dying ain't ever going to get easier. It ain't. But Golamee made a difference out here. You just gotta take it day by day."

"I hear you," Marcus said quietly. They drank for a while, watching the sun start to set over Atlanta on the video on the wall.

"You know what pisses me off, though?" Marcus said as an afterthought. "Sarjah. I saved her life, right, ya know. Well, she saved mine too, I guess. But I barely get an acknowledgment. Just this new training schedule with even more crap to do."

"Dude, she's literally cold-blooded." Grayson laughed. "What'd you expect?"

"Hell if I know. Not that."

"She is kinda hot, though." Grayson cocked an eyebrow at him.

"Oh, please."

"Man, don't act like you blind, come on," Grayson said.

"Some of these C-humans are hot. You mean to tell me the whole time you been out here, you haven't..."

"Not really," Marcus said. "There was this other ditec at training, but she was human. Earth human. But she was posted on the other side of the Society."

"Uh-huh." Grayson poured them another round. "So, you saving yourself for Rahel? You only got a thing for the sistahs?"

"Pff, whatever, country boy—besides, she too old," Marcus took a drink but had a thoughtful look on his face.

"I see that look." Grayson laughed. "Old or not, I'd be all over that; she's gorgeous. And don't think I haven't noticed how Sumiko looks at you."

"We're just friends; she—"

"Is into you. What? You don't like that she hooked up with that orange guy? She's a freaking astrobiologist, dude, what'd you expect?"

"Wait, who'd she hook up with?"

"Ha!" Grayson pointed at Marcus, the whiskey in his glass dangerously close to spilling. "Why you asking if you ain't into her?"

"Ya know what—" His door chime cut off what else he was going to say, and Marcus signaled it to open without seeing who it was.

When Sumiko walked in, Marcus's drink went down the wrong way and he started coughing.

"Doctor, come in." Grayson beamed. "Your ears must've been burning."

"My ears?"

"You want some?" Marcus offered her his glass to change the subject, thankful she wasn't familiar with the idiom.

"Sure." She took it. Sniffed it. "I just got off duty. Sorry I couldn't check on you sooner." Then she downed the whole drink in one gulp, to Grayson's and his surprise.

"American, Japanese, whatever. I swear, you boys and your bonding rituals." She shook her head. "I bet you were in here talking about women, too, huh?"

Marcus couldn't help but laugh.

"Oh, I suppose you do different?" Grayson asked.

"Actually..." She went over to the fabricator, but Marcus missed what she asked for because Grayson was giving him an *I told you she liked you* look.

Sumiko came back over with three bowls of chocolate ice cream under hot fudge and a bottle of wine. "Now, this is how you deal with stuff." She smiled.

15

With the trip to Jupiter finally underway, the rest of the day on the ship went by in a haze for Nina. The reality was, after they passed the moon, there was nothing to see except stars, and the most exciting part was being onboard with C-humans. So, people got settled in their bungalows and explored the ship. There were no official functions, and the delegates and staff were encouraged to relax, enjoy the trip, and get to know each other, the latter of which she had no interest in at the moment. She didn't have it in her to sit around socializing while pretending like nothing was wrong. The more time that passed, the more she felt that maybe it had just been her imagination. Then she would convince herself it had been real. Back and forth.

The only people who had official work to do were some in the psych department. Consul Dr. Romashenko scheduled counseling for every staff member who had been inside the station when the attack occurred. Nina knew all the right things to say, so she wasn't worried about being flagged to be sent home. In fact, she was so focused on the synesthesia episode that she hadn't even thought about the attack.

She spent much of her time video-chatting with her family. The fact that everyone's phone still worked even though they were hundreds of millions of miles from Earth was one of those novelty perks of the Society that she found herself taking for granted. It seemed like every aunt, uncle, and cousin, plus one, had made it by her parents' house at some point.

Her parents' place was still under siege by reporters; all the delegates' families were news interests, but because of what happened to Nina, her family was extra popular. It bothered her that they had to have their privacy invaded because of her decisions, but it also made her more determined. If she accused the Society of something, it would be heard, so she had to make sure. One of her aunts was there only because she had been cured of cancer with Society medicine; almost every family had a story like that now. Looking out the screen as she (on the phone) was passed around, seeing views of the ceiling, the floor, kids running, and all her family laughing, cooking, and arguing made her feel more homesick than she had ever been in her life.

And more alone.

Not that people didn't try to include her. Over the course of the day, Manaia had tried to get her to join a game of soccer in the park, Omoni had tried to get her to come to lunch with her and a few other scientists, Fresh Snowfall on the Lake had wanted to meet up with her to get a drink, and Endless Green Sky had invited her to meet some of his friends, but Nina had talked her way out of everything. The only thing she didn't brush off was a tour of the medical bay for any members of the medical contingent who were interested, which was most.

The group was given a small tour as they walked through the corridors of the ship, but Nina was too anxious to pay much attention. If she was going to have any chance of scanning herself, it would be there. The medbay had the feeling of an ER and research lab mixed together. Nina had seen most of the equipment before. When the C-humans first started helping Earth, it was with medicines and knowledge, but over the last couple of years, more and more hospitals had been given access to advanced biomedical equipment. The Society kept tight control over technology, but they worked closely with the UN to provide medical care to Earthers.

"Dr. Rodriguez, there you are." Dr. Kandahar, her immediate supervisor, approached. While Consul Dr. Romashenko was head of the entire medical contingent, Dr. Kandahar was one of the many specific department heads, in this case neuroscience.

Nina started to greet him but then stopped because she noted he didn't look well. "Are you okay, Dr. Kandahar?"

"I'll be fine," he answered with a touch of irritability. "I just need to rest. Anyway, you know that tomorrow, embassy personnel will be getting these...communication devices."

"Yes, I heard."

"I was informed Ambassador Isaacs wants to be the first one to get an exso. And I think it would be comforting if he and the consuls general had a brief update on what to expect. I would like you to do that."

"Gladly," Nina said, an idea coming to her. "Sir, I think it would be helpful if one of us is scanned to show the delegates everything the process entails."

"Scanned?" From the look of trepidation that crossed his face, Nina knew she had guessed right. "I don't think—"

"I'd be willing to do it, of course."

"Oh, well, in that case, yes, maybe. I'll discuss it with Dr. sa'Xeen."

Whatever was going on with Dr. Kandahar, Nina could tell he didn't want to be bothered with doing more than necessary and figured he would pass off extra work onto her. Now she had one possibility for scanning herself, but she still wanted to try sooner. She saw Endless Green Sky talking to some doctors across the room. She didn't want him to see her getting scanned, so she decided to try again early tomorrow, and she left.

The dome of the ship gradually lost its daytime brightness and slowly went completely transparent for a stunning view of the stars. Many people were out in the park and walking about, but Nina turned in early and spent a couple of restless hours thinking about everything. She started to log in to her social media, then thought better of it. The thought of wading through hundreds or thousands of posts just depressed her. A certain amount of fame was something that she knew was coming, but that still didn't mean she could understand how media stars adapted.

Nina browsed around the web for a bit, then decided on *Jha, Loves!* It was a guilty pleasure, as she didn't follow many celebs—especially reality-type stars—but ever since Ishani Jha had done that vlog about her trip through New Mexico, Nina had found that she had some interesting things to say. And since Ishani had been chosen to ride on *New Gaia*, her popularity had skyrocketed. The first person to ever have a billion followers, Ishani Jha was from Goa, India, beautiful —as many reality stars tended to be—and mid-twenties, a little younger than Nina.

Nina saw her most recent episode of *Jha, Loves!* The vlog had been uploaded just a couple of hours earlier and already had two hundred million views. And sure enough, it included the clip of the scene from the train station. As Ishani talked about the video, Nina scrolled through the comments for a few minutes. They were typical, full of people supporting and condemning the Society, and of course a flood of trolls just trying to spark a reaction from people. Nina tossed her phone aside and closed her eyes. Sleep was a long time coming.

THE NEXT MORNING, she got an early start, hoping that... She wasn't sure exactly what, but she couldn't just sit around. It was Wednesday, and the ship wouldn't arrive at Io until late that night, so she had all day. She decided to go back to the ship's medical bay. Nina didn't see anyone in the hallway when she left the apartment-style bungalow, but there were a number of people out and about as she walked down the street. There were joggers and people hanging out in the park. The dome above had taken on its semitransparent blue hue again, which made it feel like a nice early, sunny day. Nothing at all to worry about.

A few buildings down, she stopped at the elevator that would take her to the other levels of the ship. She presumed the design was another thing done to make the trip comfortable. The elevator was the same style as typical street elevators that led down to the subway in any major city on Earth. When it arrived, two C-humans got off, saying good morning, and went about their business. Nina got on and selected the level with the medical bay. Her phone beeped, and she saw a text from Omoni, asking if they were still on for breakfast. Nina barely remembered agreeing to that yesterday but knew if she didn't try to talk to somebody, it was going to weigh on her more and more. She responded to Omoni, telling her she may be running late but would be there.

The elevator opened, and Nina stepped out into a wide corridor with a high ceiling that glowed with soft bioluminescent light. As they had been shown yesterday, the surface of the walls was interactive, and asking a question out loud could bring up any info needed. She asked about the medbay, and a green arrow moved along the floor's surface a couple of feet in front of her, adjusting to her pace. The corridor wasn't nearly crowded, but there were a good number of C-human crew going about their task, as well as many Earthers, like her, seemingly exploring. While the upper level of the ship was the park, residential area, and dome, these levels were dedicated to ship operations and looked like the normal interior of a ship. If *normal* included a biological spaceship.

Nina absentmindedly played with the piece of stationery with the numbers written on it. It was her reminder that it wasn't all in her head, so to speak. Reporting it was the obvious choice, and, if she was objectively honest, the smartest. In fact, she was in violation of her contract by keeping quiet. About half of the delegate training had little to do with their actual jobs and a great deal to do with cultural-sensitivity training—in other words, not doing something stupid that would have consequences for Earth. And while spying wasn't in the job description, anything, *anything* out of the ordinary was always to be reported.

She didn't fundamentally disagree with that, but she wanted—needed—to be sure. And most importantly, it hadn't happened again, even though she had seen both Endless Green Sky and Fresh Snowfall on the Lake yesterday on the ship, although she hadn't been alone with or talked to either long, so that didn't necessarily mean anything. Perhaps the closed environment of the ship meant they couldn't take the risk. Perhaps it wasn't either of them at all but someone else she had met.

"Nina," a familiar voice said, dashing her hopes.

Nina looked to see Endless Green Sky coming down the corridor from the other direction with a couple of C-human colleagues. They reached the wide entrance doors to the medical section at the same time, and the Nethean told his friends he would catch up with them.

"Do they have you working all day?" Nina asked to cover up her frustration.

"Nothing official yet, thankfully," Endless Green Sky said. "Some of my colleagues are going to be showing something to a few delegates. I didn't get to talk to you yesterday on the tour. Why don't you join us? I know biochem isn't your field, but I'm sure we can make it interesting."

"Tempting," Nina said, trying not to be obvious as she fought for an excuse. Truth was best. "But I was just texting with Omoni, and I agreed to meet for coffee. I'll stop by later."

"That's fine," Endless Green Sky said. "I probably won't be here. I have to meet with the consuls general. Of course, you're welcome anytime. We should be back around one o'clock with the ambassador for his fitting."

"Oh, okay," Nina said. "I'll see you later, then."

Endless Green Sky said his goodbyes and went inside. She had a timeframe; now she just had to test herself without raising suspicion.

THE "OUTDOOR" café that Omoni sat in was across the street from the park where everyone had watched the ship leave Earth the day before. This side of the "street" was lined with restaurants and more apartment-type buildings. The dome above emitted a soft light that made for a morning feel but was still semitransparent, allowing the stars beyond to barely be seen.

"Sorry I'm late," Nina said, breaking Omoni from her thoughts and sitting down.

"That's fine," Omoni said. "I realized with the time difference, it was pretty late in Lagos, and I still hadn't talked to my parents. I promised to call them every day until we left for the Orion Complex."

"How are they holding up?"

"They're good. My brother would tell you since their favorite child is still there, everything's fine." Omoni smiled. "And my little niece posted some of the pics I sent of the ship, and she got a few thousand likes. God, she was so excited. I remember... Nina?"

Nina blinked, realizing she had been lost in thought that quickly. "Huh?"

"How have *you* been holding up, hon?" Omoni asked, putting her hand on Nina's. "You looked like you were a million miles away. I know you went through more than most of us. Did you talk to the psychologist yet?"

"Yeah, yesterday," Nina answered.

"I figured it was that when I didn't see you."

"I know it was important, but... God, that attack seems like so long ago now," Nina said. She liked Omoni—they had hit it off from the start, and she could easily see them becoming good friends—but to be honest, Nina hardly knew her. She really wanted to confide in someone, but how could Nina explain that the attack might not be the worst thing that had happened to her? She wasn't trying to mini-mize it, but considering everything else, the attack was something she hardly thought about. So, even though Nina felt she could trust Omoni, she didn't want to put Omoni's career in jeopardy, also. "I'm just thinking about everything going on. I guess I wonder if any of us truly realize what's at stake."

"It is a lot to take in," Omoni said, squeezing Nina's hand before she let go. "I'm a good listener if you need it."

"Thank you," Nina said, genuinely grateful.

Omoni sat looking up at the "sky" for a moment. "You know, as excited as I am about all this, I mean really I can't wait to go, but still, there's a part of me that's just sad."

"Sad?" Nina asked. "Not scared?"

"Well, of course scared." She shrugged. "But sad because everything's changed now. Like our innocence is gone."

"Hasn't it been changed since the Crash?" Nina asked.

"True, true," Omoni conceded. "But... Well, look at the park." Omoni pointed across the street. People—Earthers and C-humans—could be seen walking around, playing sports, and picnicking on the grass. "Those are oak trees, actual great oaks! And they didn't take them from Earth; they grew them here. In what, a couple of weeks, just to make our trip more comfortable? Not to mention Sahara City and just...everything. It's like going away to college for the first time. You can't wait to go, and yet you don't realize that a whole chapter of your life is closing. Never to come again. Now it's like the whole world is about to go through freshman year. Which isn't inherently bad, just...different."

"Growing up whether we want to or not," Nina said, holding up her cup to a passing, floating fabrication sphere, which stopped to pour coffee in it. They sat for a moment, drinking in silence, then Nina asked, "Do you think the Society's dangerous?"

"No. No, I don't think so," Omoni said, looking around at all the other people in the café talking and laughing. "Like you can feel the excitement of everybody, but at the same time a part of me thinks that nobody wants to act scared because we're all, well, scared. Scared that we might not be able to cut it and get sent back home. Scared that we won't represent the Earth right. Scared this is all too good to be true."

That hit Nina harder than Omoni could have realized. Was her real reason for not telling anyone simply because she didn't *want* it to be true? "You know, that's probably right. I didn't think about it because I guess the terrorist attack just gave everybody an excuse to freak out for a moment."

"Right," Omoni said. "And then, at the reception, when they introduced the other aliens—that freaked everybody out even more. Sorry I squeezed your arm so hard then."

"Huh? You squeezed my arm?" Nina laughed. "I was too busy squeezing Endless Green Sky's to notice."

Omoni gave Nina a knowing look. "Speaking of which, our Nethean doctor seemed quite taken with you."

Nina waved the comment away, but Omoni gave her an exaggerated eyebrow raise as she sipped her coffee.

"He's nice," Nina finally said, carefully navigating her feelings and suspicions. "And I won't lie, I do find him interesting, but that's the thing. I've been so focused on getting out here and experiencing all these amazing new medical things that I might just be projecting that onto him. Liking him more for what he represents than who he is. Does that make any sense?"

"Of course, hon," Omoni said. "And it's a valid question. You do seem a little doe-eyed when it comes to the Society. Not an insult, just saying." She held up her hands to keep Nina from interrupting. "I've met so many people who have loved ones who are alive now because of Society medicine; it's kinda hard not to be grateful."

"Yeah," Nina said, thinking about her aunt and her grandmother. Just as there were groups like True Human who hated and feared the Society, there were also a number of cults that sprang up to worship them. People who wanted to proclaim them as gods, angels, or prophets. Indeed, over the last few years, as Society technology helped poor countries with agriculture and basically ended starvation—just as it had most disease with their medical tech—it was hard not to see them as saviors. "Their medical tech was a few years too late for me, but I know what you mean."

"Oh, God, I didn't know," Omoni said.

"No, I get it," Nina said. "And it's still the reason I'm here."

"How so?"

"I got into neurology, and then neuroscience, because of my... My abuela had Alzheimer's." Nina paused a second. It was almost fifteen years ago now but still painful to talk about. "I was young, so it was a while before I understood. I had noticed she asked the same questions a lot, but it wasn't until I was like fourteen that I really learned what was happening."

"That's young to have to deal with that," Omoni said. "Not that any age makes it easy."

"True; it tore my mother apart," Nina said. "They came to a school play of mine, but a few days later, my abuela didn't remember it at all. I just thought she was playing around with me at first. Afterward, my parents sat me down and explained what was going on. And as the years went by, it just...got worse and worse."

"I'm so sorry," Omoni said.

"I knew I would never be able to help her, but just the chance that I could keep another family from going through the same thing kept me motivated." Nina had also been afraid that if it ran in the family, her parents might be faced with that one day. So, she had excelled in her job.

"That's why you decided to apply to the embassy?"

"Only partly," Nina said. "After arrival, I kept working hard, got a good position. But there was a part of me that knew we had to be willing to bridge both of these worlds if we really wanted to help people. I just didn't know how to give a voice to it.

"Near the end of my residency, there was this car accident. It was only a couple of years after the Crash, so C-human medical intervention was happening but not exactly common. A man came in with a fifty-fifty chance at best, with our tech, at least, but with the Society's knowledge, he could've been saved. No question. But the head surgeon was too arrogant and proud. He manipulated the family into thinking Earth medicine was the best option, and the patient died. I'll never forget the man's daughter crying. How would I have felt if it was my dad? And the doctor didn't even get fired. The hospital supported him; they were just scared of change, of becoming obsolete.

"You spend most of your life learning how to do something that can now be done in minutes. Like it's magic. That's hard to come to terms with." Nina took a drink from her coffee as she looked at the people walking through the park, some too far way to tell how different they truly were. "I don't just want to learn to do what the Society does. I want to help us, Earth, be ready to accept it. I know that sounds corny, but..."

"No, it doesn't." Omoni squeezed Nina's hand again. "Not at all. Our president's wife had just been diagnosed with stage-four cancer when the Society came, so in Nigeria the government accepted the new medical technology fairly quickly. Maybe a selfish reason, I know, but it worked out for everyone in our country. But I remember the news showing all the protests worldwide—for and against. And even though most governments accept it now, obviously there are still a lot of angry, scared people. Trying to do something about that is a good thing, Nina."

"I hope that's enough." Nina couldn't ignore the feeling that she might be doing the opposite of what the doctor she knew had done. She didn't want to believe she was blindly trusting C-humans.

THE MEDICAL BAY of the ship was a good-sized series of rooms that currently held a lot more than staff. While the trip to Galileo City was officially down time for all embassy personnel, most of the medical contingent had shown up. Many of the Earther doctors had congregated into small groups with various C-humans who had similar professions. Nina could see Omoni on the other side of the room, looking like she was in heaven, talking and laughing with a few different C-humans. Everyone was excited to get tech that would allow them to interact with Society technology. Most C-humans used biowebs, but for now only select Earthers—like dimensional technicians—were allowed to get those. Everyone else would get an exso, a type of extrasensory device that was noninvasive, albeit far less interactive than biowebs. And even with everything going on, Nina couldn't deny she was also excited. Back home, she had been involved in extensive research on exso and bioweb effect on Earthers, studies she would continue once they reached the capital, Sapher.

More than once, another staffer had asked her if she was okay, and she did her best to try to relax and play it off as excitement. She didn't like all the cloak-and-dagger stuff and would be happy when it was over. She saw Dr. Kandahar talking to an A'Quan doctor, and he waved Nina over when he saw her. Dr. Kandahar still didn't look great, but it seemed more like anxiety, and Nina wondered if he had been in the station during the attack the other day.

"This is Dr. sa'Xeen. She will be... Ze will be helping set up the procedure, and I would like you to assist...zer with what we discussed yesterday."

"Absolutely," Nina said, glancing at the A'Quan. She knew their race had three sexes, yet for Earthers it could be hard to tell them apart. They all had a similar sculptured beauty and lithe figures. Ze didn't seem offended by Dr. Kandahar's pronoun slip or the mildly exasperated sigh he gave when he corrected himself. "Nice to meet you, Doctor."

sa'Xeen led Nina away, talking cordially with her, and Nina tried to respond as casually as she could. She was too focused on trying to control her emotions for small talk—it was finally happening. In her pocket she gripped the piece of paper with the numbers on it, as the blue-skinned doctor had a floating medsphere scan Nina's head. Once the scan was ready, Nina would be able to see any residual traces of Society influence in her brain's neural map. She would finally know the truth, which scared her more than she realized.

She was still briefly concerned that Endless Green Sky would guess what she was doing if he saw her—if he indeed was the one who had accessed her memories. But since he was arriving with the ambassador, he wouldn't be aware she had scanned herself until she accessed the results in front of everyone. Now all she had to do was wait.

16

Zachariah sat back in his chair as he looked at the image of the man on his monitor. "Well, I appreciate you taking the time to talk to me, Captain Stanley. I wish I had gotten a moment to visit the ship before we left."

"Not a problem, Ambassador Isaacs," the captain replied, looking around off-camera. "These so-called emergence vessel–class ships are more like a small city than a spaceship, but I like her."

"And are you still on schedule?"

"We are." Captain Stanley nodded. "We'll be launching in six weeks."

"Well, I look forward to seeing it when you reach the embassy," Zachariah said, glancing at his aide Peter, who had just walked in.

"Absolutely. *New Gaia* out."

"Mr. Ambassador," Peter said. "It's time, sir."

"I'll be right there," Zach said as he stared at the blank screen. So far, he had spent much of his time on the trip to Jupiter talking to everyone he could who had spent time in the Society. Once he had been selected as ambassador, he had spent the first few months having countless meetings with Earther envoys, who happened to be back on Earth, because he wanted to have a good idea of what embassy personnel would be facing in day-to-day life. But after his talk with Envoy n'Dala, he felt the need to see if there was anything he had missed. He had reported what he learned to the UN Secretary-General and American president, but to his astonishment, they weren't surprised. They had suspected the Society knew a great deal more about anti-Society movements on Earth than they let on. And the Secretary-General had even implied that True Human might indeed be backed by powerful political and corporate entities and that an investigation had been underway for a while. It upset him that he hadn't been included in the loop because, if true, that meant the embassy may have also been compromised.

Zachariah had hoped to learn something from the captain of New Gaia. Victor Stanley had been one of the First Six Hundred, the first envoys from Earth allowed into the Society. He was also one of the first groups of Earthers to serve on a Protectorate ship. Something had happened on one of their missions, and an Earther and some C-humans had died. The event was classified by the Society and the UN Secretary-General, which led to a lot of rumor-mongering, and many nations objected to Captain Stanley's getting another assignment. But the South African had been the Society's only choice to captain Earth's emergence vessel. And if the UN wanted an Earth-led ship, they had no choice but to accept him. That was plainly another reminder that while the Society said Earth was free to choose their own path, if Earth wanted to use their technology, then the Society had final say.

New Gaia would tour the solar system and then stop at Nethea on its way to Earth's new embassy on Sapher in the Orion Molecular Cloud Complex. Hopefully, Zachariah would be able to learn something more when he talked to the captain in person.

Zach also knew another envoy who had served with Captain Stanley, who he might be able to get information from. But he hadn't spoken to her since before his wife passed away, and he wasn't sure he wanted to open that door.

"Mr. Ambassador," Peter prompted.

"Coming, coming." He stood to leave. This was the part of his mission he was looking forward to the least.

ZACHARIAH INVOLUNTARILY GRIPPED the armrests as the chair he sat on in the medical bay leaned back.

"There's nothing to worry about, Ambassador Isaacs," Dr. Endless Green Sky said, standing next to him. "This is completely painless, quick, and temporary."

The medbay room they were in was large and spacious, even with Zachariah, all the consuls general, and most of the embassy's medical contingent present.

"I think you choosing to do it first so everyone could see was a great choice, Mr. Ambassador," Consul Dr. Aleksei Romashenko said from his other side.

"I felt it was important for people to know it's safe," Zachariah responded, his hands still gripping the chair. He believed what he said, but he was still a little nervous.

The Nexus was the Society's version of the internet—although whenever that analogy was made in front of C-humans, they just smiled as if having to explain something to a child with a limited vocabulary. And just like a smartphone was integral to being able to connect on Earth, in the Society, a bioweb was used to interact with the Nexus.

"You remember Dr. Rodriguez, of course," Aleksei said.

"Of course," Zachariah said, nodding to Dr. Rodriguez as she walked over. Zachariah had briefly talked to the doctor after the launch ceremony yesterday morning and congratulated her on her actions during the terrorist attack.

"Mr. Ambassador. Consuls general," she greeted them. "I know we've been exposed to Society technology for years, and our training has gone over this, but we thought it might be helpful if I walked you through what's going happen."

"I appreciate that," Zachariah said.

Nina typed something on the small pad she was holding, and an image of a brain appeared in the air between them. It was larger than real life and obviously some type of hologram, but Zachariah had no idea how it was being generated.

"This is a normal brain," Nina began, speaking loud enough for everyone to hear. "It's actually my brain, in fact. Earth-human brains have about eighty-six billion neurons, or nerve cells. These neurons receive, process, and send information, and most can fall into three broad categories of sensory, motor, and interneurons." As she talked, Dr. Rodriguez manipulated the image with her hands, turning and enlarging it. "Now, Society medical technology is used to stimulate a C-human's brain to grow an additional layer known as a bioweb. This so-called bioweb produces a new type of neuron known as a metaneuron. And just like any neuron, the metaneurons receive, process, and send information, but across metaspace instead of just the brain and central nervous system.

"And charting the neurons in my brain, you can see that...there are no metaneurons present." Zachariah thought Nina sounded surprised—relieved?—by what she had just said, but she continued quickly. "Which is as expected, since I don't have a bioweb. What you can see is some increased activity in my sensory neurons. That's because earlier, I got the exosensory device you're about to get, and the increased activity is simply my brain processing the new data. But the exosensory device is not part of our physiology like a bioweb. It's really multiple external organic-based devices that are colloquially known as an exso. The exso covers various places on the body, like contact lenses for the eyes, buds for the ears, and the main sensory patch on the back of the neck."

Zachariah had heard all the technical talk before, especially about the bioweb, which to him boiled down to something grown in his brain that enabled connection to the Nexus. When he had first learned about the process, he was going to decline the ambassador position. The thought of aliens putting something in his head was just a nonstarter. Then he found out that only those people chosen as envoys and dimensional technicians would be allowed that technology. The situation had caused a long debate in the UN. The fear was that the Society would control and have access to all the delegates' information, as if an embassy went to a foreign country and gave the host government access to everyone's smartphones and computers. The argument, of course, was that the Society already had the ability to get that, and since they would be thousands of light-years away, Society tech was the only means to communicate with Earth anyway. Zach had been in this camp, and his recent talk with n'Dala had made him realize how true this was. Still, Earth tried to protect itself as best it could, so not everyone in the embassy would get the tech, and what was used had to be simple and noninvasive. So, embassy staff, and those traveling on *New Gaia,* had a choice of both interactive glasses and earphones, or the recommended exso.

Unofficially, Zach had found out that the exsos were dumbed down considerably to make the UN Security Council happy. The sensory patch could receive info from the central nervous system but not transmit to their brains, thus the need for contacts and earphones to access the data. The science consul had compared it to getting one of those basic phones with big buttons for seniors—smartphones made as simple as possible. Something Zach could relate to, since he had gotten one of those phones for his father, who he had finally accepted was never going to learn text messaging or how to use his voicemail. Some old people wanted to learn new things, but some didn't want to be bothered with all the confusing things kids were doing.

Earth scientists said the concepts behind the exso were things already being tried on Earth since before the Crash. Much of the basic science was there, but the technical side of manufacturing was still decades, if not more, away. It was even suspected that the Society had created exsos based along those lines just to make Earth users more comfortable. Apparently, it didn't give nearly the same level of functionality as biowebs, but it would allow Earthers to access the Nexus and interact with Society technology.

"Just turn your head to the left, please," Dr. Endless Green Sky said. Zachariah startled some when the single drop of liquid went into his ear, and was silently grateful he didn't yell. Then the doctor had him turn his head the other way so he could do the other ear. While this was going on, another nurse ran a device over the base of his skull, which added a thin skin-like layer, like a flesh-colored tattoo that would be invisible to the naked eye, which would process signals from his brain.

"Now eyedrops," Dr. Endless Green Sky said. Zachariah was grateful an actual person was doing it and not one of the floating spheres, which he suspected was more standard. He blinked a couple of times when the doctor used a small cylinder to put one drop in each eye. He had worn contacts for years before he had laser eye surgery, so he was still reluctant about them.

"And these don't need to be changed daily?" he asked.

"No, sir," Endless Green Sky said. "You won't even feel them after a few minutes, and they completely biodegrade into simple proteins that our bodies absorb. But they last for a few months."

Zachariah almost laughed at his squeamishness; living spaceships and cities on other planets he could accept, but he found true long-term contacts hard to believe.

"And we're done," Dr. Endless Green Sky said, raising the chair back to a sitting position. "It'll take a couple of days for you to get fully used to accessing stuff, but Envoy Last Rain in Autumn has organized training sessions for everyone during the remainder of the trip."

"So," Zachariah glanced from the Nethean to Aleksei. "That's it?"

Endless Green Sky smiled. "That's it, sir. You can understand me okay, can't you?"

"Yes," Zachariah said. "Of course."

"Good, because I'm not speaking in English anymore," Endless Green Sky said. "I'm speaking in Nethean, my native language. The eardrops translate everything for you in real time."

"Well, damn," Zachariah said, getting up.

· · ·

ZACHARIAH AND DEPUTY Chief Xian Xu were sitting on the balcony of the office he had been given for the trip. It was three stories up in a building near one end of the park, in which they had all stood to watch the launch yesterday. With no official duties yet, he could see people strolling by and sitting on the grass. One group had a football game going, and he could smell barbecue from one of the neighboring rooftops. It was all very local-holiday-feeling until you looked up to see the clear dome providing light while still allowing the stars to be seen.

They weren't close enough to see Jupiter as a planet yet, so it still looked like just another bright star in the sky. Secretly, he had been looking forward to seeing the solar system's asteroid belt until one of the scientists explained to him that even though there were many millions of asteroids in the belt, space was so vast that the average distance between each rock was about a million kilometers, meaning they wouldn't be visible together to the naked eye like in the movies. All in all, the trip was almost as boring as a cruise was to him.

"Do you miss being mayor?" Zachariah asked. He knew Xian's resume, but he hadn't gotten a chance to know her. He had been surprised to find out that like him, she had been a mayor. He had been even more surprised that even though there were far more male mayors than female, the majority of major cities in China had women mayors. He knew it was an unjustified conceit, but he had just naturally assumed the West would be more progressive in every way when it came to women in politics. It had been a refreshing reminder that no matter how open-minded he was, unconscious bias could still skew his view of the world. And he couldn't afford to have any of that with the Society. He had to see them for what they were, not what he wanted or feared.

Xian looked at him for a moment before answering. "Honestly, I've been wondering that myself the last few weeks." She breathed deep and took a drink from her coffee. "I don't think so. I like what we have the ability to accomplish here.

"I won't lie, though," she continued with a smile. "I did want to be ambassador. Why? Are you thinking about abdicating and going back?"

"Not just yet." He chuckled. "I was surprised they didn't choose you as the Asia consul general, considering your record."

"I didn't want it." At Zachariah's questioning look, she continued. "It was too specific."

"You mean like region-specific?"

"Yeah," she said. "I know we're all here for Earth, but the consuls general mainly rep their respective areas back home: Asia, North America, Africa, et cetera. But for us...for us, it's more global. Our focus is everybody, our whole species—sorry, planet. I still slip up with that. They're humanoid, no doubt, but thinking of them as human is still a conscious effort sometimes."

"It is," he agreed, looking at some C-humans below, two green-skinned and a yellow—furred?—one, playing Frisbee with some Earther delegates in the park. "And I don't know if we as a planet would have a harder or easier time accepting aliens if they all looked like the Z'tainian or Nui from the orientation reception."

"That was a shock to me," she said, glancing at him. "Did you know there were...beings like that in the Society?"

"No." He shook his head. He didn't mind that she studied his face, apparently judging whether she could believe him. They needed to learn to trust each other. "As far as I can tell, no one knew. Not even previous Earth envoys. A number of scientists had speculated that it had to be possible, but that was the first time the Society told us."

"Logically, I see the reasoning for waiting," she said. "It does make them seem more human in comparison."

"It does," Zachariah said. He had video-conferenced in on a number of meetings with the UN Security Council since the orientation. The two nonhuman aliens were due to address the UN General Assembly later today, and there was still no clear consensus on how the news should be delivered to the public. "I try to never let myself forget they're not from Earth, but sometimes one of them—Ambassador As the Gentle Wind, or Envoy Last Rain in Autumn, or somebody—will do something random, a phrase or a look, that is so human—Earth-human—that I find myself imagining I'm just looking at someone in a costume."

"That's easy to think," she said, nodding to a group of C-humans and Earthers walking by on the street below. If Zachariah didn't know better, he would think it was a couple of people in blue and orange body paint.

"I'm excited and afraid for Earth at the same time," she said.

"Me too," he admitted quietly.

They both sat in silence and drank for a moment. Then she spoke again. "You know, I read your book."

"Really?" He was surprised.

"Yeah," she said. "I came across it about a year after I was in office, and I always remembered it. I mean I never would've thought that I could relate to a Black man growing up in the West, but it's about so much more than that. And I started to see a surprising amount of analogies as a woman in a male-dominated field. Hell, I don't know. I guess anybody, be it religion, sexuality, or whatever, can find common ground if they really look. It just resonated with me."

Zachariah absently rubbed his empty ring finger with a faraway look. "That feels like a lifetime ago."

He had written *Voiceless* when he was still a local council member—when he was still married. It had started out as a statement on how poor residents often had no real voice in government. While it had started out specific to Trinidad, it had morphed into including race, religion, and gender. The book didn't try to offer a solution so much as it presented a non-confrontational way to acknowledge the problems—without assigning blame—and open the door to dialogue. The solution would take everyone working together. It had become so popular, it propelled him into the mayor's office. That was a few years before the Society ship crashed in Hawaii. After the Crash, his life had turned upside down. His wife...

"You miss it?"

For one breathless moment, he thought she was talking about his wife. "...Being mayor?"

He cracked his finger to keep from rubbing where the ring had been. "No," he said slowly. "No, that time in my life is past.

"Don't get me wrong; I love my country. And my parents and sister are still there, but this..." He waved his hand in a gesture that took in the room, the ship, and space outside. "You had it right. This could help everybody. And the thought of somebody like Richard influencing how Earth deals with the Society doesn't sit well with me."

"Yeah, the North American consul general is gonna be a

problem." After a beat, Xian seemed to realize who she was talking to and added. "No offense."

Zachariah was starting to see they had a similar sense of humor and he appreciated that. "No, I get it. But I'm just as worried about Europe. Running blindly into the Society, arms open, is just as much a recipe for disaster."

"Do you think they're not benevolent?"

Zachariah took a drink as he considered. "No, I think they are," he answered honestly, but it wasn't lost on him that they—the Society, if they could be thought of as a *they* —could easily hear everything. "I'm willing to believe the Society can be good, maybe even is good. I don't think a civilization could last fourteen thousand years without a solid foundation. And I really don't think that fear, or exploitation, could be that foundation. No, I think they're close to the utopia they claim to be."

"But," she prompted.

"But with something this big, this old..." He shook his head as he considered the scope of what was before them as a people. "I'm not naïve enough that I'd fail to recognize that things can get lost in the shuffle. And I wanna make sure Earth isn't one of those things."

"I think we'll get along fine." She tipped her cup to him. "The consuls general for Africa and South America will be our biggest allies. Like you said, Europe, and also Oceania, are too optimistic and eager, while Consul General Bakti would love to get some weapons. He's pure military."

"Yeah, the Asia consul general is going to be a handful," Zachariah said. "No offense," he added with a smile.

They both had a good laugh.

"I think we can handle them," she said.

"True," he answered. "You know, I didn't realize your English was so good."

"Hmmm." She gave him a puzzled look, then smiled, tapping her exso. "Oh, I've been speaking Mandarin."

THE REST of the last day of the trip to Jupiter was as uneventful as the beginning. Zachariah trained using his exso. It was simple but took practice. The contact lenses displayed information that appeared in his field of vision, as if floating in the air before him. The data could be controlled with voice commands, hand movements, or just focusing his eyes.

He spent most of his remaining time talking with various world leaders, all wanting to remind him how important his job was and subtly reminding him—or once or twice blatantly telling him—how he was there to represent the world, not just his country. To some, it didn't matter that he was Trinidadian and not from the continent; to them, technically he was considered North American, and that was still a sore spot. He didn't take it personally or waste time getting offended. The Society might have its own agenda, but experience had shown it certainly wasn't playing favorites with Earth's nation-states.

Now he and Last Rain in Autumn were alone in his office. Evening had come, the trip was almost over, and the ship was making its final approach to Jupiter.

"So, she's being demoted?" Zachariah asked Last Rain in Autumn. She had just told him that n'Dala was going to be envoy to *New Gaia*, and that a new envoy to Earth would be appointed.

"No, not at all," Last Rain in Autumn said with the typical lighthearted attitude that Netheans displayed. "Being envoy to your world's emergence vessel is a very important post."

"But it's because she confessed to me about the Society knowing about the attack, and your ability to monitor our communications."

"Confessed," Last Rain in Autumn said, stifling a laugh. "That's a pretty strong word. And I would say inaccurate."

"You know what I mean."

"I do. I do, Zach. And I'm not trying to make light of it. n'Dala really shouldn't have told you that, although I understand why she did."

"I sense a 'but' coming."

"Wellll"—She stretched the word out, her smile never diminishing—"your leaders already knew about True Human, correct?"

Zach reluctantly nodded.

"Aaaand," she continued, "many of your top scientists have repeatedly told your leaders things in regards to the technology disparity that they simply refused to accept."

"Speculation is different than confirmation."

"True. But..." She laughed lightly when she said it. "All of this would've been told to you once you reached Sapher. So we say."

"So you say," Zachariah said. Even though he had been thinking that, he hadn't planned on saying it out loud. He knew several politicians who actively did not like the casual nature of Netheans. They claimed it was unprofessional and an intentional sign of disrespect toward Earth. Zach thought the simpler answer was that some folk just didn't like people who seemed happy with life. "But why wait?"

"Because certain knowledge, outside of context, is more harmful than helpful."

"n'Dala made some similar points," Zachariah said. The UN had been told that there was a lot of information the Society would share with Earth Embassy only once Earthers had been living in the capital for a couple of weeks and had a chance to adjust to life on another planet.

"And I understand the UN's frustration. With all your envoys, Earth learned a lot of things about the Society through reports and debriefings. But this is the first time actual elected officials will be able to immerse themselves in our culture. You and the consuls general will be helping to shape the policy of Earth's developing relations with the rest of C-humanity. And there is no substitute for firsthand experience."

"I'm inclined to agree," Zachariah said. He started to say more on it, but an alarm notified him they would be arriving at Jupiter soon. "Shall we watch from the balcony?"

"Yes, let's."

They moved to the balcony of his office, where he and Xian had talked that afternoon, and looked out over the park. A lot of people had gathered there to watch the final approach. It was the night cycle of the ship, so the dome was completely transparent. There was heavy light pollution where he lived back home, so Zach rarely saw many stars. But here, in the subdued lighting of the ship, stars shone brightly. The Milky Way stretching across the sky was beautiful, but what Zach focused on was the reddish spot that was Jupiter. It was just big enough to start making out bands of color, and it was getting larger the closer they came. Then the image of the lead officer's face appeared in the corner of Zachariah's field of vision—along with a giant image of him above the park. The Nethean's voice seemed to come from the walls and floor itself.

"Greetings, cousins," he said. "We are on our final approach to Jupiter. First, if this large image annoys you, you can turn it off with your exso and even turn off the audio and just enjoy the view.

"For the rest of you, the science consul of your embassy thought it would be fun to give you a little bit of background on Jupiter and Io."

A giant image of Jupiter filled the air, surrounded by dozens of ellipses representing the orbits of its moons.

"As you know, Jupiter is the largest planet in your solar system, and it has seventy-nine moons...that you know of." He winked, then the image changed until only four orbits remained. "The four major moons were discovered by Galileo Galilee in 1610." Each orbital ring pulsed brightly for a moment as the Nethean said the moon's names. "Callisto, Ganymede, Europa, and Io—our destination. There are a few smaller moons closer to Jupiter, but of the major moons, Io is the closest." The image zoomed in to focus on Io, and the lead officer went on discussing some of the features of the moon and showing the large domed structure of Galileo City on its surface.

Soon, the image of Io faded away, and people were left looking at the real thing with their own eyes. The moon was a burnt yellowish sphere with splotchy patches of orange, ocher, and black, and dusty swaths of white. To Zachariah, it looked like a molded ball of cheese left to rot in a forgotten refrigerator drawer. It was just a touch larger than Earth's moon but felt far more vibrant and alive, holding its title of most geologically active body in the solar system. Sporadic bright spots showed on the moon's surface, where volcanoes spewed sulfur and silicate materials into the thin atmosphere, only to fall back to recoat the hellish landscape. It was so different, it was almost beautiful.

And for the first time, Zachariah really appreciated the travel schedule the Society had made them adhere to. Instead of just portaling to Io from Earth, their long journey —from the train ride to Sahara City, to the flight here—

helped to give them an idea of just how vast space was and how far they were from Earth. They were moving into something that was far larger than any worldview humans had before. Now they just had to survive it.

"I'm glad we didn't just portal here," Zach said.

"Experience the Way," Last Rain in Autumn said, still looking at Jupiter.

"Huh?"

"A Nethean philosophy. We are nomadic and curious by nature. So, taking time to truly experience the moment, the journey, is important to us."

"Well, this is a moment I won't soon forget."

Zachariah watched the colorful surface of Io grow beneath them as they descended. Jupiter's famous orange-and-reddish-striped body felt almost uncomfortably large in the sky. But what really took Zachariah's breath away was the Society's presence there in the Jovian system. Galileo City was about the size of Dallas. It was enclosed by a dome that, depending on the light, occasionally had a faint shimmer across its surface. In orbit of the moon were a lot of bioships of various sizes and a couple of super fabrication spheres, whose shifting surfaces sometimes made them look like rounded flower buds. As the ship slowed, the reality that they were about to set foot on another planetary body was overwhelming. On the horizon a volcano erupted, ejecting another plume of sulfur into the sky. The absence of sound made the scene seem even more surreal.

The ship lowered itself into the dome and seemed to pass through it as if it were a thin layer of water. Zachariah could see the surface as it rose along the edge of the ship until it closed above it once they were completely through. Even watching the horizon and surrounding buildings, it was hard to tell when the ship fully landed, as there was no jolting halt or bounce; it was as smooth as takeoff had been.

Zach glanced at Last Rain in Autumn, who was smiling as usual. In the park below, no one seemed to know what to say; they just stood around and looked at each other. They were on Io.

17

After they landed on Io, the delegation had been transported directly from the starport to their lodging by subways that connected to the hotel, meaning they barely got to see the city. And with the exception of Manaia, who had no fear and wanted to run right out exploring the nightlife, Nina and some others wanted a moment to let it all sink in, and they had decided to settle in and unpack first. Half of the embassy contingent was housed on the top few floors of the Jovian Hotel, with the other half in another hotel across the plaza.

As their guides had explained to them, Galileo City had the same atmosphere and gravity as Earth. In fact, most of the city's architecture was the same as Earth also. The whole place was designed to give C-humans a taste of what Earth was like. Outside the domed city, Io's harsh sulfur dioxide atmosphere, minus-two-hundred-degree Fahrenheit surface temperature, and one-fifth Earth's gravity all reigned supreme. But within this little bubble of life, if she didn't look up to the sky, she would never know she wasn't in some city back home. When she did look up, it took her breath away. Jupiter dominated the sky, far larger than the moon seen from Earth, and it made the view in Galileo City one of uncanny beauty.

As Nina stared out her room's window, she caught a glimpse of her reflection in the glass and almost laughed out loud at her big, stupid grin. She had been so relieved when the scanners in the ship's medbay showed she had no metaneurons in her brain that she hadn't stopped smiling for the rest of the trip. She hadn't consciously realized how much stress she was under until it was gone. The worry and fear that the Society wasn't what it claimed had eaten away at her over the last two days until she could barely focus on anything else.

Now she could finally let go. Let go and enjoy the trip in a way she hadn't been able to since the train station in Cairo. For a giddy moment, she even wanted to call her mom and say *I told you so*. She smiled more at the thought of how that conversation would go. But Nina was grateful she didn't have to act like a detective doctor anymore.

If she were to play devil's advocate, of course, it wasn't outside the realm of possibility that she had experienced synesthesia, but that was bordering on the paranoid. She knew from her research on Earth that the residual traces of metaneurons dissipated at different rates in different people but could usually still be detected three or four days later. Since the synesthesia episode had happened Monday night and this was Wednesday night, that was just two days, so she was fairly confident she had been wrong. The most likely answer was that imagination, stress, alcohol, and exhaustion had taken a toll on her. Now it was over, and they didn't have any obligations until tomorrow's lecture. She took her time putting her clothes away even though they were only going to be in the city a couple of days. She hadn't unpacked at all on the flight, and she felt doing it here would help give her a feeling of normality.

NINA NAVIGATED her way through the semi-crowded hotel lobby, seeing familiar faces but no one she personally knew. She, Omoni, and Manaia had agreed to meet in front. The different embassy departments would have various tours, meetings, and lectures tomorrow, but there was no official delegation ceremony until they were scheduled to leave on Friday. Unofficially, Nina knew this was the last phase of making sure all the Earthers were comfortable with living on another planet. If people couldn't handle Galileo City, they would never last on a real Society world. Technically, all the various C-humans living in Galileo City were, in some kind of capacity, workers who dealt with new human cultures and their transition into the larger C-human civilization, which, to Nina, sounded very dry and bureaucratic. The professional manner of the few living hotel staff—who, Nina suspected, were only there to baby the backwater Earthers who didn't even have the proper implants to control modern technology—hadn't changed her opinion. That's why she expected the city to be full of C-humans, in whatever their equivalent of a business suit was, rushing around focusing on important galactic matters: prim, proper, and boring. So, when she stepped from the hotel, she wasn't prepared for how biased and wrong her thinking was.

The transit time on the ship had been scheduled to coincide with the day-night cycle of the city. And Galileo City appeared to have a vibrant nightlife. The glow of the city's lights, combined with Jupiter overhead, made the plaza in front of the hotel awe-inspiring. The diameter of the circular plaza was about the length of a football field, with many streets leading out in a radial pattern. Instead of pavement or cobblestones, the plaza was covered in thick, lush grass dotted with small ponds and fountains with arcs of colored water dancing above the surface. And at the plaza's center was a small grove of redwoods. They stretched into the sky, higher than all the surrounding buildings, yet their tops still fell short of the city's dome.

But it was the people who drew most of Nina's attention. Even on the trip from Earth, there had only been about half as many C-humans as there were Earthers. But the crowds here were, by far, mostly C-human, walking around casually and seemingly taking in the sights like tourists. A lot were Netheans—about a third of all she saw—everyone else was a rich diversity of various colors, sizes, and skin types. Even though it was well known that there were C-humans of various animal classes, like reptile, amphibian, or avian— most that had been to Earth were mammal, like the Netheans and A'Quan. So, seeing the sheer amount of differences firsthand left Nina a little overwhelmed. She stopped counting the different C-human races she saw at fifteen.

She took her phone out and was about to call her friends when something flashed by her eye. Nina waved her hand about, thinking it was an insect. It took a few seconds before she realized it was text floating in her field of vision. The letters *LOL*, with a little picture of Manaia floating next to it. Nina had forgotten about her exso. Then a ring in her ear and Omoni's image popping up in her face let her know she had a call. Nina focused on the image to answer the call, and the sound of Omoni's and Manaia's laughter filled her ears.

"You should see the expression on your face," Omoni's image said.

Nina glanced around and saw her friends off to the side, grinning. She walked over, making a couple of attempts before she remembered the correct gesture to turn off the call.

"Glad to see you two getting along," Nina said, coming up to them.

Manaia shrugged innocently. "Hey, it's not our fault you were standing there with your mouth hanging wide open..." Her voice trailed off as they all got distracted by a seven-foot tall C-human covered in beautiful feathers walking by and chatting with a couple of other Earthers.

"You were saying?" Omoni bumped Manaia, then said to Nina, "And it's about time you got here. Manaia was just about to start another ex-boyfriend story, and I don't think I can laugh anymore without breaking something."

"Hey, at least I learn from my mistakes," Manaia said. "And why do you even have your phone?"

"To call y'all, obviously. It still works out here."

"Yeah, but why not just transfer the data to your exso and use that?" Manaia asked.

"I actually forgot about that," Nina said, realizing she had missed a lot of information during the trip because of her single-minded focus.

"Wow, the elderly really are resistant to change," Manaia said.

"Elderly!"

"Maybe she had to take a nap. That's why she's late."

"You're, like, the same age as me, Omoni."

"I'm young at heart, dear."

"Anyway, I'm late because I invited someone mature to join us," Nina said, noticing the other person approaching them.

"Ladies, this is Fresh Snowfall on the Lake, a cultural

historian." Nina introduced the smiling Nethean as she came up. "And these might, or might not, be my friends. Dr. Omoni Akande, an astrobiologist from Nigeria. And Manaia Harris, an anthropologist from New Zealand."

Both women tried to speak at once, and Fresh Snowfall on the Lake smiled even more, if that was possible, as she greeted them. Nina was glad she had taken a moment to reach out to the Nethean. At first, Nina had done it because of guilt. She didn't tell Fresh Snowfall on the Lake what she had suspected of her, of course, but that didn't change how Nina had been acting the last couple of days. On the trip out, when everyone had been relaxing and getting comfortable living with C-humans, she had been so wrapped up in her fear that she had distanced herself. Now she had catching-up to do. Nina had also reached out to Endless Green Sky but hadn't heard back from him yet.

"So, are you all ready to..." Manaia stopped and cocked her head, looking Nina up and down. "You look different."

"I changed, hello." Nina laughed.

"No, she's right," Omoni said, looking at her closely. "You're definitely happier than you were on the trip."

"I thought so too, when you called me," Fresh Snowfall on the Lake said. "I presumed it was a part of your culture I wasn't familiar with yet."

"I'm just excited about—"

"Oh my God," Manaia grabbed Omoni's arm, but never took her eyes off Nina. "Did you get laid?!"

"What?" Nina asked.

"Nooo." Omoni's hand came up to cover her mouth. "Did you and—"

"No!" Nina said louder than she meant, glancing around, knowing it made her look guilty. "I haven't even seen him since the ship."

"Mm-hm." Omoni's pursed lips said it all.

"Seen who?" Manaia asked, looking between them. "Wait, are you talking about that doctor from the other day? What was his name—Endless Green Eyes or something?"

"Sky," Nina said, crossing her arms.

"Whatever." Manaia brushed off her mock anger. "He was a cutie."

"And those eyes." Omoni grinned.

"Not to mention his—"

"Laid?" Fresh Snowfall on the Lake said. "Like lying down to rest, or a nap?"

"Lying down. Standing up. Reverse—" Manaia started.

"Oh, stop," Nina said.

"It's slang," Omoni said. "For when people—"

"*I,*" Nina emphasized, "did the same thing you guys did. Got changed and came down here."

"But you like a Nethean? This Dr. Endless Green Sky?" Fresh Snowfall on the Lake's smile was a little infectious.

"No. Yes. Not like that."

"Your cheeks have increased redness and temperature, though," Fresh Snowfall on the Lake said. "Isn't that a sign of embarrassment for Earthers?"

"Ha, she's got you there, hon," Omoni said. "Wait, do Netheans blush? Is that common among C-humans, the mammals at least?"

"And of course you want to turn it to biology," Nina said. "We're supposed to be sightseeing."

"And of course you're trying to change the subject," Manaia chided. "So, what's got you so happy?"

"Nothing, he's just—"

"A hottie," Manaia said.

"Hottie?" Fresh Snowfall on the Lake asked, looking at Manaia.

"Really attractive person," Manaia said.

"Oh, I want to see him," Fresh Snowfall on the Lake's eyes lost focus, and she seemed distracted for a moment. "I just looked him up; he is a...hottie."

Nina just shook her head.

"What do you say on Nethea?" Manaia asked.

"Umm...oh, a blank spot."

"An attractive person is a blank spot?"

"Well, you know we remember everything, right? So, it kind of comes from the assumption that this person is so beautiful that you just forget everything for a moment when you stare at them. So, they're a blank spot in your memory."

"I'd like to forget this conversation," Nina said.

"Fine, keep your secrets," Omoni teased.

"Whatever." Nina laughed, feeling more relaxed than she had in days. Apparently, finding out you weren't at the heart of an interstellar conspiracy was as good as sex.

EVEN THOUGH THE architecture of Galileo City was an imitation of Earth, it was still flavored by the tech of the Society, like the redwoods in the plaza. So, while there were streets, there were no cars, not at ground level at least, but she often saw capsule-like vehicles flying about above. When Nina and her group first left the plaza, she assumed they would just be walking down the streets and looking at the city. Then they noticed that although people on the sidewalks moved at a normal pace, the people in the street, while still walking, were moving much faster. Fresh Snowfall on the Lake explained to them that the material of the streets was made of numerous walk pads, which were essentially sections of the street that moved with you. Similar to the moving sidewalks at large airports, but they moved with the individual or group.

They spent the next few minutes enjoying the excuse to let their inner kids out and played around: walking faster or slower, jumping from street to sidewalk, or even just standing still, but still being carried along by the others walking around them.

At one point, Omoni and Manaia's walk pad split off as they slowed their walking to admire a street performance, and Nina found herself alone with Fresh Snowfall on the Lake for the first time since talking to her on Earth.

"I'm sorry if I brushed you off on the ship," Nina said, thinking of how she had avoided her and Endless Green Sky. "I just had a lot on my mind."

"Don't be silly," Fresh Snowfall on the Lake said. "With everything going on, that's to be expected. Especially considering the attack. You have heard there were no casualties, right?"

"Yes, thank God." She immediately realized how that might sound. "No offense. I know it was Society medical tech that saved everyone."

"Not at all," Fresh Snowfall on the Lake said. "Netheans aren't religious, but there are plenty of C-human races that are. And physical injury isn't the only kind of injury, of course. How have *you* been since the attack?"

"I'm..." Nina was automatically about to say *fine*, then she really gave it thought. "I don't really know how to answer that. I feel like I should be a lot more bothered than I am. I know I should be. But it's just..." She shook her head, not sure where to begin to put everything into words. She had known all the right things to say to the psychiatrist. Anybody who really wanted to go wasn't going to admit anything was wrong. But now that drama was over.

"Well, it did happen on another planet than you're on now," Fresh Snowfall on the Lake said. "I'm sure it's hard to even accept as real."

"Not just that," Nina said. "It all happened so fast. I'm thinking about something silly one second, and then the next, the world is turned upside down. Honestly, Envoy n'Dala living was more of a surprise to me than the actual explosion."

"Really?"

"Not in the moment, but after. All that blue blood, and then those bullets floating up out of her..." Nina shook her head." I remember it clearly, but even still, it's hard to believe it wasn't a movie."

"Was that the first time you had seen Society technology save a life?"

"Kinda...not really...I mean, that's part of it. I've never seen it happen in a situation like that, but the first time I ever worked with C-human medicine was also strange."

"Really?" Fresh Snowfall on the Lake squeezed Nina's hand in a very Earther-human way. "Was somebody hurt?"

"No, saved, actually," Nina said. "After some soul-searching, I stopped working at a hospital and went to a medical research lab in the private sector. I was focusing more on research than treatment, anyway. I had written a few well-received papers but, like most people, had only seen a C-human on TV. Then my team was sent to a military base. I knew we were going to be reviewing some Society technology, but I was surprised when we were introduced to a terminally ill Earther. They had..." Nina paused, the memories of that time bringing up memories of her grandmother. The regret that she didn't live long enough to be saved by the near-unbelievable technology of the Society still touched Nina.

"If it's too painful—" Fresh Snowfall on the Lake began.

"No, no, it's not that," Nina said. "The patient, a Marine, had a brain tumor and was only expected to have a few days left to live. This was still early, before anyone had received biowebs yet. So, he had volunteered.

"That's when the Society doctors came in. Two Netheans." Nina glanced at the cultural historian. "I admit I couldn't stop staring."

"I'd be surprised if you could."

Nina smiled at that. "After all the redundant meetings and drawn-out paperwork, once they were finally allowed to work, it was about a fifteen-minute procedure. I tell you, seeing that man recover from a brain tumor was the most incredible thing.

"Learning about the biowebs, seeing them put in, and the subsequent research and tests we did was a great experience. But it was seeing Corporal Barnes go from this bedridden shell at death's door to a noticeably healthier person in twenty-four hours that impacted me the most. Within three days, he was healthy enough that you would've never guessed he had been dying. I had known before I wanted to help Earth accept Society technology, but it was then that I knew to really make a difference, I wanted to come to the Society itself. About eight months later, they announced the Earth Embassy positions, and I knew I had to join.

"And it's that same type of magical healing that I saw when Endless Green Sky saved Envoy n'Dala. If people had died in the attack, I would probably feel different, but the whole thing is just so dreamlike in my memory that it hasn't really affected me. And then with the stress of—" Nina caught herself before she said something about her crazy fears. They would probably laugh about it one day, but for now, she didn't want to come across as the backward local who was afraid of fire. "... Just the stress of everything, you know."

"I get it. And I'm glad you're handling it well."

"This place is amazing!" Manaia said as she and Omoni caught up with them, their walk pads merging as they got close enough. "And do people ride in those?" She pointed into the sky at the car-sized capsules that occasionally flew by overhead.

"They sure do."

"There don't seem to be enough of them for a city this size," Omoni said. "I mean, this is a great walking city, but what about when people need to get somewhere quickly?"

"Oh, we use portals," Fresh Snowfall Lake said. "The air cars are mostly just for tourists and the view, really."

Nina realized then that she had missed some of the basic info people had learned on the trip out because she had been so caught up in finding a way to be tested. Back on Earth, people knew about Galileo City, but there wasn't as much news and info about it as there was on Sahara City or *New Gaia*. Another source of numerous conspiracy theories.

She vaguely remembered one of the informal meetings on the trip out, when someone had talked about how they used portals in the city for most public transit, but it hadn't registered until now. And judging from the look on her friends' faces, they had forgotten that as well.

"Uhhh, you can't just drop a bomb like that and not show us," Manaia said.

"Drop a..." Fresh Snowfall on the Lake took a second before she got the idiom, then she laughed. "Well, how else do you think I'm going to show you around the city?"

The Nethean motioned with her head, and Nina noticed, as they approached the intersection, that one of the buildings on the corners had a lot of people going in and out. Only then did she realize that the large "doorways" were actually portals.

Fresh Snowfall on the Lake laughed as she realized she had to slow her walking so her walkpad didn't separate and leave them behind; the Earther ladies had slowed as they approached the building. "Come on, slowjabs; there's nothing to worry about."

"You mean *slowpokes*?" Omoni asked, not taking eyes off the people coming and going through the portal.

"No, I think it's *jab*," Manaia said, playfully sticking her finger into Omoni's side. Then she jogged forward and turned back to look at her friends excitedly. "Well, come on, old ladies; are we doing this or not?"

It wasn't crowded, and the women stopped near the entrance. The portal wasn't an actual doorway but what looked like a flat wall with a slightly luminous sheen. A couple of Netheans walked out of the surface, like ghosts through a wall. They smiled at Nina and her friends; one waved, but they didn't stop as they moved past. Another C-human excused himself as he moved by them and walked into the wall without breaking stride, vanishing from sight in the same way the other two had appeared.

"How does it know where to take people?" Omoni asked.

"You just use your bioweb, or in your case your exso, to set a destination. As simple as pressing an elevator button," Fresh Snowfall on the Lake answered.

"But with your brain," Manaia deadpanned.

"Do we all have to go through together, like holding hands or something?" Nina asked.

"Oh, no," Fresh Snowfall on the Lake said. "It looks like a solid surface, but it generates a portal opening for each individual person."

A message icon popped up in Nina's exso. When she

focused on it, it was a simple address sent from Fresh Snow-fall on the Lake.

"You send that address to the gate, just like if you were sending a message to someone. Then step forward and boom."

"Boom?" Omoni asked.

"Figure of speech." Fresh Snowfall on the Lake smiled.

Manaia ran forward, laughing. "See ya on the other side, ladiesss—" Then she was gone.

"The fearlessness of youth," Fresh Snowfall on the Lake said.

"You know she's only a few years younger than us, right?" Nina said.

"Sure, hon, sure." Fresh Snowfall on the Lake patted Nina's hand like she was consoling someone, her smile even bigger. "I would never argue with my elders," she said as she walked backward toward the wall. "You're really not going to let Manaia loose on the city without supervision, are you?" A smile and a wink, and she was gone.

Nina glanced at Omoni, who looked like she was about to say something, then she shrugged and held out her hand. Nina clasped it and they stepped forward. She involuntarily held her breath and blinked, thinking for a second that the portal had just turned them around. But no, the building across the street was different, and Fresh Snowfall on the Lake and Manaia were off to the side, looking at something.

"Well," Omoni said, "that was anticlimactic."

Nina laughed with her. How had she ever been afraid of the Society?

THEY SPENT the evening portaling to different areas, exploring the city, and trading stories about life on Earth and in the Society. Looking at all the different C-humans walking about, Nina had never felt so tall and so short at the same time. There were just as many four- and five-foot-tall people walking around as there were those seven and eight feet tall. She and her friends would occasionally see other Earthers enjoying the nightlife, but the majority of people were C-human. And to Nina, it appeared like any late-night in a major city. Crowds of people going about their business, milling in and out of restaurants and bars, groups of friends hanging out and laughing.

While walking down one street, Nina thought it was lined with stores until Fresh Snowfall on the Lake explained to her that the Society, at least on most worlds, didn't have retail stores. With their fabrication technology, there was no need. Most of everyday life's necessities were created on demand and recycled if no longer needed. The "stores" were more like galleries where people showed things they had created by hand: art, sculpture, inventions. There were café-type places that specialized in food from all over the Society, which strictly weren't necessary because fabricators could also make any food, but people ran them for the simple pleasure of cooking. It was more of a social thing, like coffeehouses on Earth—you could easily make it at home, but a culture had grown up around the business. And there, it was all free and open to everyone, which made Nina feel a little uncomfortable on a level she didn't care to admit.

Consumer-based capitalist society had ingrained in people that cost was associated with quality. Nina knew if she had grown up in her grandparents' era, the thought of everything free would cause some knee-jerk reaction, imagining hippie communes and socialist regimes. Hell, even her parents' generation had dealt with those fears. In fact, many of the Society's most vocal opponents in Western culture already made such claims. The civilization the C-humans had built was definitely post-scarcity, but it didn't mirror any governmental ideology on Earth, certainly not socialism or communism. And given how she had almost misjudged them herself, so far, she hadn't seen any real evidence that the Society was anything other than what it claimed to be: a damn near utopian civilization.

Nina was so lost in thought that as soon as they turned onto a new street she bumped into the back of Omoni who had suddenly stopped.

"Oops, sorry I...wow." Nina forgot her words for a moment as she stared at the broad avenue that stretched out before them. It had a gentle uphill slope, stretching for about two blocks, and ending at a huge arch monument about twelve stories high. The shops that lined each side of the boulevard were the same types of eateries and special-ized galleries they had seen all over. The sidewalks were wide, lined with trees, and held many outside dining areas. And there were many hundreds of people walking about.

Like the view from everywhere else in the city, Jupiter was prominent in the sky. The planet's reddish-orange, yellow, and white bands seemed more colorful than any picture she'd ever seen and it was so large that it was hard to accept as real. But what really impressed Nina was how the wide avenue was strategically placed so that the gas giant was positioned centrally to the street and seemed to hang above the arch monument at the end of the block.

"Is that a copy of the Arc de Triomphe?" Omoni asked.

"Yes, but this one is called the Arc de Jove," Fresh Snow-fall on the Lake said.

"So, this street is just like the Champs-Elysees?"

"You're right," Nina said.

"The what?" Manaia asked.

"It's a famous avenue in Paris," Omoni said. "There was this one café Nina and I loved to go to when we were at a conference there."

"God, they had the best crapes," Nina said looking over to the far side of the street even though she knew the café wouldn't be there.

"Didn't they, though."

"Well, I'm sure we can find something just as tasty here," Manaia said. "Let's explore."

THEIR NIGHT ENDED in a local bar called *Oh, God Not Again!* that Fresh Snowfall Lake said was one of her favorites. It wasn't quite a dive bar, but Nina felt it might be what C-humans thought a dive bar was on Earth. There were Netheans, A'Quan, the avian Zythyans, and at least a dozen other C-human races that Nina had never seen before. There were no fabricators floating around, giving out drinks; there was a bar with actual bartenders making drinks by hand. On one side, there were a couple of tables that apparently could adapt for a variety of games. A group of C-humans and one Earther were playing pool; at least, the Earther was trying to show them how to play between their laughter. Another table had two multicolored C-humans playing something that appeared to involve pushing around light beams.

They were all at a table, relaxing after hours of exploring but still too wired to just go back to the hotel. Omoni and Fresh Snowfall on the Lake were drinking martinis; Nina had chosen a Nethean drink that she swore was just mango juice with a kick. Manaia had an Axlon beer that, even though cold, bubbled and churned like a witch's cauldron.

"How did this place get its name?" Nina asked.

"It's named after the bartender-owner," Fresh Snowfall on the Lake said, indicating a Nethean behind the bar laughing at something a patron had just said. "Oh, God, Not Again."

"We learned a little about Nethean names from Endless Green Sky," Omoni started.

"Nina's boyfriend?" Fresh Snowfall on the Lake asked innocently.

"No," and "Yes," Nina and Manaia said simultaneously.

"Sorry," Fresh Snowfall on Lake said. "Dr. Rodriguez's interstellar crush."

"Anyway," Nina said over their laughter, "what's the owner's name short for?"

"Actually, that's his whole name. He was a third child."

That was said so matter-of-factly that Nina paused before she asked, "Is that significant?"

"Oh, Netheans rarely have more than one child," Fresh Snowfall on the Lake said. "Some say it's because we are so nomadic."

"Well, if I had perfect memory of childbirth, I wouldn't have more than one either," Manaia said.

"Some people say that, too." The Nethean smiled. "I guess a good analogy would be how Earthers may react to someone who has, say, eight kids. On Nethea, you occasionally meet somebody who has two kids, but three is rare."

"Can I ask what's your full name?"

"Of course. She Reminds Me of the Fresh Snowfall on the Lake the Morning of Our Honeymoon."

They talked for a while about names, and then the conversation turned to careers and jobs in the Society.

"But what do they do?" Manaia asked.

"I don't understand," Fresh Snowfall on Lake said.

"I mean..." Manaia stopped and stared for a second,

then shook her head as she looked around. "We know the Society doesn't use money, so...the people here aren't working. I guess I'm just wondering what they are doing."

"Oh, I see. Well, some *are* working," Fresh Snowfall on the Lake said. "Hm, how to explain it. You're an anthropologist, and Omoni is an astrobiologist, right?"

"That's right."

"And I've learned that on Earth, depending on your country, your gender, even your skin tone, it affects how much money you make?"

"Unfortunate but, in general, true," Omoni said. "My parents were pushing for me to become a doctor. They didn't believe there would be enough opportunities for me in science as a woman."

"But you were able to?"

"I worked hard, but the job I landed was just as much luck. Things have changed a lot in the last decade, but still, I know a lot of women who haven't been nearly so fortunate."

"So, even though a doctor's job paid more and was more likely to be achievable, you chose your passion," Fresh Snowfall on the Lake said. "Now imagine you don't have to pay rent, buy food, pay for your health, or anything like that; would you quit your job and do something else?"

"No, never."

"Even though you don't need it to survive? You would still do it?"

"I would," Omoni said. "I love my work."

"And so do I." Fresh Snowfall on the Lake took in the people around them with a gesture. "If someone wants to spend their life studying geophysics, or plants, or music, then they can. Right now, I'm hanging out with new friends, but technically I'm also working. I've always been fascinated by the history of other cultures. So, every story you tell me is part of that work. Since I'm with the NHCD it may seem a little more official because I have reports to write, briefings to give, or meetings to attend, but even if I got fired today, I feel the same as you."

"You'd still study Earth."

"Exactly. Even before I started at the NHCD, since the Crash I've studied everything I can about your culture, and that interest won't change anytime soon, whether I'm doing it *officially* or not. Maybe in another decade some new aspect of a different culture will draw my attention, and I might devote myself to that. Time will tell, but that's the point. It's all up to the individual."

"I don't know. I think if people had that type of opportunity on Earth, we wouldn't do anything but sit around and stream TV all day." Nina said.

"I do have some shows I need to catch up on," Manaia mused. "And some chilling"

"You would," Omoni playfully elbowed her.

"But, no, I get it. That's why NHC status last so long," Manaia said. "If overnight our civilization changed to one where you could fabricate anything you desired, we wouldn't know what to do with ourselves. Culturally that would be a disaster, at least for a long while."

"Manaia's right," Fresh Snowfall on the Lake said. "If you grew up seeing your parents work long hours or multiple jobs just to support your family, and then you have to do that too, well, then it's how you expect life to be. So to overnight be able to do whatever you want, may be overwhelming. But remember we grow up that way."

"Manaia and Right are two words I don't think go together—" Nina started.

"Hey!"

"—but I see what you're saying." Nina continued. "Back

home we tell kids they can grow up to be anything they want. But the reality is most people never get their dream job, they settle for what they can tolerate to make a living. But if you grow up knowing you never have to settle, literally not metaphorically. Then you can simply pursue your passion for as long as you like."

"Yes, and that doesn't mean that sometimes I don't like mindless entertainment. But I don't need it to decompress from a stressful job. I'd much rather be here than lying on a couch watching TV. And this is my job."

"That's something," Nina said, looking around. "So, this is like daily life out here?"

"In some places. Most people on Io are involved in working in Sol System somehow, either in building Sahara City, your emergence vessel, or here in Galileo City. Tourism hasn't really started in earnest yet, but that's what everyone else is, mostly."

"And they'll be going to Earth?" Omoni asked.

"Oh, my, no." Fresh Snowfall on the Lake laughed. "Can you imagine thousands of C-humans going down to Earth? Your governments would think you're being invaded. They've accelerated a lot of NHC protocol, but I doubt they'll relax that. No, real tourists to Earth won't be allowed for another generation at least; even then, there will be a twenty- or thirty-year period with limited visas. For now, when Sahara City opens, only C-humans in an official capacity will be allowed to live on Earth. And just like Sahara City is a place for Earthers to become more familiar with wider C-human culture, Galileo City will serve as a place for C-humans to get a better grasp of Earth culture. I think there are only about ten thousand C-humans living here now."

"It seems bigger. This city feels so much more alive than

Sahara City did," Omoni said. "I mean, I know we never got to see much of it, but still."

"It's the people, I think," Manaia said. "Sahara City was vibrant only in the workers building it, but it lacked the feel of a living, breathing city—which only residents can convey. This city is lived in."

"I can see that," Nina said, then looked at Fresh Snowfall on the Lake. "Didn't you tell me Nethean cities are different?"

"Yes, we're very nomadic by nature, so we don't have large cities. We—"

Nina startled when a ring tone chimed in her ear, and an icon showing Endless Green Sky's face appeared in her field of vision.

"Okay, it's going to take me a minute to get used to this," she said. "I got a call," she said to Fresh Snowfall on the Lake's questioning look.

"From who?" Manaia smiled.

"Don't start," Nina said, squinting at the answer icon to take the call.

18

The next morning, Zachariah sat sipping coffee as he took in the view of the horizon from the mayor's office. Galileo City was formed as the major portal hub for travel from the solar system to the rest of the Society. It had a class-three mega-portal that could take travelers five thousand light-years, with another one under construction. And, of course, smaller portals that dealt with traffic up to hundreds of light-years. It would be the major base of operations with the Society until Earth had reached a point where class-one portals could be built on the surface without causing mass panic.

Galileo City was mostly run by Society personnel, but major positions were given to Earthers. A lot more people from Earth would arrive once the emergence vessel *New Gaia* launched, but for now, there was a small contingent. Mayor Nursel Sezer had been a politician in Turkey before she took the post on Io. Her office was on the top floor of one of the central plaza buildings, but this window faced away from the plaza and redwood grove. From this side Zachariah could see Gaia Park, a splash of green juxtaposed next to the harsh, reddish Ionian landscape outside the environmental dome. There was still some considerable debate among Earth's scientists as to why Galileo City was built on Io and not Europa. And this led to a great deal of speculation that Europa's subsurface ocean—which, to Zach's surprise, contained more water than Earth—probably had life, and that the Society was allowing Earth to discover it for themselves, which was a very Society thing to do. Once *New Gaia* launched in six weeks, one of its stops would be a science mission to the icy moon.

"It's taken care of," Mayor Sezer said, having ended her call and coming back over to sit with Zachariah.

"Thank you for that," Zachariah said. Xian Xu had let him know that two of the embassy delegates had decided they couldn't handle the trip and wanted to return to Earth. One was a management office staffer, not a critical position that would delay them leaving. The other was the senior neuroscientist Dr. Kandahar, a position high enough that Zach would have thought anyone who couldn't do it would have been weeded out in the selection process.

"Honestly I'm surprised it's only two," the mayor said, taking a drink of her coffee. "I've already had five myself who went back."

"Really?"

"Yes, for all the testing and questions people endure to get posted, not to mention the Society's screening process, it's not foolproof. I suspect that's part of the reason for the long transition period before you actually ship out to the embassy in the Orion Complex, winnowing out those last few who can't do it. Apparently, there are still some people who get out here, find themselves living, working, and socializing next to...aliens—genetically human or not, still alien by what we on Earth have called it—and these people realize they can't handle it. It's just too..." She trailed off, at a loss for the word.

"Alien," Zachariah added after a moment.

"Yeah." She smiled.

"So, you believe there will still be more people in the embassy who will decide they want to go back?"

"Absolutely," she answered. "I think—and this is just personal observation, mind you, but I think some of the people who aren't accustomed to dealing with a lot of... diverse types of groups find it harder to adjust."

Zachariah nodded. She was a born politician, carefully skating around current buzzwords and not directly insulting anyone. Not that he hadn't said something similar to the UN before he was chosen as ambassador. "It's going to take a lot of adjustment for all of us."

"Honestly, I think with a little time, most people will be able to adapt," she said. "It was strange at first, but working with them, more often than not, I see similarities now rather than differences."

Zach raised his cup to her. "Here's to hoping we can all learn that attitude."

ZACHARIAH MOVED around the elevated outdoor patio and mingled with the various C-human officials and Earther delegates. While the two days they were scheduled to be in Galileo City were packed with functions, nothing was official. In a sense, the whole city was serving as a convention center with numerous activities planned that allowed all the Earth Embassy delegates the opportunity to pick whatever interested them and pursue it. There were tours of the hospital and ship garden, sports events, food tasting and winetasting, meditation retreats, museum shows, and a dozen other things all designed to allow the Earthers to get comfortable being in a city not on Earth and surrounded by aliens.

As casual as things were, Zachariah knew everything was being closely monitored. The fact that two of his people had already opted to go back to Earth showed him that this was a necessary stage to their trip. Although he wasn't sure if only a couple of days would be enough, he felt confident that after a few months of living on Sapher, most would adjust to a new normal.

"Look at that," Achut Rai, the Earth Arts consul, said, pointing outside the clear city dome.

Zachariah and the others he was talking to turned to see plumes of erupting volcanoes in the far distance across the reddish-orange landscape.

"I feel like I'm looking back in time at some ancient Earth epoch, before life bloomed," Achut said.

"Or some future time if we don't clean up our mess," Dr. Eun Jeong Park, the Earth Science consul, said.

"After all this, I really don't think the Society will let our environment down," Achut said. He was a famous poet and painter from Nepal. Zachariah felt like the consul romanticized the Society a little too much.

"They will not save it, either," Dr. Park said.

"They just saved that town from wildfires last month," Achut said. "And they stopped that tsunami that would've devastated Indonesia last year."

"They stepped in to save lives in imminent danger from a natural disaster, Consul Rai," Zachariah said. "That's a little different."

"Exactly," Dr. Park agreed. "They've made it quite clear that we have the technological means to fix our own environment if we really want to. And that if we don't do it ourselves, it won't really mean anything."

The Earth Arts consul still looked a little skeptical and gave a noncommittal reply.

Zachariah could understand his reticence, given how much the Society had done for Earth, especially in terms of medicine. But Zachariah was well aware that they always pushed Earth to solve its own disputes and problems. After the Crash, things had been crazy, but when Earth realized invasion wasn't an imminent threat, the most powerful nations tried to take point in speaking for Earth, and the disputes, sometimes physical, had turned into a year of being on the brink of war with each other. In all that time, the Society only communicated with Earth from orbit, and whatever was said was sent to all governments. Back then, Netheans and A'Quan were the only two races ever seen, although the Society said there were many C-human races.

Then some of the poorer nations started requesting help directly from the Society. A drought was devastating the Sudan, and an outbreak of a new coronavirus happened in Laos. That was when the Society started sending down medical supplies. And that was when a Russian sub launched its first nuke. Before it could hit the Society ship, it vanished and appeared outside a Russian military base, deactivated, along with the sub that had launched it. That was when Earth first truly understood how much more advanced the Society was. And it generally marked the end of The Long Year and when nations realized they needed to stand together to confront the problem. It was also when the Society decided to allow people from Earth to go out to see things firsthand as envoys and to form an embassy.

Earth Embassy was almost five years in the making. Its creation was guided by the restructuring of the United

Nations that had taken place since the Crash. Before, each nation's leaders chose their ambassadors to the UN. But as countries agreed to give the UN more authority and a greater role in Earth's future, each nation's ambassadors were chosen by a national vote, like heads of state. Then all the elected UN ambassadors chose from amongst themselves the Secretary-General and Earth's first ambassador to the Society.

The next few years saw the disappearance of most diseases on Earth, as country after country asked for help. Now, almost at the sixth anniversary of the day the bioship crashed, Earth would have an official presence in the Society.

"Mr. Ambassador, we have a problem," Last Rain in Autumn said.

The voice was so clear that Zachariah half-turned around looking for her before he realized it was coming through the ear component of his exso.

"Envoy Last Rain in Autumn?" he asked while silently motioning for the group he was speaking with to give him a moment.

"Sorry to cut you short, sir," Last Rain in Autumn said. "But the deputy chief and I need to brief you on an important issue that just came up."

19

Nina stood outside the front of the hotel and watched the egg-shaped vehicle descend to the ground before her. Last night, when Endless Green Sky had called—to the delight of her friends—he reminded Nina that before they left Earth, he had said he wanted to show her something on Io, so they made plans for him to pick her up this afternoon. This wasn't quite what she had been expecting. The ovoid vehicle had a transparent upper half while the rest was an opaque porcelain-like shell. It came to rest in front of her, hovering about half a foot above the ground, then its side dilated revealing the interior.

"Good afternoon," Endless Green Sky said from one of the two seats inside.

"Hey," she said, climbing in. The interior was similar in size to a two-door car, but the seats were more like high-class recliners. Once she sat down, its petal-like shape molded to fit her body.

She watched as the vehicle rose smoothly into the air. The part of the car that was opaque from the outside was see-through from the inside. She gripped the seat tightly for a moment as the city stretched out beneath her, and she had the feeling of flying in a comfortable chair. They were still within the environment dome and had an amazing view of the city. The skyscrapers, parks, and plazas were all laid out in a beautiful pattern that seemed to juxtapose nicely with the barren, volcanic landscape outside the dome. It took a moment before Nina noticed Endless Green Sky wasn't using any hand controls to steer the car; when she asked about that, he said he was doing it virtually with his bioweb. After a short flight, their vehicle descended toward a building at the base of the city's dome. A large section of the building's wall dilated, and the vehicle glided into a well-lit tunnel. It reminded Nina of the drive-through carwashes she used to love to go to with her dad.

"The car is a self-contained environment," Endless Green Sky said, turning to her. "But it's still standard to wear a voidskin when going out on the surface."

"Ahhhhh, what skin?" Nina asked.

Endless Green Sky smiled and explained what the environmental suit was and how it worked. She listened but also wondered where she was going to change. He told her to sit back and relax. When she did, the seat itself seemed to shed a layer that flowed around her body. She was too amazed to be scared as the voidskin finished forming around her head, and she looked to see the same happening to Endless Green Sky. She touched her face slowly. She knew her head was enclosed in the suit, but it was completely transparent from the neck up, with only the slightest shimmer of reflected light showing its outline.

"Ready to see Io?" he asked as the vehicle approached the end of the tunnel.

"Heck, yeah," she said.

The wall in front of them dilated, leaving only the shimmer of the dome, which they passed through as they slid out onto Io's surface.

THE OVOID VEHICLE sped across the harsh yellow-orange landscape of Io a meter above its surface. The view of the surrounding moon was both awe-inspiring and intimidating. Manaia had joked that who would have thought hell could be beautiful, but she wasn't far off the mark. As bleak as the landscape looked, the ever-different colors of the terrain as it transitioned between yellow, rust, white, black, and orange-red made it look like something out of a painting. She could see at least two volcanoes on the horizon spewing sulfur and sulfur dioxide hundreds of miles into the thin Ionian air. Even closer, there was a caldera erupting lava in a half-mile-long vertical sheet. It was a fearsome sight but beautiful all the same. The horizon was closer than on Earth because of Io's small size, which made it hard for Nina to get her bearings. She could not tell how fast they were going but was sure it was well over one hundred miles per hour.

"That's where we're going," Endless Green Sky said, pointing to something that started as a bump on the horizon but rose higher and higher as they got closer.

"What's there?" she asked, realizing it was another volcano.

"There's an e-kite race," he said. "The E stands for eruption. I guess you would classify it more as an extreme sport. It's quite dangerous, actually, since the kiters don't use regular voidskins for protection, but that's the appeal for some people."

"You've never done it?"

"No, never. Medicine is more than exciting enough for me. Anyway, it's more the aftereffects of the eruption that I thought you might enjoy."

"What happens after?"

"We go skiing."

"Skiing?" she asked, casting him a skeptical glance. Outside the window on his side she could see another volcano spewing lava into the air. "On a moon full of volcanoes?"

"Yeah," he said matter-of-factly. "Unless you prefer lava-boarding, but I figure that may be a little much for a beginner. I got the idea when I saw the picture of your cousins skiing and thought you might enjoy this.

"Are you messing with me again?" She gave him a look.

"Ha, no, I swear." He held his right hand to form a circle with his fingers, like he was holding a can, and put his hand against the center of his chest, a gesture she recalled him doing at the reception.

"Oh." Nina blinked as a small icon and text appeared in her field of vision, highlighting his hand gesture: it read that it was the equivalent of an Earther crossing their heart.

"You okay?" he asked.

"Yeah," she said. "I still get surprised when my exso interprets body language signals as well as speech. But back to skiing. Where's the snow?"

He chuckled like a kid with a secret he was dying to tell. "You'll see."

Nina was about to give him crap for that when another glance outside took her breath away. The landscape they were flying over had changed significantly; it was mostly black with glowing cracks. It reminded her of the flagstone patio her dad and uncle had laid out in their backyard when she was young, that age where kids still think working with their parents is fun. Irregular black sections of the surface, larger than their vehicle, were separated by glowing jagged lines; air above the surface undulated from the heat, but it wasn't until bright orange-white bubbles forced their way out of the cracks that she realized their aircar was flying over a lake—a lake of lava.

She stared at the slowly undulating surface that stretched into the distance until data tags popped up in her exso, telling her it was over three miles wide. Off to the side she could see a solid shelf of rock, as wide as a city block, that sat in the lake like an island.

The car swerved suddenly to avoid a particularly large series of lava bubbles. Nina's heart thumped in her chest, but then they were past it and speeding on.

"Amazing, isn't it?" Endless Green Sky asked. "Sights like these always make me feel in awe of creation."

"I remember watching some stuff like this on the news when I was a kid and one of Hawaii's volcanoes erupted, but it wasn't this big." Nina then looked at him. "I thought Netheans weren't religious."

"Huh? Oh, we're not. I meant as in *created by nature*," Endless Green Sky said. "We tend to live in less urbanized areas, so I guess we appreciate nature a little more than some. Are you religious?"

"Kinda, but not really. I don't know."

Endless Green Sky glanced at her with a questioning look.

"I guess most Americans, most Earthers probably, are religious. But sometimes you just... Most people just go through a point in their adult life when they aren't neces-sarily practicing. You might only go to church a few times a year. It's not even that you don't believe; you just figure...you got time."

She paused for a moment, thinking of the past. "I grew up religious, but after my grandmother got sick, it was never the same for me."

"I didn't mean to bring out painful memories," he said.

"No, that's fine; it's been years." It had been hard for her as a young woman to see herself forgotten by someone she loved. But she did her best to turn it into something positive by becoming a neurologist and helping others.

"She had Alzheimer's, but she passed away before the Crash."

"I'm sorry to hear that."

"The hardest part for me was when she started to think I was my mom," Nina said. "Or sometimes she would think my mom and I were her younger sisters. Then one day, it occurred to me that I...that I no longer existed. Not to her, at least." The sound of fabric scrunching made Nina release her tightening grip on the seat. "Everything we had together, my whole life with her was just gone. Forgotten. Like it had never been."

Endless Green Sky looked at her, the compassion clear on his face. "I can't imagine what that must've been like."

Nina watched the landscape slide by outside, lost in thought. "I guess Netheans never have to worry about anything like that, huh?"

"Not...specifically, no," Endless Green Sky said. Something in his tone of voice told Nina there was more to it.

"I didn't mean to come across as callous," she said.

"No. No, it's not that," he said. "Your question just got me thinking about my own family. There are some mental issues we don't have a real cure for, even with our advanced technology."

"I hadn't even considered that. With you-all's memory, forgetting things must be even worse."

"It's the opposite problem actually. Remembering too much."

"I'm not sure I understand."

"It's only Nethean's innate curiosity for new things that keeps us from living solely in our memories. It's like..." Endless Green Sky paused and thought for a moment as the capsule glided across the hellish landscape. "Think of the first time you had your favorite food."

"Favorite food?"

"Yes, and not just the taste but every part of the experience. The surprise you felt when you had the first bite, the amazement of a flavor you've never experienced, the satisfaction as you chew, the contentment of the aftertaste, the anticipation of the next spoonful.

"Now imagine you can relive that exact moment whenever you want—the exact same feeling you had while doing it—as often as you want, just by thinking. That can be tempting to do all the time. And of course it applies to all experiences. The feeling of holding your newborn child for the first time, that winning score you made in the last minutes of the game, the first time you fell in love, the best orgasm you ever had, the best laugh you ever had, the most exciting night out with friends, everything. Every moment you can recall and experience over and over in perfect detail just like it's happening then."

"It would make it hard to live in the present," Nina said. "I know some people who would do nothing but live in the past."

"Exactly," Endless Green Sky said. "We call it reliving syndrome. Where a person relives past memories more and more instead of living in the present moment. In the most severe cases these people stop eating and drinking in the day-to-day world as they spend all of their time reliving the past. Technology can keep their bodies alive, of course, but they no longer really live in the now. To their families they are gone."

"Oh no, and this happened to your family?"

"My aunt," he said. "She lost her son and husband in a tragic accident when I was a kid. At first she just relived her memories of them occasionally. And then more and more until to her living with them in memory was better than living without them in the real world. And one day she just...never came back to the present."

"I'm so sorry to hear that," Nina said reaching over and squeezing his hand. "I don't even know how to process that. It's so different yet so similar in what the families go through."

"It is. Our civilization has progressed so far and achieved so much," he said. "But sometimes it's those little things that affect the individual that matter most."

They drove on for a little while in silence, then Endless Green Sky squeezed her hand back, and she realized she was still holding his. "I wish... I wish we had been able to help your grandma."

"You know, I think that's what my mom's main problem with the Society is. That you didn't arrive sooner." Nina turned toward him in her seat. Their hands came apart, but there was still a companionable closeness to the moment. "She's not stupid; my mom's one of the strongest women I know. She knows how silly it is to blame the Society for that. And that makes her upset with herself for thinking like that, which just comes out as more anger against the Society. God, the arguments we used to have when I first told her I was accepted."

"She better with you being out here now?"

Nina stared at the huge form of Jupiter in the sky as they

continued to speed across the alien landscape of Io. "She's getting better, but she's still more traditional than her mom was. My grandmother had always encouraged me to follow my passion and make the most of whatever life I chose. And this is my dream. Being out here, learning. Knowing I can take that knowledge back to help others who may be going through things like I did."

"I didn't know your grandmother, obviously, but it seems to me like she would be proud of all you've accomplished."

"I like to think so."

AS THEY GOT CLOSER, Nina could see that there were actually two volcanoes within close proximity to each other. They stopped about a mile from the base of the largest volcano, on a small hill that gave them a clear view to the close horizon. There were a few dozen or so other vehicles parked there, floating a couple of feet above the ground. Some people were sitting inside, while others stood around outside in voidskins, talking and looking up at the volcano. Nina realized that the background hum she was hearing over her exso was a type of community channel and specific voices became clear if she looked at a particular group. To Nina it felt like a scene from some old film where the young people were at a drive-in movie. As Endless Green Sky lowered the car to park, she held back a laugh, imagining him yawning—stretching his arms up, then slowly dropping one down around her shoulders.

"What's so funny?"

"Um...oh, nothing. Just thinking of an old movie I saw."

"Uh-huh." He glanced at her questioningly, and she simply shrugged innocently.

Endless Green Sky returned her smile and nodded

outside. "Do you want to watch from outside? The view isn't any better, but psychologically, you feel closer to the action."

"Sure."

The wall of the vehicle seemed to melt open, and her chair simultaneously lowered to the ground and stretched out, adjusting her to a standing position.

"Take it slow," he warned, his voice sounding in her exso. "The change in gravity can be disconcerting when you're not used to it."

"God, you're as bad as my mom," Nina joked as she stepped off the footpad onto the surface of Io—and immediately fell forward. Outside the car's grav field, Io's gravity, which was one-fifths of Earth, embraced her. She froze for a second as her body lurched forward, just a little too slow to seem real, then she panicked and jammed her foot forward, which was way too much force as it caused her to bounce a few feet to her right. Her arms pinwheeled in an effort to keep balance. She overcompensated, stumble-bounced again, tripped on a rock, and fell on her face, a fall which took enough seconds in the low gravity for her to feel thoroughly embarrassed before she hit the ground and bounced again, finally coming to rest another two feet away, lying in the slowly drifting cloud of yellow sulfur dust she had created.

A few of the people outside were looking at her smiling; one waved, but nobody really laughed.

"You were saying?"

Nina looked up to see Endless Green Sky smiling over her and holding his hands up like a camera. He made a clicking sound. "I'll be sure to send that video to your cousins."

"Don't you dare!" She laughed, taking his arm as he helped her up. She seemed to float for a second before she got her feet firmly planted. He laughed as she took another step that almost sent her flying again, but she grabbed him at the last second.

"Might be worth it." He smiled, helping to steady her and, she noticed, keeping his arm around her even after she was stable.

"There are a lot of people here," she observed. "Is this a popular sport across the Society? What'd you call it, eruption kiting?"

"An e-kite race. It's popular on volcanically active planetary bodies, but it's not a type of spectator sport that's popular on most worlds."

They started walking toward the groups of people. Endless Green Sky's arm slowly came from around Nina as they moved, but they were still comfortably close as she learned how to walk. Io was just a little larger and more massive than Earth's moon, so the gravity was similar. Her exso showed her that there, she only weighed about twenty-three pounds, compared to about one hundred and thirty on Earth. Nina had expected to wobble and bounce around like in the old videos she had always seen of astronauts on the moon, but the voidskin was more like outerwear than the Michelin Man look of old NASA suits, giving her less mass and a greater range of movement. After a few tries— feeling like she was slow-motion jumping with each step— she started to get the hang of it.

She would step in and push forward slightly with her foot and glide a moment before taking another step and repeating the process. She remembered the feeling of accomplishment she had had that first time her dad had let go of the handlebars and she was able to keep going on a bike without falling. It had that same childlike wonder making her grin from ear to ear.

"This is amazing," she said, glancing over at Endless Green Sky, who was hovering along beside her using the voidskin's propulsion to glide along. "Hey, that's cheating!"

He smiled. "I believe you have a saying: you have to learn to walk before you can fly."

Another voice came over her exso. "In other words, he's saying you already walk better than he does, so he doesn't want to embarrass himself."

Nina looked up to see they were approaching three C-humans, two women and a man. The women were Nethean like Endless Green Sky, their light-purple skin enhancing the yellowish highlights of the landscape reflecting on their faceplates. The man was tall, like a pro basketball player seven-feetish tall, and green.

"Don't give away all my secrets," Endless Green Sky said, landing in front of the Nethean and touching his palm to hers.

"Dr. Rodriguez, may I introduce some of my friends," Endless Green Sky said giving names she promptly forgot.

"This must all be a little overwhelming," the woman who had spoken said.

"A bit," Nina confessed. "Even with all I've seen, it's still a little hard to process that I'm here standing on one of Jupiter's moons talking to...uh."

"Aliens?" The woman smiled. "Don't worry; that's normal for any NHC person. It will pass, especially for a doctor. Once you get used to the science of studying C-human brains, you'll see."

"How did you know what I do?"

"The Nexus, of course."

Before Nina could respond, there was a murmur of excitement that visibly moved through the onlookers. Then everyone's attention turned to the volcano.

"Almost time now," the green man said.

"What's happening?" Nina asked Endless Green Sky.

"We made it just in time. The volcano is about to erupt," Endless Green Sky responded, then caught himself. "I'm sorry; tell your suit you want to monitor the race, and whatever you focus on will be zoomed in."

"Okay." She felt a little silly talking to her clothes, but oh, well. "Suit. Uh... I want to watch the race."

"Acknowledged," the voice of her suit said, and immediately a number of overlays popped up in her exso's field of vision. Statistical info on the volcano, icons showing the players around the top, graphs showing a buildup of pressure within the volcano and estimated time of eruption. Anything she focused on came to the forefront. Even the onlookers had markers that provided community tags if she looked at them. It was a bit overwhelming.

"Is this what the world looks like to you?" she asked with mild trepidation. She knew to fully be able to do her job and experience the Society, she was going to have to get a bioweb eventually. It wasn't mandatory—the selectors on Earth had made that clear—though it would make things a lot easier. But if it meant this constant barrage of data before her eyes, she wasn't sure she wanted to get used to that.

Endless Green Sky looked at her for a second as he figured out what she was talking about. "Oh, no, nothing so crude. The interface is made for someone only accessing data visually, similar to your exso. With a bioweb, I can incorporate graphics if I want, but think of it more as remembering something you know extremely well. The information is just there when you want it."

Nina found that when she focused on the icons hovering outside the rim of the volcano, her sight zoomed in to show they were dozens of C-humans, the kiters. Then the images from the kiter's own suits and the satellites in orbit above incorporated to form an image for her as if she was standing level with them and watching. Floating in the air, above the volcano, high above the kiters, were artificial rings of various sizes and other shapes like spirals and spheres. They encircled the volcano but were placed in no discernible pattern that Nina could recognize. Data on her faceplate showed a few were hundreds of meters above the rim, and when she focused, the image zoomed in to show shapes as far as ten miles above the volcano. These floating objects were also around the other smaller volcano and the areas between the two.

Each kiter had a line going from their voidskin to the rim of the volcano. When Nina queried that, schematics popped up on her screen, showing the lines were connected to a membrane of material that stretched across the entire mouth of the volcano.

The kiters were making final checks on their equipment. Gossamer-thin wings of some fabric spread out from their forms, then retracted. Nina noticed an icon asking her if she wanted to join the group channel. When she accepted, she could hear everybody on the hill, not just Endless Green Sky and his friends. It wasn't overwhelming, really no different than if she had been standing outside with a group of people and could hear various conversations.

"It's about to start," Endless Green Sky said; almost at the same time, a chime sounded in her ear.

Then the volcano erupted.

The membrane covering was pushed upward as the expulsion of gases and molten lava emerged from the vent at over fifteen hundred miles an hour. Nina's data tags showed her that on Earth, even the most violent volcanoes had eruption speeds of only two hundred miles an hour.

The kiters were snatched up into the Ionian sky, pulled along by the gossamer lines attached to the cover. It was a testament to Society materials technology that the membrane wasn't vaporized instantly. As it slowly burned away, the kiters released their lines before their momentum could carry them into the rising plume.

Nina's view zoomed in to see the kiters' thermal wings turn on as they started to spiral around the violent ejecta. The volcano's plume was already at a hundred and forty miles and still rising. One group of kiters continued straight up, flying around the ejecta, dodging sprays of lava and the hovering geometric obstacles. Another group of kiters peeled off toward the other volcano, letting their suit's absorbed thermal energy propel them as they twisted and turned, flying through the aerial rings and around the solid obstacles that hovered in the sky between the two volcanoes.

Then the second volcano erupted, and the kiters flew close enough that their voidskins glowed from the heat. The crowd clapped and cheered at the aerial acrobatics. One kiter's wing clipped a ring and it cut off. Nina caught her breath as he started falling, but his suit's EM field cut on, and he glided to the ground, safe but disqualified. The kiters circled the second volcano plume and came back, again dodging around the original obstacle course. It wasn't a race; kiters were simply having fun and showing off their moves.

Nina was so focused on watching the show that it took her a moment to register the flakes that were starting to fall around their group on the hill. She turned to Endless Green Sky in open-mouthed awe as the white snow fell from the sky. Jupiter was fully above the horizon, dominating the star-filled sky. That, plus her standing with a group of aliens as the snow fell across the yellow-red landscape, gave everything a magical quality. She held her hand out and watched the snow drift onto her palm.

"Told you." Endless Green Sky had his usual big smile on his face.

"I don't understand," she finally managed to say. "How..."

"It's not actually water ice like on Earth," he said. "When the hot sulfur dioxide gas released from those volcanic vents hits the cold vacuum of space, it crystallizes into these white 'snowflakes' as it falls back down to the surface. Here, it won't get nearly deep or compact enough to ski, but with a little high-tech cheating, we can—"

The rest of what Endless Green Sky was going to say was cut off by a scream. Nina looked up and saw two kiters narrowly miss each other as they tried to avoid a piece of ejecta. The near miss sent one of the kiters out of control, and he slammed into two other kiters. The force of their impact sent one of them, she couldn't tell which, into the volcano's eruption. The kiter managed to avoid most of it, but some of the high-speed ejecta hit his outstretched arm, destroying the thermal wing, and his arm, in the process. The group watched in horror as the kiter's body was violently thrown up and outward, crashing through one of the hovering rings in a shower of sparks.

The kiter's limp body fell to the surface with the wreckage of the ring. His EM field came on, and the body slowed, then it cut off, and the kiter fell to the surface below, a couple hundred meters away from them.

Endless Green Sky was already flying down the slope as Nina started running forward. She moved in great antelope-like strides in the low gravity as she covered the distance. Several other C-humans flew past her in their voidskins, but she didn't bother to try to figure out how. She just kept running to where the body lay.

She gasped in shock as she reached the spot where he had fallen and saw the broken body of the C-human. Nina unconsciously raised her hands to her mouth but was stopped short when they banged into her faceplate, causing her to take a surprised step back. The kiter's suit was blackened and charred, like burnt meat. Most of his left arm was missing, one foot was attached more by suit fabric than tendons, and the two remaining limbs were twisted at odd angles.

Endless Green Sky was kneeling next to him, running his hands over his chest plate as if he could feel something. "His kite suit sealed off the amputations and stopped the bleeding, but he has massive internal trauma."

"I'll help you carry him to the car," Nina said, even though she knew moving him would be dangerous. Waiting for a ship to fly out there would take too long; time was what he needed. She had no doubt that Society medicine could cure him.

"No need, I called for an emergency portal," he said still examining the kiter. "We should have transport any second now."

Before Nina could respond, the air around them began to shimmer and warp. For a split second, it seemed she was seeing the landscape through some type of twisted glass; then she was looking at the inside of a medical room.

She had no idea they could open a portal without some type of physical door structure.

The doctors inside were prepping a table. Two spheres floated over and came to a stop, hovering over the injured C-human, one at his head and one at his feet. Then the kiter was slowly floated into the air and moved over to the bed, where his voidskin begin to melt off him and parts of the bed molded over to cover the worst injuries. Endless Green Sky stepped over to a wall mount, and his suit began to dissolve from around him, also. Nina just stood there for a moment, unsure what to do. This was happening.

"Let's get you out of that," another C-human said, leading Nina to another alcove. She stepped in and felt a tingle of energy as the voidskin slid from her form.

The area of the room where the kiter lay on the surgery table was behind a slight shimmer in the air. Some type of sterilization field, Nina guessed. Endless Green Sky finished getting prepped, a type of medical skin forming around his clothes, and stepped through the screen.

The yellow furred C-human nurse with Nina led her into an adjoining room. At first, she thought there was a window looking into the surgery room, but she realized the viewing angle was too high for that. This was a wall-sized screen showing a video of the operation from a slightly elevated view.

Nina watched, enraptured—it wasn't like any surgery she had ever seen. Endless Green Sky and the other two doctors worked over the injured man, sometimes pointing where a floating tool should go, sometimes moving their hands, sometimes just standing and looking. She knew now that much of the data they used was directly implanted in their minds. Even most of their communication was in the Nexus, although a doctor would occasionally say something out loud. She made the decision right then that she would get the bioweb implant; there was no way she would be able to be an effective doctor in this new world without one.

The ability to directly image real-time scans of the patient's body and coordinate with the rest of the team was unparalleled. She was envisioning a time when people on

Earth didn't have to die from anything but old age. For all she knew, the Society already had life-extension tech but just hadn't shared it yet.

The kiter's partially severed foot was reattached in a gel case, as was the stump of his arm. Spheres like the one Endless Green Sky had used when he saved Envoy n'Dala on Earth floated around, providing tools, shots, and so on when requested. In one larger transparent sphere she saw what looked like a lung being grown at an exponential rate. Part of the C-human's chest had been cut open, and when Nina focused on that area, the image zoomed in, and she could see Endless Green Sky reattaching veins and sealing ruptured organs. Data scrolled across her field of vision, listing drugs being released into the patient and showing the status of knitting bones. Another doctor operated on the kiter's neck where new nerve clusters were being grown in situ; the third doctor was using a noninvasive probe on the kiter's cranium.

Nina had only doubted once that the man could be saved, and that was when they had first seen the accident, far away from any help. She should have known better. On Earth, the kiter would've been dead already, but there, in a Society facility, she could only watch and imagine the day she would be able to save people like this. She felt ashamed of, and pity for, those doctors and hate groups on Earth who were so reluctant to see the truth. She knew kids would never have to grow up seeing their grandparents suffer. She knew a new age of wonder was happening, and she was a living part of it. The Society was the best thing to ever happen to Earth.

Then reality set in.

Endless Green Sky was becoming agitated. He and the other doctors were talking quickly and picking up the pace of their work. The bed under the kiter glowed in areas, while a couple of spheres zipped around, directing beams of light at the body. There was a brief flurry of activity for a minute, all three doctors working together like it had been choreographed, then suddenly they all stopped working at the same time. Endless Green Sky stepped back, his arms covered in pink blood up to his elbows. He looked defeated. The C-human on the table was no longer breathing, the sphere covering his face floated away, and there was a moment of stunned silence in the room before it was pierced by a woman's scream.

An orange-skinned woman with yellow hair dropped to her knees, crying uncontrollably. A couple of nurses moved to help her.

Endless Green Sky's eyes seemed to catch the camera for a moment, and Nina wondered if he could see her. As alien as he was—purple skin, bone ridges, different facial struc-ture—in that moment he looked as stunned and alone as any doctor who had lost a patient. The continuing screams and sobs of the woman didn't bring to mind spaceships, alien science, or other planets, just that deep, cavernous grief that comes from losing someone you love. And it finally hit Nina that for all their technological advances, truly different-color skins, different biologies and cultures, for all of that they were still only human. Cousins.

Nina started to leave the observation room, not fully sure if she should talk to Endless Green Sky or not, but she stopped short when she noticed the words written on the door. Not what they said, but the fact that some of the black letters were colored! Only then did she realize she also had a headache—had for a while—which she had been ignoring in all the excitement. Her hand shook noticeably as she gestured her exso off, to be sure it wasn't some graphic. No. Some of the text was still colored.

She was having another synesthesia episode like back on Earth. That could only mean her memories were copied. Again. Even though the scans on the ship hadn't shown anything, there was no doubting what she was experiencing now. She had been right all along. Had he done it on the ride out? Or maybe it happened last night exploring the city with Fresh Snowfall on the Lake? Her heart sank with what she knew she had to do.

Nina didn't even remember making the call until she heard Aleksei's voice in her ear. "Consul Dr. Romashenko," she said in a daze. "We have to talk."

20

Zachariah, his aide Peter, and a Nethean escort exited the portal on the top floor of the building where he had been provided temporary offices. It was a little disconcerting to think he was on the other side of the city with just one step from the museum he had been in moments before, but he focused on the issue at hand. Zachariah thanked the Nethean. She and Peter stayed in the outer office as he entered his main room.

Deputy Chief Xian Xu was already inside, talking to a tall, orange C-human. Very tall; she must have been seven feet. Zachariah couldn't remember her races name but his momentary focus on her brought up ID tags in his exso's field of vision. The C-human was a Ta Wei, one of the amphibious races. Naturally hairless, with a slightly elongated face, she wore a type of partially sheer cassock with a more concealing wrap underneath around her waist.

"Mr. Ambassador, good, you're here," Xian said. "This is Investigator K'lalaki of the Protectorate Metatech Division. She and her partner will be joining us for this meeting."

Zachariah greeted the agent and looked around. "Where's Last Rain in Autumn?"

"I'm here, sir." An image of the purple envoy appeared in the room next to him.

Zachariah caught himself before he cursed in surprise. The image wasn't a hologram in the air but directly generated by his exso on his lenses. Other figures appeared next to Last Rain in Autumn, and the partially rendered background suggested they were all in a medical room somewhere. He believed the A'Quan was the same doctor he had met when he visited n'Dala on Earth. He recognized Dr. Rodriguez easily. Her image was seated on a medical table, and a worried-looking Aleksei was standing next to her, along with an Earther man Zachariah thought was of Aboriginal descent.

"Envoy. Consul Dr. Romashenko." Zachariah nodded to their images.

"Mr. Ambassador," Last Rain in Autumn said. "I believe you met Dr. sa'Xeen on Earth. And this is Ditec Jiemba Smith of the Protectorate Metatech Division, who will also be stationed at Earth Embassy."

Zachariah greeted each of them. His exso pulled up minimal ID tags that floated in the air next to them.

"Mr. Ambassador," Xian started. "Just a little while ago, Consul Dr. Romashenko notified me that Dr. Rodriguez may have been the victim of...a mental assault."

"A mental..." Zachariah glanced bewildered at the image. "Explain that."

"Mr. Ambassador," Aleksei began. "You know that a lot of Society technology involves interacting with the brain. We've always known that different C-human races can experience subtle side effects, and over the past few years of research, we have noticed certain residual effects in Earthers, in limited cases."

"What kind of effects?" Zachariah asked.

"Synesthesia, for one," Aleksei said, giving Zachariah a brief explanation of what it was.

"And you believe this happened to you, Dr. Rodriguez?" Zachariah asked.

"Yes," she answered slowly, but her voice was certain. She glanced at Aleksei before she continued. "Right after the reception party. Possibly once before."

"That was four days ago!" Zachariah said, shocked. "And you just now reported it?"

"Mr. Ambassador." Aleksei spoke up. "This isn't as simple as it sounds. In fact, if it had happened to anyone but Nina or a couple of others, it probably wouldn't have even been noticed."

"Which isn't an excuse," Zachariah said. "And all the more reason it should have been reported."

Aleksei started to speak again, but Nina put her hand on his arm to quiet him. Her crystal-clear image looked at Zachariah, not challengingly but honestly. "Ambassador Isaacs, you're right. I should've reported it when it happened, even though I wasn't sure. But...well, honestly, sir, I thought about what would happen if the person living their fifteen minutes of fame for helping save a C-human suddenly came forward and accused them of reading her mind. I just... I just felt I needed to be one hundred percent certain."

"Reporting it to your superiors and posting about it online are very different," Zachariah said, even though he found he could understand her logic. The political fallout from this would be bad, but the most serious implications were even more frightening.

"Let's table that for a moment," he said, looking at the images of the different people. "What's the endgame here? What were they trying to achieve? And why Dr. Rodriguez?"

"They were greedy." Jiemba spoke for the first time.

Last Rain in Autumn's image gave him a look and turned to Zachariah. "Ambassador Isaacs, you are aware that we monitor UHCs, uncontacted human cultures, to make sure their natural development is not influenced by the Society."

"I'm aware that's what we've been told, yes." Zachariah wasn't trying to be rude, but they hadn't even left the solar system yet and this was the second disturbing thing he was finding out about the Society.

Last Rain in Autumn nodded her understanding of what he said, and then she continued. "We monitor, but we don't study or record. Our belief is that UHCs have the right to privacy without their neighbors spying on them. We also scramble any signals that come out of UHC systems."

"To hide us?" Xian asked.

"No, UHC locations are all easily accessed in the Nexus so citizens can avoid them. We scramble..." Last Rain in Autumn seemed to search for the right words. "When you live in a society without the same economic drive as...less-developed planets, wealth and status take on different concepts."

"Like what, exactly?" Xian asked.

"They have a hard-on for our TV," Jiemba said, then shrugged at his partner's look. "Well, it's true."

"One example is entertainment," Last Rain in Autumn said. "Gathering the entertainment media of an uncontacted human culture is highly illegal. This has given rise to people known as story brokers, who deal in this."

"And they sell these stories?" Zachariah asked.

"Not sell, sir, no, in a post-scarcity civilization the idea of economy changes. These stories are shared freely between the collectors who follow such things. It's more the acknowledgment that they were the first to get it that matters to them."

"But Earth is no longer under UHC status," Xian said.

"True, and when a new human culture enters the Society, their entertainment is highly popular to C-human cultures that enjoy similar taste. Your stories, music, movies, et cetera. Once a planet receives NHC status, any Society citizen can access some of its output."

"But personal stories are still restricted." Investigator K'lalaki joined in. The tall orange C-human looked from Xian to Zachariah. "Naturally, Earthers' personal views will be seen more and more as your embassy, emergence vessel, and envoys become more active in the Society. But for now, that type of personal entertainment from Earth is rare, so it's still highly sought after by people who deal in these types of things."

"And they wanted Dr. Rodriguez's memories about the attack." Zachariah filled in the blanks.

"Exactly," K'lalaki said. "The attack was seen throughout the Nexus, by tens of billions of people, but it was seen through the experience of the C-humans there. And the aftermath can easily be followed in the various news communities on the Nexus, but no Earther with a bioweb was present, so that type of firsthand experience by a local was missing."

Zachariah thought it was a little morbid to need to feel the emotional state of victims, but he knew he couldn't count the number of times he had seen some video go viral because it captured a tragic attack.

"Considering the amount of time it would take one of their agents to get involved with the NHCD, it was sloppy to try so early," Last Rain in Autumn said. "It's most likely just coincidence that the agent was able to meet her. But the attack at the station and Nina's involvement made her too tempting a target to pass up."

"Copying her experience would be more impactful if done quickly instead of waiting weeks or months and slowly gathering it," K'lalaki explained.

"Like I said," Jiemba spoke. "They got greedy."

"And who is 'they'?" Zachariah asked. "Is this some type of organized crime?"

"Not as you know it, but that analogy will serve for now," Last Rain in Autumn said, then looked at Dr. Rodriguez. "As for who exactly, that's what we still have to determine."

Zachariah listened as Nina related her experience. The first headache she had brushed off, the synesthesia episode in her room, her belief that it had to be Dr. Endless Green Sky or Fresh Snowfall on the Lake, her attempt to diagnose herself, her belief that it had all been in her head, then ultimately deciding to tell Aleksei after the last episode. Who in turn notified Deputy Chief Xu, who contacted Last Rain in Autumn, who brought in the Protectorate.

"The doctor's attempt to scan herself was the right idea, but the limited power device her assailant would have had to use to avoid detection meant any traces would have dissipated within twenty-four hours," K'lalaki said. "We ran a backtrack analysis of her movements and agree with Dr. Rodriguez that it must be one of those two people, but we'll have to wait until they try again to be sure who."

"You are not going to use my people as bait!" Aleksei said.

"No one said—" Last Rain in Autumn started.

"I need to know who did this," Nina interrupted.

"Would Dr. Rodriguez be in any danger?" Xian asked.

"No," K'lalaki said, then explained what they intended to do.

"And how successful do you think this will be?" Zachariah asked Jiemba directly. Given the man's bluntness so far Zach didn't think he would hold back the truth.

"I don't think the doc will be in any physical danger," Jiemba shrugged. "Organized crime really isn't a good example, even though it might be literally accurate. These people who do this aren't like drug dealers or sex traffickers back home. Think more obsessed nerds downloading the newest movie to brag to their friends. It won't turn into a firefight."

Zachariah hoped it didn't. He gave the plan his go-ahead.

Investigator K'lalaki left and Nina's group signed off, but Zachariah spoke to Last Rain in Autumn before her image could vanish. "Envoy, I hope you can appreciate how troubling this news is to us. And it feels like vital information that's been kept from us—just like the knowledge about the attack. Are they in any way related?"

"No, sir. And while most don't agree with Envoy n'Dala divulging that so early, it is contact policy to never deny truth."

"So, you won't tell us everything, but if we find out, you'll admit it?" Xian said.

"The terrorist attack was done by the group True Human and had no outside influence from the Society; of that we are sure," Last Rain in Autumn said. "And we didn't mention story brokers because they are rare. Cousins, even with all our technology and advance predictive models, we aren't perfect. No humans are. And this is as much a learning process for you as it is for us. It's not meant to seem deceitful or overprotective, but in terms of its civilizational advancement, Earth isn't even at the stage of teenager yet;

it's more like a toddler. Please don't take offense at that. So, we try to be very careful in what we do. The only other time accidental contact turned out good, the C-humans in question also had an advanced NHC schedule."

After Last Rain in Autumn signed off, Zachariah looked at Xian. "I'm not happy about the doctor not reporting this."

"Agreed, and I really came down on her about that," Xian said. "But I do understand her reasoning."

"Yeah, but I think we can't ignore it," he said. "I just hate to lose another person before we even get to the embassy."

"Actually," Xian said, "I have an idea about that."

21

That evening, the Protectorate team had Nina contact Fresh Snowfall on the Lake and Endless Green Sky and ask to meet them for dinner at different times. The open-air restaurant was right next to Gaia Park; glancing at the shimmering hue of the dome above, she mused it was really an open-dome-air restaurant. Fresh Snowfall on the Lake was going to come first, and Nina sat sipping water while looking around at the other patrons and waiting. K'lalaki and Jiemba were nowhere to be seen, nor could she pick out anyone else who might be with the Protectorate. The place had a number of C-humans but only one other Earther, so Nina drew some looks.

Nina wasn't nervous at all because of a drug they had given her to level out her physiological responses. Jiemba had said that when the agent tried accessing her memories, subtle clues in Nina's stressed-out body chemistry would give her away, so the drug would mask that. It was something of a dreamlike experience to be sitting there knowing she should be afraid, but not be worried in the slightest. She was completely calm and focused. If people ever got ahold of this drug on Earth, it would be abused like crazy.

The cultural historian arrived a few minutes later, and Nina waved her over to the table.

"I'm glad you called," Fresh Snowfall on the Lake said, giving her a hug before she sat down.

Nina returned the hug without any hesitation, still amazed at how calm the drug was keeping her. She was thinking about it so much that she missed what the woman said next. "I'm sorry, what?"

"I see you're already a thousand light-years away." Fresh Snowfall on the Lake laughed. "I said you just beat me to it. I was going to invite you to dinner since I probably won't get to see you tomorrow before you leave."

"Oh, you're not assigned to the embassy?"

"No, unfortunately," she answered. "I'll be working with our embassy here."

"Well, I guess we'd better order drinks." Nina smiled.

"Absolutely!"

They sat at the restaurant for the next half hour, talking and laughing about cultural differences and how they were both coping. Nothing seemed out of the ordinary to Nina at all. More than once, she forgot her real reason for being there and was tempted to ask the other woman outright. She liked Fresh Snowfall on the Lake, and if the drugs had let her, she would have started to worry that Endless Green Sky must be the one. And even though she knew it wasn't possible, her real hope was that it was simply a false alarm and it had all been in her head somehow. All told, it was a pleasant experience, and she was starting to enjoy herself. So, she was caught off guard when the predetermined icon popped up in her field of vision, dashing her hopes with cold reality.

"I have to go to the bathroom," Nina said, collecting herself. "Will you excuse me?"

"Of course, hon," Fresh Snowfall on the Lake said. "I'll order more drinks."

"Great," Nina said as she left.

Jiemba had drilled into Nina that they would be monitoring the meeting, and if they sent that signal, she should make an excuse to leave. She waited in the hallway leading to the bathroom, where she could just make out Fresh Snowfall on the Lake still at the table. As Nina watched, a number of C-humans who had been sitting at different tables near them stood up and approached Fresh Snowfall on the Lake.

Nina unconsciously held her breath as she saw K'lalaki walk up to the Nethean and say something. Nina still wasn't able to feel anxious, but she couldn't get the dozens of action movies she had seen out of her mind. She imagined Fresh Snowfall on the Lake fighting and running, and a big chase through the city with laser guns, jet packs, and some type of daring escape in a spaceship.

So, when Fresh Snowfall on the Lake calmly stood and left with K'lalaki, surrounded by the other Protectorate agents, Nina wasn't quite sure what was happening at first.

"Told you it'd go down like that," a voice said from her side.

Jiemba stood next to her with a cocky grin on his face.

"Wait," Nina said. "So, it was her? It did happen?"

"Yep," he said, walking her back to the table. "We had monitor programs in the Nexus. As soon as she touched you, she used a mini-biosphere in her bag to scan you continuously. We waited so long to move to see if she would contact anyone we could trace."

And just like that, it was over.

All the days of worry and fear, all the stress and lying to her friends. The fear that she was going to start a political incident. All that was finished now. Her thinking was clear, but Nina knew the drug was still suppressing her emotions. She chastised herself for even thinking there might be a fight; the Society was better than that, even considering what Fresh Snowfall on the Lake had done.

Now there was nothing keeping her there. She would be fired and sent back to Earth, and once that happened, the story would get out. And then...Jesus, she would be eaten alive by the media. There was no way some people wouldn't call her a traitor. Her parents were still being hounded by the news because of the attack in the station, but once this came out—she hadn't really considered how it could blow back on her family—they would probably have to move. Her career would be over, except maybe working in some secret government lab more as a test subject than a researcher.

Yet given the same situation, the same choices, she would do it again. She really felt it would have been worse if she had come out on Earth, not for her but for relations between the Society and Earth.

"What will happen to her?"

"Honestly, I have no idea," he said. "I'm still new to this myself. I'm pretty sure they don't have prisons the way we do back home, though. But don't get too sentimental, doc. That lady is a criminal who violated your mind because she felt like she was entitled to something."

"Yeah..." Nina knew he was right, but it was still hard to accept.

"Anyway, are you still good to go for the other guy? He should be here soon."

"Endless Green Sky?" Nina was confused. "But...if it was

Fresh Snowfall on the Lake, why do we still have to go through this with him?"

"Just to be sure. Don't worry, doc; we probably won't have to interrupt your date this time." Jiemba smiled as he left her at the table.

NINA STOPPED outside the door to breathe deep and try to calm her racing heart. The drug the Protectorate had given her was well worn off now, so she had to face her future on her own. And she could only presume her summons to the ambassador's office would be her last official duty. She had met with Endless Green Sky as planned and felt like a complete fraud for pretending while he was obviously interested in having a companionable dinner. They slowly started to talk about the kiter who had died, but Nina had quickly excused herself and ended up dry-heaving in the bathroom. She had lost patients herself, so to sit and hear him talk about it under false pretenses made her sick. Apparently, the drug did nothing about self-loathing. As soon as Jiemba had sent her a message over her exso that the doctor was what he appeared, she had felt so relieved that she almost confessed right there. She needed time alone to just process everything that had happened, so she claimed her boss had just called her to an important meeting. Endless Green Sky's understanding made her feel even guiltier. Then right after she left the restaurant, she really had been instructed to report to the ambassador.

"The ambassador is ready, Dr. Rodriguez," Peter, the ambassador's aide, said from his desk.

Nina nodded to him, knocked once, and went inside. Ambassador Isaacs, Deputy Chief Xu, and Aleksei Romashenko were there. They were sitting in a group of chairs next to one of the big windows looking out on the domed city, and after a brief greeting, she was invited to sit.

"I won't make any problems for the embassy with my resignation," Nina said, trying to remember everything she rehearsed on her way over. "And I'll take full responsibility for what I did...didn't do. But so many people are looking for ways to vilify C-humans that I didn't want to add fuel to that until I... I... There's no excuse. I know I should've notified Consul Dr. Romashenko, but that's honestly why I didn't at first."

"Yes, you should've told someone," Deputy Xu said. "I can understand your reasoning, but you didn't consider the entire picture."

"I'm sorry?" Nina didn't follow her.

"You looked at it from the point of view of not embarrassing the Society, or thinking it was a mistake that people would blow out of proportion," Xian said. "Or maybe even as an isolated incident—"

"And it was an isolated—" Aleksei started.

"But," the deputy chief continued over him. "You didn't really consider it from the global angle. Yes, it might have been a mistake. *Or* it might have been a prelude to something bigger, something that could have affected our entire species. Something only you knew about. If this had turned out differently, you might have been the only person in a position to save lives, perhaps all our lives."

"Now, Deputy Xu," the medical consul interrupted again. "I think that's something of an exaggeration."

"Aleksei." Ambassador Isaacs spoke for the first time. "A living spaceship crashed into Hawaii, and we found out we're not the only intelligent life, or humans, in the galaxy. From that moment on, nothing was farfetched or impossible.

"We have no idea what the future holds for Earth. Oh, we have hopes. We have dreams and speculation." He leaned forward a little, looking from Aleksei to Nina. "But we have no freaking idea what will happen. None. We are out here to represent our entire planet. Everyone. And every choice we make, no matter how small, could affect that. I need to know that you understand that."

Nina looked from the ambassador to the deputy chief, really taking in what they said. She still didn't believe that humanity was at risk from the Society. If anything, Earth was more at risk without their help. She genuinely believed that contact was the best thing for everyone, but this wasn't about just what she believed. And honestly, she hadn't considered the larger-scale implications of what happened. Not once. Fresh Snowfall on the Lake was taken into custody so easily, Nina had brushed it off, but there *had* been a lot of Protectorate agents present to apprehend her. They had obviously taken the situation very seriously, meaning so should Nina. If she was going to trust the Society, she couldn't pick and choose. While her overall belief might be positive, she had to acknowledge that there could be dangers.

"I do understand, Mr. Ambassador," she said. "I do."

Ambassador Isaacs looked at her for a long moment, his dark brown eyes seeming to find what they needed, before he sat back, looking to Xian. "Good. Now that we have that out of the way…"

"We'd like for you to take over as head of the neuroscience division," Deputy Chief Xu said.

Nina's mouth hung open as she looked between the three people. She started to speak but couldn't find the words. The thought that she was being promoted instead of fired, or arrested, was crazier to her than aliens reading her mind. "You're not...sending me back? I don't... I..." She sat back heavily in her seat. "Why?" was the only thing she could get out without breaking down.

Aleksei smiled. "I told you Dr. Kandahar was sick, but in reality, he's decided that he can't handle being out here."

"Can't handle it?" Nina asked, remembering how he had acted strange on the trip out. "Is he okay?"

"Nothing happened to him," Aleksei said quickly. "But he started to notice that he didn't feel comfortable with... well, everything. C-humans, the exso, traveling to other planets—he just never felt like he was able to adapt."

"And there are others who feel that way," Xian said as she explained how the mayor of Galileo City was having the same issue with her staff. "So, I was able to convince the ambassador, barely, that you would be a bigger help to us here than as a disciplinary example."

"Thank you," Nina breathed. Xian's use of the word *barely* hadn't been lost on Nina. But still, this was more than she had hoped. The fact that they were not shipping her back to Earth had her confused and excited. And a part of her couldn't wait to tell Endless Green Sky, which made the fact of how she had doubted him come to the surface. Feelings she would have to face eventually. "Thank you. But help in what way?"

"We want to reexamine Society technology, specifically biowebs in human—Earther—brains," the ambassador said.

"But that's part of what we're doing anyway."

"True," Aleksei said. "But we will be taking a more proactive, in-the-field approach. Before, we were going to focus on embassy personnel who got a bioweb and, of course, continue studying it in other C-humans. Now we will be responsible for examining *all* Earthers in the Society with the tech. Not just delegates."

Nina was glad the leaders were finally going to address this. All envoys and ditecs were checked out by the UN on Earth. But she, and others, had always argued that the embassy's medical contingent should also be involved in testing, researching, and monitoring, since they would be out in the Society. Now it was happening.

"Being able to recognize what happened to you, and the possible cause, isn't something most people would've connected, Nina," Aleksei went on. "I wouldn't have. I doubt Dr. Kandahar could have either. You've put in more work on biowebs and C-human neurology than just about anyone on Earth. So, we definitely need your skills out here."

"Currently, only Earthers who the Society accepted as dimensional technicians, some envoys, and Protectorate observers have been given biowebs. So, for now, you will examine Ditec Jiemba Smith," Xian said. "But once we get to our embassy on Sapher, you and Consul Dr. Romashenko will work out the best way to proceed. Some of the Protectorate starships that have Earthers on board will be the first people you examine."

"Nina, I'm willing to believe that the Society is good for Earth," Ambassador Isaacs said. "Lord knows I hope it is. But I can't take that for granted. None of us can. The stakes are too big. I need you to use what you've learned from this experience to help us know if things like this happen again."

"I won't let you down, sir." Nina's mind was already racing ahead to all the work they would have to do. And she couldn't wait to meet Earthers who were using the tech in everyday life.

22

When he wasn't training with Sarjah, Marcus spent the almost two days' travel time immersing himself in various task around the ship. At first whenever he had a free moment he would relax and watch the ships transit. There were no windows on *Fulcrum's Light*, but connecting to the ship sensors allowed Marcus to watch the travel as if he were flying through the void. When not enmeshed in metaspace himself, Marcus couldn't truly perceive the dimensions they traveled through, and his brain interpreted it in different ways. The field of stars seemed to warp and twist around him, not as if he were flying through a tunnel but more like he was part of a strong current that twisted around itself. Sometimes stars were just points of light, and other times he could see entire star systems bubble and churn past him. It was hard for him to conceive that as he watched they were flowing past dozens upon dozens of light-years, countless kilometers. The impossible vastness of space was humbling.

They were still running dark, so the ship was cut off from the Nexus. The shiplink still worked, of course, which

Marcus found was a blessing and a curse. Sometimes, it felt like a song stuck in his head that he could ignore when busy, but the first moment of quiet, it pounced right back on him. He didn't want to turn off emotional sharing completely, because learning to deal with it was a part of his training and why he was a ditec. And on some level, he had to admit it was comforting. It was hard to feel anxious when there was unconscious emotional support around you—with you—at all times. Conversely, because people were thinking about the mission, to him the shiplink had the feeling of a slight undercurrent that he felt might sweep him away at any moment.

He tried explaining it to Sumiko once, but because she didn't have the same level of access, she couldn't really relate. Grayson spent most of his time training or introducing C-humans to video games. And Majid was practically living in bioneering. Rahel was the only Earther who could understand.

He had finally talked to Rahel about the accident with Golamee, and she wasn't as preachy as he thought she would be. But she wouldn't open up any more about her own personal experiences with pre-Society tech, either, except to say it was nothing like his had been.

"The thing that weirds me out a little is, I'm not sure how much of these feelings are strictly mine," he said after lunch in the mess hall one afternoon.

"Just because you can sense others' feelings doesn't mean yours are any less real. It can be a confusing line to see past."

"I mean, I get what we're doing and why," he said. "We shouldn't let the people on the planet be taken advantage of. And I absolutely want someone to pay for what happened to Golamee. I know that might seem petty—"

"It doesn't"

Marcus nodded as he sighed. "You know, I can tell everybody on board wants to stop the bad guys, but there is something else. I just... I can't put into words."

"Show me."

Marcus let his perception slip into the shiplink, and he felt Rahel mirror him. He paused, letting the flow of connectedness wash over him. He felt people having general conversations that they didn't bother to use private links for. He felt the status of the ship, its health as various people on duty went about their task. And there it was, the subtle feeling from the crew, but it was about...him?

"Not just about you," Rahel said. "You have to realize this is an unusual mission. A lot of strange things happen in border space, but within the Society, an event like this is very rare. The last real time was when the ship crashed into Earth. And I believe what you're feeling is a collective sense of shame *and* protectiveness. Having Earthers on board, I think, reminds them of the Society's failure and success at the same time."

"Because even though they messed up when they exposed themselves to us, we have, for the most part, been able to adapt and maybe even grow a little."

"A little," she agreed. "For Earthers, aside from a few select envoys, your group is the first to have full dimensional technician access. There is going to be a learning curve; everyone accepts that but in their own way. The UN is afraid of what they don't know and are trying to find out everything they can. But because of the NHCD contact protocols, they can't just send soldiers or spies; they have to rely on regular people like us. The Society is afraid of causing irreparable damage to Earth and, I suspect, sometimes falls

over itself, trying to avoid the mistakes of the past. We're all
figuring it out, but it will take time."

THE SHRUBBERY on each side of the path was about the
height of him standing with his arms raised, so Marcus
couldn't see over it. The garden wasn't strictly a maze, but
the numerous paths curved, turned, and twisted in no
discernible pattern, which made it easy to get lost if you let
your mind wander instead of paying attention to where you
wanted to go. But no matter how often he lost his way,
Marcus never felt trapped or confined. The garden complex
was a place of beauty and peace; the walls of shrubs were
filled with flowers and colored leaves that flowed together in
intricate patterns. Some paths were wide, some narrow, and
they all led through larger areas with fountains, trees,
brooks, and small alcoves with plush petal-like benches
where one could sit and relax.

He never saw anyone else, but he knew all the other
ditec trainees from Earth were also there. The only thing
they were asked to do was explore the garden, walk the path,
and, when they were ready, to come back out. Day after day.

So, he explored. The path forked ahead of him, and he
took a left, admiring a few purple iris-like plants. Marcus
took another left at a T intersection, then he turned right,
which led him past a small fountain. From there he took a
!%$, then a #^*-down, and after walking a while followed a
branching path to the *$@, then a right, and a @!%-right.
While in the garden, the nonuniform spatial dimensions
were as easy to follow as the standard ones like left and
right. It wasn't until he came out of the garden and thought
about paths he had taken that he realized there were certain
things he had no words for. He could remember that he had

gone straight, but not straight. And it wasn't as simple as thinking diagonal or some other direction that could be charted on an x, y, z Cartesian coordinate system. Something might be analogous to straight and feel perfectly natural while doing it but still not be a direction that existed in three-dimensional space. The same way a two-dimensional person on a plane couldn't go up or down.

But in the garden he could go anywhere. He turned left and saw Sarjah farther down the path in the distance, which confused him for a moment because he hadn't met Sarjah until after his training. He didn't worry about it after he lost sight of her around the bend, and he turned !#&-left. He forgot all about her when his grandparents called. Marcus had been wanting to talk to them anyway, so it was easy to look past the small part of him that knew he had never had a phone in the garden.

"Hey, Pop-Pop, Nana."

"Hey, honey," his grandmother said. "I was wondering if we would get to talk to you."

"Hey, Marcus, this ain't a collect call, is it?"

"You called me, Pop-Pop." Marcus laughed. "How y'all doing? Did you get the last check?"

"I went to the bank yesterday. Rhonda helped me," his nana said. "I told her you said hi. Oh, she got a promotion. And you know she goes to Mount Zion, right? Lord knows not enough young people still go to church."

"Leave the boy alone; he probably got a space girlfriend," his pop-pop said. "You got a space girlfriend out there yet?"

"Not yet." Marcus smiled; his nana really thought she was a good wingman.

"How's your studying going?" his nana asked. "They not working you too hard, are they? You look like you lost some weight. And I still don't know why I can't send you some-thing. They got all this fancy technology; you telling me they can't keep some food fresh?"

"I'm fine, Nana," Marcus said. "Besides, you looking like you done lost some weight; maybe I should be sending *you* some food."

"Dr. Burns got me seeing this new nutritionist. I'm trying to get your grandpop to go, but he acting like just 'cause they cured him of his diabetes, he don't have to exercise or nothing."

"I got enough exercise yesterday carrying your heavy purse. Marcus, do them space women be packing a whole closet in their pocketbooks?"

"I didn't hear you complaining when you wanted a bottle of water to take your pills and I had it, did you?"

"That's not the same."

"Uh-huh." Marcus smiled, knowing the look she was giving his grandfather. They reminded him of his parents.

"Are you still traveling, honey?" his nana asked. "I can't believe my grandbaby is out there walking on other planets!"

"I seen a couple," he said. "But mostly we stay on Ya'sung. It's a nice planet, smaller than Earth. The sky is roughly the same color, but the vegetation is more colorful. We do a lot of training in metaspace, though. Remember I explained about the Nexus and stuff to y'all?"

"I don't know, son," his pop-pop said. "The thought of your mind flying all over space just gives me the heebie-jeebies."

"The heebie what? I don't speak last-century English, Pop-Pop."

"Tell 'im, Marcus." His nana laughed.

"You wasn't worried about last century when you were

sneaking my jazz records out to impress that DJ girlfriend of yours."

"That's not the same!"

You will get to speak to them again, Marcus, a woman's voice said in his mind. *But you need to come back now. It's dangerous to get this caught up in a mindscape.*

"Nana?" Marcus shook his head, a little confused. Had he just been talking to someone? He couldn't remember. He was walking on the garden path. Training. At least, what his teacher claimed was training. Two weeks he had been on this planet, and all he did was wander in this damn garden.

He turned the corner and came upon a tree dappled in sunlight. He stopped, a thought at the edge of his mind that he couldn't quite grasp. The way the shadows and light moved across the leaves reminded him of something. He knew there had been a hundred people total accepted in the dimensional technician program, but they hadn't been allowed to meet each other before they left. His grandparents drove him to the air force base the day of his departure. He reminded himself to call them; it'd been a while since... No, hadn't he just talked to them?

That was a memory from before, Marcus. Focus on my presence. On talking to me now. In this moment. This was a different woman's voice. But different from who?

He glanced to the side when he thought he heard someone coming along the path, but no one was there. He rarely saw anyone even though he knew there was only one garden and all the Earther ditecs went in it at the same time. He stepped closer to the tree, holding out his hand, and watched the play of sunlight filtered from leaves above on his open palm. The patterns of the shadows could be from one leaf or many; he couldn't tell looking at his hand, because they blended into one shadow. Was it one shadow, or a hundred blended together, or were they both the same? Like metaspace. It was one thing; it was many things. This was part of his training to learn how to perceive metaspace! This was—

Months ago, the purple-skinned reptilian woman said as she stepped out from another path that hadn't been there before. *This is the point. Exist here. Let everything else fall into balance.*

You're still on Fulcrum's Light, *Marcus,* the other woman who stepped out behind the purple woman said. She was a mammal like him, but the first woman was... Marcus stumbled to the side as everything came back to him. When he hit the ground, he realized he was in the training room with Sarjah.

Marcus, are you okay? Rahel's voice over the shiplink and the feeling of concern he felt from her were an immediate comfort to him. He also felt Sarjah there, next to him, but also in his mind. The three of them were in a grouplink, although he didn't remember how it happened.

"What the hell was that?" he asked.

A normal part of ditec training, Sarjah said as matter-of-factly as ever, but she did allow a moment of calm to come through their link.

"Since when?"

Always, Sarjah said.

Just breathe, Marcus, Rahel said.

He felt Sarjah say something to Rahel, although he didn't know what.

Rahel paused for a moment and Marcus felt a brief bit of reluctance on her part, then she said, *Listen to Sarjah, Marcus. I'll talk to you later.* Her presence vanished from the link.

You understand why the other Earthers on board don't have the same difficulty with a bioweb that you do? Sarjah asked.

"Huh." He was still a little out of it. "Yeah."

Explain it to me.

"What? Why?"

Sarjah's mental presence didn't say anything, but Marcus knew she was waiting.

"They only access the Nexus and other biowebs."

Which is the same for the vast majority of people in the Society. The Nexus is a platform created within metaspace. Dimensional technicians' biowebs give them the ability to manipulate certain levels of metaspace. Your mind interprets that in a variety of ways. So, for someone with a normal bioweb, a mindscape is simply a mental projection that they can interact with in their mind. The safeguards of the Nexus protect users. But a ditec using a mindscape can inadvertently use it to represent different aspects of metaspace. Not realizing they have entered metaspace, a ditec can sometimes be unable to distinguish their mental creation from the actual reality of standard space.

"And when exactly was this covered in the training?"

Right now. And it can't be trained, Marcus; it can only be experienced. The more comfortable and proficient you become in using metaspace, the more you can do and learn.

"So, did I, like, graduate? I've mastered ditec training?"

Sarjah actually laughed out loud. Marcus had barely even seen her smile, so her laughing was outright weird.

That's the first truly funny thing you've said, baby culture, she said, no sign that she had laughed. *No, Marcus, now you're ready to spend the next few years mastering what you know.*

There was a ghost of amusement from her as she closed the link and vanished from his mind. Only then did he even realize she hadn't been there in the flesh, either. And Marcus was certain she was going to enjoy working him to death after the mission, even though she would never admit it.

AFTER RESTING in his quarters for a while Marcus decided to get some food. As soon as Marcus stepped out of his quarters into the corridor, he heard the shouts and yelling. Even as he turned his head, his mind was searching the shiplink to see what was wrong and how he had missed an alarm. There was nothing wrong; the ship was still in transit to the target system, about nineteen hours away now.

"Take that, little mammal!" a booming voice called out, and Marcus realized all the noise was coming from Grayson's open doorway down the corridor. And from the continuing sound of explosions, gunshots, and curses, Marcus knew exactly what he would see as he walked to the door.

Inside the main room area of Grayson's quarters, the interior had grown one big couch along one wall, and the room was full of C-humans. Marcus caught himself looking to see if anyone was orange skinned. He still hadn't figured out who Sumiko had hooked up with, and he refused to give Grayson the satisfaction of asking. On the couch, Grayson looked almost comical squeezed between Kleedak's eight-foot huge blue bulk on one side and Ky'Gima's seven-foot-long, lean feathered form on his other side. They were holding what looked like game controllers in their hands as they yelled at the image projected on the opposite wall. They were playing a first-person shooter game, but not some high-tech Society thing. It looked like a typical FPS from back home.

"Is that that PlayStation game that just came out?" he asked.

"Dude, I downloaded every console and PC game I could before I shipped out," Grayson said, then cursed at something onscreen.

"Marcus, welcome," Sinju said from where he was leaning on the wall next to Ditec Yeizar of Eleven.

"Sinju, what up," Marcus said. He smiled because the white furred four-and-a-half-foot-tall Yotara reminded him of his friend's little brother waiting to play as the bigger, older boys hogged the game system. His long, pointed ears, more elf-like than cat-like, twitched at the different sounds in the room, and his thin tail swayed slightly. "I'm surprised Grayson got you to play this."

"Oh, I was just checking to see if things were working okay," Sinju said. "Kleedak asked me to grow a system that could run these antiquated files. It's been a pleasant distraction, surprisingly. And I'm quite proud of the custom controllers that can adapt to multiple C-human hand sizes."

"How Axlons ever get anything done with those big, unwieldy hands is a wonder," Ky'Gima said, then her blue and yellow feathers ruffled as she yelled. "Ahh, I died."

"Ha, how's that for unwieldy, skinny avian!" Kleedak laughed.

"I guess that means you had to convert the programs," Marcus asked, looking over to Yeizar of Eleven. His multi-hued green skin was darker than Ujexus of Seven, but their head, shoulder quills, and short tails were the same yellow-ish-orange, as were their eyes.

"I did," Yeizar said, and Marcus could see he was still tweaking code over the shiplink. "It reminded me of some programming I did when I was little."

"And I thought you were just hiding out from Sarjah."

"Ha, a Oodandi hiding from a Xindari." Kleedak boomed in laughter. "She could smell him from across a star system."

Ky'Gima laughed, but Marcus had no idea what to make of that, since as far as he could tell, Yeizar had no real odor. Grayson saw the confusion on his face and said, "Dude, don't ask. Tuhzo's got some crazy stories."

"Tuhzo jokes?" Marcus asked. The Xindari lead security officer wasn't there, and Marcus had a hard time picturing it.

"Not so much a joke as a..." Grayson rapidly pressed buttons on his controller and leaned his body in response to something on the screen. "Headshot, ha."

"Boneless wretch," Kleedak cursed.

"Uh, yeah, not jokes," Grayson continued. "More like well-timed statements."

"Our little reptile cousins always see to the heart of things," Kleedak said.

"Sarjah is a very good ditec, though," Yeizar said absently, still messing around with the game code on the shiplink. "If you survive training, I'm sure you'll be quite skilled."

"Huh? What do you mean if I..."

A pulse over the shiplink cut Marcus off. It wasn't a direct message only to him, but a specific feeling to everybody in his vicinity that Sarjah wanted him.

"Uh-oh." Grayson laughed.

Marcus would swear she was spying on him, but he never felt her presence on the shiplink.

Hey, I'm in Grayson's room. He's showing some people Earth video games, Marcus sent to her.

Yes, I know Earthers find entertainment in the simulated murder of others, she said. *But we still have enough time to train again before we go on duty.*

He really didn't have a comeback for that at the moment, as he watched Grayson gun down enemies, but Marcus swore he would think of one.

"Dude, at least you don't have to deal with security," Grayson said. "Oh, damn!"

Just as Kleedak was yelling, "Ha, skull penetration!"

⁜

IN THE SILENT void between stars, reality seemed to ripple for a moment as dimensions coalesced and *Fulcrum's Light* emerged into standard space a full light-day's distance from the edge of the target star system. It was located deep within Society space, just to the south of the galactic plane but not near any inhabited areas. More Protectorate ships were en route, but they were the first to arrive.

Marcus and Sarjah were stationed in the ditec cavity, working in tandem with the sensor-analysis team. Marcus scanned metaspace, the same as he had done in the Travanis system, looking for the slightest evidence of a portal. The data Golamee had retrieved, before she died, showed a trace signature that was probably caused by a planet's magnetic field, so their search was focused on the system's planets. It was a standard red dwarf system, the most common type of star in the galaxy, so basic it didn't even have a name, only a star-chart number. There were three terrestrial planets, two gas giants, and a few dwarf planets. The terrestrial planets were barren rocks in a tight orbit about the central star, the innermost planet so close, it grazed the star's photosphere and would probably be consumed in a few tens of thousands of years. One gas giant had some larger-than-average debris in its ring that analysis determined was from a couple of its moons colliding in the recent astronomical past—about twenty million years ago—

which wasn't unusual. Marcus ran filtering algorithms to correlate everything, but he still didn't detect any discernible dimensional signatures.

"We're not reading any traces of dimensional technology in-system," Sarjah reported. "But from this distance, it could be lost in regular stellar noise."

"On the surface, it seems like a completely ordinary system with no habitable worlds and no reason for anyone to travel here," Lead Officer Ja Xe 75 05 said, accessing the results of the scans over the shiplink. "No doubt why they chose this spot."

"No doubt," Captain Ahmon said. Marcus could feel the captain's and other officers' presence over the shiplink. Even without emotional sharing there were enough similarities between most of the C-human races that Marcus could still detect an unspoken tension among the crew.

"Take us to the edge of the star system, Nav Tech Ky'Gima," Captain Ahmon said.

"Aye, Captain," Ky'Gima said as she set course. The dimensional field enmeshed the flesh of the hullskin, radiating inward to protect the bioship and its crew as it transitioned through dimensions. Moments later, *Fulcrum's Light* reemerged from metaspace a few light-minutes from the system's Kuiper Belt.

They went through another long round of analyzing data but still found nothing conclusive. So, the captain made the decision to take them in closer to the periphery of the outer system. This time, Sarjah saw it, a small fluctuation of dimensional energy. It was somewhere around the largest gas giant, and an intense search of the area showed a ship parked deep in the planet's ring.

"We got it, Captain," she announced.

"Good." *Attention, senior staff.* The captain's words over the shiplink got their focus. *Sim meeting in two minutes.*

MARCUS WAS SURPRISED when he was included in the summons to the meeting. Some meetings were done in the physical, but most were done over the shiplink so participants could join from wherever they were on board. He relaxed back into his chair in the ditec cavity and closed his eyes. The simulated environment of the meeting wasn't simply a re-creation of a conference room or some other physical place. It was more the understanding of being in a group. Marcus thought it was akin to sleeping in bed with someone and knowing they were next to you even when you weren't physically touching. All the subtle things that one is rarely consciously aware of about their partner: the weight of their body pulling the bed, their breathing, smell, body heat, just that *feel* you have when someone is next to you. That's what the conference was like, simply *knowing* who was there with you in your mind.

But to Marcus it wasn't creepy like being in a dark room with other people. It was more comforting in a way, like being around a group of close family or friends. Even without looking, you know your sister's facial expression to what your mom just said, or your cousin's body language while he's telling a joke. You can tell your best friend's emotional state by the sound of their voice, or your lover's feelings by the way they absentmindedly touch you. In many ways, the sim was disturbingly intimate, even with the default safeguards that kept people's emotions from being shared without conscious intent. This was another reason why some technologies were slowly introduced to NHCs:

there was no guarantee how a race would adapt unless they already possessed something similar.

Let's get started, the captain said. *Metatech, report.*

t'Zyah's presence took center focus in the sim. One benefit of not visualizing themselves in a room was that whoever was talking was presented as the main focus for everyone's awareness.

Further analysis indicates that it's a stationary portal base, not a ship, t'Zyah said. *So, most likely it's on one of the moonlets, or larger rocks, within the gas giant's ring.*

When she spoke, Marcus couldn't resist peeking at the sitting form of t'Zyah, as he sat in between her and Sarjah in the ditec cavity. His bioweb's safety protocols kept him from being disoriented, but it was still a strange experience, seeing her next to him in person but mentally still feeling like he was with a group of people who weren't in the cavity.

And while we can't be certain from this distance, Sarjah said, *we believe this portal is for receiving only, not transmitting. No way to say why that is until we examine it, but no doubt it has something to do with the third-civilization encryption.*

So, whoever is responsible will have to physically come here to retrieve the data, Ja Xe 75 05 said.

Yes, Sarjah answered.

Sensor Tech Ujexus. Ahmon focused on the Oodandi. *Recent ship activity in the area?*

The data from the recon probes that were portaled here show no ships have visited the system while we were in transit, Ujexus said. *And, sir, whoever chose this system was smart. It's roughly equal distance from all surrounding inhabited systems, and there is just enough ship traffic in the general vicinity that D-signatures are not uncommon in the area. We can say with eighty-seven point three percent accuracy that there haven't been any*

ships visiting the system in the past week, which isn't unusual for
this type of system.

Marcus knew that most travel throughout the Society
was done by portal. Traveling by ship was generally recre-
ational, so the majority of it was done by civilians. There
were world ships that could hold billions and were just that,
self-sustaining worlds that casually migrated around the
Society between systems; there were community ships of all
sizes where people of similar interests traveled together for
the company (physical meetings hadn't become obsolete
with the Nexus); and there were even personal ships that
people traveled in for the novelty of it, like the one that
crashed on Earth.

Ditec Greer. The captain's voice drew his attention back
to the sim environment.

Sorry, he said, feeling all the others focus on him. And
even though Sarjah's presence in the meeting didn't react or
say anything, he clearly heard her whisper, "Focus," from
her physical body next to him, loud enough for only him to
hear.

Ditec Greer, it is...unusual for C-humans from NHCs to be
involved in certain missions, the captain said. *But the facts are*
of everyone on board, with the exception of Ditec Sarjah, you
have the most hands-on experience with third-civ technology.

Marcus had never given that conscious thought, but he
realized the captain was right. The whole reason Golamee
had come aboard was because studying tech from previous
C-human civilizations was a specialized field.

So, I won't order you to go, the captain continued. *But I*
believe you would be an asset to the recon team.

Marcus's first thought was of Golamee's mind being
sucked away into metaspace. He didn't think any trace of his
fear slipped into the shiplink, but he did feel Sarjah focus

on him. And that led to his second thought—that she would be dead too if he hadn't been there to help. He had spoken to Rahel earlier, and she had warned him this might happen and that he shouldn't feel forced into anything. He appreciated her looking out for him, but it wasn't just about getting revenge, or closure, for Golamee. Earth was part of something far larger now.

It's okay, Captain, he said. *I volunteer.*

Good, Captain Ahmon said, as his presence then became the focus of the meeting. *Primary objective: a recon team will infiltrate the portal base, retrieve the data, and return to the ship. Then* Fulcrum's Light *will remain here stealthed until our unknown thieves arrive. Commander Ja Xe, contact the backup ships and tell them to hold off at least twenty light-years. We don't want anyone coming to realize we are waiting on them.*

Aye, Captain.

Listen up, everyone. Given the fact that the target system is so deep in Society space, it is highly improbable that an outside species is behind this. Meaning, as unlikely as it sounds, a group of C-humans willing to commit genocide is behind this. Captain Ahmon paused a moment to let that sink in. To Earthers, violence and terrorism were commonplace, but Marcus had come to know that this type of act in the Society was very, very rare. *This has far reaching implications, people. So, let's avoid any mistakes. t'Zyah, get your team together. I want you to leave in one hour.*

Aye, sir, t'Zyah said.

Dismissed, the captain said, and the sim environment dissolved.

23

Zachariah stood at the window of his suite and looked out over Galileo City. He took it all in: the massive planet Jupiter in the sky, the dome of the city, the C-humans, the sheer unbelievability of everything that had happened since contact. It had been a long day. A long week, really, and it was only Thursday night. Tomorrow would be the real beginning. He could only imagine how much stranger things would become once they actually left the solar system. He didn't doubt that he wanted to be ambassador, but meetings like the one he just gotten out of with the consuls general made him realize how much work was before him.

Briefing them on the situation with the story broker agent and Dr. Rodriguez had gone as expected. Anger, fear, confusion, and accusations were all evident. Consul General Saputra had even floated the idea of a vote of no-confidence in Zachariah. Deputy Xu quickly quashed that, and Bakti relented when he realized he wouldn't get the votes. The main thing had been that the UN Council accepted what happened.

"Sir." An image of Peter's face popped up right in front of Zachariah, causing him to step back in shock.

"Dammit."

"Sorry, sir," Peter said, struggling hard to keep a smile off his face.

Zachariah didn't feel old, but he had to admit that the younger generation staffers in the embassy were adapting to the exosensory device better than he was. He tried to keep his annoyance out of his voice. "What is it?"

"The Secretary-General of the UN is on the line again, sir."

"Put him through," Zachariah said.

"Um, you want to take it on the phone or your exso, sir?"

"The phone will be fine," Zachariah said.

The phone on the desk rang, and Zachariah pressed the talk button. The image of the Secretary-General appeared on the screen. The fact that it was still a video did not make Zach embarrassed. It would take him a bit before he was comfortable talking to floating images.

"Zach," the Secretary-General said. "I only have a minute. I'm about to have another meeting with the American and Chinese presidents. The UN will make an official statement to Ambassador As the Gentle Wind later tonight, but I wanted you to know that the mission is still a go."

"That's good to hear, sir," Zachariah said. After his initial report of what had happened, some members of the UN Security Council had talked about postponing the embassy mission. Zachariah had made it clear he thought that was the worst thing they could do, since the main purpose of the mission was for them to better understand the Society's civilization, and actually being there was the only way to do that.

"It will be a while before we decide how we want to

approach this," the Secretary-General continued. "There is definitely a vocal group calling for this agent to be tried on Earth, but it's the usual players more interested in political points and making a name for themselves than in addressing the problem."

"Are there still people trying to combine this with the attack in Cairo?"

"Of course," the Secretary-General said, looking off-screen as he signed something for an aide. "And we all know it's only a matter of time before it *leaks* to the media. But the intelligence community was already making progress on the True Human group and some of the things you learned from Envoy n'Dala. Right now, we're operating as if it isn't a larger conspiracy, but no one's discounting anything yet."

"That's good."

"There are some who want to interview Dr. Rodriguez, but we'll trust your judgment for now. I must say I was surprised you fought so hard to keep her."

"She made a mistake, but I believe she will be a more valuable asset here," Zachariah said. Her promotion wouldn't go through until they were on Sapher. He knew he would take some flak for that from the consuls general, but it would be a done deal by then. "And sending her back, I think, would play into the hands of the anti-Society factions."

"That may be true. Well, it's on your head," the Secretary-General said. "We'll talk again before you leave."

Zachariah signed off. He used a memorized hand gesture to call up a contact list on his exso. He might as well try to get used to it. With a squint, Xian Xu's name was selected from the list hovering in his field of view, and in a moment, she answered his call.

This time, she appeared full-size standing across from

him. He knew that sensors in his room recorded him and projected a life-size image of him onto her exso wherever she was. Supposedly, they didn't record all the time, but he was already accepting the fact that they had no guarantee of privacy, even though Last Rain in Autumn assured him they did. Zachariah could control the opacity of Xian's image as needed, but at full resolution, he couldn't tell she wasn't actually standing there except for the telltale reaction of her eyes looking at things in her environment that he couldn't see projected, and the subtle differences in ambient lighting on her person.

"I just spoke to the Secretary-General," he said. "The mission is still definitely a go."

"Good. I'm finalizing Dr. Kandahar's return to Earth," she said. "And thank you again for trusting me about Dr. Rodriguez."

"I'm willing to wait and see how it works out," Zachariah said. Even more than Aleksei, it had been Xian Xu who had argued the case for Nina not being sent home and instead replacing Dr. Kandahar. Zachariah actually agreed with her reasoning, but he knew without her insistence, he would have probably fired Dr. Rodriguez, simply so it didn't seem like he was playing favorites with another North American. "For now, I want to—"

Zachariah paused when another icon in his field of vision indicated Envoy Last Rain in Autumn was waiting to speak with him. "Go ahead with the preparations for departure, Xian. I'll meet with you later about specifics."

They ended the call, and Zachariah used his exso to tell Last Rain in Autumn to come in.

"Ambassador Isaacs," she said, coming into the office with her typical smile and followed by Ditec Smith. "I realized because of circumstances, you haven't officially met the dimensional technician who is assigned to the embassy, and I wanted to introduce you."

"Mr. Ambassador," Jiemba said, shaking Zachariah's hand. "I didn't meet you on Earth because I was on the other side of the Society."

"Not a problem," Zachariah said. After finding out about Dr. Rodriguez, Zach had looked up Jiemba. His official file said he was a cop. But Zach had found out Jiemba had been on suspension when he was chosen for the ditec program. Not for anything bad, but he had apparently had some choice words for some government officials when he was protecting an Aboriginal site from corporate developers.

"Mr. Ambassador, there is a more important reason I wanted to speak with you," Last Rain in Autumn said. "I've gotten a report from the Protectorate Council. As you know, some Earthers have been stationed on Protectorate ships so Earth can see all aspects of the Society. Well, one of those ships was recently engaged in a conflict where one crew member was lost."

"My God," Zachariah said.

"Not an Earther," Last Rain in Autumn went on quickly. "Although still a tragedy. Normally, any NHC crew would be transferred in the event of a life-threatening situation, but time is of the essence. The situation may or may not escalate, but it's our policy to let you know if anyone from your planet is in danger."

Zachariah listened as Last Rain in Autumn proceeded to tell him what she knew about *Fulcrum's Light* and the events with the exploding moon. "These are the files on the Earthers on board. By the time you get to Sapher, you should be getting a full report."

A list of names and profile pictures scrolled up in his field of vision, surprising Zachariah, but what caused him to catch his breath was that he knew one of the names. Envoy Rahel Ashenafi. Zachariah stared at her name and picture, but his thoughts were lost almost twenty years before when they had met at college in Washington, DC. They had dated seriously for a while before she had to go back to Ethiopia because of a sick parent. They had kept in touch at first but finally agreed long distance wasn't going to work out for them, and eventually Zachariah had moved back to Trinidad, met his wife-to-be, and moved on with his life. Naturally, he had known Rahel was an envoy, but there were so many of them, he had never expected to see her.

"I'd... I'd like to speak to the Earthers on board, as well."

"Of course," Last Rain in Autumn said. "If you'll excuse me, I have some things to follow up on. I'll keep you updated."

The Nethean envoy left, and Zachariah tried to process what he had learned. He appreciated the info but felt like there was more to the story.

"Do you think this could have something to do with another power outside the Society?" he asked Jiemba. The Society had never hidden the fact that there were other alien civilizations, but they hadn't given Earth info on them, either. It wasn't impossible that they were engaged in a war somewhere thousands of light-years away; Earth would never know.

"I hope not," Jiemba said, looking around the office. "Gut feeling is that it's a local thing."

Zachariah mused, "I suppose there are so many different cultures in the Society that conflict is bound to happen, although they have always said otherwise."

"I haven't seen any real cultural tension yet, in my travels, but doesn't mean it isn't there," Jiemba said. "I should also point out that I know one of the Earthers on that ship."

"Really?"

"Their ditec, Marcus Greer. Good kid, and fairly talented with Society tech, as I recall."

"You trained together?" Zachariah asked.

"After a fashion," Jiemba said. "You know there were only one hundred Earthers chosen to be dimensional technicians, so we've all met. And while we were on the same planet, our training was very personal and usually one-on-one with C-human ditecs, so most of us Earthers rarely got a chance to socialize with each other.

"I figure whoever you recognized on that list, you know much better than I know Marcus," Jiemba finished.

"How..." Zachariah was lost for words.

"From the reaction on your face, I'm guessing you're not much of a poker player."

Zachariah paused a moment, lost in thought. "The envoy on board, Rahel, she and I used to...know each other...in college."

"Um, she was one of the First Six Hundred," Jiemba said. His eyes had a faraway look, and Zachariah guessed he was accessing some info. "An envoy while you were still mayor and before you ran for ambassador; probably coincidence, but worth keeping note of."

His comment troubled and sobered Zachariah; he hadn't considered it was anything but coincidence. If it wasn't, the Society was playing a long game indeed. "What's your take on the Society?"

Jiemba took a while to answer. "Well...I don't think they want to destroy us. With some of the technology I've seen, that would be laughably easy. I know that's kind of a taboo subject among you suits, and that governments back home don't really appreciate the truth of it. Too many decades of movies with us fighting alien bugs and robots, I suspect. But really...they wouldn't even need to come into our solar system to destroy us if they wanted. It's hard to swallow, but we really are the proverbial anthill to them."

"Well, that's never a comforting example, but I agree with you there." Zachariah watched a volcano erupting in the distance. "So, you're not one of those who think they want more territory and resources?"

"Nah, the Society is not expansionist. It would be bigger if it was."

"You don't think eleven thousand light-years is big?"

"To us, hell, it's practically unimaginable. To them..." Jiemba shrugged. "It's a step through a class-one portal. I know it's hard to appreciate when you haven't seen it first-hand, but this is a civilization that doesn't have needs. Wants, yes, but not needs. Certainly not resources. They can draw all the energy they ever desire from stars, as well as harvest them for heavy elements for their fabricators. And that's not even mentioning the fact that they can tap into metaspace. To be honest, this whole incident with Dr. Rodriguez has made me more trusting of them."

"How's that?" Zachariah asked, the expression on his face clear that he didn't follow.

"Criminals I understand," Jiemba said. "Greed, envy, status-seekers; the fact that they have people who experience those things makes them feel more...human, I guess. No money is bad enough, but a society with no type of crime would make me very suspicious."

"I suppose." Zachariah nodded as he thought about everything. "I'm sure they would say that's a very Earther viewpoint, but I get it. And they do like their secrets."

"Very true. Have you gotten a straight answer as to how many different C-human races there are in the Society?" Jiemba asked.

"No one has, that I know of," Zachariah said. That wasn't something he had given a lot of thought to lately. "It is strange, the things they choose to keep secret, things that seem trivial to us, while on the other hand being open about things that could cast them in a negative light."

"I noticed that also," Jiemba said. "I can only guess that they want to show us they can be trusted without overwhelming us. I tell you, the first time I saw a Saaorish, I had to put my hand in my pocket to keep from making the sign of the cross."

"A Saaorish?" Zachariah asked.

"I have it on good authority that when the Society was deciding which C-humans would be our mentor race—or older cousin, as they like to call it—it came down to Netheans and Saaorishi."

"Really?"

"Yeah. Saaorishi have extremely similar bone structure and musculature to us. More than any other C-human I've seen. So much so that they look almost just like us."

That was news to Zachariah. "So, why Netheans instead of them?"

"Well, the thing is, they're red."

"Red? So? We've seen every other color; why not that?"

"No," Jiemba said. "I mean straight-up the devil red. And given our civilization's myths and religions, especially in the West, well, the Society realized that red people coming to Earth would have a negative impression, to say the least. I'm not religious now, but it's kinda hard to completely forget that forced Catholic upbringing. And the one I met was a woman. Drop-dead gorgeous. Succubus type. But the whole time I was talking to her, I could hear my old headmistress counting her rosary and praying for my soul. So, we got the purple guys."

It was a strange story, but Zachariah believed him. He was also aware of the fact that it showed how skilled the Society was at shaping the narrative that Earth saw when dealing with them. Netheans instead of these Saaorishi was a perfectly logical choice, and he understood it, but still, it was calculated.

Zachariah noticed Jiemba watching him, seeing if he had worked out the implications of what he was saying, and realized the man was cleverer than he had given him credit for.

"They are very good at showing us what they want us to see, no?" Jiemba said.

Zachariah nodded, looking at him. "Do you think you'll be able to find out more information about *Fulcrum's Light*? If there's...some colors we're not seeing."

"I believe I can, sir," he said. "I won't be portaling with the delegation tomorrow, but I'll meet you at the embassy on Sapher in a few days."

"Godspeed," Zachariah said, shaking his hand.

"To all of us," Jiemba responded.

24

F ulcrum's Light shrank to an indistinguishable dot as the shuttle accelerated away in space. The organic transport was a smaller version of the bioship but not strictly a "child" of it. The seven-person recon team sat in the seats that lined each wall, while the pilot flew from a smaller cavity up front. Lead Metatech t'Zyah was in charge, while Sarjah and Marcus served as the ditecs. Sinju was the bioneer, and like a lot of C-humans with thin tails the white furred Yotara kept his wrapped around his waist while in a voidskin so it wasn't in the way. Lead Security Tuhzo, along with Grayson and Kleedak Pah—the Axlons large frame easily taking up two spaces—sat along the opposite wall in their bulkier ultra-voidskins. Marcus squirmed in his chair again, trying to get comfortable with the way his voidskin adhered to the seat in place of straps. Every time he did, he noticed Sarjah's shoulders roll slightly back, which his bioweb told him was the Xindari equivalent of an exasperated sigh.

Sorry, he said on their private link. *I'm just not used to this, man. I keep thinking of the beginning scene in all those war movies that start out quiet, then bam!*

Your race has a higher-than-average use of referring to others as male. It says a lot about your hierarchical structure and how you place lesser importance on the female in your society.

Jesus Christ, dude, it's just a... Marcus realized he had said it again and changed gears. *It's just colloquial English. It doesn't mean anything.*

Everything means something.

"And what does you being a pain in the ass mean?" He didn't realize he had spoken out loud until a few people around him turned to look. Marcus swore Sarjah did that on purpose, goading him in their private link so he lost focus and started verbalizing. Another way of subtly showing him that he had far from mastered the bioweb.

"Dude," Grayson said from across the aisle. "Don't start freaking out now. Too late to go back." He had a big grin on his face.

"Ditec Greer?" t'Zyah was walking down the aisle, checking that people were secured.

"I'm fine, Lead," he replied. The A'Quan nodded and kept moving.

Then a still image of a crocodile—colored purple and eating a gazelle—popped up in his mind's eye, a message from Grayson with the caption *Girlfriend troubles* ;-). Marcus barely caught himself from saying something else out loud and casually rubbed his eye with his middle finger. Grayson smiled wider as he relaxed in his seat.

Then his private link with Rahel, who was monitoring from the ship, opened. *You're not a soldier, Marcus; it's natural to be nervous. But this isn't a firefight. Stick with Sarjah, and you'll be fine.* Her words were accompanied by a feeling of shared understanding and confidence in him.

Marcus was mildly shocked. Rahel rarely intentionally shared emotion over the Nexus.

Thanks, Rahel. He sat back, letting his gratitude flow through the link. She acknowledged and closed the channel.

Your envoy also did not tell you I wouldn't have requested you come if I did not think you would be of use, Sarjah said over their private link. *And the captain certainly would not have permitted it.*

Marcus did a double take. Private links were supposed to be unhackable. Sarjah still sat calmly in her seat, eyes closed, not having moved at all.

Spy much? he asked.

Encrypt better, was the simple reply.

Marcus was about to respond when he thought about that. He delved into his bioweb and examined his Nexus connections. The continuous open link to the ship and the grouplink of the recon team were stable. As were the comm tags for each member of the crew and all ongoing open channels. Studying the protocols closer, he realized the link he maintained with Sarjah had a slight back channel that could give her access to any comm link he received, private or not. He examined it, saw how it worked and the simple mistake he had made when opening the original private link. With a thought, Marcus adjusted certain parameters and fixed it, careful not to close the actual link with her itself.

Sarjah didn't say anything or open her eyes, but her hands moved in a gesture analogous to an Earther's nod of approval. That made him prouder than he wanted to admit.

It wouldn't be until much later that he embarrassingly realized she must have also seen the picture Grayson had sent.

. . .

THE RINGED GAS giant was breathtaking. It was bluish in color with bands of azure and white encircling the planet, broken only by the occasional purplish storm clouds. The planet's ring was a swirling mass of ice, ice-coated rock, and dust particles. Marcus could remember watching the Cassini probe's images of Saturn, when he was a little kid, with his parents. Saturn's ring was two hundred and eighty-two thousand kilometers wide. This planet was larger, and its ring stretched out on the plane of the ecliptic for over three hundred and forty thousand kilometers but was only a little over fifty to a hundred meters thick on average. From the outer edge to the inner edge nearest the planet was almost one hundred and ten thousand kilometers. The scale was more than he could easily imagine. In comparison, Earth was only about twelve thousand seven hundred kilometers wide. The entire planet Earth. It was a stark reminder to Marcus of how immense space was.

The shuttle approached from south of the ring's plane, and the crew was silent as they accessed the view from the shuttle's sensors. The closer they got, the more the ring took up their entire field of view, stretching from horizon to horizon. At that scale, it didn't so much get bigger as it just became the *sky*. But it wasn't so thick that they couldn't see through it. They were near enough now that only the bottom of the planet could be seen clearly; the upper half was slightly obscured by the ring but still easily visible.

Planetary rings only looked solid from a great distance. This close, it was easy to see the ring was not a uniform sheet, but made up of thousands of closely spaced bands, or ringlets. It reminded Marcus of the grooves on the records his pop-pop still played—if the record was over three hundred and forty thousand kilometers wide. He could also see the many gaps in the ring, made by small shepherd satellites, or moonlets, that orbited the planet on the same plane as the ring. The moonlets' gravitational forces affected the particles outside and inside their orbital path, clearing large areas and creating gaps within the ring itself, some only a few kilometers wide and some many thousands of kilometers wide. Saturn's most famous ring gap, the Cassini Division, was almost five thousand kilometers wide, which was wide enough to hold the planet Mercury.

Ice particles in the ring glittered, reflecting light from the system. For a moment, the angle of their approach and the ring's reflected light made it seem to Marcus like there was a vast sparkling ocean above his head and the bottom half of the gas giant—seen in the distance—was like a sun rising from it. This perspective made him feel upside down, like the empty void of space beneath them was the sky, which he supposed it was.

Entering the disk, the pilot said over the grouplink. *Ride might get a little bumpy.*

The material of the planet's ring ranged from small ice and rock particles less than a centimeter wide to chunks bigger than houses that the pilot had to fly around. Even the ring gaps weren't truly empty up close but full of small dust particles, all of it swirling slowly in orbit around the gas giant. The shuttle's grav drive could generate enough of a field to repel the ring material, but the pilot was using it for maneuvering only, to minimize the chances of being detected as much as possible.

The gas giant was emitting a huge magnetic field, and what little radiation the grav drive didn't reflect Marcus could feel striking the hull. Feedback sensors gave him the impression of getting a sunburn in the cold, while damaged hullskin ablated away as new material was grown to replace it. The shuttle eased fully into the disk, and Marcus felt they had submerged—upmerged?—into a murky sea.

The shuttle was now in stealth mode, running without shields and forming an extra hardened layer of skin on the hull. The constant collisions sounded like they were inside a washing machine with rocks, but minimizing their active signature would mask them as just another large chunk floating around. The stars above and below were still easily visible from within the ring's thin layer, but horizontal visibility dropped drastically. Marcus cycled his viewing spectra to also see in infrared and ultraviolet. Ring material continually bombarded the ship, its minimal grav drive field causing smaller particles to swirl around it like a vortex.

Eventually, sensors showed a large, somewhat elongated moonlet, a pitted chunk of ice and rock about the size of three football fields. In tens of millions of years, it might accrete sufficient material to become large enough to clear a gap in the ring like some of the other moonlets, but for now, it was just one of the larger objects in the drifting material of the ring. As it slowly rotated, a structure came into view. There was a dome on the surface, and deep scans showed at least one level below the ice.

On final approach, the pilot said. Marcus was listening to t'Zyah report to the ship when suddenly he was hit with an absence, a sense of loss and isolation that left him confused until he realized their Nexus connection had cut out. Their shiplink was also gone. He could still access metaspace with his bioweb, but the connective structure/plane that made up the Nexus was lost to him. He felt like he had just walked out of a forest, turned around, and it was gone.

"Okay, people," t'Zyah said. "We knew this would happen. The base is putting out a jamming field, so no comms with *Fulcrum's Light* till we turn it off. It also means they can't portal us out if things go bad, so stay alert. Grouplink will still function as long as we are in reasonable proximity to each other."

Everyone acknowledged as the pilot brought them down. The shuttle landed just over the horizon from the base to block any sensors in case they picked up their grav drive flux. And Marcus found himself for the second time in a few days going into open space.

THE SEVEN FIGURES skimmed over the landscape in their voidskins, surrounded by seven recon spheres. The group stayed close to the surface of the moonlet, not so much to avoid scanners but to minimize debris impact. Grains of dust and ice particles permeated the area like a haze, giving their surroundings a foggy, overcast feel. Large chunks floated by, but the icy rock they were on was the largest in the area, and soon enough the structure came into view.

Scanning, Sinju said. *I don't think we've been detected.*

The portal base was an opaque dome about the size of an average house. Its bluish-gray surface blended in with the surface of the ice-coated moonlet, and there was only one apparent entrance. t'Zyah sent out perimeter orders, and Kleedak, Tuhzo, and Grayson moved. Marcus watched through Grayson's POV as they circled the compound. The ultraskinned figures sometimes used bounding hops in the minimal gravity, and sometimes flew low over the rough terrain. Readings indicated nothing around them for at least as far as the near horizon on the icy surface. Sixty-some meters above, the ring material gave way to the relative emptiness of space. And although its middle was slightly obscured from view by the ring, the gas giant's upper and lower halves were still visible, and its bluish-purple luminance gleamed through the disk, reflecting off ice particles and casting a dusty glow across the horizon.

Sarjah, t'Zyah said.

Sarjah glided toward the base. *Let's go, baby culture.*

t'Zyah and Sinju took up positions covering their rear as Marcus and Sarjah drifted to a halt in front of the door, a square two meters by two meters. The measurements made Marcus assume that races like the Axlons or Zythyans were not responsible, because he believed no one would make a doorway they had to stoop to get into.

Off to the side of Sarjah, one of the recon spheres hovered in the air. Its similar shape gave Marcus uncomfortable reminders of Golamee, but the recon spheres were smaller, and random areas of their shape seemed to pulse and fluctuate as parts of it were always in metaspace. Sarjah stopped in front of the door's access panel, and he observed through their link as she studied the traces of energy flowing through the organic circuits. Then Sarjah directed the recon sphere forward, and its surface morphed to cover the access panel as nano filaments eased into the dome's circuitry.

While Sarjah mapped the system access, Marcus monitored for any countermeasures. He bypassed two defensive attacks, then isolated the code, killing any further attempts to sound an alarm.

Well, done, Sarjah said. *We're in. Tuhzo, I'm opening door in three, two...*

The Xindari and Kleedak readied their guns as the door dilated on one. Drone spores slipped inside at the first crack and started scanning the area. Tuhzo took point as he and

Kleedak moved through into a wide-open space. The entire building was one room with a data portal in the center. This portal had the same coral reef appearance, but was about the size of an SUV, larger than the data portal on Travanis 4's moon.

t'Zyah led the others inside. Grayson and Kleedak took up positions at the door, watching their backs.

Pilot, are you getting this? t'Zyah asked, her signal relayed by the drone spore network behind them.

Copy that, the pilot answered. *Recording.*

Marcus stared around. He wasn't sure why he had been expecting a big structure full of machines; he supposed even living on a biological spaceship, he still fell into twenty-first-century thinking sometimes. Rising from the center of the data portal was a meter-wide column that stretched to the ceiling and branched out like a tree at the top. At its base, the floor had traces of organic circuitry patterns—similar to the lifecore chamber on *Fulcrum's Light*—spreading out to the walls. When he queried his bioweb on that, he could see that the entire structure was used to power the portal. The chamber they had detected under the base held a small lifecore. Sarjah was scanning the portal, and he moved to join her.

Lead t'Zyah, Sarjah said. *Looks like whoever did this will definitely be coming here anyway.*

t'Zyah bounded over to her in the minuscule gravity. *Is that a cycore?*

Marcus was looking at what they were talking about even as Sarjah confirmed it. The transmissions being received from the data portal in the Travanis system were being stored in a third-civ biomechanical dimensional-storage device. A quick index search showed Marcus this meant the information couldn't be transmitted through the

Nexus. In fact, the cycore couldn't safely be sent through a Society portal at all. The incompatible tech could destabilize the connection, causing feedback capable of tearing dimensional space. A lot of third-civ technologies, even though they might have originally been innocuous, were now highly illegal and classified as weapons of mass destruction because of their interactions with Society tech. So, someone had to retrieve a physical copy to collect the data in the cycore, a cylindrical shape about the size of lipstick tube.

Marcus felt the slightest wave of disbelief and disgust from t'Zyah as she studied the device. *This isn't a small operation by someone trying to grab some UHC entertainment.*

Agreed, Sarjah said. *But I can't imagine what it is, though.*

Sinju, t'Zyah said to the Yotara who was accessing telemetry from the lifecore under the base. *Can you tell the last time someone was here?*

Door code wipes entry logs, he answered. *But from residual sensor readings, I would say close to a month. No way to be more specific. No genetic traces inside, so whoever they are, they worked in vacuum and kept their voidskins on.*

Can you disable the base's jamming field? she asked.

I can, Sinju said. *But there would be no way to disguise that. Someone would be able to tell we had been here.*

Okay, we can't portal out with a cycore anyway, so we take it with us on the shuttle, t'Zyah said. *Since the other portal sent signals out on a monthly cycle, we have to presume they could be showing up any day now. Sarjah, Sinju, copy what you can, but discreetly. Best-case scenario, when the perpetrators show up, they will come all the way to the base before they realize anything's amiss.*

Already working on eliminating traces of our entry, Sinju replied. *I'll do a final sweep once Sarjah is done.*

Marcus joined Sarjah as she examined the portal's protection code. *It's not Protectorate-grade, but just barely,* she observed. *I can copy directories without a problem, but we will need to get the cycore back to* Fulcrum's Light *before we can even have a chance to decrypt the data.*

Ditec Greer, monitor the portal's ancillary code junctions while I focus on the cycore, Sarjah said.

Copy that, Marcus said after a moment. He was taken aback because for just a moment, he felt what Sarjah did, just a small peek, then it was closed off. It wasn't outright fear but extreme caution. They still hadn't talked about what had happened on the moon of Travanis 4, but he was sure it had shaken her up more than she let on.

They both touched a recon sphere that floated over to land on the data portal and serve as a firewall. Their void-skins connected with the device, allowing them to access the cycore's metaspace presence. To Marcus, it was a distinctly different feeling from when he used Society biotech. Sometimes, things manifested in recognizable analogs, but really, it was more about focusing on the flow of the energy patterns and what they did. The third-civ source code that created the foundations of algorithms and operating parameters could be molded intuitively but not as easily as Society tech. Patterns that resisted change might run, dispersing the code throughout the portal matrix, or attack using viruses. Viruses would try to follow the trail of his consciousness and access the pico filaments and organic-chemical facets of his bioweb, overloading or corrupting it, which would result in brain death. Still preferable to what happened to Golamee. Subjectively, they worked for a long while—their biowebs speeding up their thought routines to hyper fast speeds—but objectively, within a few minutes, Sarjah broke through the defenses and copied the data she could. She then shut down the data portal, making it look like a local system error.

We got everything, t'Zyah, Sarjah said.

Pilot, we're ready, t'Zyah said. *Fly by and pick us up here.*

Copy that, the response came.

25

"Commander, what's the update on our back up?" Ahmon asked. He and Ja Xe 75 05 were in his captain's cavity reviewing the mission status. Zin Ku Lai were taller than Xindari by about half a foot on average, but also thinner. And unlike the captain's purple larger scaled skin Ja Xe 75 05's smaller silvery scales sometimes fluoresced with his body's EM field as a second layer of communication. Over the shiplink Lead Bioneer Jahnas, Lead Doctor Haxi Leikeema, and Ditec Yeizar of Eleven had also joined the briefing. They didn't appear as physical images, just presences in everyone's minds.

Fulcrum's Light was twenty light-minutes out from the planet, resting in a pocket dimension. Instead of traveling through the different dimensions of metaspace, the ship entered metaspace and stayed still in one localized, curled-up dimension. The ship's D-field maintained an open connection to standard space to scan the outside universe, but the microscopic fluctuations this caused in standard space were next to impossible to detect. So, *Fulcrum's Light* was effectively stealthed; it could monitor what was happening but would have to transition back into standard space to do anything.

"We've established ultra-secure metaspace links to ensure no data of our movements are in the Nexus," Ja Xe 75 05 said, his blue eyes unfocused as he accessed info. "*The Casual Diver* is the closest ship at just under seven hours away. The other four backup ships will arrive over the next fifteen to twenty-six hours."

"Good. Liaise with Captain Sarda, and have *The Casual Diver* remain stealthed on the edge of the system when they arrive," Ahmon said. "And have the other ships hold off at least twenty light-years distance. We might have to wait here for days or weeks before anyone shows up, and I don't want to take the chance of an increase in activity in this area being detected. If the recon team finds definitive evidence on who is behind this, we will reevaluate, but for now we will operate on the presumption that we need to catch the perpetrators in the act."

"Aye, captain."

"Ditec Yeizar, even ditecs who aren't on duty should be on full alert," Ahmon said to his presence over the shiplink. With t'Zyah and Sarjah off ship, Yeizar was the senior dimensional technician on board. "We have to operate on the presumption that they will have third-civ weapons."

All ditecs have absorbed third-civ weapons knowledge memories and are currently running simulations in preparation, Yeizar said.

I don't want to believe they would be stupid enough to use those types of weapons, Dr. Leikeema said. She started to say more, then stopped, her emotions clearly showing she was upset.

Ahmon knew that while the doctor had no combat experience, on a previous assignment in border space she had been on a medical ship that had spent a year dealing with the fallout of a third-civ weapon that had caused an epidemic among the crew that had inadvertently activated it.

"I can say that the Protectorate Council deems it a lower probability, but it is an unfortunate possibility, Doctor," Ahmon said. "And the fact that the perpetrators have access to and have used third-civ tech means we must expect it. I also want you to monitor the Earthers on board," Ahmon continued. "The next few days will be far outside their experience, and they may need additional support."

I will, Captain, the doctor answered. *But do you really think it will come to actual combat?*

"I do, Doctor. I hope not, but I do," Ahmon said. "And we must be prepared for that eventuality. Which means you also have to be prepared for casualties."

Understood, Dr. Leikeema said.

On Earth, Mr. Ebrahimian served in his country's military in the past, so I think he can handle it, Jahnas said. *But I will make sure he has tasks suitable to his level of expertise.*

"Jahnas we should also have a bioneering team versed in the effects of third-civ weapons on lifecores," Ja Xe 75 05 said.

I have some of my best specialists on that. We'll be ready, Jahnas said.

"Very well," Ahmon said. "I know this isn't the type of mission our ship is used to. And while Lead Jahnas, Lead t'Zyah, and myself are the only crew who have been in actual ship-to-ship combat I have confidence in the crew and their training. Everyone stay focused, and we will get through this."

They all acknowledged Ahmon, and then their presences disconnected from the meeting, leaving Ja Xe 75 05 alone with the captain.

"Captain this whole situation disturbs me a little," the lead officer said, his silver scaly skin fluorescing in simple colored patterns of mild anxiety. "Whatever this is really about, the spying on Travanis 4, the use of third-civ tech, it feels bigger than what we're seeing. And I feel it will have far reaching implications. Especially for worlds like mine."

"I believe that is truth, although I cannot see the pattern yet," Ahmon said. He knew Zin Ku Lai were more homogenous than many races, and there were some talks among their leaders about them taking a less active role in the Society. "I know there are other worlds like Zin Ku 000 that feel the Society has too many weapons, even if they are for defense."

"Even that bothers some," Ja Xe 75 05 said. "Did you know my entire family pod was against me joining the Protectorate?"

"I did not," Ahmon said. Even though they had only recently joined the Society, Zin Ku Lai had a stable civilization going back almost ten thousand years. It was argued their stability was also a form of stagnation, which was why it had taken so long for them to develop space travel, but Ahmon agreed with the belief that they hadn't bothered with it because they hadn't needed it.

"We don't do well with change on a macro scale, myself included," Ja Xe 75 05 said. "And there are more of the younger generation who come out into the Society for a while to take back what they have learned firsthand. But I fear the more we face conflict the more my people will want to withdraw."

"But there hasn't been a battle in Society space in over four thousand years."

"Some of my people think that is still too recent."

"Perhaps it is," Ahmon said, but before he could continue the alert came.

Captain to the bridge, Ujexus called over the shiplink, and they saw the sensor data he included with the summons.

An unknown ship had just entered the system.

ON THE BRIDGE Captain Ahmon studied the visual of the star system in the shiplink. It was centered on the gas giant, with the image's outer edge just showing the primary star. The path of the enemy ship showed as a glowing line from where it had materialized in-system a few minutes earlier, just outside the orbit of the gas giant, and moved in toward the ringed planet. He focused on the planet's ring, and the image switched resolution, zooming in. The enemy ship soared above the northern plane of the ring. It was a bioship, definitely Society in origin, but not a design Ahmon recognized. Its hullskin was gray with streaks of green. The ship's ellipsoidal shape was similar to *Fulcrum's Light*'s two-hundred-meter-long body, but its stern had two additional tendril arms to the standard four of the *Fulcrum's*.

"Captain," Ujexus said. "Energy output and hull analysis indicate that that ship is equivalent to a cruiser-class Protectorate ship."

"But that's a custom design," Comms Tech M'zazape said. The tall, orange amphibian looked around the bridge, disturbed by the implications. "That would mean they have access to their own ship garden."

"Possibly," Ahmon said. "Let's keep speculation to a minimum until we have more facts. Ujexus, can you tell where it was grown?"

"Not without giving away our presence, sir."

The icon showing the portal base's position within the disk phased and then disappeared.

Sir, M'zazape said over the shiplink. *The ship is putting out a jamming signal.*

"We won't be able to portal our team out now even if they disable the base's jammer," Ja Xe 75 05 said. "Has the enemy ship detected us?"

Comms and sensor techs conferred for second, then M'zazape said, "No, sir, the jamming appears to be standard metaspace interference focused on the portal base to disrupt any communications."

"I think they know someone's down there, sir," Ujexus said, his shoulder quills and tail twitched anxiously. "They just launched a heavy shuttle. Definitely combat-capable."

"Red alert," Ahmon said. *Nav, set a course to bring us in above that ship. I want a high-dimensional transition to get us there quickly. Comms, contact the backup ships and let them know we are about to confront an unknown ship. Send full sensor logs.*

Aye, sir, they both answered.

Ahmon immersed himself in the shiplink, letting his consciousness expand. The entire bridge crew was linked now, able to make decisions in nanoseconds. Ahmon saw/felt that his lead officer was confirming the status of the rest of the ship. There was a great deal of anticipation, even a little fear, but the crew was well trained and ready. Protectorate ships in Society space very rarely were faced with a combat situation, but they were up to the task.

Within four and a half seconds, all was ready, and Ahmon ordered navigation to take them in. *Fulcrum's Light* slipped into higher dimensional space and moved toward the enemy.

26

Marcus and the group exited the building to wait for the approaching shuttle. The constantly moving ice and dust particles of the ring felt like a windy light hail, or the spray of a waterfall, as it struck their voidskins. Marcus watched as the shuttle came over the near horizon, flying close to the surface to avoid most of the larger ring material. His second mission in space, and Marcus hadn't performed as badly as he had feared. He figured that a lot of his nervousness was an unconscious refusal to accept that what had happened to Golamee had scared him a lot more than he wanted to admit. And he knew Grayson was right when he said Marcus would never forget it—but he felt he might be able to learn to live with it. Marcus was still lost in thought as he watched the approach, so he was completely surprised when about fifty meters away, the shuttle blew up.

The force of the explosion caused an expanding sphere to blast away and melt the surrounding ice debris. While there was no atmosphere for a true shockwave to propagate through, the vaporized moonlet surface and ring material provided enough of a medium for the blast to hit them with the force of a hurricane. Their voidskins automatically compensated for the sudden force, pushing them forward against the torrent and balancing them out. A debris cloud was kicked up, spreading across the boiled surface. And for a moment, visibility dropped to almost nothing.

Inside! t'Zyah yelled. *Back inside now.*

Marcus felt himself dragged along by Sarjah. Grayson took position just inside the door as everyone stumbled past. Kleedak and Tuhzo, who had been farther away checking the perimeter, took cover behind some rocky outcroppings.

There! Sarjah yelled, pulsing an image over the grouplink. A comprehensive image of the surrounding environment was formed by the sensors of all the voidskins, drone spores, recon spheres, and the final shuttle logs. It was like watching themselves from the outside and being able to move the POV around as if they were in a video game. Reviewing the video showed an area about half a kilometer off, to the ten o'clock of their shuttle, where another ship emerged from the ring debris and opened fire. Without the shields up, their shuttle had stood little chance.

Sarjah, disable the base's jammer and get a signal out to Fulcrum's Light, t'Zyah ordered. *Sinju keep the shield up. Tuhzo, Kleedak, fall back here.*

Hostiles incoming! Kleedak said, and everyone saw from his POV as he watched the enemy shuttle's bottom iris open and four ultra-voidskinned figures drop down to the surface. Marcus's voidskin was allowing him to process information faster, but he still almost missed what happened next. Two of the recon spheres with Kleedak and Tuhzo flew at the shuttle, their field displacement drives propelling them to hypersonic speeds in a moment. The spheres exploded against the shuttle's shields—which had barely turned on again after dropping off their strike team—causing the shuttle to be knocked aside just as it fired again. The shuttle's particle beam carved a trench out of the icy rock next to the base's door. Then two more recon spheres launched, their passage causing wavelike ripples as they sped through all the swirling debris thrown about by the explosions. One was shot down by the shuttle's guns as it tried to stabilize its flight; the second exploded against the ship's aft section. The shuttle careened out of control for a moment, its shields straining in multicolored sparks as it skidded along the top of the base's shields before it righted itself and flew out of sight overhead. Their exterior drone spores showed four more enemies drop down from the shuttle when it was behind the structure.

Shuttle didn't fire on us again, Kleedak said. *Probably don't want to risk destroying the cycore until they know for certain we don't have it.*

Contact! Tuhzo yelled, the shields of his ultraskin sparking as a barrage of X-ray beams from the enemy ground troops struck him. He rolled and dodged, his gun destroyed by one lucky—or very accurate—hit. Kleedak, Grayson, and the last recon spheres opened up on the enemy, giving Tuhzo a moment's reprieve. He rose from behind an outcropping, arms stretched before him to direct the field, and his ultraskin manipulated energies to fire X-ray beams back at the enemy.

Marcus continued scrambling into the room. There was so much going on, he couldn't focus. The grouplink was starting to overwhelm him: the feed from the spores outside showing the attack from multiple viewpoints, somebody's emotional state leaking in, the people yelling around him in the real world, the attackers firing on them.

t'Zyah grabbed his arm, banging her face membrane next to his, making him focus on her blue fluorescing eyes. *Damp down Grayson. Now!* Then she was moving, yelling to Sarjah.

Marcus wasn't sure what she meant then he saw that a lot of the confusion on the grouplink was coming from Grayson. His emotions were flooding it. Not fear really, but the high rush of feelings when in a life-and-death fight. Grayson wasn't even intentionally trying to send messages; he was just subconsciously transmitting, and it was causing chaos on the link.

As Kleedak and Tuhzo fell back toward the doorway, the lead security officer had a repeating signal sent to Grayson to stop leaking. Grayson was on one knee, at the opening to the main door, laying down fire, his ultraskin's shield incandescing as it took hits from enemy energy weapons. Marcus wasn't a soldier, but this he could do. The trick he had used on the shuttle to fully block Sarjah was exactly what he needed. Marcus couldn't actually go in and control Grayson's bioweb, but he was able to access Grayson's metaspace protocols and patch them by providing filters that would keep non-intentional emotions from transmitting. Grayson was so focused on fighting that he wasn't even aware of what Marcus had done.

Good job, Marcus, t'Zyah said, crouching next to him just inside the doorway of the base. *Help me with the shuttle!*

What? Marcus asked.

Without *Fulcrum's Light*'s lifecore as a processing hub, their grouplink could never provide the hyper fast perception of the shiplink, but biowebs still allowed users to process information at speeds far faster than a normal person. So, Marcus was consciously aware of the simultaneous things happening now that Grayson's emotional leakage was no longer an issue. Sarjah and Sinju were at the portal station in the center of the room. She was trying to bypass the portal controls to get them back to the ship, but they were heavily encrypted, and the metaspace jamming field was still up. Sinju had hacked the bioneering systems of the base lifecore and had already stopped the enemy from remotely shutting the shields down. Kleedak and Tuhzo were falling back to the entrance, but drone spores showed him that the enemy shuttle, while damaged, was still in play and was just coming back from behind the base. He was immediately aware of the danger.

The shuttle couldn't portal anyone from inside because of the base's shields, but Kleedak and Tuhzo were still about twenty meters from the base's doorway and outside the protected radius. Their ultraskins didn't have enough power to take out the heavy shuttle's shields, so they focused on the enemy on the ground and left the shuttle to the ditecs. Marcus was scared and a little overwhelmed, but he had trained hard, so when t'Zyah's perception expanded into metaspace, he mirrored her automatically. Even though the base's jamming still blocked access to the Nexus, that was only the dedicated area that served the Society—one dimension of metaspace. This close the enemy shuttle's D-signature made it easy to locate and focus on it, in metaspace. He let his conscious perception of what was happening in standard space take on background status. His and t'Zyah's bodies were kneeling on the floor just inside the doorway, but in metaspace a different battle raged.

Marcus could feel the shuttle's dimensional energies as its portal narrowed in on his teammates' metaspace coordinates. He instinctively knew t'Zyah's plans from their link, the knowledge opening in his mind like a well-rehearsed memory, and they attacked at different points. She focused on the shuttle's link to metaspace itself, trying to hack the code and disrupt it. Marcus focused on the shuttle's portal, creating dimensional interference keeping it from opening in standard space around his people as they moved for the entrance.

Kleedak's massive shoulder carbine fired depleted-heavy-element shells, and thousands of rounds struck the ground with such force, they reshaped the landscape. Kleedak's and Tuhzo's shields fluoresced brightly as the attackers tried to overload them with concentrated energy beams. They were almost to the doorway when the shuttle changed tactics. Marcus felt t'Zyah's shock as she warned Kleedak. The last two of their exterior recon spheres swarmed around them and created a repeller field just as the shuttle fired. If the enemy couldn't capture them, apparently, they wanted them dead. The repeller field held for a moment, dispersing the worst of the particle beam, then collapsed as the recon spheres were destroyed. The continuing beam destroyed the ground with such force that the explosion threw Kleedak toward the doorway, while Tuhzo was thrown in the other direction. His ultraskin's shields finally failed, and he died screaming in a storm of high-energy particles.

Through the drone spores, Marcus watched in horror as Tuhzo died and his presence on the grouplink winked out. So much debris and steam from the icy surface was kicked up that the visual spectrum was almost useless. Marcus froze for a moment hardly believing what had just happened, until alerts from the last exterior drone spores showed that the attackers behind the building were not moving around to flank them but instead were focused on one area of the dome. A quick scan showed that it was a hidden door.

I know! t'Zyah said as he pulsed the image to her. She switched from hacking the shuttle to the actual enemy ditec on board. *Help Sarjah. I got this.*

He could still perceive her in metaspace, but the immediate danger of the shuttle was over. Marcus saw Kleedak struggle up and fly the last few meters to the doorway, adding zer attack to Grayson's. Kleedak's shoulder carbine was gone, lost in the last explosion, but zer ultraskin was still functional and ze raked the enemy with gamma beams. The four attackers in front were about twenty-five meters away and slowly advancing now that they only had two opponents left.

Inside, Sinju was next to the data portal, trying to keep the dome's rear door closed. Sarjah was kneeling in front of the portal, touching it, not even using the last recon sphere as a buffer. Marcus saw through the link that she was manipulating the portal controls itself, but she was ignoring every safety measure she had used before. He quickly mirrored her crazy assault. A virus she had passed started creating a back door in her metaspace link, and Marcus was able to relink it to another portal subsystem, saving her from getting brain fried.

Marcus was only dimly aware of the other stuff happening in the room until Sinju pulsed a warning. A back section of the room dilated, and ultraskinned figures filed through. Sinju activated the recon sphere next to them, and it shot forward, its organic shell morphing as it slammed into the lead attacker, strands and tendrils wrapping around him and contracting. It was unable to slice through the ultraskin, but it still immobilized the attacker and discharged a large enough burst of energy to fry the body within. Marcus pulled Sarjah a little farther behind the data portal as cover, not sure if she was even fully aware of him because she was so focused in metaspace.

The attackers didn't use explosives, but their energy weapons poured over the edges of the portal, causing the defenders to take cover. Then Marcus's sensors registered an energy field form between them and the enemy. Sinju had control of the base's lifecore and was trying to establish a force field to block them off, but it wasn't solid. The three remaining attackers took a centipede formation, one behind the other, and their shields merged to focus on the front-most figure. Another blast shot through a weak area in the shield and struck t'Zyah in the back, knocking her down even though her shield protected her for the moment.

Anytime, Sarjah, t'Zyah yelled from where she had fallen. Kleedak turned from the doorway to stand over her, extending zer shields to cover t'Zyah's less-durable voidskin. Ze launched mini seekers; the small rockets spiraled up and out, swirling around the room and hitting the enemies from multiple sides, the explosions designed to drain shield energy.

t'Zyah, the base jamming field is disabled, but there's another one. Probably their main ship, Sarjah said just as Sinju was finally able to close and lock the main door. *No way to break through and contact the* Fulcrum.

Grayson immediately turned from the now-closed main doorway and dove to the side; he landed, rolled, and was up firing at the attackers inside in one graceful move, drawing their fire to the left. Kleedak grabbed t'Zyah and pulled her behind the data portal. Both groups were hindered in the enclosed space. But the attackers were even further hampered by trying not to destroy the data portal, at least not yet. The attacker in back stumbled as his shielding was overwhelmed by weapons fire, then a shot to the head caused his body to fall back out the doorway.

With only two attackers left Marcus had a moment's brief hope that they would survive. Then he detected a shift in local metaspace; something about the attacker's ultra-skins changed, some type of unchecked energy buildup.

Suiciders! t'Zyah yelled as she shifted her consciousness into metaspace, with Marcus just a moment behind. He knew the shot she had taken had hurt her, because of the briefest wave of pain he got from their link. He followed her guide, and they were able to establish a local dampening field to override the enemy's self-destruct process, at least for a few seconds.

Kleedak charged forward, zer eight-foot hulking form moving past Marcus like a tank. The Axlon slammed into the front attacker, their shields flaring bright. No sound carried in the airless base, but Marcus felt the force of the impact through vibrations in the floor. Grayson and Sarjah continued firing at the other enemy. Kleedak focused the full force of zer shield forward as ze unleashed gamma beams. Any unprotected life in the room would've died from all the radiation at play. Sinju used his new control of the base's lifecore to boost Kleedak's power levels. Marcus registered traces of energy flowing along the floor's organic-circuitry veins, leading right to the Axlon's feet and flowing into zer ultraskin. And step by step, the enemy gave ground to Kleedak's onslaught. Within moments, the two attackers were pushed back out the door, and outside the dampening field, their ultraskins exploded, just as Sinju got the entrance closed.

Now they were trapped.

27

"Captain," Ujexus said from sensors. "The enemy ship's jamming makes it hard to verify, but I'm fairly certain I detected explosions from the portal base area."

"Any contact with the recon team yet?" Captain Ahmon asked.

"No, sir," Comms Tech M'zazape answered.

Ahmon breathed, centering himself as he reviewed their options, but he knew what choice they needed to make. If the recon team was under attack, then they couldn't wait for backup. Xindari always looked for another solution before fighting, but given the events that had happened so far, he didn't think they would get an option to talk. He glanced at his lead officer.

"If they can field a cruiser-class ship, they'll fight, not surrender," Ja Xe 75 05 said.

"Agreed," Ahmon said, his green eyes studying the map for a moment, using his bioweb to lay out possible areas for confrontation. The portal base was located closer to the inner edge of the gas giant's ring. Tactical scenarios opened in his mind; he settled on one and sent it to the navigator. "Ky'Gima, bring us out along this vector."

"Aye, sir," Ky'Gima replied, her feathers ruffling briefly in excitement. The nav tech took the captain's path and molded it until it was an ideal trajectory, adjusting the ships transition through metaspace as they approached their new exit point.

Captain, we've just been scanned, Ujexus reported over the shiplink when they were still twenty light-seconds out from the enemy.

"Hail them," Ahmon said, and when M'zazape noted the channel was open, Ahmon continued. "Attention, unknown vessel, this is Captain Ahmon of the Society Protectorate ship *Fulcrum's Light*. You are ordered to stand down and prepare to be boarded."

Sir, there is a gravitonic buildup in their forward section, Ujexus said studying the sensor data. *Looks like a standard gravity lance projector.*

Targeting us? Ahmon asked. He wasn't worried; when ships first emerged from metaspace, the manipulation of local spacetime dispersed most energy weapon damage.

No... Goddess, I think they're targeting the portal base.

If there was a firefight and our people held theirs off, Ja Xe 75 05 said, *they might be willing to blow the entire portal to keep us from getting anything.*

"That's crazy," Ujexus said out loud.

Focus on the job, people, Ahmon said. *Tactical, I want a lock on that ship as soon as we emerge from metaspace. Message pattern fire protocol.*

Aye, sir, Zeinon, the tactical technician, answered, programming the message the captain sent to him.

Fulcrum's Light reentered standard space three thousand kilometers from the enemy ship, above and behind them on the plane of the ecliptic. The planet's ring stretched away beneath them from horizon to horizon. Even at this distance, the gas giant dominated the view, its bluish-purple color slightly reflected across the ring.

"Unknown vessel," Ahmon said. "Stand down. I repeat, stand down. You are suspected of UHC violations, crimes against humanity, and will—"

Sensor Tech Ujexus pulsed an alert on the shiplink as the enemy fired. *Fulcrum's Light* rocked slightly as a particle beam struck their shields.

Fire, Ahmon said. *Evasive action.*

Ten missiles launched from *Fulcrum's Light*, and grav drives boosted them to a fraction of the speed of light. The speeds were so high that if he had been viewing it in standard time, the missiles would've seemed to explode around the enemy ship almost simultaneously with the moment they launched. But in his hyper fast combat state, Ahmon saw the ocular orbs open on the enemy hullskin and the ship rake the area with gamma beams, so only a few missiles got through to hit their shields and explode. The thermal and luminal output of the explosion would easily be seen from within the ring. Exactly what Ahmon wanted.

A gravity lance strike—fired by the enemy less than a second after the attack—warped *Fulcrum's Light's* shields as they sped over the ring, but damage was minimal. Through the shiplink Ahmon showed Ky'Gima the course he wanted her to take. Things were happening too fast now for verbal communication. Almost a full three seconds had passed since the enemy had first fired.

Fulcrum's Light sloped downward toward the ring at high speed, while it also rotated to keep its nose pointed at the enemy, its forward cannon actualizing a path of high-energy virtual particles that bombarded the enemy shields.

They're barely maneuvering, Ja Xe 75 05 said. *Did we damage their engine?*

Negative, Zeinon said from Tactical. *Only a fraction of our attack penetrated their shield bubble.*

Captain Ahmon studied the display. The enemy ship had risen and spiraled a little to give their point defense gamma cannons a better shot at *Fulcrum's Light*'s missile barrage, but it had stayed within one hundred kilometers of its original position. At the speeds ships traveled, space battles rarely happened in visual range of enemy vessels. With projectiles moving at fractions of lightspeed, energy weapons traveling *at* lightspeed, and exotic weapons being superluminal, battles could be engaged over thousands to hundreds of thousands of kilometers or more. *Fulcrum's Light* was already eleven hundred kilometers from where it had first fired. So, for a ship to move only a few tens of kilometers made it practically a stationary target. But given how much planning and resources had gone into the enemy's operation, Ahmon didn't believe for a second that he was facing an incompetent captain.

Ahmon studied the enemy ship's patterns with the full processing power of the lifecore and saw the obvious. *Nav, take us in. They're going to destroy the base.*

28

Marcus cringed involuntarily as the portal base shook under the continued enemy shuttle's attack. When the actual fighting was going on, he didn't have time to worry, but now that they were trapped, he couldn't stop thinking about the fact that he had almost died. Again. It was the most intense feeling of his life, but it was also completely surreal. And looking around him at the others only reinforced that weirdness. Here he was on a moonlet in a distant star system surrounded by people who, while human, also weren't—at least not as he grew up understanding it. And he wasn't afraid, or he was so afraid that he had pushed past fear and was... He didn't know what he was—everything had happened so fast. Life happened so fast. One minute you're fine, and the next your loved ones are gone before you can say goodbye to them, or you're gone before you've made the effort to call them.

Boom.

He startled at the explosion. The enemy shuttle's particle cannon struck the portal base again, causing the building to rock even within the protection of the shield.

Marcus watched the scene from the sensor data—his point of view looking out on it like he was an intangible, disembodied giant standing on the landscape of the small moonlet.

You did good work with the shuttle, Marcus, Sarjah said on their private link.

He nodded to her but didn't say anything. He was focused on not letting his feelings leak into the grouplink like Grayson. She was about to say more, then stopped as they all accessed the exterior view and saw the light of the explosions seen high above the ring. Marcus's voidskin alerted him that there was a structured pattern to the radiation from the warhead's explosions, and his bioweb automatically revealed that it was a message from *Fulcrum's Light* detailing the situation in orbit and that help was coming. Then Marcus saw the suited figures of the remaining enemy outside leave their positions and fly back to their shuttle.

"They're leaving!" Grayson gave a shout of triumph.

The enemy shuttle turned and flew away as fast as it could, given the ring material.

t'Zyah gasped, then yelled to Sarjah, *Portal us out of here, right now!*

We can't. Sarjah said. *The cycore will mess with transfer.*

No choice, t'Zyah said. *You saw the message; they didn't just suddenly give up. They're falling back so the main ship can fire and take this place out. They'd rather lose it than let us get it, which means we must save it.*

t'Zyah, Sarjah said, holding the cycore. *Worst case, trying to portal with this could kill all of us. There's a forty percent chance it could cause the formation of a dimensional rift. And if—*

If we don't portal, we all die. Guaranteed, t'Zyah said. *Do it* now!

Within seconds of Sarjah's activating the portal, Marcus

could tell something was wrong. He and t'Zyah were mirroring her in metaspace, but they could only offer support. The portal room of *Fulcrum's Light* was there, a beacon on the layout of metaspace. At first, the sphere of the portal encompassed the recon team, but the third-civ tech resonated at a different dimensional frequency, causing interference. The portal room on their ship started to twist and warp. Then Marcus was aware of the portal room on the enemy ship as well. The feedback from the portal spread exponentially and encompassed the base, the enemy shuttle, the portal rooms on the two bioships, and to a lesser degree everything that operated on dimensional tech in a few light-years' radius.

He felt Sarjah try to readjust the portal controls. He fought through his fear to try to help, but this was different from the trap that had killed Golamee; the transdimensional forces at play were beyond his skills. Normal spacetime bled into metaspace without any of the usual protections. And for a brief heartbeat that was infinitely long Marcus was everywhere at once: onboard both ships, in the upper atmosphere of the gas giant, and spread throughout its ring. Standard three-dimensional space and one-dimensional time were, in that moment, as confusing to him as the higher dimensions, and his conscious mind began to lose awareness.

Were those screams? Pain. Was that him or someone else?

29

The first time he saw actual combat, Ahmon was a junior ditec on a Protectorate ship deep in border space. But unlike now the conflict was against another sentient species. There were a few civilizations in the Milky Way as advanced as the Society, but they had all moved past any type of conflict with each other. Occasionally, however, younger civilizations would make a technological leap, or retro engineer leftover artifacts of dead or transcended ancient civilizations and—depending on the younger civilizations culture—this would lead them into confrontation with other sentients.

The interstellar war of two younger civs using scavenged technology they barely understood, had spilled over into C-human border space. But by the time the Society had been drawn into the conflict to try to mitigate a peace, both younger civs had almost completely genocided each other. Even though the war had barely lasted three days Ahmon had never forgotten the few battles he had been in or the scale of the destruction that had occurred. Entire star systems had been obliterated. And even though he had extensive training and memory absorption, Ahmon didn't truly appreciate the role his old captain had to play until now. Now that he himself was the center.

The perceptions of the crew showed Ahmon the specifics of what he needed. *Fulcrum's Light*'s trajectory was carrying them on a parabolic course as they skimmed over the surface of the gas giant's ring, light glittering off the icy particles like a sparkling transparent sea. The enemy ship was barely a hundred kilometers above the ring and about two thousand kilometers away from and below them. Ujexus's thoughts flowed into Ahmon faster than any spoken words could sound. He was aware of all Ujexus "saw" with sensors and melded that knowledge with Ky'Gima as she moved the ship. He was aware as Yeizar's ditec team worked to disorient the enemy's metaspace abilities and weapons lock, and he melded that with tactical as Zeinon tried to get a target lock through enemy ditec interference.

Ahmon perceived the actions of the ship as a whole. Sensors allowed him to know the world around him, navigation let him move, tactical was his bite, comms let him talk to his parts. And Lead Officer Ja Xe 75 05 was like Ahmon's subconscious, keeping things running smoothly in the background like managing the immune system (making sure repairs were prioritized, that weapons were primed, that each department had energy they needed) allowing Ahmon to focus on the big picture.

Tactical options opened in Ahmon's bioweb. He analyzed and discarded multiple scenarios in milliseconds. He instinctively felt the simplest choice was their best, taking the fight straight to the enemy to allow the recon team time to get out; t'Zyah was a competent officer, and he trusted her to take care of her people.

Sir, their gravity lance is priming again, Ujexus said as they closed the distance to the enemy. *They changed target to us again.*

Captain, I have target acquisition.

Hold for two point four three seconds, Zeinon, Ahmon ordered, meshing his desired plan with Ky'Gima's flying.

They fired! Ujexus said. *Lance and missiles.*

Even with hyper fast perception and the speeds they were traveling, it was impossible to evade certain exotic energy attacks, especially within only a few thousand kilometers. Pockets of high gravimetric disturbance hit their shields again as Ky'Gima changed course to try to avoid the worst of the enemy's gravity lance attack. Ahmon perceived the strikes where the gravitic forces of the attack and their shield met as warped areas of space. Bioship's shields manipulated gravitic force creating an inverse gravity well around the ship, which graviton-based weapons tried to rupture.

One second.

By now the incoming missiles were almost on them, their grav drives propelling them at thousands of kilometers a second. Ahmon *saw* his ditecs manipulate metaspace to disorient their targeting sensors, causing some missiles to fly off into the void chasing sensor echoes. At the same time, p-tecs opened portals before *Fulcrum's Light*, and the remaining missiles vanished through them into metaspace.

Two seconds.

Ahmon ordered Navigation to do a quick metaspace jump. The ring beneath *Fulcrum's Light* seemed to fluctuate and curve outward to both sides as space appeared to wrap around the bioship. To make such a short metaspace transition required precise calculations, and mistakes could mean never reemerging. Nav and sensor techs worked in unison, and *Fulcrum's Light* emerged barely fifty kilometers from the enemy ship.

Point four three seconds.

Fire! Ahmon ordered.

Fulcrum's Light's gravity lance did massive damage to the enemy shields, which was compounded by their follow-up missile and particle beam barrage. Multiple missiles with graviton warheads warped standard space enough that a few particle beams got through the enemy shield bubble. Swaths of the other ship's hullskin split under the assault, ruptured veins spewing nutrients and biomass to freeze in space.

The enemy's particle beams deformed around *Fulcrum's Light*'s shield as the gravity bubble distorted their energies. Both ships fired another volley of missiles. Point defense ocular orbs on the hulls of both ships raked space with gamma beams as their particle cannons bombarded each other—so much energy and exotic matter was being discharged that the space in between the two ships became a high-radiation dead zone.

The enemy ship vanished from Ahmon's perception for a moment until sensors led his conscious awareness to the vessel's movement through metaspace. A second later the enemy appeared a couple of hundred kilometers away.

The enemy is back over the location of the base, Ujexus said from sensors. *They're about to fire on the base!*

Ahmon was already directing Zeinon who was targeting the enemy with the gravity lance again when metaspace seemed to explode in everyone's mind. Standard emotional dampers were wiped away, and Ahmon felt the panic of the crew as their minds and the ship itself seemed to be turned inside out. Ahmon's breath caught as he realized he was part of an icy rock floating in the ring, yet he felt no pain as his body's organs started to solidify. Then utter whiteness surrounded him, and his bodiless consciousness relived moments from his childhood and old age—simultaneously. A torrent of emotional stress, disorientation, a swirl of colors that weren't colors, and then he was on the bridge again, trying to make sense of what had happened.

The portal techs were in disorder, alarms were going off all over the ship. The enemy ship had been able to fire on the station. The sensor data showed the path of its particle beam looking like a neat tunnel carved down into the ring, that is, until it twisted and curved like a pretzel—an impossibility—before all sensor data stopped. But it was what happened just as they fired that Ahmon had to replay to be certain of.

There was an energy spike from within the ring. And for a few nanoseconds, a dimensional rift opened. Everything for a few hundred thousand kilometers was shifted in various ways through metaspace. Even processing the data at hyper fast speeds, the members of the bridge shared a moment of shocked silence at what their sensors showed them. The entire ring of the gas giant was now twisted and smeared, like some cosmic deity had taken a brush, swirled around the three-hundred-and-forty-thousand-kilometer-wide ring, and spread it through space. Tendrils made up of the icy debris of the ring curled and stretched out for tens of thousands of kilometers, looking like some giant squid was breaking out of a cosmic ocean. Tunnels and cyclones spanning the size of terrestrial planets, made up of loosely packed icy particles, slowly moved in other areas. Some parts of the ring were gone completely: there was an almost thirty-thousand-kilometer stretch of empty space in one area, like a hole in a glittering, storm-ridden sea. Other areas of the ring were thousands of kilometers thick and packed with enough icy debris that he couldn't see through it at all. The expansion of the rift had also knocked the ship about, and they were thrown into a relatively flat area of what was left of the ring, looking like a ship sinking on its side into the ocean. Gravity was still working, so there was no sensation of falling sideways, but what was happening was clearly told by the sensors.

Report! Ahmon ordered. *Was that some type of D-rift weapon?* A flood of information entered Ahmon's mind, and his bioweb filtered and prioritize the initial data.

In the shiplink, Ja Xe 75 05 was organizing data focusing on the damage reports from bioneering. The ship hadn't suffered as badly as the ring, but there was still a lot of damage. One of the ditecs was unconscious. Even worse one of the portal techs was dead and another in a coma. The feedback from whatever had happened was intense. *Fulcrum's Light* had two major hullskin breaches where standard space had fit back together out of phase, causing matter in the area to implode. He could perceive Dr. Leikeema in one smoke-filled hallway performing emergency surgery on one crew member with a missing leg. There was a long list of minor injuries and system failures.

I don't think that was a weapon, sir, Tac Tech Zeinon responded. *Analysis shows that the D-rift formed just before they fired. But I have no idea how.*

Sir, we're...almost forty thousand kilometers from our last position, Sensor Tech Ujexus said, slightly shocked, before he continued. *And the enemy ship was pushed about seventy thousand kilometers spinward and ten thousand kilometers above the ring plane.*

What's left of the ring, you mean, Nav Tech Ky'Gima said.

There's actually much more ring material now than before, Ujexus said as Ahmon and the rest of the bridge observed his calculations over the shiplink. Even accounting for the large section of ring that was completely missing from the far side of the planet—leaving what was left in a horseshoe shape—there was far more matter than there should be, which meant the D-rift had affected metaspace as well. The physical effects were the most obvious since the gas giant's ring wasn't truly a ring anymore. The violent collision of multiple dimensions had increased the ring material by many orders of magnitude. So, while some areas of the icy particles were still flat expanses, most of it looked like a twisted, deformed landscape.

We have it, Captain. Ditec Yeizar joined the shiplink, letting his data fill the captain's perception. *That was consistent with the backlash from third-civ tech and our portal technology. Especially given what we found at Travanis.*

So, the portal base exploded? Ahmon asked.

I think someone tried to initiate a portal jump with proscribed third-civ tech, which resulted in a mini D-rift.

You call that mini? Ky'Gima said.

That rift lasted three point two nanoseconds and reached a max size of eleven thousand kilometers, and distorted standard space for a few hundred thousand kilometers, the ditec said. *Compared to the D-rifts that span light-years in the Orion Nebula, this wasn't even a pebble splashing in a pond.*

And our people? Ahmon asked, a subconscious check showing that no portal activity had occurred in the ship. *Could they have survived that?*

Ditec Yeizar held his emotion from leaking into the shiplink, but his expression was clear. *I... I don't know, sir. They could have been transported anywhere in tens of thousands of kilometers. They could've been torn apart by the stretching of standard space, they could have been lost in another dimension altogether, or a hundred other things. There's just no way to know.*

Endless Dark, Ja Xe 75 05 cursed, looking at the image of the ring. Half of his perception was still organizing damage response around the ship, and his silver biofluorescent scales shifted patterns, reflecting his stress.

Ahmon joined his perception with him and Lead Jahnas.

The lifecore was severely strained, Jahnas was saying. Ahmon could perceive her in bioneering directing the repair efforts. *We have minimal grav drive ability, but transiting through metaspace is out of the question for now.*

Ahmon pulsed to Ja Xe 75 05 to focus on that. They needed to be able to get back to the portal base quickly.

What's the status on the backup ships? Ahmon asked Comms.

Residual D-rift disturbance is making communication next to impossible, sir, M'zazape said. *I believe I picked up emergency beacons for a moment, but now we can't hear anything out-system.*

The effects of a D-rift like this would've permeated dozens of light-years, Yeizar said. *It wouldn't affect anything in standard space that far, but any ship in metaspace would've probably been kicked out. And it would take some time to recalibrate their lifecore to initialize a stable D-field to traverse metaspace again.*

Ahmon knew that meant they were on their own for now.

Emotional blockers had been reestablished, so Ahmon couldn't feel anyone's emotions, but he could clearly smell the fear on some of the bridge crew. It was strongest from M'zazape; the Ta Wei's natural physiology produced scents that Xindari found quite strong. But except for some elevated breathing she was doing a good job of handling her fear as she did her job.

Ahmon's bioweb muted his own filters so he could let his feelings of confidence flow to M'zazape and the rest of the bridge crew. This was faster than any words could convey, and he reassured them with his feelings of confidence in their abilities. No one said anything as they continued their jobs, but Ahmon could tell from body language that people were a little more focused.

Captain, I'm reading a signal, M'zazape said. *The enemy ship's jamming has stopped. It's faint, but I think it's one of our team in the ring.*

Ahmon looked at the enemy ship; sensor data showed it wasn't running as he would've expected now that what they came for was destroyed. Instead, they were dropping back down to the ring.

They must be trying to pick up their people as well, Ja Xe 75 05 said as he shared the data.

Or pick up ours, Ahmon said. *Portal room, as soon as you can, get that person on board. Lead Jahnas, propulsion is the priority now. Sensors, if that ship picks up someone, I want to know who.*

As people went about their duties, Ahmon studied the weak comms signal from deep in the ring. He didn't know who it was, their crew or the enemy, but he hoped they could hold out.

30

I t was his own breathing that Marcus noticed first, slow, gasping pants that reminded him of a fish plucked from the water as it lay on the deck of a boat, trying to breathe. A complete shock to go from its universe of water to one of air. Like the shock of going from a standard three-dimensional universe to...something else. What had happened wasn't a mental transition with a bioweb's safeguards to protect his sanity, or even a physical transition within the protection of a portal or ship, with a stabilizing D-field.

It was a dimensional rift. A rip in the fundamental structure of spacetime where the local area was no longer just the three spatial dimensions and one temporal dimension but all dimensions—metaspace.

But that was all before. Before this moment. Not now. Now he was...linear? He had been with the recon team on the moonlet. The portal. And they had all been snatched through/in/around/out/away from it. Now here, he was trying to breathe, trying to remember what breathing was, trying to...

be

Marcus.

And he was back. This was now.

His breathing slowed, calmed, and then his other senses started to coalesce and come into focus. His voidskin imprinted vital signs into his consciousness, and what his eyes were seeing started to make sense. Then his nausea caught up with him. He threw up in his helmet, and for a moment feared he would choke to death, but his voidskin reacted immediately, his face membrane expelling the offending matter like pus oozing from a wound. The vomit instantly froze as it touched vacuum and broke off into icy chunks floating away from him. A special chemical boost was injected into his system and cleared his head. He reached out, holding on to the wall in front of him, and calmed himself. Marcus slowed his breathing more and focused on where he was.

The wall he was holding turned out to be a large chunk of ice about the size of a car, but there was so much debris floating around him that he couldn't see more than a meter or so. His first thought was that an explosion had completely destroyed the moonlet the base had been on, but that would've killed him. There was no way he could have been transported completely out of the system, was there? He couldn't see the stars anymore, or even a hint of the planet, which confused him. The ring wasn't nearly thick enough to obscure the view unless—the D-rift. It hadn't just affected his group; it had affected the ring itself.

Marcus tried an ultrafield scan of the area, but his skin's readings made no sense or didn't work at all. He tried to piece together what had happened. Sarjah had tried to portal them to the ship, and the feedback from the cycore had scattered the signal. When it felt like he had been in multiple places at once, he actually had been. And that was what happened to everyone else. They could be anywhere; he could be anywhere. His sensors could tell that none of his crewmates were within five hundred meters of him, and the grouplink had been severed. He was alone.

This is Ditec Greer to recon team; can anyone hear me? he sent on a general frequency. No answer. There was still no Nexus access, but not from jamming; something about the D-rift kept him from being able to access it. That unnerved him. The Nexus could be accessed from anywhere. Trying to make the connection now just felt wrong to him somehow. He considered connecting to metaspace, but without a lifecore, he had to be very careful not to go too deep, or he risked the same fate as Golamee. He wasn't sure if things were that desperate yet.

He had to stay calm. Health-wise, he was fine and could survive for at least another couple of days without worry. But since the gas giant ring was over three hundred and forty-thousand kilometers wide, he could be lost a lot longer than that. His best bet was to get above or below the plane of the ring.

Since he had no metaspace and no ultrafield scan, he had to go more low-tech. He tried using the local EM field to determine his location, but his voidskin was having a problem processing the input, so something that should be instantaneous would take minutes, which made him smile for the first time since all this started. He was getting spoiled by the speed of Society tech. He also had his voidskin analyze the drift of the debris around him, but there was no apparent pattern. The icy ring material didn't seem to be orbiting one source, like a planet, but instead there seemed to be a multitude of turbulent currents and eddies. Debris might flow past him one way, only to twist and swirl another direction a meter later. His voidskin's sensors finally finished, and knowledge opened in his mind, his bioweb allowing him to perceive the gas giant's massive magnetic field. It'd taken so long because at times, the field seemed to move or disappear completely. No doubt D-rift interference, but now he at least had a starting point. He was floating parallel to the ring plane with his head toward the planet and system north above his back. Marcus used the voidskin field manipulations to tilt his body up so instead of facing the rock, he now stood on it. Perspective was everything during EVA, and just standing on a surface with *up* above him, and the planet somewhere in front of him, helped to ease his nervousness.

The dust and ice grains in the ring blocked visibility so much, it made him feel like he was in a thick underwater fog with occasional large rocks floating past. And his voidskin was unendingly being pelted with debris. Marcus still figured his best chance was to go up, get above the ring and get his bearings, and hopefully get far enough away from the effects of the D-rift to contact the ship.

At first, Marcus tried calling everyone from the recon team again, but after a few minutes, he set a repeating message to transmit. He took a deep breath and launched himself upward. The rock he had been standing on disappeared as he rose, hidden by the thick ring material, and he fought down a momentary feeling of panic. Even though he had no sense of direction, his voidskin did. He flew through the ring slowly, occasionally altering course to fly around large chunks, as small pebbles continuously bounced off him.

As he flew, Marcus tried to ignore his voidskin's indicator of how far he was traveling: one kilometer, two, four. The original ring was only about fifty to a hundred meters thick on average, a kilometer at its thickest, so this endless fog of swirling particles and icy chunks was impossible—although clearly it wasn't. After a full fifteen minutes of flying, Marcus accepted consciously what he had known since he first realized he couldn't see out of the ring. Its structure had fundamentally changed, and he was lost. He had no idea how thick the ring was there, but it had to be at least hundreds of kilometers thick to block his view so thoroughly. He altered course and flew horizontally for a while, just in case what he thought was the planet wasn't, but no way he went made a difference.

Marcus picked a northern direction again and started flying, all the while sending signals and calling for help. He flew for almost an hour before real fear began to set in. What if he wasn't even in standard space anymore? He could be trapped in metaspace like Golamee had been, and this endless ring may be his burnt-out mind's way of coping. God, that was a depressing and frightening thought. If he was lost in metaspace then no one would ever know what happened to him. His grandparents would never know. As scarred as he was for himself the fact that he couldn't even be bothered to call them kept playing through his mind. The loss of his parents had nearly broken him, and it wasn't until he was much older that he realized the loss of a child —regardless of how grown—was just as devastating. And no matter how much they went through after losing their daughter, they had always been there for him. And if he died out there, they would go through all that again.

The only thing he could really do about that was to survive. The guilt would eat him alive if he let it. So he pushed it down for the moment. He had to focus on what he could immediately handle in the present. Marcus kept flying through the endless material of the planet's once ring.

Sometimes he could see no more than a meter away; sometimes a gap would open, and he could see many meters. But he knew better than to just try to rely on his eyes. He had his skin continuously scan the entire EM spectrum and highlight anything of interest. Eventually, after about another twenty minutes of flying, a small gap in the debris faintly showed something in the infrared, but the floating ring material blocked it again almost immediately. He didn't know what it was, but it was at least fifty meters away.

This is Ditec Greer calling recon team; come in. Can you read me? Marcus changed course and moved toward the heat source, praying it wasn't going to be a body.

Once or twice, he saw the heat signature come back into view only to be obscured again by passing ring material. He continued hailing for help but received no response. The sound of his breathing and the relentless vibrations of the ring material hitting his voidskin was the only noise. Then a small clear area opened before him, possibly caused by two larger pieces colliding and knocking each other away, but it was still full of smaller particles, like chunks of hail floating around him.

Marcus stopped suddenly when he saw the heat source. Not one of his crewmates as he had hoped but the severed front portion of the enemy shuttle slowly floating through the ring like just another ice rock. The hullskin was torn and twisted where it had been ripped apart; the edges still glowed hot in infrared—that was what he had detected. The back half was nowhere to be seen. The shuttle hadn't been that close to the portal base, so if it had also been caught in the D-rift, there was no telling how far its event horizon had stretched, or how far they had been scattered. He hoped *Fulcrum's Light* was okay.

Marcus was about to fly forward when his shoulder erupted in pain and he was flung through the ring, twisting, and spinning, until he crashed into a dresser-sized rock with enough force to get wedged in for a moment.

"What da hell?" He breathed, trying to clear his head.

Information flooded his bioweb perception. Health status, voidskin integrity, and the knowledge that he had been shot!—weapon type, location of attacker.

"Evade!" he yelled before he could even focus on the memory replay of what happened. His voidskin's bioelectromagnetic field barreled him away from the rock just as it exploded under the force of multiple projectiles.

"Shit!" Marcus banged into another large rock and went spinning in another direction until he could right himself. He put full power to his propulsion and flew away from the wreck, dodging and weaving around debris as best he could. Evasive maneuver patterns opened up in his consciousness, and he let them take over. His bioweb's memory nodes let him know what had happened; the enemy attacker had been hidden by the thermal energy coming off the broken shuttle, then he peeked over the shell of the top and fired. He had probably heard Marcus's calls for help and just waited until he got close. And like an idiot, Marcus had flown right into the trap. All this had been recorded on his voidskin sensors and transferred into his bioweb.

Only seconds had passed. A chair-sized piece of debris exploded in front of him, and he altered course. His voidskin backtracked the projectile trajectory, and he saw a rear view of his attacker coming after him—not visually, there was too much debris for that, but by the telltale traces of his enemy's bioelectromagnetic field and what he realized was his gun glowing bright in infrared. Distance pings told him he had about a forty-meter lead on the attacker, whose ultraskin seemed damaged but, unfortunately, not his weapon. That reminded Marcus to check his own skin status; his propulsion was fine, but his voidskin was too damaged to emit concentrated beams like X-rays. Running was his only option. Marcus flew with no plan in mind, just escape.

As Marcus flew through a marginally less dense area of icy particles, the new alarm that sounded in his mind focused him on the present. The enemy had just gotten a missile lock on him and fired.

The missiles flying at Marcus couldn't go nearly full speed, because they also had to change course to avoid large debris. One exploded against something almost immediately. Marcus knew he might get lucky and more large debris might still hit the other missiles and destroy them, but he also knew he might not get lucky. Alternate evasion patterns opened in his mind, and he let go and trusted his instincts. Two large house-sized ice rocks were about to collide right near him; if he could fly between them, using them as a shield, he might make it. But if he didn't clear it before they collided, as durable as his voidskin was, it showed he would take heavy damage being caught in the impact between those two rocks, and his lead would disappear. More missiles exploded behind him, unable to avoid ring material, but there were two left. He banked right hard, flying at the huge chunk of ice, and skimmed over its surface with just centimeters to spare. His voidskin showed the missiles changing course; they were seconds away.

Just as Marcus was flying out of sight around the edge of the ice boulder, he realized he cut it too close, and his shoulder banged into the rock, knocking off chunks of debris and sending him spinning. But before he could bang into the other rock and get crushed, the last missile—which tried to avoid the rocks Marcus had knocked loose—hit an outcropping and detonated.

The explosion vaporized large sections of both rocks, and the ring debris was dense enough for it to move out like a blast wave. Its force caught Marcus, and he careened and tumbled with all the other material. He was dizzy and had trouble focusing on the data his skin fed to him. His body continued spinning through the ring like all the other debris, bouncing off chunks like a pinball.

Seeing what was happening only made him nauseous again, so he kept his eyes closed and tried to make sense of what his voidskin was telling him. There was minimal structural damage, it wasn't going to keep out one hundred percent of the radiation, and his air processor was messed up, but he could still breathe for about twenty hours.

He had been knocked about a hundred meters from the explosion point and was still traveling—spinning—but there was no sign of the enemy. The chances of him finding Marcus were slim even if he didn't think the explosion killed him. There was too much ring material between them, and he had no possible way to even know which way Marcus had been knocked.

Marcus slowly uncurled from the fetal position he hadn't realized he had been in and gathered himself. He oriented himself to the rings north and south again, his voidskin stopping his spin. Visibility was still next to nothing. He knew he had to change tactics. He couldn't just fly around this once-ring, now icy debris field, and hope to come across somebody. Somebody not trying to kill him. He had to attempt going into metaspace. He flew for another half hour to put more distance between him and where he had last seen the attacker, then he settled on the next large ice rock he saw and gathered his thoughts.

Usually there was no danger going into metaspace, certainly not physically since his body didn't actually go anywhere just his consciousness. Although extreme mental stress in metaspace could cause a person's body to have a stroke or heart attack, it was exceedingly rare. The real danger was to his mind. Using his bioweb to enter metaspace without a corresponding lifecore to stabilize his awareness was dangerous. It was possible he would lose his ability to find standard space again, and since his physical self resided in standard space, it would mean he couldn't reintegrate his consciousness with his body. Meaning he would end up like Golamee. That scared him, but so did the never-ending ring he couldn't find his way out of. Going into metaspace seemed the only viable option to him.

The first time Marcus had accessed metaspace he had no idea. None of the other Earther trainees had either. About two months into their training their entire group had been gathered in the courtyard entrance of the garden. It had been one of the few times everyone had been allowed to be together.

Since they had arrived on Ya'sung they had done nothing but explore the Nexus. And every single day that started with them walking the garden paths. They spent half the day wandering the paths; the other half they spent researching specific things on the Nexus. That day the only difference was they were told to walk a mindscape of the garden instead of physically going in.

What they didn't realize until after was that the mindscape of the garden itself was constructed in metaspace. The garden's physical paths were laid out in a pattern that trainees would subconsciously memorize as they walked it over and over again. It was used to help trainees recognize patterns and thought processes that would lead them back to standard space. Marcus did his best to remember that training now.

His bioweb allowed his consciousness to perceive beyond standard space, and his awareness expanded into metaspace. It wasn't quite as bad as he had feared, like with Golamee, but there was still a feeling of wrongness. Like walking down a dark alley, deep in a shady neighborhood wrong. Now this was some shit that would give somebody the heebie-jeebies. Things seemed twisted, skewed, like a bad reflection of himself. Marcus thought there would be an utter sense of isolation, but metaspace was a maelstrom of perceptions he couldn't bring into focus. The sheer weight of the tide almost overwhelmed him and pushed him back into his mind, but he held on, trying to find any hint of Society tech. Then he felt the briefest of connections over his bioweb. Not a verbal signal but more of a presence, like walking into a room and knowing someone is there even before you see them. He focused on it, letting his training take over.

It was Sarjah! Their private link was a bit stronger and more intrusive than normal Nexus communications, but something was different. He sent encrypted pulses so they wouldn't be picked up by anyone else, but she didn't respond. It was almost like she was ignoring him, or asleep, then a stronger pulse showed him she was unconscious—maybe even in a coma. Marcus homed in on the signal as best he could, then brought his awareness out of metaspace.

He started flying toward her location. The rocks, dust, and ice still floated about him as if he were flying through a cloudy river. And in all these debris-filled kilometers were an injured crewmate, lost or dead friends, and at least one person trying to kill him.

He flew onward.

31

F ulcrum's Light limped along over the surface of the now-distorted ring, its grav drive struggling to maintain a consistent gravitational field after the damage the ship had taken during the D-rift. Comm Tech M'zazape had eventually identified the signal they had picked up as Kleedak. Ze had only been a few thousand kilometers from the ship but still over thirty-five thousand kilometers away from where the portal base was located. Captain Ahmon let Kleedak's experience, recorded by zer ultraskin, open in a memory node in his bioweb and reviewed it. Then Ahmon let his perception slow down to C-human standard and spoke to Kleedak, who was in Medical, via shiplink. Kleedak's account of the assault gave no further clues to the identity of their enemy. Ahmon could see that Sarjah had had the cycore in her possession when she activated the portal and the D-rift formed, but after that, Kleedak's data had been static until ze was deposited back into the ring where they had rescued zer. There was no way to tell where the others had come out, or even if they had returned to standard space at all.

Ahmon glanced at the bridge crew. Everyone sat calmly in an apparent meditative state. At the hyper fast speeds they thought when in the shiplink, physical movements would be far too slow to direct the ship. Everything was done mentally. Being connected to the lifecore and able to process multiple things in moments was good in a crisis, but Xindari still preferred normal speeds when possible. They felt more wisdom came from there. More genuine human choice. That's why at the end of their lives, Xindari rarely chose to transfer their consciousness into a Manifold World. Without experiencing the full cycle of life, death included, its true value was never achieved. No balance.

Ahmon stopped indulging himself, linked back up with the lifecore, and started addressing other reports for his attention. The bridge was quiet with only the occasional comment muttered out loud, as everyone did their job through the shiplink. Ahmon stood behind his chair, hands resting on the seat back as his mind examined the ship.

Damage reports and systems analysis floated in his conscious perception. The ditec that had been knocked unconscious by the feedback from the D-rift was okay, but they all had headaches. Yeizar was leading them in mapping the rift's effects on local standard space. The enemy had been closer to the portal base and thus the center of the D-rift, which didn't necessarily mean a more damaging effect. Even though they had origin points, D-rifts could have multiple epicenters across different dimensions. So, while the enemy had been displaced a greater distance, for all he knew, *Fulcrum's Light* could have taken more damage even though it was farther away originally. With so many systems still damaged, it was impossible to tell yet. Ahmon knew that time was on their side, not their adversary's; the longer it took, the closer they were to reinforcements arriving.

The most critical system affected was their propulsion. The D-rift had knocked out their metaspace capabilities, and their grav drive was only functioning at minimal power. Ahmon could feel the bioneers directing the ship's cells to hyper-stimulate and start repairing; more nutrients were directed to areas that needed mass for healing. The ditecs were stabilizing the lifecore's metaspace connections, bypassing damaged neural nodes, and working with bioneers to grow new ones. Ja Xe 75 05's presence was organizing the repairs over the shiplink, and Ahmon could perceive him and Lead Bioneer Jahnas discussing priorities as bioneering teams tackled the problems. Ahmon partitioned his mind so he could join in on the talk and still review the ship. While Jahnas gave a rundown on the grav drive damage, Ahmon allowed another part of his perception to observe medical.

He could see Kleedak, the large blue Axlon still arguing with Dr. Leikeema in the medbay. Ze wanted to portal back out to find zer team, and ze wasn't masking the anger and frustration of those feelings over the shiplink. Dr. Leikeema stood before zer, hands on her hips, and steadily shook her head. The yellow-skinned Fent'r was barely higher than Kleedak's waist, her long purple hair done in a braid down her back.

"Kleedak Pah," Dr. Leikeema said, not giving an inch. "You have been exposed to multidimensional *fields* with no more protection than an ultraskin. You might feel all right, you might be all right, but there are two more tests we must run to be sure you are all right. And you *will not* be cleared for duty until those tests are run. The more you argue the longer it will take."

Ahmon could feel Kleedak's unmasked anger and frustration, not at the doctor but at the situation. He could also feel Dr. Leikeema's undisguised empathy and understanding for Kleedak, fueled by her determination to do what was best for her patient and the ship. Ze started to say something multiple times, grumbled something under zer breath, then nodded zer acquiescence.

As one of the nurses led Kleedak away Ahmon linked with the lead doctor. *Dr. Leikeema, how are things?*

Captain, I was just going to contact you, she said. Feelings of concern, frustration, determination, and a small bit of anger flowed from her, and Ahmon realized she hadn't put up her filters again after sharing with Kleedak. He knew her previous experiences with the effects of third-civ technology made her take it very seriously. *All ditecs have been cleared,* she continued. *The headaches reported are typical in cases of mental strain from dimensional awareness. They shouldn't have any lasting symptoms.*

Good, Ahmon said. *Is that what killed Portal Technician Fahgi?*

A brief wave of sadness, regret, and anger flowed from her before she realized and shielded her emotional output again. *Sorry, Captain. People dying because of this ancient tech brings back some uncomfortable memories. I just can't understand why someone in our day and age would use this stuff.*

No apology necessary, Doctor, Ahmon said. *This isn't an easy situation.*

P-tec Fahgi, she said after realizing she hadn't answered him. *Yes, it was feedback from the D-rift. Her synapses were overloaded because she was actively working a portal at the time of the event. But the other p-tec was accessing a neural node to help with power flow, and that provided a buffer. He's come out of his coma but won't be able to work a portal for a while.*

I see. Ahmon was momentarily distracted because when she was mentioning the p-tec he naturally observed the portal chamber and noticed Envoy Ashenafi was there. He partitioned his mind again to speak with her. *Any other major injuries?* he asked the doctor.

Just minor injuries to deal with now. Some headaches, dizziness, two broken bones. And thankfully we were able to save Bioneer Jolzyn. And Dr. Ueda is holding up well for a civilian. I think having patients helps distract her.

Ahmon perceived Dr. Sumiko Ueda across the medbay, making small adjustments to the biogel cast attached to Bioneer Jolzyn's leg. A new leg was already starting to grow from his stump. At the same time Ahmon's partitioned awareness was observing Majid Ebrahimian in bioneering. The Earther was helping another bioneer working on the lifecore.

Bioneer Ebrahimian handled himself well, Jahnas was saying to Ahmon's partitioned awareness in bioneering. *A power vein ruptured right next to him, and he never left his station. I think these Earthers will do okay out here.*

Perhaps that will be true, Ahmon said to Jahnas.

I hope that's the worst Dr. Ueda has to deal with, Ahmon said to Dr. Leikeema at the same time. *But unfortunately, this is far from over.*

He covered a few more points with the Dr. Leikeema and Jahnas, then he condensed his awareness down to only two aspects, one on the bridge where he physically was and the other in the portal chamber. Through the shiplink he spoke to those on duty—a couple of p-tecs and one bioneer running diagnostics and repairing damage systems—then he manifested an image of himself to interact with Rahel. There were a number of races in the Society that didn't like communicating with biowebs, for one reason or another. Earthers tended to do well with the Nexus, but he noticed they did prefer to converse with a visual image instead of just a voice in their head. He suspected that was just because they were still new to the technology.

Envoy Ashenafi, Ahmon said.

She was off to one side, sitting on the floor in front of an open panel. Ahmon saw she was using a portable enzyme emitter to help dissolve some clots that had formed around the power veins when they ruptured.

"Oh, Captain, hello," she said. "I hope this is okay. I was in my quarters when the battle happened. And when the D-riff hit I was only disoriented for a bit. After things calmed down, I felt pretty useless sitting in my room, so I asked Lead Jahnas if I could help in any way."

No problem, Ahmon said. *I knew you were skilled with a bioweb, but I didn't realize you were knowledgeable with portal technology.*

"On the last ship I was on one of my friends was a portal technician." She absently brushed a stray lock of hair out of her eyes before she wiped some of the dissolving clot from the power vein. "Guess I ended up learning more from him than I realized. I remember the first time I saw him doing something like this, I laughed about..." An intense feeling of sadness, loss, and regret flowed from her. She sighed and wiped her hands on her suit leg as she stood up. "Well, that's in the past now.

"Has there been any news on Marcus and the others?" she asked.

Not yet. But once we complete repairs, we'll get them.

Rahel glanced over at the two p-tecs in the chamber. Ahmon noticed the subtle shift in her behavior. When he had first approached, she had been more relaxed, the way someone gets lost in thought while doing a task they are used to. Now her professional demeanor was back.

"I'm sorry, Captain," she said. "I didn't mean for that to

come across as if I was only worried about the Earthers on the mission. It's just everyone else is trained for this. Even Lieutenant Grayson is a soldier. I'm just concerned Marcus may be out of his depth."

I didn't think you meant anything else, envoy, Ahmon said. *And I know you don't have any official duties on the ship other than Ditec Greer and the program, but I would like to ask you a favor.*

"Of course."

Would you check in with the other Earthers on board? he asked. *Dr. Ueda and Bioneer Ebrahimian seem to be doing well and, like you, keeping busy. But this is still a very new experience for them and out of the context of what they have prepared for.*

"And since I've been involved in crisis situations with pre-Society tech you think I might be able to help them?" she said.

That's a likely possibility, Ahmon said. *You might also be able to help each other.*

Rahel looked at his image for a moment before she spoke. "Captain, I appreciate that you haven't pressed me for any information on my previous mission. Even now it's still a lot for me to process." She looked off in the distance seemingly lost in thought and smiled wistfully. "I don't seem to have the best luck when it comes to pre-Society tech, hmmm?"

Envoy... Rahel, I think you're handling yourself quite well. Ahmon said letting her momentarily feel the truth of his words. *All of you are.*

"Thank you. And I will speak to them."

Ahmon started to say more when action on the bridge caught his conscious attention. *You're welcome, envoy. I'll let you carry on.*

Ahmon let his image in the portal chamber disperse and

centered his perception on the bridge, where he focused his awareness on an anomaly that sensors had just detected. Ujexus and Ditec Yeizar conferred for a moment, the quills on both Oodandi's head and shoulders seeming to sway in unison, then Ujexus spoke. *Sir, the amount of D-rift interference makes it difficult to be sure, but from these readings, I believe there was some type of metaspace backwash from the location of the enemy vessel.*

Ahmon reviewed the data as it expanded in his bioweb's memory nodes.

With all the displaced ring material, there was no way to get a visual, but the enemy's grav flux was clear. They were about ninety thousand kilometers away and not moving at all, although readings said they had some power.

It looks like they tried to enter metaspace, Yeizar said. *But the dimensional feedback caused a disruption in their lifecore. If their engines weren't as badly damaged as ours before, they are now.*

Now it was a race to see who could repair their ship the fastest.

We now have minimal grav drive, Captain, Ja Xe 75 05 said. *But until repairs are complete the best we can do right now is a few thousand kilometers an hour.*

Meaning it would take them over eleven hours to get back to the base, some thirty-five thousand kilometers away. Compared to the over three-hundred-and-forty-thousand-kilometer width of the ring, they had only been displaced a fraction of the distance, but at their reduced speed, it made all the difference.

Understood. We can continue repairs en route, Ahmon said. *Nav Tech Ky'Gima, take us to an orbit above where the portal station was.*

Aye, Captain, Ky'Gima said.

Fulcrum's Light continued across the ring. To one side, a twisting column of ring material rose thousands of kilometers upward, looking like a gigantic tornado frozen in mid-spin. The ship kept on a straight line for the base as much as possible, but some areas still had pockets of dimensional turbulence. At one point, they flew over a hole in the ring, a few hundred kilometers across, where you could see completely through to the other side of space. Approaching it looked like a ship about to fly off a cliff.

Sir, Ja Xe 75 05 said on a private link, *if the D-rift explosion spread our people throughout the ring, shouldn't we see if we could find any other survivors?*

We can't afford to wait, Ja Xe, Ahmon said. *Past encounters with this type of third-civ tech indicates the device itself probably didn't portal anywhere. If it wasn't destroyed, it will still be there. Securing that is our primary objective. Our people will have to hold out for now.*

32

It took Marcus almost another hour to reach Sarjah's signal. He tried not to let himself dwell on the time, but he couldn't help it. A part of him didn't even believe he was in the same ring anymore. He occasionally had to detour to avoid areas that had instabilities from the D-rift. Marcus slowed as he got closer to the signal; he didn't know what to expect, but he would at least try to not fly into an obvious trap. A large area before him glowed faintly in infrared, and the ring debris seemed to be thicker than average for a moment, then it started to thin out, and Marcus slowed to a stop. Before him was a relatively clear spherical area, about half a kilometer across, with several huge chunks of ice rocks floating randomly about. One, the size of a bus, was slowly drifting out of the clearing, back into the denser material of the ring.

Marcus had his voidskin back him a little farther into the surrounding debris and matched trajectory with the ring material floating past so he wouldn't stand out as a stationary object. Sarjah's signal was coming from near the center of the hollowed-out area. The space was clear enough that his voidskin's sensors could see Sarjah's body floating limp and motionless on the largest house-sized chunk in the middle. Next to her was the data portal, still intact, even though the dome of the base was completely gone. But even more surprising was the enemy agent working on the portal. Instead of a ultraskin he wore a void-skin but of the same style as the ones who had attacked, so he was probably one of their dimensional technicians. That, of course, didn't mean he couldn't kill Marcus.

It took a moment for Marcus to stop thinking about how he could save Sarjah and start paying conscious attention to the information his skin was feeding him. Analysis of the surrounding area showed that this was where the portal base had been. The D-rift that had scattered them had destroyed the small moonlet. Debris-dispersal patterns showed the explosion was what had cleared out the hollow area; the speed of the expanding material colliding with the rest of the ring debris had heated it up and explained why it showed in infrared at its perimeter. But the area immediately around the portal was intact. Marcus presumed Sarjah hadn't been transported anywhere because she was the one connected to the cycore, but that was only a guess. The vitals he could pick up through their link showed she was alive, but he had no way of knowing if she was just a body that was brain-dead. He tried to ignore the voice in the back of his mind reminding him of what had happened to Golamee. And tried even harder to ignore the voice telling him he might die out here and never see his family again.

No. This moment now was all he could focus on. He almost laughed at the thought of Sarjah telling him to let everything else fall into balance. He looked at her motionless body again and shook his head. He refused to believe Sarjah's mind was lost in some higher dimension and her body was just an empty shell now. He couldn't tell any more about her condition, so he had to focus on saving her, but he wasn't sure how. His voidskin was capable of self-healing, but the damage he had taken put him at a disadvantage—especially without functional beam-emitter capabilities. He could try flying out of the ring again, to contact *Fulcrum's Light*, but he had no way of knowing if they had even survived or how long that might take. If that guy figured out whatever he was trying to do while Marcus was gone, Sarjah was probably as good as dead.

Marcus tentatively reached out with his awareness to study metaspace. The enemy was more focused on the data portal, but Marcus could feel subroutines still trying to access Sarjah's bioweb. That was what had caused the pulse that let Marcus detect her before. He adjusted his metaspace interaction to be sure the enemy couldn't pick it up and risked piggybacking a code on the pulse that only members of their grouplink should be able to pick up.

Marcus slowly moved around the edge of the clearing, trying to decide on a plan, all the while hoping he wasn't going to fail Sarjah like he did Golamee. He soon circled the entire area once but could see nothing that would give him an advantage. And Marcus was beginning to fear he didn't have much time. Even if the other ditec didn't figure out an answer, he still may try something that would make everything worse. Marcus knew he would have to do something soon.

Then a wave of emotions washed over Marcus with such overwhelming force that he cried out, his hand going to his heart as his body started hyperventilating. Surprise /fear

/anger /powerlessness. If he were standing he would have staggered, maybe fallen down, but in the weightlessness of space his body naturally curled in on itself and he floated there, knees pulled almost to his chest as he tried to catch his breath and center himself. He had turned all the filters off on his bioweb when he was trying to pick up a signal, and the suddenness of this experience caught Marcus off guard. As he established control again Marcus realized there was a familiarity to the emotions.

Grayson?

Greer? Greer, is that you!? Grayson's voice over the grouplink was so gratifying to hear that Marcus hadn't truly realized how scared he had been.

Grayson! Thank God. Are you OK? What just happened?

No, I... The mixture of anger and frustration that came over the link was strong. *I came across Sinju. Half of his body was... it was fused inside of a large rock.*

Jesus, Marcus said.

I couldn't pull him out of it, man; it was like... Fuck, it was crazy. What happened to us, Marcus? One minute, I think we're portaling home, then I'm in orbit above the freaking planet, and then I'm lost in the ring. Is this even the ring? Where the hell are the stars, man?

As far as I can tell, just what Sarjah warned us about happened. A dimensional rift formed when she tried to portal us. Marcus described the situation as best he understood it, allowing his voidskin to share visuals with Grayson, but he was careful not to access Grayson's. He didn't want to see the image of Sinju's body. And that thought reminded him that Tuhzo was also dead. *Have you heard from anyone else?*

No, and I've been looking for hours. Grayson's signal was a little choppy because of the D-rift, but it was getting stronger. Marcus could tell the other Earther was only a few kilometers away and closing.

Me too. Just home in on me. You should see this area on infrared any minute.

You sure you lost that other guy?

Yeah. I mean, I guess. Who knows in all this mess? And there were more of them than us, so no telling if anyone else is nearby, Marcus said, then he forced himself to ask what he was dreading. *Do you think t'Zyah and Kleedak are...*

Dude, there's no way to know so worrying about it won't help. We'll deal with that when we can, Grayson said. *I got you on visual, now.*

Marcus's scan showed him Grayson's location. He was on the far side of the bubble at the edge of the debris. The large mass of the leftover moonlet, in the center, blocked Grayson's view of Sarjah and the enemy, but he accessed it from Marcus's POV.

So, any idea what this guy's doing? Grayson asked.

No, but my guess is he's trying to use the data of Sarjah's attempt with his own knowledge to open another portal or at least contact his people.

Our mission's the same, then. Retrieve the cycore and rescue Sarjah. Then we look for the others.

Marcus hadn't even thought about getting the cycore, only rescuing Sarjah. But he knew Grayson was right. He could still feel how bothered Grayson was about what happened to Sinju, but he was hiding it well, focusing on the mission. And Marcus could also feel Grayson's determination.

He can't see me, Grayson continued. *So, I'll work my way around the chunk he's on. When I'm in position you cause a distraction, and I'll take him out.*

Okay, sure. Marcus was about to ask what kind of a

distraction when his voidskin picked up more movement on the bubble's boundary. Another ultraskinned enemy slowly emerged from the debris and started flying toward the data portal. Marcus couldn't tell if it was the same one that had attacked him, but he also had a big-ass gun.

Shit, Marcus said.

33

Captain Ahmon stood in the dimensional technician cavity, discussing options with Ditec Yeizar and Commander Ja Xe 75 05. *Fulcrum's Light* had been traveling for a few hours, gradually increasing their speed as the lifecore got more power, but they were still over twenty thousand kilometers from the portal base where the D-rift had originated. Engines had been fully repaired a half hour ago, but the ship had been moving through an area with high dimensional flux, and Ahmon didn't want to risk going into metaspace without the D-field fully working. And Yeizar and the others were just finishing strengthening the ship's D-field now.

The enemy vessel was still on the far side of the portal base from *Fulcrum's Light*. Ujexus had detected readings that suggested the enemy had repaired their engines as well, but since the initial explosion sensors had detected hours ago, the enemy ship hadn't moved far from their immediate location. As long as the other ship had maintained their status and not run, Ahmon had used the time for *Fulcrum's Light*'s repairs. The longer things lasted, the better for *Fulcrum's*

Light, because it meant that much sooner to other Protectorate ships arriving.

"Any guess as to how bad our backup may have been hit?" Ahmon asked.

"I had confirmation the backup ships started coming as soon as we let them know the enemy had arrived," Ja Xe 75 05 said. "But no communication since the D-rift."

"No way to be sure, with Nexus connection still down," Yeizar answered. "But since the D-rift shockwave permeated many light-years away—"

"They were no doubt knocked out of metaspace and are fixing their systems as well," Ja Xe 75 05 said, his scales fluorescing darkly with frustration.

"Yes, I suspect it will be at least another hour or so before we get help," Yeizar finished.

"Meaning, for now, we are still effectively on our own and the only ones capable of stopping the enemy from getting away," Ahmon said.

Captain! Ujexus called from Sensors. *I'm registering portal activity from the other ship. I believe they just found someone.*

A moment of anxiousness passed through everyone on the bridge with the unspoken acknowledgment that it could be one of their people the enemy ship had found. Normally, they would easily be able to pick up life signs in the ring, but the D-rift made deep scans unreliable and sometimes even misleading. They had already had two false contact readings.

Ahmon knew that their first priority had to be the data from the portal base if it still existed. The enemy ship might be responsible, but most likely it was just a piece of a larger puzzle, and the info from the data portal could lead them to the true culprit.

"Ky'Gima?" Ahmon asked, walking back into the bridge cavity and taking a seat.

Course is set for a location above the portal base explosion, Captain, the nav tech answered.

Take us in.

The distance between *Fulcrum's Light* and its destination appeared to squeeze together as the bioship transitioned into metaspace. The ring itself seemed to go from a field of debris to a solid object as the view of it was compacted.

The enemy ship is powering weapons, Ujexus reported. *And they are moving into metaspace. Looks like an intercept course.*

That must mean it was one of their people they picked up, Ja Xe 75 05 said. *If they had retrieved the cycore they would probably leave system.*

Ahmon knew that was no guarantee. There could be something else at the portal base they needed to retrieve or destroy.

Suddenly, the ship rocked with such force that Ahmon would have been thrown to the floor if his ship suit didn't adhere to the seat. Data flooded the captain's mind. For a microsecond, he thought they had been attacked, until the perceptions of the ditecs and sensor tech showed him they had crossed another pocket of dimensional fluctuation that had destabilized the ship's D-field for a moment, knocking them out of metaspace.

Fulcrum's Light spun as they reentered standard space, and Ky'Gima struggled to get them under control. The bioship plowed through one of the many tendrils that stretched up for hundreds of kilometers from the now-distorted ring, pulling a smear of twinkling ice particles in its wake like a glittering contrail, before the nav tech got the ship stabilized again.

Reports flowed through Ahmon's mind; bioneering was

strengthening the lifecore, so he let Ja Xe 75 05 handle that as he focused on the ditecs. Yeizar and his team had suffered massive feedback, and one of them was even unconscious, but they were working to reestablish the D-field. Even though the dimensional rift had sealed itself after a few nanoseconds, its impact on the surrounding space would be evident for centuries or millennia. The gas giant itself was often completely obscured from view by the once-ring's bulges, hills, valleys, columns, and twisted tendrils of dust and ice material so vast it could swallow terrestrial sized planets in its hundreds of thousands of kilometers of area. Worse than that were the small areas of instability where standard space was still weak and multidimensional forces could bleed through. There were less of these areas near the epicenter of the D-rift formation but still enough to justify caution when traversing metaspace in the region. It was an acceptable risk, especially given that the other ship was trying to reach the portal base area. So, as soon as he determined from the ditecs that they were ready, he had Ky'Gima take them back into metaspace.

Captain, Ujexus called. *The enemy ship got knocked out of metaspace also. They exited about twenty thousand kilometers from where the portal base was.*

If their lifecore is damaged enough, Ja Xe 75 05 said, *we might be able to end this before they go into metaspace again.*

Ky'Gima, the captain said. *Change our exit vector.*

Fulcrum's Light continued through metaspace, bypassing the portal base, as it now closed in on the other ship.

They fired! Ujexus said.

Ky'Gima dropped *Fulcrum's Light* into standard space early at the sensor tech's warning, just as a gravity lance strike warped space a few hundred meters in front of and below their position. The enemy had calculated the

Fulcrum's Light's most likely exit and fired, trying to hit them when they emerged into standard space.

Zeinon, fire, Ahmon ordered.

The enemy's shields radiated as they were struck by *Fulcrum's Light*'s gravity lance. Then the ship vanished into metaspace as particle beams passed where he had been moments before.

Probable exit locations showed on the map in Ahmon's mind as Ujexus tracked the enemy's dimensional signature with sensors. At the same time, Ahmon absorbed Tactical's data, reviewing what Zeinon's expertise considered the most likely emergence for the enemy and then pulsed his approval on the attack. *Fulcrum's Light* fired again then they transitioned back into metaspace also.

The two salvos of missiles *Fulcrum's Light* launched streaked forward at relativistic speeds. The first group met the enemy ship as it emerged from metaspace and exploded in a massive gravitic burst. Most of the fundamental forces released were radiated into higher dimensions, but a small portion of gravitons survived to bombard the enemy shield, causing unstable pockets in the gravity bubble.

Ocular-like orbs opened along the enemy ship's hull-skin, and gamma beams swept out, destroying the second salvo of missiles, which had altered course and were closing on the still-moving ship. Explosions expanded across space like popcorn across a hot plate.

The battling ships popped in and out of metaspace, trying to catch the other off guard, but since they were going to the same place, that meant there was little option but close combat. Even this close to the epicenter, a few areas still had high concentrations of D-rift energy, which played havoc with the battling ships' sensors, targeting, and navigation. Both ships were within one hundred kilometers of each other now. Too close to effectively use the dimensional drive for maneuvering. Their grav drives manipulated local space as they flew around the ruined ring.

Fulcrum's Light's shields sparked with twisted, intense swirls of energy where particle beams struck them, and were warped by the inverse gravity well. In the full sensory input of the shiplink, the area between the two ships was a flood of EM output—where polarizing and filtering parameters allowed for individual sight of energy beams and antiparticle explosions—that glowed like a brief star.

The enemy shields were overloaded for a moment by an intense barrage of missiles with exotic matter warheads, and they phased, allowing a number of *Fulcrum's Light's* particle beams to strike home. The enemy ship rocked violently to the side from the impact, and its hullskin blistered and cracked like burnt flesh, a dark, ugly scar carved along its side.

Fulcrum's Light's gravity lance hit the renewed enemy shields again, charged particles glowing in the visual spectrum for a second, until the enemy's momentum carried them behind a broken moonlet ripped from its orbit. The tendrils, mountains, and valleys of the once-flat ring were being reshaped even more by the force of the battle. Icy ring debris was swept up in the enemy's grav drive's wake leaving a hundred-kilometer-long streak across space, like twinkling paint over a cosmic canvas.

The battle flowed over Ahmon's mind as his heightened perception took in everything, the ship operating as one organism and he as its brain. Sensors, Tactical, Navigation, all separate, but feeling the pattern of the fight and reacting to it with one voice. His voice.

Ahmon's main focus was the attacking ship, but on the periphery of his consciousness, Ahmon was aware of Ja Xe

75 05 managing the repairs; areas that impacted the ship's abilities were noticeable to the captain as his subconscious filtered the data with his bioweb. He was fully aware of the bioneers' struggle to maintain the power output of the lifecore. He could feel the biomass and nutrients pumped through the ship's veins into damaged areas. He knew the dimensional technicians worked to keep *Fulcrum's Light*'s systems from being disoriented at the same time as trying to disorient the enemy ship and disrupt their dimensional link.

Then M'zazape's perception was marked high priority and pushed to the forefront of Ahmon's consciousness. There was another transmission from the ring. Another one of their people!

It was t'Zyah. Her signal was faint and broken. As the main aspect of Ahmon's mind directed the battle, a partitioned part monitored M'zazape as she attempted to get a clear signal. Only the occasional word and some vague emotions were distinguishable; she mentioned the cycore, but it was impossible to make out whether she had it or if it was destroyed.

Sensor Tech Ujexus's perception came to Ahmon's attention as he marked a barrage of enemy missiles that were just launched—not at *Fulcrum's Light* but at the location of t'Zyah's signal! Ahmon knew they must have picked up on her wideband distress call. *Fulcrum's Light*'s gamma cannons were able to take out a few before they were out of range, but it would only take one to destroy everything in t'Zyah's vicinity. The portal techs tried to get her, but there was too much interference that far away. And there was no way *Fulcrum's Light* could stop all the missiles and retrieve t'Zyah without giving the enemy an open shot at the portal base.

In the nanoseconds that passed as the missiles sped

onward, Ahmon replayed her message multiple times. M'za-zape ran many algorithms to clear up the signal, but nothing helped; the D-rift was causing too much interference. The comm officer calculated a fifty-six percent chance t'Zyah had the cycore. That wasn't high, but as Ahmon weighed the choices, he knew he couldn't ignore the possibility that she had the device. If she did and they killed her, then this was all for nothing. If she didn't, the enemy might be able to take out the base, but maybe the cycore wasn't there, either. With barely a thought, Ky'Gima understood the captain's orders and shifted *Fulcrum's Light* into metaspace.

The enemy's missiles streaked across space above the ring, avoiding dense columns and wisps of material when necessary. t'Zyah was ten thousand kilometers on the opposite side of the portal base from *Fulcrum's Light*, with the enemy and their missiles between them. The only way for the ship to reach her in time was to transition into deep metaspace, so deep that they ran the risk of being lost in metaspace themselves. With a deep-enough transition, a ship could travel across the galaxy, but finding their way back to their standard spacetime would be next to impossible.

They did it anyway. Ahmon experienced Ky'Gima navigating with Ditec Yeizar's help as *Fulcrum's Light* brushed the edges of dimensions that would suck them in forever. Ahmon lost perception of the target system altogether for a moment, and then *Fulcrum's Light* popped back into standard space, above t'Zyah's position. The portal techs got her on board as Tactical destroyed the last of the enemy's missiles that were almost on them now.

Ahmon knew immediately that t'Zyah didn't have the cycore. Her full report flowed into his bioweb in moments, and he had *Fulcrum's Light* set course back to the portal base.

Sensors showed the enemy ship diving into the ring itself, an expanding cloud of ice and rock debris spreading out as the massive ship plunged downward, flakes of necrotic hullskin trailing from its burning surface.

Ahmon knew they had lost the gamble but still had them give chase. *Fulcrum's Light* was too far away now, and the enemy would probably be able to fire and destroy the portal base before they could stop it. He just hoped none of their people were still there.

34

D*ammit,* Grayson said.

You see him? Marcus asked.

Yeah, but better he showed up now than two minutes from now, when he could've surprised me while I was sneaking up on his friend.

So, what now? New plan?

Little late for that.

What? Marcus turned from watching the incoming enemy to where Grayson had been. He was confused for a second because the sensors showed instead Grayson was holding on to a chunk of rock that was drifting toward the data portal. A rock not nearly big enough to hide him.

Da hell, man?! Marcus blurted out. *You couldn't even count to three or some shit?*

I was already moving, Grayson said. *Focus, dude; it's about to get real.*

Can you take both of them?

When the one next to the portal engages me, you swoop in, grab Sarjah and the cycore, and get out.

Marcus stopped himself from saying *What if he doesn't*

leave her? Grayson was about to risk his life to save them, and the last thing he needed was Marcus talking in his ear. This was happening.

The ultraskinned enemy drifting in suddenly jerked his weapon up, but too late; two shots hit his chest and shoulder, spinning his body around. On Earth, the fight would've been over, but while slightly damaged, the ultraskin was still very functional. Reacting so fast Marcus guessed it was an automatic response, the skin changed the enemy's course and turned him back toward Grayson even as his gun came up, firing a barrage of projectiles.

The rock Grayson had been behind disintegrated into dust as the heavy-element shells tore through it at terminal speeds, but Grayson was already flying away as he returned fire. The enemy dodged, flying to the side as Grayson's shots whizzed past. Both combatants were fully committed to the fight now. Their figures dodged, turned, and accelerated, trying to avoid each other's fire and land their own shots, their dark ultraskins reminding Marcus of flies buzzing around, changing directions at amazing speeds. Ultraskins didn't have enough power to generate dimensional or gravitational fields; their thrust worked by manipulating bioelectromagnetic fields. Even so, the armor had enough mass that in the void of space, they couldn't stop on a dime. There was always a minute amount of inertial drift whenever they changed course before they could reach speed again. It was that moment of relative stillness in the fight, just a fraction of a second, that each tried to take advantage of, calculating when their opponent was going to change course and which direction they were going and targeting that spot to get the maximum amount of weapon fire hits.

Their bioelectromagnetic shields sparked and flared as they worked to deflect the damage of energy and projectile impacts. At one point, Grayson's flight took him behind a large floating rock, which he used to block his course change. Enemy fire lanced by where Grayson should have emerged, but he came from below the rock, rifle firing almost before he was clear and scoring a direct hit to the enemy that knocked him spinning. A few pieces of large ring material crashed into the enemy before he could right himself, alter course, and use the debris itself as a shield as he returned fire.

Marcus realized that Grayson was slowly drawing the battle away from the data portal in the hopes that the enemy there would help his friend. More ring debris was starting to flow through the open area, and Marcus saw his chance as a car-size chunk floated past him. Marcus bided his time and breathed deep. As soon as he was certain the guy next to Sarjah was focused on the fight, Marcus launched himself from the safety of the densely packed ring, into the open area, and toward the rock three meters away. An X-ray beam, visible only to his voidskin's sensors, shot past in front of him, and he thought he had been seen.

Two meters.

But Grayson and his adversary were on the other side of the clearing. Their fight was so chaotic and erratic that there were energy beams and projectiles flying all over.

One meter.

Marcus's voidskin tagged multiple projectile hits on the ground near the data portal, but the enemy ditec still didn't join the fight.

Marcus landed on the icy rock, staying on the far side, out of view of the enemy next to Sarjah, and released drone spores that flew around to the other side and fed sensory data to him. The rock's trajectory would take him within thirty meters of the larger rock with the data portal. He lowered the energy output of his voidskin to minimum, figuring that the rock would be enough to keep him from being detected. He took a knee on the rock, shifting his perspective so that it was "down" to him; now it appeared he was on a slowly rotating slab. By coincidence, *above* him coincided with system north.

Marcus was distracted for a moment as his voidskin picked up a massive burst of energy from above. Faint glows of light filtered through the ring material, in some areas causing God rays, like sunlight peeking through a cloudy sky, as it was scattered by the ring dust. It was mesmerizing enough to make him forget for a moment how much danger he was in. When his skin analyzed it as weapons fire from a battle, it sobered him up quickly. That meant *Fulcrum's Light* was up there, fighting the enemy ship. That meant they had a chance of being rescued. Marcus shifted his perspective as data from his drone spores fed into his mind. The figure next to Sarjah was no fool. He was looking around now, not at the fight, apparently scanning to see if anyone else was around. There were so many other large icy chunks floating in random directions that Marcus's rock didn't stand out.

The enemy ditec could also see the signs of the starship battle above, and knowing time was running out was what may have decided him. He picked up his gun and glided a few feet away, taking aim at the closer battle still raging.

Heads up, Gray, Marcus said. *The other guy is moving.*

Copy, ugh, that, Grayson grunted as an X-ray blast slammed his shields.

Then, seemingly by chance, both ultraskin fighter's dodges sent them barreling into each other. They locked together a moment in a flurry of hand-to-hand combat, faster than an unaided eye could follow. Blows powerful enough to break walls landed in the soundless void of space.

Then a well-placed kick by the enemy sent them both spinning in opposite directions for a second before they resumed their flying firefight.

Marcus could feel waves of resolve and determination flowing from Grayson. Then he perceived from the data of Grayson's skin that his shields were almost gone and serious damage had been taken to the left leg. He couldn't read the enemy's ultraskin data, but he didn't look to be in much better condition. Marcus knew he had to act fast because the other ditec would definitely tip the scales of the fight.

Marcus looked at and discarded trajectories, trying to find a way he could reach the enemy ditec before he fired and without getting himself shot. He tried to hack the enemy's bioweb, but his encryption was too good, and Marcus's mind kept sliding off. Any more effort would give him away. It wasn't like when he had hacked the ditec during the portal base fight. Then he was attacking the connection the ditec was making; now he was trying to get directly into the guy's bioweb. He knew he didn't have much time but couldn't see a solution.

His link with Sarjah showed him the answer. He was trying to find a physical solution to help fight, but his strength was as a dimensional technician. And that was where he had to fight.

Marcus used his private link with Sarjah to study what the guy had been doing. The enemy had not tried, or at least hadn't succeeded in hacking Sarjah's bioweb. But he had been able to access recent command routines she had just run. It appeared he was studying what Sarjah had done to open the portal and cause the D-rift and was using that data to determine a safe course of action to avoid the same mistake. Marcus could see that even though the enemy was rushing and under pressure, he had still set up safeguards and firewalls with his connection to Sarjah. There was no way Marcus would be able to piggyback on the connection and use it to access the enemy. He just didn't know enough, and more than ever, he realized why Sarjah pushed him so hard in training. She or t'Zyah might be able to do it, but not him. But that was still attacking the problem head-on when he only needed to find a workaround. He didn't need to be a better ditec than that guy; he just had to find the best solution.

The rock Marcus was on was getting closer, and his spore drones showed him the guy starting to fire at Grayson. Marcus didn't think he hit Grayson, but it was only a matter of time now. Marcus had to stop him. The ditec had fixed basic portal function, but taking the cycore through would still be impossible. So, Marcus stopped worrying about the cycore, which let everything fall into place. He couldn't hack the enemy using Sarjah's connection, but they were both linked to the data portal, and Marcus *could* access that.

Marcus bypassed the normal startup protocols that would notify someone the portal was ready; it was already powered because of what the guy was trying to do. Marcus set random coordinates and maximum range; he didn't worry about exit location, just the origin point. He had to be sure the portal field wasn't big enough to accidentally get Sarjah or the cycore. Once he had it set up, he sent the activation command. The ditec's head quickly turned to look at the portal, but by then it was too late. The portal was already forming around him and then he vanished.

The enemy must have gotten off an alert just before he went through the portal, because the one fighting Grayson turned and looked. He was distracted just for a second, but immediately his helmet and torso were bombarded by Grayson's fire. His shields collapsed, and his limp form went flying back, out of control, fluid leaking from ruptures in his ultraskin. Marcus couldn't tell if he was still alive or not as his body floated into the denser part of the ring and was swallowed from view.

Greer, respond, Grayson yelled. *Where's the other one?*

Sent him on a little trip, Marcus replied, flying down to the data portal while pulsing an image of what he had done. *You good?*

Think I'll need a new skin, but yeah. Grayson's figure came into view, flying a little unevenly toward where the enemy's body had floated. *Is Sarjah okay?*

I... I'm not sure. She's still unconscious. But I got the cycore.

Good. I'm going to retrieve the body. We need intel on—

The rest of what Grayson was going to say was lost as the universe seemed to explode. A beam of energy shot down from above, cutting through the ring like a drill and continued down until it was lost from sight. It was so bright in the EM spectrum that Marcus's visual sensors shut off completely for a moment. His voidskin was hit with a massive burst of radiation even though he was shielded by other rocks. The ring material around the beam instantly vaporized and spread out in a blast wave.

The beam had shot in front of where Grayson was going, and even though it wasn't near him, the force of the expanding debris knocked him spinning back to crash into the moonlet fragment Marcus was on. Grayson hit hard, creating a small plume of dust about thirty meters away. Marcus flew over to him, accessing his vital systems as he did. Grayson's shields had completely failed, and his ultraskin was burnt and blistered. He had taken a massive dose of radiation. Marcus picked him up and flew back to Sarjah and the portal. Another beam shot by on the opposite side, and Marcus realized they had not been shooting at Grayson but at the portal itself. The residual D-rift energy was throwing off their targeting and affecting the beams.

Grayson tried to struggle to his feet but stopped at one knee and doubled over coughing, blood freezing as his mask expelled it. Marcus finished setting up the data portal and finally felt a tentative link to their ship. Marcus could now perceive where the D-rift interference was going to fail and allow him to get a signal to *Fulcrum's Light*. He could also see that if Grayson didn't get medical help immediately, he was going to die.

Hold on, man, he said to Grayson. *You'll get to the ship in a second.*

Another beam fired past but a little farther away.

You mean us, Grayson said weakly.

Only enough power for two, and this won't be able to portal, Marcus said, holding the small cylindrical cycore to his chest. His voidskin grew a membrane around it, holding it firmly in place. *I'll fly away, and* Fulcrum's Light *can pick me up after.*

Then I keep it... and you two go. Grayson wheezed and coughed again. *I'm the fighter; you're the egghead.*

Marcus didn't question his commitment; he knew Grayson was absolutely willing to risk himself again so that his team could escape. His father would've liked him. But Grayson's voidskin was too damaged to stand a chance, not to mention its vitals showed that he was dying.

Yeah, maybe, Marcus said, finally seeing the shiplink connections fully established so he could send a transmission. *But I got the key.*

Grayson's pain-contorted face managed a little *o* of surprise as the portal field meshed around him and Sarjah, and then they were gone. He was gonna be pissed.

Marcus launched immediately, trying to put as much

distance between him and the portal as possible. He opened up fully to the voidskin, boosting his senses to the max. As he thrust out of the clearing back into the ring, debris swirled past him, rocks and chunks of ice crashing into each other all about him. He did his best to avoid the larger pieces, but his voidskin was being bombarded by small pebbles and icy rocks from every angle. It was like he was skydiving through a hailstorm.

The enemy ship was moving so fast that even though he was ready for it, it was still completely past him before he consciously registered it. He couldn't tell the distance accurately with the maelstrom about him, but it couldn't have passed more than fifty meters away and must've gone straight through where the portal base was located. There was no air to suck him in with its quick passage, but all the disk material being displaced by its grav drive tossed him about like a pachinko ball. He couldn't get his bearings; everything was a swirl and jumble as he banged and collided with stuff.

Until finally he hit one really large chunk, and everything went black.

35

As *Fulcrum's Light* plowed downward through the ring of the gas giant, Ahmon allowed a good part of his awareness to pay attention to bioneering. The ship's shields were already stressed from the battle, but the lifecore seemed to be holding strong. They were traveling at an angle, on a course to try to intercept the enemy ship. *Fulcrum's Light*'s grav field cleared the debris before them, carving a tunnel through the ring, but the ring material was in constant movement and drifting back in to fill the hole.

I may be able to get a good shot, Captain, Zeinon said from Tactical.

Not yet, Ahmon said. *We may still have people down there, and I don't want to fire unless we have to.*

They were trying to get close enough to attempt to grab the enemy with the grav net, but the other ship still had too great a lead on them. Then the enemy started firing ahead of themselves, but sensors showed the D-rift was affecting the aim. Their particle beams twisted and turned like snakes, none taking a straight course. Ahmon realized they weren't going to make it before the enemy reached the portal base, and he considered whether the gravity lance would be able to get a true shot. Then the excited awareness of Comms Tech M'zazape caught his attention; the Earther, Ditec Greer, had the device and wounded crew.

P-tecs, get them aboard! Ahmon ordered. And he saw two figures portaled directly to the medbay: Ditec Sarjah and Lieutenant Grayson.

Sensors, do we have Ditec Greer? Ahmon asked.

Sorry, sir, too much interference, Ujexus answered.

Sir, M'zazape said from comms, *Ditec Greer's message said he would fly clear with the cycore.*

The enemy ship just hit the area where the portal base was, sir. It didn't slow down, Ujexus reported.

Ahmon hoped that Marcus had gotten clear. The fact that the Earther was willing to sacrifice himself for his crewmates and the mission spoke a great deal to the nature of his race for individuals. Ahmon still wasn't convinced Earthers as a whole would be able to adapt, but he had to acknowledge some of them could. Ahmon wanted to search for Marcus, but given the fluidity of the moment he felt this was their best and last chance to capture the enemy ship.

Tactical, fire!

Fulcrum's Light's gravity lance slammed into the enemy vessel, but their particle beams missed. Sensors showed the enemy ship made it out the other side of the ring. Ahmon allowed the data to flow as he studied the results. The enemy ship was heavily damaged, and it was no longer able to maintain consistent shields; readings also showed it would not be able to go into metaspace.

Fulcrum's Light burst from the ring a few kilometers behind the enemy ship, which was still speeding away.

Captain, Ujexus said. *They're not slowing. I think they're going into the gas giant.*

They can't think they can hide from us in there, Ja Xe 75 05 said.

I don't think they want to hide, Ahmon said, studying their trajectory. *Tactical, take out their grav drive!*

Then the enemy ship fired what had to be all its remaining missiles. They streaked toward *Fulcrum's Light.* This close, there was no evasive move a ship the size of *Fulcrum's Light* could do to avoid them without transiting to metaspace. At the helm, Ky'Gima strained the grav drive as she slowed the ship to give the particle and gamma cannons more time to destroy the missiles, the ocular orbs on the ship's hullskin firing nonstop. A good number still struck the forward shields, and they phased out for a second. The ship lurched as the last two missiles struck the hullskin, but their explosions didn't penetrate.

It's entering the upper atmosphere of the gas giant! Ujexus yelled.

The attacker hadn't hoped to destroy *Fulcrum's Light,* just slow it down enough for the ship to make a suicide run.

Follow it in! Ahmon said. It was possible they could still catch the ship and recover important data.

Fulcrum's Light plunged through the top cloud layers of the gas giant. Air friction slowed them a little as the bioship was bombarded by seven-hundred-kilometer-an-hour winds. Storms surrounded the ship as lightning slid along its shields. Off to the side a cyclone that was wider than terrestrial planets raged. From above it looked like an oval storm, but below the cloud tops the cyclonic storm descended over four hundred kilometers. While passing through the eye of another storm the relative calm made it seem like they cut through a gigantic cave large enough to hold moons.

Fulcrum's Light broke through to the third cloud layer of the hydrogen-dominant atmosphere. They were thousands of kilometers beneath the top, and fierce jet streams, powered by the planet's fast rotation, buffeted the ship. This deep in the storm-ridden atmosphere it was becoming too dark to see anything visually except when burst of lighting lit up the surrounding area. Unlike terrestrial planets, much of a gas giant's atmosphere was powered by the heat coming from the planet's interior—so wind energy increased as they went lower. The ship was plowing through fourteen-hundred-kilometer-an-hour winds now. The enemy still had a good lead and dropped below the storms, seemingly on its way to the helium and liquid metallic hydrogen region deep beneath the clouds where even the skeleton-frame of a bioship would be crushed by the pressure.

Sir, they're... The sensor tech paused, unsure he was reading the data right. *Sir, they are opening all outer pores to the ship.*

The bridge crew watched as the enemy continued its downward journey, the raging winds of the gas giant battering its hull and now its interior. Soon, the ship sank deep enough that the external pressure crushed it, its life-less hulk falling into oblivion.

Ahmon knew the fact that they chose death instead of being captured suggested that this was a highly organized and dedicated operation and the Society had only just seen the beginning of it. He couldn't be sure what that would mean for the Society in the future. But one thing he had to acknowledge was that Earthers had been instrumental in the positive outcome of the mission. Ahmon didn't know if all the people of Earth would be able to adapt so well, but obviously—surprisingly—some of them could. Maybe there was some hope for them as a species. He still wasn't certain they would survive themselves, but he was no longer certain they wouldn't.

Time would tell.

36

M arcus's eyes blinked open, and he was happy for the headache that let him know he was still alive. His voidskin was badly damaged and his sensors seem to be out, but basic systems showed he had only been unconscious for a few minutes. He patted his chest, relieved that the cycore was still there. As his damaged voidskin halted his slow tumble, he noticed he could now see the planet through the haze of the ring material. He had floated close to the ring's inner edge and was just starting to pass through into the relatively empty space between it and the gas giant.

He was too tired and in pain to be scared anymore. He had no idea how long his damaged voidskin could keep him alive, but at least he had an amazing view. The gas giant dominated everything before him, stretching from horizon to horizon. And he laughed, only realizing just now that he had never gotten the chance to see Saturn up close before he left the Sol System. He floated there for a while, just cherishing the act of breathing, and starting to accept thoughts of his grandparents and what would happen to them.

But he didn't feel guilty anymore. Sad, yes. And he knew fear would come again soon enough, but he didn't feel the same guilt he had before about not calling his family. They knew he loved them. And if he was honest with himself, he knew they had encouraged him to leave and have a life. But he was sorry he wouldn't get to say goodbye.

Then movement below him caught his eye, a speck at first, which quickly grew into the shape of *Fulcrum's Light* as it rose toward him, like a gigantic whale rising from the deep. Its hullskin was burned and marred in many places, but it was still the most beautiful thing he had seen in a while. As he saw a shuttle emerge from the ship, he let himself drift back into unconsciousness.

37

N ina was in her room packing, the mundane task barely able to keep her from drowning in her turbulent thoughts. She had so much on her mind that she stared at the rectangular object in her hand for a second or two before she realized it was her phone. After the first day with an exso, she hadn't thought about it once. Her exso had become as indispensable as her phone used to be. Before everything that had happened, she wouldn't have worried about it, but now she did recognize how quickly the Society's technology could override Earth's way of life.

The embassy would be leaving through the portal soon, on their way to the Orion Molecular Cloud Complex and whatever the future held. She had been looking forward to this moment so much before she left America that now it seemed a little anticlimactic to her, especially after the events of the past week.

She had used her exso that morning when she finally got around to calling her parents and surprisingly didn't end up fighting with her mom. Nina didn't know what tech was

going on behind the scenes that let her make a phone call
from Jupiter to New Mexico with no time delay or waiting,
but she didn't worry about that. She told them what she was
allowed to of what had happened, how it made her feel, and
that the nosy reporters might get worse before they got
better. They were nothing but supportive, which in turn
allowed her to really open up about how she hadn't been
happy before, not just with her job but in her life—Tony
included.

"Honey, I know I pushed you to excel," her mom said. "A
lot of it is fear of you having to go through similar hardships
I've had to endure. I really want you to be happy."

"I know, Mama, and for my part in that, I'm sorry. I really
am. I realize how I used to talk about the Society, and I
wanted you to know that in some ways, you were right.
They're not perfect. And I think that maybe what both of us
didn't see is that that's part of what makes them human."

"Yeah, I think I'll get there eventually. And your papa
and I are so proud of you and want you to make the most of
your time out there. But that doesn't mean I want any alien
grandbabies just yet."

"Ha, yes, Mother." They parted with a lot of tears and
laughs, and Nina had been forced to promise to come home
for the Fourth of July. Uncle Luis's fireworks and her dad's
barbecue were enough to draw anyone across the galaxy.

It wasn't until she finished packing that she even
thought of calling Tony. That part of her life seemed so long
gone that there was no way she could go back to it, even if
she wanted to. She called anyway, feeling she at least owed
him a goodbye, so, when the answering machine came on,
she was caught off guard but decided it was for the best. She
didn't go into specifics, but she got a lot off her chest and
talked until the machine cut off.

· · ·

WHEN NINA MADE it downstairs to the train station in the hotel, Manaia immediately ambushed her with a long hug. "Girl, you been through a lot this week."

"Sorry I couldn't make it last night," Nina said, hugging her back.

Manaia had tried to get Nina to join them yesterday for their last night in Galileo City, but Nina had been able to truthfully claim that she just needed a break from everything and a night off. She had also been ordered not to talk about Fresh Snowfall on the Lake and what happened, so after she had returned to the hotel, Nina found that, yet again, she had to keep things from her friends.

"Don't worry about that," Omoni said, also giving her a hug.

"Yeah, no worries," Manaia said. "Once we get settled on Sapher, I'm sure we'll have plenty of time to make up for it."

"I look forward to that," Nina said. She couldn't even talk about the promotion until they got to the capital.

"After we heard about the e-kiter accident, I knew you might want some time to process, like you did on the trip out here," Omoni said. "But honey, really, we're here to listen when you need us."

"I know." Nina squeezed Omoni's hand as they boarded the train. Nina still felt a little guilty. Her new friends were only thinking she had witnessed two tragic events within a few days, but she couldn't begin to tell them most of what she had really gone through.

They found some seats, and once the train was full, it pulled out for the short ride to the portal hub.

"I was actually watching it live when it happened,"

Manaia said. "But it wasn't until after that Omoni told me you had been there, and about the person who died."

Nina knew the e-kite event had been watched by people over the Nexus. She had had too much on her mind to think about it, but she wasn't surprised that members of the medical contingent would've also learned about the surgery. And while the news of the resulting death had been tragic, the city hadn't shut down, mourners didn't line the streets, and life had gone on. That, just as much as the death itself, had helped open her eyes.

"You know, you were right," Nina said to Omoni. "What you said to me back on the ship."

"What was that?"

"How I was kinda in awe of the Society. I idolized them without even realizing it, and only now am I starting to see them as human instead of superhuman."

"I think we all have to learn some of that," Omoni agreed.

THE PORTAL STATION WAS ENORMOUS, spreading out over multiple blocks at one edge of the city. The crowds of travelers were as large as any major transport hub on Earth. A few times Nina felt anxious, remembering the crowd at the station in Cairo before the attack, but for the most part that seemed like a lifetime ago to her now.

Nina knew the station held multiple portals of different power levels and that there was only one class-three megaportal which could send things many thousands of light-years. The portal itself was an organic vine-like frame, wider than the wingspan of two passenger airplanes and at least fifteen stories high. It was situated almost right up against the city's dome, with a large open area in front with dedicated lanes for traffic. It gave the impression of being a gateway leading out onto the moon's surface. But the portal wasn't a doorway where you could see through to its destination. The air shimmered and moved about itself, but Nina could still see the back wall of the station through the frame. Aerial vehicles and platforms glided slowly through the upper half, disappearing from sight foot by foot as they crossed the threshold. At ground level, a number of train cars similar to what they rode on Earth sat ready to transport the delegation through, and at each corner there were dedicated walkways for those who wanted to go through on foot.

On one side of the portal runway type area stood a stage in front of enough rows of seating to hold the entire delegation. The seating was organized by embassy department, so Nina had to sit separately from her friends again, but she was grateful she didn't have to be on stage this time as she watched Ambassador Isaacs and Mayor Sezer give speeches. The ceremony commemorating the last leg of their journey was a small affair. The only other Earthers in the city were those who worked for the UN under the mayor's office. And while there were no official news crews from Earth, the signal was being sent back for everyone to see, and Nina had no doubt the eyes of the world were on them.

After the ceremony, Envoy Last Rain in Autumn pulled Nina aside for a moment, to talk to her privately. "Dr. Rodriguez, I know words will never truly be enough. But I wanted to express again how truly sorry we are for what you went through. I know compared to crime on Earth, what Fresh Snowfall on the Lake did might seem weird or just alien enough to not take seriously, but she committed a crime. And we don't gloss over the seriousness of that."

"Thank you, Envoy," Nina said, noticing this was maybe

the first time she had ever seen a Nethean not smiling. "I don't blame the Society for what happened. And no matter what some people think, I still believe this is the best course forward for Earth."

"I'm glad to hear that," Last Rain in Autumn said. "There is one other thing, but I want you to understand you are under no obligation whatsoever."

"What is it?"

"I cleared this with Deputy Chief Xu already," the envoy said. "It's Nethean custom that when a person seriously wrongs someone, they give them a reason why. For us, since we will always remember what was done, knowing why, we believe, helps us to live with it. And I have a short message for you from Fresh Snowfall on the Lake, if you would like to hear it."

"Oh." Nina wasn't sure how to feel. "What's going happen to her?"

"There will be a trial, but she's confessed everything already. She will be sent back to Nethea to serve out her punishment. Nothing inhumane, but there are still things we're not allowed to share with NHC people."

"I see. Okay, yes, I think I'd like to hear it."

An icon popped up in Nina's exso, showing she had just received the message.

"I'll give you some privacy. We can talk again on Sapher if you need," Last Rain in Autumn said. Her natural smile returned, if somewhat subdued, and she moved away into the crowd.

Nina took a breath and opened the message. Fresh Snowfall on the Lake's face appeared in her field of vision. She looked contrite, and Nina realized how accustomed she had become to Netheans' smiles.

"Hi, Nina," Fresh Snowfall on the Lake began. "I'm so

sorry for everything that happened. I really am. I did it because... Well, because I love new cultures, and I truly felt lucky when Earth was made an NHC in my lifetime. I didn't mean to hurt, embarrass, or exploit you, although I know I did. I got caught up with a group of people who felt like me, enamored and obsessed with the new C-humans, and we just got carried away. I know it was a mistaken way to try to be closer to Earthers, and there's no excuse for that. I really did think of you as a friend, which makes it all the worse. And even if you can never forgive me, I hope you won't let my stupidity affect how you feel about the Society. I could really tell you love being out here, and I hope you never lose that feeling. Again, I'm sorry. Take care, Nina. I wish you a life of new experiences."

As she listened to the message once more, Nina realized she hadn't even gotten mad at Fresh Snowfall on the Lake but was sad that the budding friendship they had was based on a lie. That hurt more than anything else. She didn't hold a grudge against Fresh Snowfall on the Lake, but Nina took what Last Rain in Autumn said about it being a crime to heart. She wanted to believe she would be able to forgive her, but it would take some time.

And thoughts of forgiveness made her think of Endless Green Sky. She had put it off as long as possible but couldn't avoid it any longer, not without admitting to herself that she was afraid of what he would think of her. He had needed a friend to talk to about losing a patient, and she had been setting him up for the police. She couldn't even remember what she had said to him, the same hollow sayings anyone used when trying to comfort someone they barely knew. Nina sighed, knowing waiting would do no good—she had her exso call him.

Her subconscious hope that she would have to leave a

message was dashed when the call connected and his image appeared in her exso.

"Nina." The Nethean's ever-present smile seemed to genuinely be glad she called. "Today's the big day."

Nina started to answer, found she could only speak from the heart. "I need to apologize and explain to you about yesterday."

"Given what you've had to deal with the past few days, it's completely understandable, Nina," he said.

She looked at him surprised. "You know?"

"It's not public knowledge yet, but my position is high enough that I was briefed." He looked at her, his smile growing. "After I was cleared of suspicion, of course."

Nina knew he was making light of the situation for her benefit, but it still shamed her a little. "I appreciate your kindness, but I understand if you're upset with me," she said. "Sitting there yesterday and lying to your face while you talked about that poor kiter. I'm sorry. Everything just happened so quickly after I had that second episode...I just wasn't sure what to think."

"Nina," Endless Green Sky said softly, and waited for her to look at him before he continued. "You did the right thing."

She sighed deeply, some of the tension in her body draining away. She didn't realize how much it would mean to her to hear him say that.

"Well, I hope Earth can be as forgiving as the Society. If I was in your place, I'm not sure I would be so forgiving."

"I suspect you would be," he said. "You know, when I was five, my cousin broke one of my toys. I had spent days making it, but she was mad I had used all her paint up. I can still remember every moment of making it, painting it, and how I felt when she broke it. Now imagine that for every moment of your life, remembering and perfect clarity for every conversation, broken heart, joke, love, failure, et cetera. When you have memory like ours you have to become very good at forgiving." He smiled at her. "Not that there's anything to forgive.

"Although"—he grinned—"technically, you do still owe me a dinner. Seeing as the last one was under false pretenses."

Nina laughed before guilt could stop her, and she immediately felt better for it. "Deal," she said. "When we get to Sapher, I'll make you my mom's famous green chili."

"It's a date," he said. "You know, Nina, we're all here to make sure it works. All C-humans, whether Nethean, Earther, A'Quan, or whatever, all of us can make mistakes and have room to improve."

"I'll remember that," she said. "Endless Green Sky...I'm glad it wasn't you."

He looked at her, his green eyes studying her face. "And I'm glad you're not being sent back to Earth."

They smiled at each other a moment longer, both lost in thought, then they signed off.

Nina caught up to her friends as they all started to board the train. She was pretty sure she had the same expression on her face everyone else did—part awe, part fear, and part anticipation. It didn't matter that other humans were already out there, living and working in the Society. In a few minutes, they would ride through a gate and emerge on an alien planet around a distant star. For Nina, even with everything they had been through and seen up to this point, to her, this was the real beginning of the journey.

"And it would be nice if you find a church."

"Yes, Nana." Marcus smiled automatically. He didn't know about in the Society, but on Earth he was pretty sure no matter what culture you were from, it was best to learn early on not to talk back to grandmothers when they were talking about God.

"Don't placate me," the image of his grandmother said from the wall screen. His grandfather was beside her with a knowing smile on his face. "Just cause you flyin' around space don't mean you can't make time to pray."

Marcus had woken up in the medical bay, where he had been rushed after *Fulcrum's Light* had picked him up and retrieved the cycore. He mostly suffered only bumps and bruises; Sarjah and Grayson were in far worse condition. Some visitors had dropped by, and a lot of waves of compassion flowed to him over the shiplink.

There was also an undercurrent of disappointment on the shiplink over not capturing the enemy ship, but there was a stronger component of pride and accomplishment over completing their mission, having saved Travanis 4, and recovering the cycore and the survivors of the recon team. He and Grayson in particular were the focus of much of that. It was a very familial feeling, like the comfort of knowing the people you care about, care about you.

There was a type of shared mourning across the shiplink as well, for the lives lost on the recon team and aboard the ship during the battle. All the different C-humans and their different practices mingled into an overall feeling of comfort and protection that was beautiful. It was what he had missed when Golamee had died. And even though he didn't know most of the crew well—he had only been on board a couple of weeks—the shiplink allowed for a level of closeness that made him think of family. And now that the mission was over, they were allowed to connect to the Nexus again, and he had finally called his grandparents.

"That Earth Embassy is going out there right now; it's all over the news. They have plenty of theologians, so I'm sure come Sundays, you'll be able to find something."

"Awright, Nana, awright." Marcus had already told them as much about what happened as he was allowed to, leaving out the fact that he had almost died, of course. But they weren't stupid, and he could tell they did their best not to worry. What they didn't try to hide at all was how proud they were of him.

"And you're sure you're all right?" his grandfather asked.

"I'm fine, Pop-Pop," Marcus replied. "But what about you? Have you started eating healthy?"

His nana's expression told him the real answer even as his grandfather said, "Of course."

They fell into their old routine easily—them worrying about him being safe and having friends, and him bugging them about taking care of themselves. And even though they were thousands of light-years away, just being able to talk like this felt like home to him.

"I'm sorry it took me so long to call y'all," Marcus said. "I don't have an excuse. I just..."

"Marcus," his grandfather said, "I didn't call my grandparents when I was your age either. Son, I'd be worried if you was calling us all the time."

"And your mama was even worse than you when she was young," his grandmother said.

"Really?" Marcus asked.

"Ha, that girl," his pop-pop said. "You remember that time we had to drive out there to her college?"

His nana laughed. "Do I. Marcus, your pop-pop was about to tear that campus up, thinking somebody done kidnapped his baby. When really she was just out there rippin' and runnin' them streets with your daddy too much to think about us."

"Them kids." His pop-pop sighed, shaking his head with a sad smile.

"Honey, don't spend your time worrying about us," his nana said. "Your grandpop and I are fine, and you have to know it's okay to live your life."

"As long as you're happy, son," his pop-pop added. "And safe. That's what we want most for you."

"And church," his nana added.

"Yes, ma'am." Marcus laughed.

They talked a little while longer, and Marcus felt better than he had in a while. A part of him still felt bad for not being there for them, but he also knew it wasn't so much about his grandparents as it was about him working out his feelings about his parents not being there, and his overcompensating. He promised to call them again once *Fulcrum's Light* reached the Orion Molecular Cloud Complex, and they signed off.

They love you a lot. Rahel's voice startled him, and her image appeared to him over the shiplink.

You and Sarjah love creepin', don't you?

Whatever that means, Rahel said. *Anyway, I just wanted to give you a heads-up that when we reach the Orion Complex, we'll likely have to give a report to Earth's ambassador directly.*

Marcus felt the faintest trace of...something through their private link when she mentioned the ambassador, but it was gone so quick, he wasn't sure.

Okay, he said. Rahel had already been to check on him twice in person, and now she was doing it over the shiplink. He knew she felt responsible for putting him in danger by not insisting that he not go on the mission. And even though she was better than him at not letting emotions leak, he could still feel an underlayer of guilt and worry, which meant it had to be strong for her not to cover it all up. One day, they would have to really talk about what happened to her on that earlier mission in the Society.

And, Rahel, he said before she cut off, *I'm fine.*

She nodded, and he felt the briefest wave of relief from her before she signed off.

"DITEC GREER."

Marcus stopped as he exited his small room in the medbay, trying not to act like a kid being caught doing something he shouldn't. "Oh, Captain. Hi."

"Dr. Leikeema tells me you'll make a full recovery," Ahmon said.

"I feel much better."

"You did a good job out there, ditec," Ahmon said. "I reviewed the data on how you handled the other ditec.

There were a few obvious countermeasures you overlooked, but I'm sure with more training you will make an excellent dimensional technician."

"Ugh, thanks," Marcus said. He was still sometimes unsure how to take Xindari bluntness, but he recognized the captain was simply speaking the truth. "I did my best."

"I have no doubt of that. You're a fine example of... A fine example of humanity, Ditec Greer."

"Thank you, sir," Marcus said. The captain's pause was so brief Marcus wasn't sure it was real, but he felt like the captain had been about to say Earthers instead of humanity. He wasn't sure why, but he felt like that was an important distinction coming from the Xindari.

Marcus watched the captain leave, but before he could give it more thought loud, laughter distracted him. From the sound of it, Marcus thought a party, or a war, was going on in Grayson's room. He walked in to see Grayson in the bed on one side and Kleedak and a couple of other security personnel laughing loudly. The ceilings were high, but the blue reptilian's eight-foot frame made the room feel crowded. Standing in front of Kleedak was Sumiko, arms crossed, and barely up to zer chest.

"...and like I said, Lieutenant Grayson needs to rest," Sumiko was saying. "You can play your games later."

"You may have missed your calling as a security officer, little cousin," Kleedak said, staring down at her, then ze saw Marcus. "Good job, cousin!" Ze bellowed. "Your race is a fine example of our species."

"Thanks?"

"Be careful though, little mammal," ze said, moving past Marcus, the Axlon's ridiculously huge hand patting his shoulder. "The doctors here are fierce."

"That they are." Marcus smiled, seeing the look on

Sumiko's face as she ushered the rest of the rowdy group out.

"Should I leave?" he asked Sumiko while looking over at Grayson laid out in bed. Medical biopolymer encased his right arm, hip, and left leg, and there was bruising on all the skin he could see.

"You can have a few minutes."

"I'm surprised she doesn't have me chained to the damn bed," Grayson said weakly.

"You keep it up and that's next," Sumiko said from across the room, where she was checking some scanners.

"How you holdin' up?" Marcus had used the shiplink to check on Grayson's and Sarjah's status while he was stuck in his room, but there was no substitute for seeing someone in person. Especially when they had helped save your life.

"Man, I don't know what they gave me, but I feel great," Grayson said.

"You still pissed?" Marcus finished.

"At you for portaling my ass back to the ship and hogging all the fun for yourself?" Grayson asked. "Hell, yeah. And when I can walk, we're gonna have some words about that.

"But until then"—he smiled and took a sip of his drink—"I'm going to milk this room service for all they got."

Sumiko pulsed an image of a bedpan dumped on top of Grayson's head but didn't look up from what she was doing. They all chuckled, and then Grayson nodded toward the newsfeed he had playing.

"You seen this yet?"

On the wall next to his bed, an image of the social media star Ishani Jha was talking about the first Earth Embassy getting ready to leave Sol System and go into the Society.

There was video from Galileo City and talk about what this meant for humanity.

"You know what pisses me off?" Grayson said groggily. "That nobody back home even knows that we were just out here, fighting for our lives. These damn politicians are acting like they're going on some grand trip, and we're already a thousand light-years from Earth."

Marcus nodded. "True, but politicians are always taking credit for normal people's work." He hadn't really paid much attention to the selection process that had flooded the news cycles. And once he had been chosen to join dimensional technician training, Marcus had paid even less attention to politics.

"I'm just sick of their games, man." Grayson coughed. "You would think we woulda learned something from the first part of this century."

Marcus agreed with him, but at the same time he wasn't sure what the reaction would be back home if people knew what they were doing. He still didn't think Earth was ready for the Nexus, so did that make him as bad as the politicians who acted like they knew best for everybody, or did it make him realistic?

Marcus hung out and joked with Grayson for a while longer. For all that he had gone through, Marcus hadn't been seriously injured, although he was ordered to take it easy for a few days. Grayson had almost died, though—if he had gotten back to the ship any later, he wouldn't have made it. Marcus looked over to say something else and saw Grayson had dozed off.

"You guys did good out there," Sumiko said quietly, coming over to check on Grayson's bed monitors, and then she looked at Marcus, her concern clear over the shiplink. "Just 'cause you've been released doesn't mean you shouldn't take it easy. I can't imagine what it was like out there."

"Scary," Marcus said.

He tried to make a joke about it but couldn't. Now, in the safety of the ship, he was realizing just how scary it had been. Marcus wasn't sure he even knew how to process yet that not only had he almost died but he had saved people's lives also. Except for Golamee, of course. And Tuhzo. And Sinju. And the shuttle pilot whose name he couldn't even remember without looking it up, making him feel like more of a shit. The wave of empathy and compassion flowing from Sumiko was easing his anxiety and shame before he consciously understood it was there.

"If you need to talk..."

"I know... Maybe later," he said, knowing she could feel his desire to change the subject, just as he could feel the sincerity of her concern. It would just take time. "Can I see Sarjah?"

"Sure, but don't be too long," Sumiko said. She pulsed him a thumbs-up, like she had so long before when he first went down to the moon.

MARCUS QUIETLY LEFT and went to the next room to look in on Sarjah. The purple-scaled Xindari lay on the bed, breathing slow and steady. The shock of the D-rift transition had knocked her unconscious, but no permanent brain damage had been detected. He looked down on her sleeping form, her flat, nippleless, scaled chest slowly rising and falling. As much crap as she gave him, he was still concerned, but she looked at peace, and through their link he could feel an undercurrent of bliss in her rest. Her subconscious was gradually realigning itself, and she would be back to normal in a few days.

He smiled, realizing why that made him so happy: he was relieved she would be fine, but he was also going to take great pleasure in letting her know a *baby culture* had saved the day. He absently touched her hand; the surprisingly warm scale was smooth as glass. She slowly opened her eyes, her large green irises turning to him.

"Sorry," he said. "I didn't mean to wake you."

"I was just centering myself," she said.

"How are you?"

"Fine." She looked at him a moment, but he couldn't read the expression. "I understand I have you to thank for that. Again."

"Guess I had a good teacher."

She smiled, and to his surprise, he realized he had never seen her do that before. She really was attractive.

"Marcus," she said quietly, then after a long pause: "Thank you."

He smiled and nodded, not sure why that made him nervous. "Of course," he finally said. He forgot about all the jokes he wanted to make and was just glad she hadn't ended up like Golamee. He didn't realize until that moment how much he had feared that.

"But there is something else bothering you," she said, not a question.

"I'm just wondering if it was worth it. All the death and..." Marcus shook his head in frustration. "I mean, I haven't even heard anybody say why it happened. What they were after? Just...why?"

"Ultimately, that doesn't matter."

"How can you say that? People died!"

"Yes," she said. "And an entire planet was saved. An

entire planet, Marcus. The Protectorate will investigate what happened, but don't confuse that with our job. Even knowing what happened isn't our job. We're out here to survey and protect UHC systems. And then it was to retrieve the copied data, which we did."

A stray thought accessed the shiplink and showed Marcus that the cycore was in bioneering and being studied. And he saw it was scheduled to be taken to a Manifold World for further study. He could also see the other Protectorate bioships that had finally arrived and were searching the system for any possible enemy survivors. "But if we knew why, we could know if it was going to happen again."

"The Protectorate will find out eventually," she said. "But we may not. We'll almost certainly never know what was on the cycore. What matters is that we saved an uncontacted human culture from being exploited, *without* revealing ourselves. Without throwing another civilization into the deep end like we did with...your home."

And as she said this, for the first time since he had met her, Sarjah opened herself and let him completely feel her emotions through their link. And it revealed, or explained to him, something he had noticed only subconsciously on the shiplink: a sense of connectedness, responsibility, and compassion for C-humanity as a whole and UHCs in particular. Even though none of them had been involved, the crew felt a sense of guilt over how Earth had been exposed to the Society. So, saving Travanis 4 had been personal. And even with all the unanswered questions, they had succeeded.

"The Society knows that with our level of tech, it can be hard not to see us as a utopia," she continued. "But we're not. We're a pre-utopian civilization because things like this, while rare, still happen. We're not perfect. All we can do is our best."

"We're only human," Marcus said, thinking of the quote.

"I wouldn't want to be anything else." Sarjah smiled again as she shrouded her feelings once more.

"Me either." He smiled. They looked at each other for a moment longer, then he said, "I better let you get some rest."

"Night." Her eyes slowly drifted closed, and she seemed to fall asleep. He left. He was tired himself and realized just those two visits had worn him out. As he walked down the hall, he got a pulse from Sarjah. His imagination did some wandering before he reeled it in. Smiling still, he opened the message to read it.

It was a new training schedule.

A schedule with about twice as much work as the old one had—of course. He spent the rest of the walk to his cabin grumbling about cold-blooded aliens and cursing lizards, even while trying not to laugh.

EPILOGUE

Z achariah stood near the walking entrance to the portal. After the official leaving ceremony, he had managed to ease away from the others for a moment of peace. The consuls general, mayor, Society envoys, and others were milling around, taking pictures, networking, and politicking. He was thinking about what was next. Last Rain in Autumn had given him an update that no Earthers had been killed on *Fulcrum's Light,* but a full report on that mission would have to wait until he was at the embassy. He looked up at the stars. He was still very interested to find out what had happened out there.

Zachariah asked his exso where Earth was, and one of the apparent stars became highlighted. He stared at it for a long moment. Without the prompt, he would never have been able to tell it was Earth and not just a random bright star. He thought about his parents and family still there. And he realized, apart from the few envoys and delegates over the last couple of years, everyone he knew was there, on Earth. Everyone that anybody had ever known was there, from cave dwellers to pharaohs to influencers. All the things his species had ever created, from nations to religion, happened there. Everything that any Earther had ever done, had happened on that one little dot in the sky. And Earth civilization was just now taking its first steps out of the crib. Looking at all the other stars he realized it was the same for every civilization. Whatever stage they were at now, they had all gone through a growing phase. Learning to survive their own ignorance, selfishness, and fear, to make something better. It was staggering to him.

"Are you okay, Zach?" Xian Xu asked, having gravitated over to him.

"Humm, oh yes. I was just thinking even though we still have a long way to go as a civilization, that we *can* adapt and survive this. Just like others before us.

"So, you still think were ready?"

"I think we have it in us to flourish but..." He didn't know if any of them were truly ready. He stared at the portal for a moment and looked around the station at the crowds. The vehicles flying through the gate overhead. The throngs of C-humans and Earthers socializing and saying goodbyes. The floating spheres broadcasting everything back home. He took it all in with a nod. "All this stuff is distracting. I want... I just want to get an unfiltered view. To the limits that that's possible."

"True; this is so outside the context of anything we know that we could easily be distracted by spectacle," she said, taking in everything herself. "Well, I promise not to let that happen to you if you promise not to let it happen to me."

"Deal." He said. Behind them Zachariah saw other people were starting to form up as they all got ready to leave. "You know, I really believe this is the most dangerous and prosperous time in the history of our species."

"I agree," she said. "And we need to be ready to deal with all of it. Good and bad."

He knew exactly what she meant. For all their power and technology, the Society wasn't infallible. And neither was Earth.

Zach nodded and smiled. "To the Society...no, to humanity. Warts and all."

Xian Xu laughed. "Warts and all."

They walked through the portal together, ready to see what was to come.

AFTERWORD
RATE AND REVIEW

If you enjoyed this novel please take a moment to rate and review it. This helps immensely for new authors. Thank you.

The Orion Complex: The Society book 2

Coming 2023

ABOUT THE AUTHOR

Jonathan Sol is a lifelong storyteller who spends most of his free time creating worlds. He has lived and traveled throughout the US and abroad. He currently lives in his hometown of Washington, D.C.

www.jonathansol.com

Made in the USA
Middletown, DE
16 December 2022